THE SIXTH KEY

ADRIANA KOULIAS

ZURIEL PRESS

1st edition Paperback by Bantam/Random House 2011
2nd edition (ebook) by Bantam/Random House 2012
3rd edition (ebook) by Zuriel Press 2013
4th edition Paperback by Zuriel Press 2013

National Library of Australia Cataloguing-in-Publication Entry

Koulias, Adriana.

The Sixth Key/Adriana Koulias.
Cover Art: Adriana Koulias, Adam Kenteroglou
Image: Roy Bishop
License: Arcangel Images

ISBN 978-0-9874620-5-3

All secret societies and groups depicted in
The Sixth Key exist. All church artwork, architecture,
puzzles and grimoires of black magic are factual.

*To Serapis, who taught me the secrets of the Apocalypse.
And to Loouie, who wore Venetian masks though
she never saw Venice — you taught me
that death is truly brighter than life.*

'I was looking for divinity,
yet I find myself at the gates of Hell.
Still I may continue to walk, to fall, even in flames.
If there exists a way towards Heaven then it crosses Hell.
At least it does for me. Well then . . . I dare!'

SS Obersturmführer Otto Wilhelm Rahn

ISLAND OF THE DEAD

1

THE WRITER OF LETTERS

'What then shall I ask?'
'You must begin at the beginning.'
'The beginning! But where is the beginning?'
Edgar Allan Poe, 'Mesmeric Revelation'

Venice, November 2012

I had fallen asleep on the bench waiting for the vaporetto and woke with a dry mouth and a crick in the neck as the boat pulled up at the Fondamente Nuove. Once we were chugging lazily over the dusk-coloured lagoon, I dared to ask the boatman where he was taking me. Luckily he spoke some English and pointed to an island in the distance, saying, 'San Michele. The Island of the Dead . . . the cemetery of Venice.'

Well, I thought to myself. Why not a cemetery in the middle of a lagoon? It all made a crazy sort of sense – it was something the Writer of Letters, as I liked to call him, would do.

It was *in character*.

My publisher had forwarded his last letter, as always, typed on the same watermarked paper as the others. It contained these words:

Perhaps it is time we meet? Together, i am certain that we can find the solution to the riddle that is perplexing you:

HOC EST SEPULCHRUM
INTUS CADAVER NON HABENS
HOC EST CADAVER SEPULCHRUM
EXTRA NON HABENS
SED CADAVER IDEM EST
ET SEPULCHRUM SIBI

This time, along with the letter there was also an air ticket to Venice and 9instructions on what to do when I arrived.

Counting this one, I had received six letters in all. At first I had thought them mildly amusing; after all, what author of mysteries doesn't receive letters from shopkeepers, housewives, or even convicted criminals, offering interesting information? But I only realised *how* different these letters were when the fourth arrived. That's when I began to wonder who this person was.

At the time I had just finished a novel and my editor discovered that a Latin word, a word integral to the plot, was grammatically incorrect. This unfortunate realisation occurred just as the book was headed for the printing press and I quickly got on the phone to several Latin professors. I needed a Latin word composed of seven letters – no more and no less – that meant 'becoming'. I was on the phone to the printers trying to delay them when the fourth letter arrived. A coincidence, you might ask? No, I've come to know there are no coincidences. Inside the letter I found the Latin word I had been looking for – Fiesque.

Similarly, the fifth letter arrived when I was unable to source important details about an underground passage in an obscure castle on the border of Austria and Hungary. Once again, in that fifth letter I found a miracle – an essay written in the early nineteenth century by a Knight of Malta, containing the very information I needed. This was a mystery that could well have been written by Edgar Allan Poe!

So, you see, I wasn't surprised when I received the sixth letter containing a Latin riddle that had been confounding me for months. The riddle was found on a sixteenth-century tombstone in Bologna. It was entitled 'To the Gods of the Dead' and translated it read:

This is a tomb that has no body in it.
This is a body that has no tomb round it.
But body and tomb are the same.

I had long been certain that it held the solution to one of the most important mysteries of our time – the mystery of life and death – and I had resolved to make the solution to this riddle the pivotal theme of my next novel. When it proved more than difficult to solve, I took comfort in knowing that it had obsessed and exercised the wits of better minds than mine: men like Carlo Cesare Malvasia, Jung and the French writer Gerard Nerval had also wrestled with it. But as time dragged on, and the deadline for delivery of the manuscript loomed, I began to wonder what had made me imagine myself capable of solving it. The timely arrival of that sixth letter was compelling evidence that its writer was either intuiting my thoughts, or indeed, perhaps even inspiring them. Of course I had to accept his invitation. How could I refuse? By coming to Venice I would be solving two mysteries – the identity of the Writer of Letters and the solution to the inscription.

Now, as I looked out from the vaporetto towards that cold island overhung with Cyprus spears, I marvelled at the ingenuity of the creator of those letters. He had orchestrated a scene straight out of the Egyptian *Book of the Dead*: I was travelling on the boat of Isis, sailing over the river of souls to the Underworld. It was brilliant!

When the boat came to the landing stage on the northwest corner of the island I climbed out, paid the man what I owed him and watched him pull his vessel away into the foggy evening. Above on the upper landing I saw a light moving in the darkness – it was a monk carrying a lamp. The monk turned out to be a rather pleasant Irishman. He made animated conversation as he led me through dark arches and cloisters, beyond which lay a world suspended in a mercurial solution of fog and Carrara marble.

'Will you be staying the night?' he asked.

'Actually, I'm not certain,' I said, feeling ridiculous.

'Well, it's good you've come before the Day of the Dead.'

'That's in three days' time?' I hadn't thought about the Day of the Dead, an important holiday for Venetians, and so appropriate – I couldn't help but smile.

'Yes, the vaporetto is free all day for those who want to visit the graves of their relatives. The cemetery ends up full of flowers and aswarm with people.' He leant in. 'The definition of bedlam if you ask me! For now, it's serene, thank God!'

I looked around, taking in the size of the island. 'The cemetery doesn't seem big enough to service all of Venice.'

'You're right: the buried only stay here twelve years. After that, the bones are exhumed and the remains are moved to the Island of Bones, Sant' Ariano. Venice is built on water, you see, and there can be no catacombs, so, over the centuries a lot of thought has gone into what to do with the dead. One could even say that Venetians are obsessed with death. Did you know they once used the bones of the dead to refine their sugar! I won't be getting diabetes living here, that's for certain.' He gave an easy laugh. It sounded strange, given the present setting.

Beyond the monastery's cloister now, we entered a dark, labyrinthine corridor that led to what looked like a library. I followed the monk over oriental rugs to two winged chairs set by a great fire and here my breathing paused. After six years the moment had come, and I could hardly believe it.

I had tried many times to imagine the Writer of Letters.

Sometimes I conjured an image of a middle-aged hermit with a crooked back, a hooked nose and a lined face. At other times he was the handsome head librarian of some illustrious library, a man of letters who liked to read mystery novels on the sly. I even imagined a beautiful, erudite woman – a modern version of that Alexandrian philosopher Hypatia. Now, when the man stood and offered his hand, I couldn't have been more surprised.

The Writer of Letters was about my age but his entire manner bespoke another era. He looked at me with deep-set eyes and hair swept back from a face slightly lined but still youthful.

He gave a charming white smile. 'Thank you for coming! I had hoped you wouldn't refuse my invitation.' His English was perfect with only the slightest accent, perhaps Swiss or German.

I told him that it was good to put a face to his letters and thanked him for his invaluable help over the years.

'Please.' He gestured to one of the winged chairs. 'I hope your journey was bearable.'

'First class is as good as it gets, thank you. Perhaps we should exchange names?' I ventured to say.

He hesitated and I felt that I'd made a faux pas.

'Names get in the way,' was all he said.

There didn't seem to be room for argument and I decided to let it go for now. 'Do you live here at the monastery?'

'I am not sure if you could call it my home,' was his ambiguous answer.

Before I could say anything in response the Irish monk entered the library again, carrying a tray of coffee and pastries, which he set down before us.

When he was gone, the Writer of Letters poured me a cup and offered the sugar. I declined, smiling to myself.

He settled back in his chair. 'So, what do you think of my library?'

I glanced about, taking in the many bookshelves. 'It's remarkable.'

'This monastery once housed a famous scriptorium as well as

a school for theology and philosophy, but that was before Napoleon. In those days it held as many as forty thousand volumes. After the invasion of course, there was little left, everything was looted . . . War is not a friend of books, you see. At any rate, they say Napoleon was looking for something and when he didn't find it he punished the monks by converting the whole place into a prison.'

'And now it's a cemetery.'

He looked at me with those hooded eyes. 'It guards corpses. A book is a corpse in a way, wouldn't you say?'

I sipped at the coffee. 'That's an interesting way to look at it.'

He raised one brow. The gesture made me uncomfortable.

'When the Franciscans became the caretakers of the cemetery,' he continued, 'they opened the library again and began making careful acquisitions here and there, slowly filling the shelves again. I'm happy to say that now there are over twenty thousand volumes here, many of them first editions or very rare copies. From reading your books I can tell that you are not only fascinated with libraries and labyrinths but also with puzzles.'

'Puzzles are my living,' I told him.

He leant in to poke at the fire a moment. 'Have you read Jorge Luis Borges?'

'Yes . . . but that was years ago.'

He sat back again and crossed his legs, elegant and cool, as far from my image of a Franciscan monk as you could get.

'Borges' "Library of Babel" is one of my favourite short stories,' he said. 'I love his idea of a universe that consists of endless interlocking galleries, in which are kept all the books ever written, and even those likely to be written. Books whose content and order is random and meaningless.'

I thought about it a moment. 'Do you think Borges was trying to convey the opposing ideas of chaos and order, or the futility of accumulating knowledge?'

He smiled. 'Perhaps both, perhaps neither? It might just be

the learned Arab coming out in him.'

'But I thought he was Argentinian?'

There was an awkward silence.

'I am speaking of one of his previous lives.'

My disquiet must have been palpable. I realised he was playing a game and that everything he was saying had been calculated to make me feel slightly uncomfortable. I decided that I wasn't going to give him the satisfaction.

'I see.'

He wasn't put off. 'Take "The Book of Sand", for instance,' he said. 'An infinite book that changes every time you look into it. Then again, there is "The Garden of Forking Paths", where one confronts several alternatives and these create several possible futures, which are again full of alternatives, and these proliferate and fork to make more futures, endlessly.' He sat forwards. 'Do you think Borges understood the idea of karma and destiny?'

'I don't know.'

'Well, he certainly managed to illustrate, quite perfectly, the experience of crossing the threshold.'

'What threshold do you mean?'

'The threshold that separates life from death, time from space; where the past and the future converge in the present; where the dead exist.'

My smile must have looked increasingly foolish. 'I suppose you are going to tell me how one crosses the threshold? Is that the solution to the riddle – initiation?'

He looked at me without humour, clearly annoyed. 'To taste a good brandy one must sip slowly, savouring the complex flavours on the tongue! A man who drinks it down in one gulp tastes nothing and burns his throat. Isn't that so?'

I nodded pensively. He was right – I was being precipitous. Still, his tone had been harsh

He looked a little repentant. 'I do apologise. I've been away from society for too long, I'm afraid. I don't mean to be ill-mannered.' He paused, thinking a moment, or perhaps he was just giving me time to forgive his shortness. 'Yes, all initiations are a form of death. One's consciousness of the world dies and one enters the realm of the spirit, the realm of the dead, as you have intimated. But do you know this: that every time one goes to sleep one also enters the realm of the dead, leaving behind one's personality to enter a labyrinth, a hall of mirrors, a universe of galleries, wherein lies a record of all the personalities that one has been through the aeons?' He watched me, measuring the effect of his words. 'Tell me, what do you think has brought you here?'

'You invited me.'

'No,' he said with a curt tone that once again caught me by surprise. 'You invited yourself!'

'If this were so, then it would mean that I am you.'

He considered it. 'Do you find me familiar?'

I looked at him. 'Are you asking me if I feel a sense of déjà vu?'

'Not as it's understood in the usual sense. Do you think that my sitting here and your sitting there, the fire, the lagoon, this evening, this old monastery, this library, this moment, could have been created by you?'

I didn't know what to say.

'Think of how meticulous you are in creating the milieu of your books, down to the smallest detail. Now imagine you could do the same thing in the realm of death; that you could create what would surround you in your next life; this would make you the writer of your own story.'

'You're referring to reincarnation?'

'Yes. You are here at this point because centuries ago you did something which made this moment possible, and this moment will lead to another moment, and so on. Like the "Garden of Forking Paths" – every decision creates a fork in the path of your futures.'

He paused, giving me time to digest his philosophy. 'Think of it in ordinary terms: suppose someone calls you and this makes you late and you miss a train that catches fire, in which many people are killed. What do you do?'

'I would thank the caller for saving my life.'

'Ah, but perhaps you wouldn't have been killed at all? Perhaps during the course of events you would have met someone of great importance, someone who would have led you to a different fork in your path, a fork that would have led to another and another? In any event, imagine that because you did not take that train you are now crossing the road at the exact time that a car's brakes fail and it ploughs into you, killing you. Karma was the caller – but the choice was yours to take the call. Freedom lives in that choice. One can't imagine how many choices one makes in the course of a day, choices that affect not only one's future, but the collective future of all humanity. No, you are here because you have made a choice to be here.'

I looked at him, trying to see where he was going with this, but his face betrayed nothing. 'But what about you – you also made a choice when you invited me to come here?'

'Did I?' he said.

'Aren't you also free to create your own forking paths?'

'Sometimes we do things not out of our own need, but out of a desire to further the evolution of the world.'

'A sacrifice, you mean?'

He nodded. 'Take the sniper who had Hitler in his sights and who decided, at the last moment, to let him live. Imagine how different the world would be now: how many writers, artists, poets, musicians, scientists, mothers, fathers and children would have contributed to the world had it not been for one man's poor choice. Perhaps when that sniper died he had to relive that moment over and over again, until he realised that his own personal goodness was a puny concern, in comparison to the many lives he could have saved.'

I sat forwards and set down my cup. 'You are saying that if

the sniper had pulled the trigger and killed Hitler, he could have secured a different destiny for the world, even if it meant sacrificing his own personal karma?'

'Precisely. That soldier was there to kill Hitler, that was his karma, you see? He chose not to follow it.'

I had to smile. This strange man intrigued me.

'You find this interesting?'

'Yes, I do.'

'The moment that lies between what drives us from the past and what pulls us towards the future is the one moment in which we are completely free, completely conscious and completely alive. So, imagine we are in this moment. If this were a novel as yet to be written by you, and I were your character, poised in that moment, what would you have me do?'

'I would have you tell me why I'm here.'

'Touché!' He was pleased. 'I would say you're here because you want to know how it begins.'

'How *what* begins?'

'Your new novel.'

'And how does it begin?'

'It begins with a telegram, an invitation to meet someone mysterious. Now, let's say your character guesses the invitation must be from a fan of his work, because the telegram offers the prospect of a patronage. Let's assume that the message could not have arrived at a better time. His last book isn't selling well, and he needs funds to research another book. Let's imagine that in the meantime, he is surviving by the barest margin, living hand-to-mouth. So when the offer comes to meet a generous benefactor in an apartment in Berlin, well, he does the only logical thing a man in those circumstances could have done – he finds himself in Prinz Albrechstrasse.

'The street has changed little since his childhood, except these days it houses the Gestapo and the headquarters of the SS, and everywhere on shop front doors and on walls two words are written: "Juden Unerwünscht" – *Jews Unwelcome.*

'When your protagonist arrives at the fashionable apartment building, he checks the address against the telegram and the time against his pocket watch and looks up. The sky is steel blue and the sun is cold. He stands like that, in his rather shabby double-breasted suit that does little to keep off the swift breeze, trying to resist the impulse to turn around. But where could he go? The financial embarrassment that led to his rather hasty expulsion from France meant he couldn't return. At least not until his circumstances had improved enough for him to pay his creditors. *It's no wonder the poor are all Communists!* He sighs, looking again at the telegram.

> YOUR BOOK SUPERIOR WORK STOP
> A THOUSAND MARKS A MONTH FOR SECOND STOP
> FURTHER SUM TO SETTLE AFFAIRS STOP
> BERLIN FEB 18 15:00
> 7 PRINZ ALBRECHTSTRASSE STOP

'Shortly after receiving this telegram, a small fortune in deutschmarks was wired to him and a letter followed, containing a first-class train ticket from Paris to Berlin. How could he resist such a generous offer? It was a balm to know that someone appreciated his work enough to pay for it. Still, he was full of misgivings. Why had the publisher or benefactor not given his name? Why did he want to meet in an apartment? Could he be one of those Jewish publishers that had been shut down by the Nazis?

'Perhaps I should say something about the state of Germany at that time. Your character had arrived back in his homeland when there was a general feeling of enthusiasm for the promise of a new life and for the return of German pride. After all, the re-arming of Germany had been achieved without conflict, and the endless political wrangling of Weimar was over. These events were like the herald of a new age.

'The supposed Nazi vision of cultural rebirth should have fitted quite nicely with your character's own idealistic views, had he been a man of his times. But he was not a man of his times. If you were to ask him about the war against the Cathars, or something concerning Spanish politics at the time of the Reconquista, he would have expounded clear and concise views that were based on genuine insights; if you had asked him about Don Quixote, or Parzifal, or even Sherlock Holmes, he would have had you listening for hours! You see, when it came to the happenings of his day, he could tell you about the latest Georg Wilhelm Pabst film, or the most recent jazz recordings by Django Reinhardt – and not much else. The truth is, talk of politics sent his mind into a fog and for this reason he was not in the least bit interested in Hitler. This confounded his friends and irritated his family. They argued that Hitler had united the nation by erasing inflation and reducing unemployment and poverty; they even pointed out to him the language of symbolism used by Hitler, as a way of raising his interest, but your character was simply not convinced. He felt there was something rather sinister about the way the little moustached man used the ideal of oneness that all Germans longed for, and the symbols that they only half-understood, to gain power over them. These things your character sensed, in the same way a deer senses the presence of a hunter. It was an instinctive disquiet. For the ruthlessness of the new leaders had not yet become outwardly apparent – except for the issue with the Jews.

'In his view, Hebrews were as well educated, as polite, astute, sensitive and cultured as any other race. In fact, quite a few of them were exceedingly talented in diverse fields and were, for the most part, possessed of impeccable ethics and moral dispositions. He couldn't understand Hitler's obsession with blaming them for everything, from the "stab in the back", to bad weather. On top of that there was the regime's stern attitude towards homosexuals, Communists and artists. In France he had grown rather fond of bohemians and, he had to admit, since his return to Germany he had found it rather bland. He was starved for good conversation! Where were the intellectuals? Where were the poets, artists and philosophers?

'Right now, standing before that apartment, he weighs the risks. Who would believe him should it turn out to be a Jewish publisher, or an enemy of the Reich, or a homosexual, or a liberal, or a Communist waiting for him in that apartment? On the other hand, he knows he can't continue his research into the Cathar treasure without money. After all, there are only so many radio interviews he can do – and only so many times he can recount his exciting experiences potholing in the caves of southern France looking for the Grail – without feeling like a parrot. Moreover, his scripts for the filmmaker Pabst have come to nothing, and he's had enough of traipsing about the country working on film sets for a pittance. No, this interview is his last resort and he resolves that should he not like the look of the publisher, he will thank him politely and simply walk out. He need never see the man again. After all, no one is going to hold a gun to his head!

'He knocks on the door. There is no answer. This is the fork in the road, so to speak.'

'What does he do?' I said, watching the fire.

The Writer of Letters allowed a little silence to pass. 'If he had done differently, perhaps you wouldn't be here? Perhaps there would be no need for you to write this book at all? No, he knocks again and when he hears nothing, a sudden relief washes over him. Providence has saved him, he thinks – but from what? The truth is, had he left one minute earlier he would never know, but his hesitation on descending those steps now means that he is visible to the man who has, by now, unlocked the door behind him. When he turns, he recognises the uniform. Who in Berlin wouldn't have?'

2

IN THE BELLY
OF THE
DRAGON

'But the good champion Ethelred, now entering within the door,
was sore enraged and amazed to perceive no signal of the
maliceful hermit; but, in the stead thereof, a dragon of a scaly
and prodigious demeanour.'
Edgar Allan Poe, 'The Fall Of The House Of Usher'

Berlin, 1938

A long corridor led to an elegantly furnished room overlooking the street. At the threshold to this room a peculiar calmness came over Otto Rahn. He could have screwed up the telegram or even refrained from knocking on that door, but he hadn't, and now he had to surrender to the moment, for good or ill.

In a chair by the window sat a man dressed in full uniform: black hat with the Death's Head emblem; long black leather boots; shining buttons; sig runes; swastikas – the whole regalia of the SS. His face turned only slightly, and he looked at his visitor with those small myopic eyes ensconced behind pince-nez. To Rahn he looked like an accountant, someone who, at another time, might have lived an inconsequential life, perhaps as a disliked but tolerated clerk, a civil servant with shabby domestic cares. Rahn could see him riding a bus to work, thinking about money or illness, shuffling through his life unperturbed by the great problems of fate and goodness. But destiny had dealt him different cards and here he was.

When the man smiled – white, thinly spread and shrewd – it caused a tremor to pass over his left cheek. He blinked and blinked again, adjusting his lenses.

Rahn realised he must do something, so he stiffened his back and raised his right hand in what to him felt like a rather comical version of Hitler's salute.

The other man didn't stand. He gave an effeminate little wave and said, 'Heil Hitler.'

Rahn waited while the seated man stared with an expression much like that of the mouse that has tricked the cat in those American cartoons. He almost expected the man to say, 'Boo!' and laugh heartily, but he didn't. Instead he looked Rahn over, scanning him from head to toe, no doubt ticking off a mental check list of features that displayed the Aryan ideal: green-grey eyes; smooth hair; fair skin; tall with good bones; not terribly athletic but nothing that a good stint in training couldn't cure.

When he spoke, his voice sounded small, as if it were coming from inside a radio speaker. 'Otto Rahn! Delighted to meet you at last. Will you take a seat? I did wonder if you would answer my mysterious telegram. Sorry about that – it couldn't be helped, I'm afraid. Correspondence in and out of Germany has to be considered carefully these days. One never knows who is listening in. Still, I had a feeling you would come and here you are! Tell me, are you astonished? It isn't every day you find the Reichsführer waiting in an apartment to greet you?'

Rahn faltered. To say he wasn't surprised might seem to be acknowledging some form of guilt. On the other hand, to say that he was surprised might sound as though such a thing as Heinrich

Himmler coming to meet a man in an apartment in Berlin was altogether ludicrous. So he said nothing. He simply returned the smile and sat down. It was an impossible situation. Beyond his fear and awkwardness he began to speak, but Himmler interrupted him with a raised hand.

'There's no need. Your anxiety is perfectly understandable. Many people feel sick when they see this black tunic,' he said. 'But this is the desired effect, you see! Our aim is to be as much feared by the criminal, as we are regarded by the German citizen as a trusted friend and helper.'

With immense effort, Rahn answered, 'Of course, in truth, Germany has never felt a safer place.'

'Correct.' Himmler gazed at him, his eyes laconic and expressionless and his features stagnant.

For a moment, the only sound Rahn heard was the passing of a streetcar below. This situation was far outside his experience and he hadn't the slightest idea what to do next. He had a terrible desire to let go a nervous laugh, but he coughed politely into his hand instead.

'Let's get to the point, shall we?' Himmler reached for a book on the table. It was a German copy of Crusade Against the Grail, Rahn's book. The Reichsführer leafed through it for quite a time, pausing now and again to read something before speaking. 'When you wrote this, you brought yourself to the attention of the Führer. The Führer is very attentive, always on the lookout.'

'If I have offended—'

The man laughed a small, clipped laugh. 'Are you listening, Wolfgang?' he called to his bodyguard. 'Our author believes he is going to Dachau!'

The guard nodded as if such a thought did not go beyond the realm of possibility.

'Well, I shall let you in on a secret – you are off the hook, as the Americans say.'

Rahn felt a sneeze coming on, which he tried to suppress.

'No, our Führer agrees with me that your work is erudite and Aryan to the highest degree, an example of the German creative spirit and an inspiration for our men. In actuality, he believes you are closely connected to the Reich, through your destiny . . .'

Rahn didn't know what to say to this, nor indeed if anything was required of him, so he said nothing.

'You are not only an expert on history, Herr Rahn, but you also have a good working knowledge of the occult – something we regard highly. In fact, we believe that many lives have prepared you precisely for the moment when you could offer your gifts to the Reich. And I am here to tell you, personally, the moment has now arrived.'

The reischführer stood and Rahn followed.

Himmler was tall, with long legs and arms and a short body marked by a potbelly. Everything about him seemed immaturely made and awkward, as if the bones had grown faster than the muscles that supported them. Rahn imagined Himmler as a boy, being made fun of by his peers for running into desks and for tripping over carpets because he couldn't see where he was going.

'What is your next book?' he said, breaking into Rahn's thoughts.

'I am writing about the siege of the Cathar castle at Montsegur, comparing that massacre with the crucifixion at Golgotha,' he said.

Himmler went to the window. 'Well, you must forget that. The Führer would like you to write two books, which you will produce over the space of two years. He is interested in the lineage of the Grail and how it is linked to the Aryan peoples. He is also impressed by your ideas on the Cathars and your knowledge of mythology.' He turned around again to face Rahn with an impassive expression. Rahn sensed that the niceties were over. 'You will receive a handsome advance and ample freedom to do what research you need. We might even send you back to France, or to the north, to Scandinavia. In a few days you will be given an office at headquarters and you will meet your superiors. Until then I would suggest you sort out your affairs and prepare yourself for the tasks ahead. In time you will be accepted into the SS, but for now you can consider yourself a provisional member. No need to thank me – I know what an honour it is.' He looked about him, his eyes quite far away. 'I sense you will accomplish great things, Otto Rahn. I trust you will not disappoint me.' He looked at Rahn penetratingly for a moment before saying, 'Heil Hitler!'

He walked out then, snapping his heels on the polished wood floor.

3

CALM BEFORE THE STORM

'Make yourself honey and the flies will devour you.'
Miguel de Cervantes, 'Don Quixote'

It goes without saying that Rahn was agitated after that meeting with Himmler. To refuse the man's offer had not been an option, so he decided to make the best of it, burying into the deep recesses of his mind the nagging doubt that he was walking into a trap. After all, there was something to be said for his move from the flea-ridden guesthouse to the Grand Hotel on Wilhelmstrasse, and he was able to use part of that large sum, left by Himmler with the desk clerk, to purchase a good black coat and a new pair of boots – he could now walk without undue concern for rocks and puddles. In fact, he didn't know how much he had missed having doors opened for him, beds made for him, and dinners cooked for him! And to not have to wash out his shirt and socks one day, so that he could wear them the next day, was an exquisite luxury.

In the following days he threw himself into the multitude of tasks that began to crowd his new life. His boss was Brigadeführer Karl Maria Willigut, or Weisthor, as he liked to be called. Weisthor was a corpulent man who claimed to be descended from ancient German sages, a peculiarity that apparently afforded him a powerful ancestral clairvoyance. But right away Rahn could see that Weisthor was simply mad. Rahn was not surprised, therefore, to hear later that his superior had only recently come out of a mental asylum, something Himmler had not been told when he first met Weisthor at the Nordic Society in Detmold. At the time, Himmler had been so impressed by Weisthor's outrageous claims, that he had immediately installed him at the SS headquarters in Berlin with the task of running the archives of the Principal Race and Population Bureau.

On his first day, Rahn was ushered into Weisthor's cramped office to find the man behind a desk buried under papers, curios and statuettes. Every spare surface in his office was taken up with files and strange artefacts, and every available wall was either covered in shelves that sagged under the weight of so many dusty books, or wallpapered with an assortment of exotic maps.

When Weisthor's pale eyes looked up, his face broke into a jovial smile. 'Welcome! So this is Otto Rahn? Sit down, sit down, Otto! Well, well, you are a handsome fellow!' he said. 'Look at you! A German through and through!'

For his part, the man's face was fat, his nose bulbous, and his greying hair, despite the short haircut, was not of the mind to be tamed, poking out of his head at odd angles like little radio antennas. His eyes, strangely askew and weighed down by bags of skin, stared with great intensity at Rahn who, on the other hand, tried not to stare at the crumbs that littered his superior's uniform and short moustache.

'Just having lunch, do you mind?'

'Not at all.'

'Good . . . good . . . I have a ravenous animal inside me that I must feed at regular intervals, or it becomes quite violent! So — you're from Michelstadt?' Those bushy brows were arched and waiting.

Rahn removed a half-dozen books and a thighbone that looked curiously human from a chair and sat down. 'Yes, Michelstadt is my home.'

'Ahh, the forests of Odhinn-Alfadir, home of the grand god of the North, the town of Michael the Dragon Slayer!'

'My mother used to tell me stories about him,' Rahn said, with a polite smile, feeling uncomfortable under that mismatched stare.

Weisthor picked up his half-eaten sandwich. 'Well, the woman certainly inspired you!' He underlined his statement by taking a bite. Between chews, he observed, 'You know, a father may be the backbone of a man's life, but a mother is the voice that encourages him to walk tall!' He stared for a moment, perhaps remembering his own youth and came out of it with a start. 'So! You're a philologist, a scholar of the German Romances, an expert on the Cathars and caves, the Holy Grail, the occult, history and mythology! Impressive for one so young – how old are you?'

'Thirty-one.'

'Oh! A fine age, a fine age! And your book on the Grail, I must tell you, has created a sensation, a real sensation. As a matter of fact you're quite in vogue, and you'll have to thank my surrogate daughter, Gabriele, for that, because she was the first to tell me about you.' He leant forwards. 'You can thank her in person; she is quite a catch, you know.' He allowed this to hang in the air between them before continuing, 'At any rate, I have to say, when I read your book tears came to my eyes – tears! I agree with everything you wrote; the Cathars and their terrible struggle against the evil power of the church is an image of our own Aryan struggle. Needless to say, I passed your book on to Himmler, and here you are! The entire book will soon be required reading for every man entering the SS. What do you think of that?'

Rahn quickly came to realise that Weisthor's questions were purely rhetorical, and in this case, gave him pause to tease out something caught between his two front teeth. 'As to your task here, your knowledge will be of great help to me. You see, timing is of the essence.'

'Timing?'

He looked at Rahn with a fiery eye. 'The Führer has plans. We are to reinvigorate the old cults and resurrect them into a new, all-embracing religion! We've been ordered to bring back the gods of the Underworld, Rahn! That is what this department is about. What do you say to that? Your books will help support, through your scholarly research, what we already know – that the German race is superior to all others and that the Grail lineage, the knightly bloodline of Saint Odilie, courses through our veins. In fact, the blood of the German people is the Grail itself! We are the *beloved* of God, just like the Bogomils and the Cathars! But we have other work . . . yes . . . yes . . .' He sifted through his papers. 'As well as coming up with new rituals and festivals, we have to find evidence for our conclusions! We must find the links between our people and the Tibetans, the Romans and the Persians – what do you think of that? And we haven't much time. We'll have to create a map library and visit the old pagan shrines, because the Reichsführer wishes us to conduct our research in the most scientific way. Science is *everything* these days, Rahn! For this reason I will be sending you to many places of interest, so that you can supervise our scientific archaeological work.'

'But what of the books I have to write for Himmler?' Rahn asked, tentatively.

'Books? Yes, those too, you can do them in between everything else. You will see, you will not be idle.'

And he wasn't.

The weeks turned into months. Rahn travelled to the Odenwald, the Westerwald and to the hilly Sauerland; he trod through the Wildengerb ruin, near Amorbach, where there was a dig in progress. He went to the Leichtweis cave near Wiesbaden and then onto Sporkenburg, where there was an important historical ruin. In between journeys to this place and to that place, he moved into an apartment in Tiergartenstrasse, he was given a small office at SS headquarters in which to work, and a nervous young assistant, Hans, to help him.

Whenever he was in Berlin, Rahn spent a great deal of his time compiling that map library for Weisthor, who had started calling him a 'surrogate son' and even invited him to visit the Villa Grunewald, to meet his 'surrogate daughter', Gabriele.

Gabriele turned out to be a rather vivacious young woman, highly intelligent and fun to be with but, unfortunately, not at all his type. Thereafter, whenever Weisthor spent a weekend away at the Schloss, the castle on Lake Malchow, he invited Rahn, and Gabriele always seemed to turn up. Rahn began to wonder with some discomfort whether his invitations had been at Gabriele's insistence. She certainly seemed to be growing quite attached to him, and although so far he'd managed to divert her frivolous advances into intellectual channels, he knew the situation was likely to grow increasingly awkward.

At the Schloss Rahn mingled with the elite of Berlin, a strange mixture of Nazis, foreigners, businessmen, and members of the flying squadron who were billeted nearby. He drank a great deal, danced until his feet were sore and fascinated the guests by recounting his escapades in the caves of the Lombrives. On the odd occasion, he even took over the bar to make those cocktails he had learnt to mix from the Senegalese barman, Habdu, at the old hotel he once owned at Ussat-les-Bains. To the delight of all, he told stories of the guests he had served: Josephine Baker, Marlene Dietrich, even Pabst himself. What he didn't tell them was that he had bought the place on a whim and had spent so much money on renovations it had sent him bankrupt.

At the Schloss he met an enigmatic man, a Georgian named Grigol Robakidze, a poet and playwright. Robakidze was in his mid-fifties and wore his short hair plastered to his head with pomade. When he looked out from under his well-shaped brows he exuded a decadent urbanity and an evil indolence that reminded Rahn of Bela Lugosi's Count Dracula. Later, Gabriele would tell Rahn that rumours were always circulating about Robakidze. Some said he was a magician, others that he was a Russian Merlin or a genteel Rasputin. Some even went so far as to call him a spy.

Whatever the case, in the coming months Robakidze would prove a most congenial and interesting friend to Rahn, inviting him to sumptuous lunches or splendid dinners, during which they would sit for hours, locked in conversation. Whenever they met at the Schloss, the Russian behaved as though a meal with Rahn was a sacrament. Robakidze even became rather upset if Rahn was ever absent for the weekend.

The last time Rahn saw him at the Schloss, Robakidze seemed unusually subdued and suggested they abscond from the castle to a little restaurant in the township, where they could be alone. They ate their meal in a strange monastic silence and it was plain to Rahn that Robakidze had something on his mind. When they were finished and the plates were cleared away, the Russian lit a thin, Burmese cheroot and sat back, observing Rahn and saying nothing for a time.

'You must be wondering,' he began, finally, 'why I have taken you away from excellent food and champagne bubbles to eat soggy strudel and to drink ordinary house wine?'

Rahn calculated his words, sensing something strange afoot. 'Too much perfection can be tiresome.'

Robakidze raised one brow very high and his eyes narrowed. He seemed to be assessing Rahn. 'I simply wanted a different milieu for what I am about to tell you.'

'I see,' was all Rahn could say.

'You know from our conversations that long ago I was a pupil of Nietzsche,' he said. 'What you may not know is that one day I came across Goethe's teachings and they have since become the basis of all my thinking, my poetry, and my prose. Goethe led to an illumination. I woke up to a strange species of knowledge: I knew, without a doubt, that Nietzsche was driven by a demon to write his work on the Antichrist. Yes, I can understand why you smile, but it is true!' He leant forwards to whisper, 'I believe that the very same demon has entered into German hearts.' He sat back again and took a long drag of his cheroot, letting this sink in. 'Why were the German people not inspired by Goethe?' He shrugged. 'Who can say? But they have made their choice and so Germany is headed for doom. One day, perhaps sooner than you think, you will understand. When that day comes, if you are in need of a friend, or if you find yourself in *trouble*, you can call this number. It is the number of the Black Swans.' He took a card out of the inside pocket of his flawless suit and gave it to Rahn. *Black Swans?*

At the time Rahn couldn't imagine what Robakidze meant by 'trouble'. Later, on reflection, he understood that to continue to have any association with the Russian and these Black Swans, *whomever they were,* might prove dangerous to his health, so he stopped going to the Schloss altogether. In any event, his workload had increased so much that he had no time for pleasant weekends away.

It all began when he asked Weisthor for more time in the office, so he could concentrate on reworking an old travel diary he'd kept for some years into a book entitled *Lucifer's Court*. But soon he was overseeing a number of additional projects, including reviewing an article written by the alchemist Gaston De Mengel.

De Mengel's research into pre-Christian, Indian, Persian and Chinese religious documents was of a sudden interest to Himmler, and Rahn's job was to check and to translate the article with the assistance of the flamboyant mathematician, SS Sturmbannführer Schmid.

Despite his growing workload, other items kept landing on his desk for consideration: treatises on Tibetan Buddhism and tantrism; books by the alchemist Arturo Reghini; articles on the lost Atlantean civilisation; pamphlets on the goddesses of Earth and

Moon; works on Sacred Geometry – the science of grids, harmonic mathematics and Earth energies; as well as various texts on alchemy, witchcraft, ancient mythology, numerology and the science of symbols.

The list was seemingly endless, and he wondered how he would ever find time to finish his book. When he asked Weisthor why Himmler wanted so many reports, his superior had answered him with a puzzled expression.

'Don't you know, dear boy? Why, it is for our Führer. He has had many visions of his past lives. In truth, he remembers one particular life, which was foremost among them: his time in Atlantis when he was a great magician and a man unsurpassed in his abilities! What do you think of that? Now, as you no doubt know, in each life one must relearn the knowledge of the past before one can begin to work on future abilities. So to this end, the Führer has been amassing a great number of books on magic and sorcery. He has a voracious appetite for knowledge but, you see, with all he has to do, he has no time. Your reports will save him having to read through everything. Do you understand the great honour he has bestowed upon you? I believe, if you please him, he might even show you his libraries one day.'

'How many libraries does he have?'

'There are three separate libraries. But it is at the Berghof that he keeps all his magical works – some five or six hundred of the rarest volumes on the occult. Everything is managed by his librarian, a man called Herbert Döhring, whose fervent hope it is to increase the size of the collection to sixty thousand volumes! In that library, our Führer has nearly everything written about magic and witchcraft, torture and ways to summon devils. You will never see anything more beautiful.'

Ways to *summon devils?*

Rahn walked back to his office feeling that Weisthor was living up to his reputation for lunacy.

In the coming months, Rahn worked through the Olympic

Games to publish *Lucifer's Court*, and had a run-in with his assistant Hans. The stupid man had interpolated anti-Semitic remarks into the narrative without his permission! When Rahn complained to Weisthor, he was warned against going to Himmler – after all, Hans was the Reichsführer's brother-in-law.

Disheartened, Rahn observed the remilitarisation of the Rhineland and the Anschluss of Austria from his windowless and therefore airless office, rarely noticing whether it was day or night. He also did his obligatory dismal time as a guard at Dachau, where he saw happenings that disquieted him and where he heard of even worse things: the murder of Jewish prisoners and the torture of Marxists and anyone suspected of speaking out against the Government. He only cheered when he saw the snow begin to melt, because it meant that he would soon be leaving the camp. But when he returned to Berlin he not only found it cold, damp and smelling of boiled cabbage, he also witnessed the same cruelty and inhumanity he had seen at Dachau, placidly tolerated and even encouraged by ordinary German men and women alike. Sometimes even children would go out of their way to kick an old Jew who had been struck to the ground by a Gestapo officer.

From that time, Rahn began to consider ways of ending his involvement with Himmler and the SS. What could he have been thinking? How could a tolerant man continue to live under such a government? He was pleased, therefore, when he was given the task of fine-tuning the Reichsführer's genealogy because this meant he had to travel to Switzerland. Once there, he was seized by a sudden overwhelming sense of liberty. He wanted desperately to see mountains again, hawks flying overhead and caves below. He had sorely missed the villages, the lakes and the cool freedom of being awake beneath a pure, early morning sky.

On impulse he looked up an old Swiss friend, Alexis La Dame, but learnt from La Dame's mother that he was working at the university in Paris. Rahn hadn't seen him for almost two years but La Dame was the sort of friend who remained close despite distances and the vagaries of fate. They shared a love of the mountains, caves, detective novels, mysteries, music and, during their potholing days in the south of France, had both developed a taste for brandy.

Full of excitement, he secured a certificate from a Swiss doctor to lengthen his stay, citing exhaustion. He then set about petitioning the French Embassy for a new passport, all the while writing to Himmler lies of the wonderful book he was writing, a great tome some two thousand pages long.

The day he was denied entry to France he was feeling particularly low and his spirits became decidedly lower when a German officer arrived at his door wearing plain clothes. He was carrying orders from Weisthor, signed by Himmler. A new assignment was waiting for him, something of great importance, and he was to leave with the man immediately. At this point Rahn realised his situation – he was not a free man.

When he returned to Berlin he waited cheerlessly for Weisthor to call him to his office and to give him the particulars of his mission, but the days passed with no word. To make things worse, while working on his own genealogy, to fulfil the requirement for racial acceptability, he discovered something alarming. His mother's maiden name was Hamburger, apparently a name frequently used by European Jews, and to top it off, his grandfather's real name was Simeon! Rahn's ignorance of these particulars did not surprise him. What parent discussed such things with their children? But now he was in a mess and the situation grew even more acute when Gabriele called him one night to warn him that the Gestapo was secretly investigating Schmid – the mathematician who had worked with him on the De Mengel article. Rahn took himself to Schmid's apartment and found the door unlocked and Schmid gone. Everything was still in its place and even the table was set expectantly, waiting for a dinner that now lay cold and rotting on the stove. Rahn made discreet enquiries about Schmid but to no avail – the man had disappeared without a trace.

The day Rahn confronted Weisthor on the matter, he was feeling rather unwell from a bout of the flu and this made him incautious. Weisthor heard his words in a blank silence and afterwards remained quiet, as if undergoing some internal debate.

When he spoke his voice was serious and conspiratorial. 'Tell me, Rahn, are you the sort of chap whose ears are disposed to hearing extraordinary things?' He blinked and blinked at Rahn, quite full to the brim with a fierce form of enthusiasm.

'I would like to think so,' Rahn said, blowing his nose.

'Well then, close the door, dear boy. Sit down and listen.' He regarded Rahn heavily. 'I like you, I think you know that,' he said. 'I feel that when I talk to you I am speaking to an intellectual equal. You're different from the empty-headed puppets that walk about this place and so I want to tell you something that might save your life. Can I trust you to be discreet?'

Rahn nodded, trying to appear the very model of prudence.

'In the coming months, Rahn, you must get used to the idea that Germany is going to have to kill an inordinate number of Jews. But not just Jews,' he said. 'You must get used to the idea that the master race has no time for the sick and the ailing and the degenerate. Do you know what Eugenics is? Darwin's half-cousin came up with it. It is the science of racial hygiene, the science of culling out riffraff; a kind of enforced natural selection. You see, the weaker races can only survive by breeding with the stronger ones, and this weakens the stronger race. Simple really. We become less than animals because even animals do not mix together. Have you ever seen a monkey mating with a zebra? Of course not! If this were allowed to go on in the human race it would be headed for doom!'

Rahn felt this comparison distasteful in the extreme and it bristled his every sensibility. 'But you and I know that this is nonsense!' he risked saying. 'Science shows that when races mix they become stronger, not weaker. Look at what happens in small

German towns where inbreeding is rife – you see nothing but imbeciles.'

Weisthor's face grew very serious. 'Well, Reichsführer Himmler would disagree with you. Certainly it has been known to happen that imbeciles are born this way, because negative faults are emphasised, but so are positive traits accentuated! At least that is what he is trying to prove. He wants to show that this is so because our Führer himself comes from such a small township. So, he has our department investigating our Führer's genealogy for evidence that he is a product of such a union, which one would have to say, in his case, has bred a genius. To his mind, it is no wonder that the church continues to decry incest, considering it fears the birth of Nietzsche's super-human man!'

Robakidze's words now returned to Rahn and he felt a chill.

'My advice to you, Rahn, is to forget what has happened to your friend Schmid. It would have happened sooner or later, believe me. This is a new Germany. The curse on society will be scourged: astrologers, mediums, Freemasons, clairvoyants, Jews and gypsies will be rounded up; and the disabled, the elderly and the insane will be despatched in their hospitals.'

Can the man hear himself? He who has not long been discharged from a sanatorium?

'But if you go around asking too many questions, Rahn, you will be tarred with the same brush. That is the danger.'

Rahn blew his nose. 'What do you mean, the same brush?'

'The same brush, Rahn. Why would a normal man befriend a homosexual?'

Rahn looked up. 'Are you suggesting . . . ?'

Weisthor's eyes narrowed a touch. 'This is the question that will be asked. One might think you don't seem to fancy women. Look at my dear Gabriele, for instance; she spends all her time swooning over you, throws herself at your feet and you are, how should I say it, as cold as a seal. Be careful, Rahn! Do you think they don't know everything there is to know about you? For instance, they know you are intimately connected with a certain Raymon Perrier.'

'I've known him for years and love him as a dear friend!'

'But what are you doing mountain-hiking with him? You even shared a house with him in Switzerland!'

'As a friend!'

'But that is not all, Rahn! What about Dietmar Lauermann, who is associated with the outlawed Grey Corps?'

'Lauermann? I met him when I was at university! I've had nothing to do with him for years.'

'And what about your Jewish connections?'

Rahn felt his palms grow moist. A bead of sweat was forming on his brow.

'The shopkeepers, where you buy your groceries, Rahn! You should not be seen in such places owned by Jews!'

Rahn wanted to faint from relief.

'Listen to me.' Weisthor sat forwards with a mad look in his eye. 'The Sicherheitsdienst spies on everyone, not just bohemian artists, or Marxists, or the morally perverted – like Schmid, with his apartment full of statues of nude men. The slightest remark, or the smallest activity deemed questionable by the SD will have you hearing a knock on the door in the middle of the night. Before you can blink, you will find yourself in Dachau and I won't be able to help you. The Gestapo SS are not subject to laws. They are above the law and can place any man in protective custody. You don't want to know what happens to those who go there, Rahn. A bullet in the head is the pleasant alternative. At best your parents will have to ransom you and nurse you back to life after the Waffen SS have had their fill of you. Be pragmatic, Rahn! No one is safe!'

'You make the Gestapo sound like the Inquisition!' Rahn blew his nose again.

'Look, if you're not careful you too will be considered nothing but riffraff, and riffraff has to be eradicated! Mark my words,

Rahn, they will take comfort in knowing that such an act comes as an inspiration directly from the gods.'

Rahn, bewildered and feverish, asked, 'Why would the gods inspire the killing of innocent people?'

Weisthor sighed, as if Rahn had just made the most naïve statement in the history of the world. 'You're a historian! Surely you can see how the gods have always needed their sacrifices, be it on an altar of stone or on a battlefield. The sacrifice of weakness is what our Führer believes will make our race perfect, and only a perfect race is a vessel capable of containing the spirit of its people – like the Grail, Rahn!'

He stood and went to the window to look out at the dreary day. 'This now brings me to your next mission. New information has come to light. Gaston De Mengel has sent me a letter that has me quite excited. I have shown it to the Reichsführer and he is similarly invigorated!'

'What is it?' Rahn said.

Weisthor didn't turn around but began tapping one hand over the other behind his back. 'It is of the utmost importance and completely top secret. De Mengel tells of a certain text, a grimoire of black magic, very rare . . . He has a contact for you in Paris. Himmler is quite elated since this text is one that has been sought after by our Führer for some years to complete his collection. It is the only one he doesn't possess. At any rate, the Reichsführer would like to give it to the Führer for his birthday, so there's no time to delay. Himmler has expedited matters by signing a request for your journey. All you need do is append your signature.' He turned around. 'Now, to details.' He looked about his littered desk and produced an envelope. 'In here you will find your new papers. Knowing of your difficulties in Ussatles-Bains, I appealed to the French Embassy here in Berlin and they have issued a new passport. You will also find quite a sizeable sum, enough to provide you with meals and accommodation and anything else you might need for a month or so. If you need more it will be wired to you, but you must note down every expense, the smallest amount must be accounted for. Himmler is a stickler for detail, as you know by now. Oh, and inside there are also train tickets and the address of the man whom you are to contact in Paris. A certain Vincent Varas.' He sighed. 'Think, Rahn, how overjoyed the Führer will be to have that book! I need only say that we are full of enthusiasm for your positive findings . . . *if you know what I mean.'*

'If the Führer is so interested in occult matters why is he persecuting astrologers and gypsies?'

The old man raised one brow. 'His reasoning is beyond our comprehension because he is a giant and we are dwarfs. Now, before you go, the Reichsführer would like you to take his genealogy to him at Wewelsburg, the spiritual centre of our nation. Have you finished your own one, by the way?'

Rahn shifted. 'Not yet, I've been so busy . . .'

'Watch out, my boy.' Weisthor lowered his voice. 'Every man must show that his blood is free from impurities – make it a priority on your return from France or face the consequences. Now, your train leaves tomorrow and afterwards you will travel to France directly from Wewelsburg. I expect you to report in from time to time on how you are getting on in the south.' He looked at Rahn with paternal affection. 'Be careful, son, do your duty, and, Heil Hitler!'

Rahn left the office with his mind spinning. His body was aching and his head hurt but in his heart there was a little leap for joy. He was leaving Berlin with its sodden dampness and its noise and the all-pervading smell of boiled cabbage. He would soon see mountains again and with any luck lose himself in France, leaving this terrible business with Himmler behind him.

He went to his desk and cleared it of pressing matters, sorted through his papers and left early to make arrangements. And if he felt at all uneasy he ignored it, like one ignores a small cloud that mars an otherwise perfect sky. After all, no man who knows history would care to look a gift horse in the mouth. Well, at least not until he was very far away from it.

4

DOG AND WOLF

'They entered the chief court of the castle and found it prepared and fitted up in a style that added to their amazement and doubled their fears . . .'
Miguel de Cervantes, 'Don Quixote'

The journey to Wewelsburg was particularly bleak. Low, grey clouds coloured the world in their image: grey buildings gave way to grey fields, grey farmhouses and grey villages, where grey people waited at grey stations. He watched the scenery pass, feeling sick, melancholic and anxious. His previous elation had succumbed to the reality that he had to get over one more hurdle: Himmler.

On the train he tried to work on an idea for a new book but his thoughts were scattered. What if Himmler didn't like his genealogy and decided to send him back to the drawing board? What if Himmler were to guess his intentions? He had to get a hold of himself! He couldn't present himself to Himmler looking desperate. Bad enough he didn't look an example of the robust healthy Aryan, what with his red nose, pale complexion and sunken eyes. He went to the lavatory and washed his face and pinched his cheeks and told himself, *Calm down.*

When the train arrived at the ragged little station of Paderborn, a car was waiting to take him to the rural village of Wewelsburg. It rained heavily most of the way but as the fortress appeared, a crack in the clouds allowed the dying rays of the sun to illuminate the building's west face. It lent the citadel an otherworldly gleam that made Rahn nervous, for it recalled to his mind not the castle of the Grail, but the castle of the sorcerer Klingsor, Chasteil Marveil, which on the outside appeared to be the most resplendent castle while inside it was full of traps. He was so taken by this thought that he was half expecting a number of virgins to greet him, those whom the neutered Klingsor had kept imprisoned for the pleasure of it. Instead he was met by silent Waffen SS guards with humourless faces, who opened the door to the car. They escorted him over the sodden threshold, into a cheerless courtyard still under construction. Another two guards then led him directly ahead to the north tower and some moments later, he was standing at the threshold of a great circular hall.

He waited for his eyes to adjust. At the centre of the hall stood a round table festively laid with white linen embossed with sig runes and adorned with lit candles, silverware and crystal glasses. Around it sat a large number of SS officers and Himmler himself, talking and laughing, while in the background pleasant music played, Bach perhaps.

All activity paused on his arrival and Rahn waited, uncertain as to whether he should enter.

'Come in, join us!' Himmler said, quite like a jolly Arthur surrounded by his knights.

Rahn's breathing paused. *What now — couldn't he just drop off Himmler's genealogy and be on his way?*

A servant appeared from some hidden corner and showed him to a seat. In a moment there was wine in his glass and a crisp white napkin in his lap. He was trapped! There came now a brief introduction, expounding the merits of his books and his talents as a writer and Grail historian.

Himmler said then, 'Before you came, we were talking about

the salamander. Perhaps you can tell us something about it that we don't already know?'

All eyes turned to Rahn and he felt his heart pound in his ears. Not only did he feel a sneeze coming on, but the inner activity required to prevent it caused his fever to spike, leading to a cold sweat, which he could feel trickling over his temples. He gathered to him his wits and smiled faintly.

'The salamander is a mythical creature,' he began. 'It dies and yields its blood, and from its blood it wins immortal life . . . death has no power over it—'

'Correct! Did you hear that, gentlemen? Death has no power over immortal life!' Himmler said, expansively. 'And the Grail also keeps death at bay, isn't that so? So tell us, what is the Grail?'

Rahn looked around the circle at the matching vacant smiles and he guessed there must be thirty or so SS officers gathered here. 'The Grail is the vessel that holds the life-giving blood of Jesus Christ, the god who overcame death through sacrifice.'

'You see! The Grail holds the immortal Aryan blood of Jesus, because Jesus was not a Jew, was he? Is there support for this idea that Jesus was Aryan?'

Rahn's mouth was drier than a stick and he sipped at the good Bavarian wine, but it only made him more parched. 'Well . . . it is a contentious issue,' he said. 'There are two genealogies: one in Matthew and the other in Luke. The Matthew lineage suggests a dark Jew child; the Luke lineage suggests a fair Galilean Jew child of mixed heritage.'

Himmler was so pleased his eyes twinkled behind his pincenez. 'You see, gentlemen! The Roman church and the Jews have deceived us! Jesus was an Aryan! Even so, he was only one symbol of sacrifice. Germany has its own Aryan symbol, our Führer! He says that this, above all, is Germany's destiny – to live in the fire of sacrifice, like the salamander.'

'What is it that I say, Heinrich?' The voice echoed strangely in the high-vaulted room. Suddenly all men stood and Rahn followed by reflex; his stomach lurched and he forgot to breathe. The air in the room grew still and the torches flickered and seemed to wane as the man in the grey suit crossed the threshold.

The glow of the great torch in the arch under which he stood marked out the bones of his face and threw shadows under his eyes, eyes that were as wild as a winter sky at midday, wild as those of a wolf caught tearing at its prey. He came to the table, straight backed with the self-absorbed mien of a mythological god, and a dumb, astounded silence grew around him until it was thick and awkward. Rahn, with his sense for unspoken things, knew that the newcomer was proving to them that they could exist simply by basking in his presence. He did not need to speak: his very greatness alone should hold them.

Satisfied that his presence had achieved the desired effect, Adolf Hitler scanned the group before him, and in his eyes there glittered the promise of unfathomable mysteries, both miraculous and magic. The Führer drew a smirk upwards over the scored bones of his face, stretching at his short moustache, but it was an action neither touched with irritation nor amusement. It was the expression of an automatic intelligence that was fast, cold, merciless. It swept over his men, as if to say, *I am neither your friend nor your foe and by you I am completely unaffected. But by me you are fully enthralled.*

Rahn felt a sudden surging of his blood, a feeling confusingly and quite disturbingly sexual in nature. A primal magnetic love of kin for kin, of the deepest blood ties. A part of him was disgusted by it, but another part was exhilarated.

'Well?' Hitler said, turning his eyes to the Reichsführer.

Himmler cleared his throat, the loyal dog cowering before a superior wolf. 'Mein Führer!' he said with passion. 'We were just saying that it is your desire that all Germans come to know the true meaning of sacrifice!' Himmler adjusted his glasses, as nervous as a schoolboy.

'IT IS NOT MY DESIRE!' These words exploded from

Hitler and sent a shockwave around the table. His face moved over every man with fury in his eye and hatred about the lips. 'IT IS WHAT THE SPIRIT OF GERMANY DEMANDS!' he cried, taking in a strangled breath as he thrust one fist into the air. 'THE SPIRIT THAT SEEKS TO MAKE GERMANY GREAT!'

The candles glowed, the torches flapped, a draught blew in and circled the group. Adolf Hitler stood perfectly still, reining himself in. He looked about him at the arid landscape of blank faces with his hands behind his back now, his eyes probing and his lips working inaudible whispers.

His eyes fell on Rahn.

Rahn's blood paled and his bones felt like lead under his skin.

A deep fatigue seized him, as if the light had gone out of the world and his heart was touched by a shadow.

'So, the Grail historian is here. Otto Rahn!' Hitler said, serenely now, stretching his neck as if to adjust the tightness of his collar. 'I have read your books. Sacrifice is written in blood in all history books, do you not agree?'

'Yes, mein Führer!' came Rahn's immediate reply, which was followed by a sudden terrifying thought that sent him into a palsy of uncertainty: *Was this the reply the Führer wanted?*

'Look at this castle, for instance.' Hitler swept the room with a hand, his back stiff, his chin raised and his jaw jutting out. 'It has an interesting history. Witches were tortured and put to death here, and the shedding of blood has made this place more powerful. In fact, all the ancient people understood the value of human sacrifice – the Mexicans, the Druids, even our own ancestors. Is this not true?' he asked Rahn again.

Oh! Rahn could find no breath in his lungs! He glanced about. 'Yes, mein Führer,' he managed to say.

Hitler gave a nod of his head and made a gesture with his hand and there was the collective scraping of chairs as they were drawn into the table and the circle of men sat down.

Rahn breathed a sigh of relief, but his hands were shaking so he held them in his lap beneath the table to keep them still, lest the wolf smell his fear and discern from it his unfaithfulness.

'Heinrich was right,' the Führer now confirmed, coming to his own chair. 'It is the destiny of the German people to become the consciousness of Europe. Such a responsibility comes only by way of great sacrifices, and more sacrifices will come before the world will see that it must, either willingly or by force, unite under the rulership of the German Reich and its supreme leader . . . in the same way the limbs, if they are to function properly, must come under the governorship of the mind's supreme consciousness! But consciousness, gentlemen, comes at a price!' He turned in Rahn's direction, and the historian felt as though he had plunged his head into a torrent of water chilled by melting snow. 'We are at the outset of a tremendous revolution in moral ideas and man's spiritual orientation; a new age of the magic interpretation of the world is coming, an interpretation in terms of will instead of intellect. The Freemasons once knew this secret, as did the alchemists and the magicians of old, like Solomon, Basil Valentinus and Faust: control over evil, harnessing evil – this is true power, gentlemen! The man who sacrifices evil is nothing to me, but a man who can sacrifice his goodness – such a man can become the instrument of the one destined to fulfil the plan of the gods. You are such men . . . and I am the destined one!' He scanned the circle of faces. 'I am the ideal of the Grail, gentlemen! And you are the true ideal of the knights of the Grail – the Brotherhood of the Grail. You are the limbs through which I will one day work my magic, as Christ performed his magic through his disciples. And I *demand* of you the sacrifice even of your goodness!'

Before he sat down, he gave the signal for the meal to begin.

It was a solemn affair. Rahn could barely touch his venison. He watched Hitler, askance. The man ate a plate of steamed vegetables and drank nothing but water and seemed to take no pleasure in it. Rahn sat half listening to the occasional footfall of the servants, the clinking of cutlery, the muted music, feeling the slow-burning terror of intuition rising up to his temples.

How was he going to get out of this?

He looked furtively around him. He didn't belong to this circle of SS officers and, more to the point, he didn't want to belong to it. Once again, he told himself to calm down. Soon he would be far from Himmler's reach and a free man. He would be his own master. All he had to do was to get through this night, give Himmler his damned genealogy and get out.

When all were finished, Hitler looked about his table for a long time, staring at each man in turn.

'A moment ago,' he said, 'you were speaking of Jesus, but I say you must forget Jesus – for the final saviour of the world has come; the one who will replace Jesus and lead you to the Apocalypse and the renewal of the world! Satan, the creative, fertilising spirit principle of the world, will reign through me in the same way Christ reigned through Jesus. And those who wish to follow me into the glorious light of a new Reich must be willing to sacrifice everything: brother, sister, mother, father – the very death of God and even Jesus Christ himself! They must be willing to supplant Christ with Satan. For a man cannot follow two masters!'

He tamed his ecstasy by replacing some strands of hair that had fallen over his eyes. When he stood, all followed again by reflex, but he was finished with them.

'We are awake, gentlemen. Let others sleep!'

Rahn remembered this line. Philip le Bel, that demonic king who had tortured and sent so many Templars to the stake, had been in the habit of saying these very same words.

With a gesture of disgust Hitler walked out of the hall as if to say, *I have tasted your souls and found you bitter!*

Himmler woke them from their reverie. It was time, he said. Rahn had no idea what he meant.

Only later would he learn that what had gone before was the

customary ritual before a man could be initiated into the circle of Ritters, or knights. They called it The Last Supper, because the ordeal that followed was death, and it marked the beginning of a new life.

5

THE CRYPT

'There are moments when, even to the sober eye of reason, the world of our sad humanity may assume the semblance of a Hell...'
Edgar Allan Poe, 'The Premature Burial'

Rahn moved with the others out of the castle entrance and into the darkness, not knowing what would come next. He descended a long staircase to a lower court-yard and followed the group over a path lit by torches to a door. Beyond it another set of narrow steps took them to what looked like an underground chamber or crypt of sorts. Years of orienting himself in caves led him to the calculation that they were in the north tower and directly beneath the circular hall where they had just eaten. The space was fashioned into a round crypt of about the same size as the hall above, lit only by torches placed beneath arched windows set high and recessed deeply into the thick stone walls. In this strange otherworldly penumbral light, Rahn shivered from cold and fear. He could sense something sinister afoot, but he didn't know what it could possibly be.

Ahead of him the officers took their places around a large circular depression cut into the crypt's floor. Rahn was filled with dismay when he realised, as he approached it, that in this central depression there lay a man, battered, bruised and bleeding.

'What do you think of this, Rahn?' Himmler said cheerily at his side.

Rahn didn't know if he meant the poor wretch in the centre of the room, or the room itself. He decided on the latter; if he could keep things scholarly he might not lose his nerve.

'It looks like an initiation chamber,' he said, 'a cross between a Mycenaean tomb of ancient Greece and a Mithraeum used by the Romans. It has the same vaulted, domed ceiling.' He followed its arc with a trembling hand. 'It is also rounded with a central depression for—' He paused then, unable to say the word. He felt the undigested venison and the good Bavarian wine do a somersault in his stomach.

Himmler looked at him with paternal concern. 'You did not finish your eloquent conclusion? Is something the matter?'

'No . . .'

'Well, as the Führer said, this castle has an interesting history of human sacrifice. Perhaps it is a little like Montsegur, where so many good souls were burnt to death by the agents of the Catholic Church.'

Indignation replaced revulsion. Rahn bristled at this comparison.

'Not far from here in the Teutoberg forest there is a mystery centre, a temple eighty feet above the ground. Weisthor says this makes Wewelsburg a most propitious geographical location for the centre of our new Reich. He says that it is at the head of a long ley line that connects Germany to France – a line of powerful energies called serpent currents, which channel the forces of death. For this reason I will soon have twelve basalt pedestals located around the perimter of this vault. Onto these pedestals I will place urns containing the ashes of those esteemed dead knights who have sworn an oath that binds them to our order for eternity.' He stared pointedly at Rahn. 'But before one gives this oath one must sacrifice even one's goodness. Do you understand, Rahn?'

A little patch of meaning floated out to Rahn and caused the hairs on the back of his neck to stand on end and a bead of sweat to form on his brow. That same moment the man in the central depression began moaning.

Rahn's heart burned with alarm. He stared at Himmler. 'What are you going to do?'

'It is not what I am going to do, Herr Rahn, but rather what you are going to do. This is a test of your loyalty. This man you see here is a malcontent. He has been inciting the people of the township against us and we were forced to arrest him and his family. I give you my word that I will spare this man's children if . . .'

Rahn frowned. 'If?'

Himmler sighed, like an impatient parent who must instruct a slow child. 'If you will show your willingness to sacrifice your goodness, Rahn! The time has come for you to stain your hands with blood!'

Rahn turned the request over in his mind. He had obviously misunderstood it. 'Stain my hands with blood?'

'Of course!' Himmler replied, happily. 'I know you are an intellectual, for whom the word is mightier than the sword, but you may find consolation in saving the lives of three children who, beyond the error of their father, are of good German stock. It would be a shame to waste them, wouldn't you agree? One life in exchange for three – a fair price by any estimation.'

Rahn, confronted by this monstrous proposal, fell into a panic. He looked about. He was surrounded and there were guards at the door. Even if he could get past them there was nowhere to go.

'This man is an enemy,' Himmler continued, 'his children will be adopted by one or two of our own members. Soon you will hear of a program I am creating for such children. I've named it Lebensborn.'

The moans of the man in the pit turned to howls and tears

made tracks through the blood on his face. Rahn could make out the words 'Spare my babies!'

Himmler rocked backwards and forwards on polished heels. He looked to Rahn as if at any moment he might do a little dance. He was enjoying the macabre ritual, and Rahn despised him.

'You see?' his superior continued. 'Even this man understands what you have to do! Sacrifice must come before illumination can begin.'

Rahn felt a distortion of his focus. Perhaps he had been drugged? The wine? The food? Was this a hallucination? Some strange mock initiation, using suggestion and lighting, smoke and mirrors. He summoned his defiance. This was surely a test of his moral fibre.

'I will not do what goes against my conscience!' he said.

'Conscience? Well, I have underestimated the strength of your conditioning, Herr Rahn. I think you need a little encouragement. Once you see the children's cherubic faces you might change your mind. I had wished to spare them the sight of their father's execution, but you leave me no choice.' He made a signal and one of his ritters came forwards, a man with a scar on his cheek. The man caught Rahn's eye as he handed him a large dagger adorned with the Death's Head.

The dagger felt impossibly heavy in Rahn's hands. The skull's grin mocked him.

'Why don't you kill me, you coward!' the man in the pit cried.

A tremulous indecision overtook Rahn now. The man staring at him in the pit; Himmler with his fatherly grin; the dagger in his hand; the circle of ritters: all of it seemed to drop away like a rock thrown into a chasm in the caves of Lombrives and he felt himself rising. He would surely have fainted, he realised, had he not been startled to awareness by the appearance of three children ranging in age from twelve to two. They were brought down the stairs and into the chamber. The youngest was screaming, wrestling with her captor, while the older ones wore vacant faces until they saw their father. There was a struggle and they were reined in. The father cried and the children responded. The father turned away in shame and the children called out to him.

Rahn was gripped by a species of terror and indecision.

Himmler glanced at his pocket watch. 'You have thirty seconds to spare their lives.'

Rahn decided to try reason. 'Listen to me – I don't know anything about killing a man! Let the children go – they are good German stock, as you said.'

Himmler regarded him, and in that passage from eye to eye Rahn saw a man who was beyond history, beyond civilisation, beyond humanity; he was nothing but a shadow without substance. In a matter of seconds Rahn understood that he alone in that chamber had the freedom to choose, even though he would not escape guilt, no matter what his choice. That was Himmler's little joke, the illumination he had promised.

Himmler said, 'You are an expert on mythology, and mythology is steeped in violence. Just pretend you are Achilles and this man is Hector – kill him. You have twenty seconds.'

A strange calm descended over Rahn.

'Fifteen seconds . . .'

He glanced at those terrified little faces; three lives about to be shattered or finished, one way or the other. He went down into the pit. He looked into the man's encouraging eyes. Perhaps he had worked all day and had gone to a tavern and voiced his opinions about the Nazis over a beer? Now he was facing the unthinkable – not only his death, but also the death of his children.

'What are you waiting for?' The man pushed out his chest like a cock in a fight. 'Do it!'

'Ten seconds . . .'

Rahn brought the dagger to the man's unguarded abdomen, but his arm was paralysed.

'Do it, Nazi bag of horse-shit!' the man growled, slapping his stomach, working up a hateful panic.

'Five seconds . . .' Himmler said, consulting his watch.

What would the Cathars have done? To kill even to save a life was to commit moral suicide. He could not do it! Moreover, he would not do it! He brought his arm down and dropped the knife.

The man shouted and made a grab for the blade but the guard was in the pit before Rahn could think and in a moment the captive was lying on the ground sobbing.

'For pity's sake! My children!'

The moment had passed and Rahn closed his eyes, certain he would be executed along with the man. He held his breath and when the shots came they were deafening. Images now danced before Rahn's eyelids: he saw himself as a child, running after lightning in the forests near his home; he saw his father reading the paper and heard his mother in the kitchen, humming to the faint sound of Wagner coming from the gramophone. He saw the snow on the pines outside and inside, on the Christmas tree, flickering candles throwing their light on the fresh pfeffernusse cookies and marzipan covered in schokolade that were hanging from the branches. He saw himself inside the village church, a boy of five, urinating into his shoes because churches were spaces with no end, where there was no light, and where he could hear the creaking of evil stepping over the stones with the patience of a pendulum.

He waited for the reproving, interminable darkness to digest him then but it did not and when he opened his eyes he found he was standing as before and the captive was dead at his feet, lying in a pool of his own blood. Beyond the circle he glimpsed those three small bodies slumped on the ground, one over the other, lifeless, still.

'So how does it feel?' Himmler asked in his high-pitched voice.

Rahn couldn't speak for a moment and then gall rose up with suddenness and he leant over and discharged the venison and

good Bavarian wine all over the dead man. There was the fire of
bile in his nostrils and in his throat. He looked up at Himmler.

'Why?' he managed to say.

'So that you could come face to face with the beast, the power
of pure egotism inside you.'

The meaning now came and with it a piercing shame: faced
with making a choice between moral annihilation and the lives of
those children, he had decided to let the children die.

'You chose what was right for you, you see? That is pure egotism, don't you think?'

Anger welled up in Rahn. 'No!' he spat. 'You were wrong to
give me that choice! Wrong in the eyes of God!'

'I don't believe you were thinking of God for one moment!
When you made that decision you were thinking of yourself, of
the picture of yourself that you hold so dear. At that moment,
you were your own god and so God, as you have imagined Him,
is now dead for you!'

Rahn swallowed acid and wiped his mouth. 'I am a free man!'

'When you believe you possess freedom, that is when you
understand it the least. Freedom comes from knowing the evil
within and embracing it. I told you it would be illuminating! Only
now do you truly know yourself, and your life will never be the
same. You see, now that you know your egotism, you are free to
act as you will – unlike most people, who go about thinking they
are so good and proper and god-like. The truth is, Herr Rahn,
given the choice, a man will always choose himself – this is natural. Those who wish to join our circle must be willing to sacrifice
the false image of this God that is inside them for an ideal that
is higher, no matter what the cost to their soul. This is the first
step to a new life. Until now, to the outside world, you have been
SS-Unterscharführer Rahn, unofficially a member of the Allge-
meine-SS. Now, you are made SS-Oberscharführer. To those of
this circle, you are a member of the Blood of the Schutzstaf-
fel-SS. One day your name will grace a plaque fixed to the back

of one of those chairs in the hall above.' He gave Rahn something. 'What you hold in your hand is the Totenkopf, the Death's Head ring. It is only given to those few whom I feel deserve it.'

Rahn wanted to throw it into that pompous little face but that would not have been wise. His hand was shaking. He looked at the ring. It was a silver band with several runes and oak leaves cast into the exterior, topped off with a skull.

'Look inside it, go on!' Himmler said, excited.

Rahn wiped his eyes. 'I can't see.'

'Inside is your last name, today's date, and my own signature. You see how I have faith in you, Rahn – even before you bring me your genealogy? Keep the ring safe. It is the visible sign of your devotion to our community's inner code and your loyalty to the Führer and his ideals. However, you must not wear it until you have made the final oath to replace the Christian cross with the Swastika – only then will you be wedded to this order. But remember, Herr Rahn, even now you are united with us in such a way that you can *never* resign. Do you understand?'

The group returned to the castle and Rahn was shown to a room where he spent what was left of the awful night unable to sleep, sitting on a bed vacantly waiting for the dawn. When it came, he was taken by car back to the station where he caught the next train out of Paderborn for Berlin.

As the train left the station Rahn opened the window and threw the Death's Head ring as far as he could into a field. He recalled a fairytale about a man who was so good he allowed one mosquito to bite him. He thought, 'Poor little mosquito, let him suck until he is full,' and the mosquito was so happy with the man it then told all the mosquitoes in the city. Soon the sky grew black with mosquitoes wanting to taste the good man's blood and they bit and bit and sucked and sucked but they couldn't get full because there were so many of them, and in the meantime the man had died.

Rahn had given his blood to the Nazis and he could throw

that ring all the way to the moon but it would make no difference now. He was forever tainted with their madness.

Somehow he knew he wouldn't get out of this alive.

6

SERINUS

'This is a very unexpected turn of affairs.'
Sir Arthur Conan Doyle, 'A Scandal in Bohemia'

In the train, Rahn dozed and had a dream in which he was floating in blood. It woke him with a start and to his surprise he found that someone was sitting beside him reading the *Völkischer Beobachter*. The man closed the paper and folded it neatly. He was wearing a blue suit, a hat to match and a party pin in his spotless necktie. He looked like a respectable middle-class gentleman who lived a middle-class life in a modest house in Berlin with his plain Bavarian wife and his fine Aryan children. What would he say if he knew the madness of the man he called his Führer?

The man looked at Rahn now as if to say, *Who are you?*

Rahn wanted to tell him that he didn't know who he was or what had happened to the legend he had created for himself, as an adventurer, a writer and historian. Everything had fallen to pieces the moment those shots were fired.

When the gentleman spoke, he said, 'Are you alright?'

'Terribly sorry,' Rahn said, 'just a dream.' He looked out at the grey day and it stared back at him.

'You were saying something in your sleep,' the man ventured.

'Was I?'

'Oh yes, you said, "The children."'

Rahn laughed nervously. 'Did I? Strange . . .'

The man adjusted his glasses. There was something familiar about him.

'Do you have children?' he asked.

'No.'

'Indeed. That is good, in times like these.'

In times like these! There was a world of meaning hidden in such a phrase. It said all there was to say.

'What are you going to do now?' he asked as plainly as if he had said, *What do you think the weather will do now?*

'I beg your pardon?' He felt his temple for a fever.

'You're in a bit of a pickle, Herr Rahn.'

Rahn sat up. 'I'm terribly sorry, have I met you before?'

'Well, yes and no.'

'I don't remember, I'm afraid . . .'

'I'm not surprised. After all, we weren't formally introduced. One could say it was just a brief encounter.'

'When did we meet?'

'Last night.'

It took a moment for this to sink in. He had seen this man before. This was the man with the scar on his cheek! The man who had given him that knife when he was standing in the pit!

'I am a friend,' the man said.

'I don't understand.' Rahn's heart was pounding. Was this a trap, one of Himmler's trials to gauge his loyalty?

'I can offer you . . . restitution.'

'I'm sorry but I—'

'Do you want to make good what you've done? I am here to offer you an alternative. You don't have to say yes or no right away. Perhaps you think this is a test, but I'm here to tell you that no, it isn't. We understand your caution and we advise you to trust no one. For now, all you have to do is go to France and continue as instructed – to hunt for that grimoire. I wish you luck on your hunt. Keep your ears open in Paris and you will soon learn more. Perhaps you still have a chance to do something fine for the world.'

The train began to slow down. The man stood and tipped his hat slightly and left the compartment, leaving his newspaper behind. Rahn picked it up and a card fell out.

On it was written a single word:

Serinus.

7

SANCHO

'Tell me thy company and I will tell thee what thou art.'
Miguel de Cervantes, Don Quixote

Rahn changed trains in Berlin and from there his journey was therapeutic. With each hour that passed, Weisthor, Wewelsburg, and the memory of that chamber of blood became, at times, unreal to his mind, like a distant point, a pause at a station that one soon passes, thinking how good it is that one doesn't live there. But something told him that he could only put aside the horror temporarily. Sooner or later he would have to face it and he wondered whether he could live with the guilt. For now, he leant on those words spoken by the man on the train – that he *might still have time to do something fine for the world*. This thought kept him sane.

Sometime in the night his papers passed inspection and he boarded another train for France and its fields, its houses, its farms, mountains and vales, vines and trees. Nothing had changed in that beloved country and he found this profoundly reassuring. In Paris, he dozed again in his hotel until he was well enough to go out to find coffee and food. He walked about the old city with convalescing affection, hearing his own footsteps on the leaf-littered pavements as if they belonged not to him but to a disembodied ghost. Paris! Embalmed by history, happy among its Napoleonic monuments and its obelisks, its cathedrals, its squares and streets; its river meandering in a seductive pulsing of life.

As soon as possible he contacted his friend Alexis La Dame on the number La Dame's mother had given him. La Dame was pleasantly surprised. Rahn asked him for a favour: Could he gather information on a certain individual called Vincent Varas? They agreed to meet and that was that. In the meantime, the galleries and the restaurants, jazz clubs and bookshops reclaimed him.

On the day of their meeting, Rahn looked in the mirror to shave and found himself taken aback. He saw a thin man with high cheekbones jutting out of a pale face. Gone was the look of one for whom the entire world is a riddle waiting to be solved and in its place was a sad resignation – a spectre of death looming behind the façade of life.

Looking at himself, he recalled how, as a child, when dark clouds scurried over the horizon in autumn and there was the sense of an impending storm, he and his friends would gather in the forest near his home. They would wait and, when the storm came, feeling their hearts in their chests and the wind in their lungs, they would run through the trees in the rain, flying over the ground, weightless, invulnerable, using lightning as swords, playing at being Michael slaying the dragon, with a feeling of sovereign protection in their hearts. Michael always triumphed, the good had always won and Rahn had always been on the side of the good! Now he no longer knew which side he stood on, nor what ground he walked. He understood that this meant he had lost his innocence, as clichéd as this sounded.

He tried to put these thoughts aside as he approached the intersection of St Germain des Prés and rue Bonaparte where the Café de Flore was situated, to plan roughly what he was going to tell La Dame. He would likely be sitting at their usual table near the window reading the paper but in any case Rahn could have found him in a crowd: the combination of straw-coloured mop of hair; gold beard; suit and tie; cigar in one hand and brandy balloon in the other, was unmistakable.

They'd met eight years before as extras on the set of a Pabst picture, filmed on the border of Austria and Poland, called *Vier von der Infanterie*. But, as it turned out, they discovered the happy coincidence that they had met once before, albeit very briefly, at an obscure bookshop in the rue Montmartre, where they had both been in search of the same, very rare Mexican edition of *Don Quixote*. So, after the day's filming, they took themselves to an old pub run by a one-eyed madame, where, compelled by Dionysian inebriation, they drank toast after toast to the memory of Miguel de Cervantes. When they ran out of money, they turned to warm beer and after singing a number of discordant songs, Rahn announced that he was leaving to look for the Holy Grail in the caves of southern France and La Dame was welcome to come along. La Dame, citing years of working with his brother, a mining engineer and geologist, as credentials, said he would be only too happy to assist. La Dame, in fact, turned out to be rather good with a lamp and rope, and even taught Rahn French, interpreting for him until he was proficient.

And so for the next two years La Dame played Sancho Panza to Rahn's Don Quixote, and their friendship, having survived cold nights and wet caves and the inevitable frustrations, disappointments and dangers of treasure hunting, had grown as comfortable as a pair of old shoes.

Those endless, careless days now seemed to Rahn like another life. In his pocket sat Weisthor's envelope and the card from the man on the train, side by side, as if to underline to him how much things had changed. Even so, he would have to go on as if nothing had happened until he could figure things out.

He was about to cross the street when he had a strange feeling. He looked around but saw nothing out of the ordinary, and put it down to his mind playing tricks. Still, the feeling remained with him until a sudden downpour interrupted his thoughts and forced him to make a run for it. Once inside the café, he removed his soaked black coat and his fedora and looked around. It was early and the café was quiet. In one corner, a man ate an omelette, his poodle beside him on its own chair, lapping at a bowl of soup. At the far end of the room two lovers sat entwined, kissing. Behind the bar, the waitress argued with the manager and threatened to leave, both ignoring a middle-aged blonde, perhaps a femme de la nuit, asking for a glass of wine. All in all, an average afternoon.

As expected, La Dame was at his usual table by the window and when he looked up from reading the Paris-Soir, he cried, 'Rahn!'

He was shorter than Rahn but more athletic and so when they embraced warmly it was rather a mismatched affair.

'The reason for your unreasonable treatment of my reason so enfeebles my reason that I have reason to complain of your beauty!' he said, quoting Cervantes and bowing graciously.

'And the high Heavens, with which your divinity divinely fortifies you with stars, makes you the deserver of the desert that is deserved by your greatness!' Rahn returned with a courteous bow.

'I took the privilege, knowing your tastes.' La Dame sat down and poured Rahn a glass of brandy with one hand while he puffed on the cigar he held in the other, a Hoyo de Monterrey, purchased, as usual, from the oldest tobacconist in Paris near the Louvre in the rue Saint Honoré. La Dame liked Cuban cigars, fast women and expensive clothes because it made him feel less Swiss, which in France was another word for prosaic, or, as some would say, l'ordinaire.

'I see you still possess your vices,' Rahn said, sitting down.

'Consistency, my dear Rahn, is the last refuge of the unimaginative. Who said that?'

Rahn sniffed the brandy; the note was comforting. 'Oscar Wilde.'

'You look wretched!'

'Thank you.' Rahn took a good sip and let the fruity fire sit on his tongue a moment. 'And you, my dear La Dame, look a little portly.'

There was a flash of panic in La Dame's eye and his hand explored his middle to test the veracity of the vile statement.

Touché! Rahn thought.

There was a narrowing of the eyes and a shaking of the index finger of the hand that held his cigar. 'You almost had me believing it!' he said, with a smile, straightening his tie and biting into the cigar with a virile ferocity. He took a glance at his reflection in the mirror opposite and sat back, satisfied that he cut a good shape. 'I've been working at teaching imbeciles to think logically, a task that, I have to say, is starting to lose its lustre. At this rate I'll die of boredom before I'm forty.' He watched Rahn drink the remaining contents of his glass down in one gulp with amusement and blew smoke rings in the air. 'Hold on, Rahn! That's expensive, you know.'

'I'll pay.'

La Dame raised a lazy brow. 'Well, in that case . . . bottom's up!' He drank his glass in one gulp too and set it down for a top-up.

Rahn poured another for both of them, then held up his glass and looked at La Dame through the golden liquor. 'Nice colour . . .' He sniffed it. 'Oak casks, extra old; Napoleon or Vieille Réserve; aged at least six years. So you haven't been cheap, La Dame, but you haven't spent all the rent money either!'

'How can you know so much from one mouthful, Rahn?'

Rahn ignored him. 'Do you know how they tested brandy in the old days? They put gunpowder in it and set fire to it. If the gunpowder took, the brandy was good.'

La Dame sat back. 'How you manage to retain so many completely useless but terribly impressive facts in that head of yours simply astounds me. Lucky for me, I have my looks to fall back on.' He sighed. 'This is good, isn't it? Just like those nights at the Leila in Montmartre! The only difference is we're not waiting for the bartender to turn around before running out of the place without paying. Things do change, thank goodness. But we did have rather a lot of fun, didn't we? Drinking brandy and la Fée Verte.'

Rahn nodded. 'Yes, I also remember those days with fondness.'

'That reminds me of Etienne – have you seen her lately? Are you and she, still . . . you know?'

'We were never an affaire de coeur,' Rahn said, 'but I keep expecting her to turn up wearing a suit like the old days, carrying a bottle of absinthe in one hand and a gun in the other.'

'I'll take the absinthe . . . She was rather odd.'

La Dame had a fashion of calling everything 'odd' and seemed to live amid a legion of oddities.

'A Marxist with good taste is a rare species,' he continued. 'Speaking of Marxists, you certainly did send me on a chase! And exceedingly odd it was too!'

Rahn sat up. 'What did you find out?'

'Actually—' He warmed his words with another swallow of brandy. 'There was a bit of hole-and-corner work involved. This Vincent Varas is an alias for a man called Pierre de Plantard who works for a group called Alpha Galates, which has some connections to the French Union. They have a nasty periodical called Vaincre, which they use to disseminate their anti-Freemason, anti-Marxist, anti-Jew, anti-*everybody* diatribe. Alpha Galates purports that its secrets come from ancient Atlantis. Moreover, they're more Catholic than the pope and are expecting the so-called Apocalypse sooner rather than later, after which there will be the creation of a New Jerusalem – where, incidentally, there are no Jews but only good Roman Catholics.'

Rahn sighed. 'How big are they?'

'As far as I can gather, there are only a handful of members and this Plantard is only a boy really, no older than nineteen, but there are others. The interesting thing is that behind Alpha Galates there is another group run by a man called Gaston De Mengel.'

'So,' Rahn said, 'that's the connection.'

'What connection?'

'I'm here at De Mengel's suggestion.'

'Really? And you didn't know that he and another man called Monti ran that group?'

'No.'

'Well, the group behind Alpha Galates is called Groupe Occidental D'etudes Esoteriques. They are highly secretive and dedicated to bringing peace to the world . . . and the Eiffel Tower is also made from Meccano! Whatever the case, this Monti was apparently Péladan's pupil. You know Joséphin Péladan – the Rosicrucian?'

'Yes, I know of him, I acknowledged him in my book. You know – the book you never read?'

La Dame ignored Rahn's sarcasm and said happily, 'The plot thickens, Rahn! Some months ago, the Masonic Grand Lodge published an article denouncing Monti. It said he was a fraud and a supposed Jesuit agent and soon after he winds up dead.'

'Dead?'

'Dead as a doornail, dear Rahn! And his close associate, a certain Dr Camille Savoire, apparently rushes to his side, examines him and claims that he has been poisoned – his body was apparently covered in black spots.'

'Let me see if I have the gist,' Rahn said. 'Alpha Galates is a front for *another* society started by De Mengel and Monti, Groupe Occidental D'etudes Esoteriques. Some months ago Monti was murdered because he was a fraud and a spy.' Rahn tried to think through the brandy fog. 'Could it be more complicated?'

'Yes, indeed, it could – I told you it was bloody marvellous! This Dr Savoire supposedly took up the vacated chair left by Monti and he runs the society now, along with this De Mengel fellow. So Plantard, or Vincent Varas, or whatever you want to call him, must be working for them. But the word is, there is a little friction between De Mengel and Savoire.'

'And Plantard is caught in the middle? That's good to know.' Rahn raised his glass. 'You've done well. I think you've missed your calling – you should have been a private eye or journalist, not a minor professor of science!'

La Dame shook his head dismissively. 'Too uncomfortable, Rahn. All those nights standing in the rain, waiting for something to happen. Not *my* style.'

'Alright, but how did you find out so much?'

'I have one or two friends in the periodicals.' La Dame took a long puff of his cigar. 'So, are you going to tell me what this is about and why you need to see this Pierre Plantard?'

Rahn heard La Dame but he was distracted by that feeling again – that they were being watched – and found himself scanning the room. 'I don't quite know how to start,' he said, with a strange laugh that sounded nervous to his ears. 'It's all rather a long story really. But to cut it short, I have a new publisher.'

'A new publisher?' La Dame puffed away. 'Congratulations, that's wonderful. This calls for a celebration!' He poured two more glasses and regarded Rahn with an admiring eye. 'That explains why you're dressed like Clark Gable. You're clearly not the man who left Ussat-les-Bains hounded by creditors! So, who in God's name is it?'

Rahn looked at La Dame; his smile behind that gold beard was all eagerness. The last thing Rahn wanted to do was drag his friend into this messy business. He drank down his brandy before tackling an unpleasant abridged confession, which now seemed to him, all things considered, to be unavoidable.

'When I saw you in Munich, do you remember me telling you

that I had an appointment in Berlin?'

'Yes, a mysterious telegram – and money if I remember correctly?'

'Well, who do you think sent it?'

'I don't know, Marlene Dietrich?'

'Cold, La Dame,' he said. 'Take another guess.'

'Well, I'll look for an antithesis then. Was it the pope?'

'Close. Hitler's Black Pope.' He leant forwards and whispered, 'It was the Reichsführer, Himmler.'

When La Dame's disbelief turned to comprehension he laughed. 'You're not serious, Rahn!'

Rahn shot him a look.

'Could it be true? What did he want? I was just reading about that weasel. I have to say, people here are talking about nothing else these days – Hitler and his cronies. Wasn't he a chicken farmer? I dare say! I wouldn't want to see him coming for me with an axe. Are you going to let me prattle on, or are you going to tell me what he wanted?'

Rahn's smile was weak. 'Himmler made me an offer I couldn't refuse.'

'Sounds dangerous?'

At that moment a man entered the café: medium build, medium height, wearing an expression that was so benign, so plain and commonplace that it made an immediate impression on Rahn. The man sat down and began to roll a cigarette. Rahn tried to remember that saying from one of Arthur Conan Doyle's celebrated Sherlock Holmes tales and found it: *There is nothing so unnatural as the commonplace.*

'So, are you going to drag it out? Make me beg you to tell me what it was?'

Rahn wrenched his eyes from the man to look at La Dame.

'They want two books, nothing more than propaganda for the new regime. They gave me an office at SS headquarters and I've been writing reports, doing errands, which include some archaeological work, you know, looking for evidence of the Aryan forefathers. All a lot of rubbish, really.' He felt sour now, saying it out loud, and he didn't like the look in his friend's eye. 'Recently, my superiors received a letter from De Mengel; apparently this Pierre Plantard knows something about a grimoire called *Le Serpent Rouge*. The fact is, I'm supposed to find it so that Himmler can give it to Hitler on his birthday.'

'Well, burn my beard!' La Dame said, rubbing it absently. 'A grimoire? Isn't that a book of black magic? What sort of nut-bags are you working for?'

Rahn drank a good mouthful of brandy and wondered what La Dame would say if he knew about Wewelsburg. 'Nuttier than anyone gives them credit for, I'm afraid.'

'And you're working for them!'

'Look, a man has to eat, La Dame!' he said, suddenly defensive. 'You, a man of means, have no idea how cold it gets in winter without heating, nor how difficult it is to walk in the snow when your shoes are full of holes. It's not comfortable, let me assure you! Do you see how I look? I've been under the weather and the weather has been rather appalling. Besides, if you think that I could have said no to Himmler to his face, well, you are sorely mistaken! By now I'd be buried under a mound of rubble at Dachau.'

La Dame turned sombre and looked at Rahn with unfocused, gloomy eyes. 'Well, you do realise, Rahn, that you have fulfilled the prophecy of the locals at Ussat-les-Bains – they always said you were working for the Nazis.'

Rahn stared out to the street slashed by rain: the traffic was busy and the streetlights came on. He sighed. 'I'm not working for the Nazis. I'm working for myself.'

'Oh, yes, I forgot your first rule: you always work for yourself.'

'Look,' Rahn said, ignoring his obvious reproof. 'All I wanted was enough money in my pocket to continue our search for the Cathar treasure.'

'What about this *Le Serpent Rouge*, then?'

'I'm undecided; perhaps now that I'm in France I'll just disappear in the mountains and hope that sooner or later Himmler will forget about me.'

'I don't know about that! He sounds like the type to hold a grudge, if you know what I mean. So, you're not going to see Plantard tomorrow?'

'Well, I'm a little curious about it, and my train doesn't leave until the afternoon.'

'It all sounds rather diabolical to me.' La Dame threw the last of his brandy down his throat, exemplifying how much he needed it.

Rahn tipped his brandy in La Dame's direction before he drank it down. 'I'll be the Faust of my generation and you can be my Wagner!'

'Doctor, to walk with you is ever an honour and a profit, and yet . . . to aid and abet your work for the Devil would, I'm afraid, lead me astray. Facilis descensus Averni and all that! It is far too easy to enter Hell, but getting out is another matter entirely. I'm afraid I'm of rather a different constitution to you.' He poured more brandy into their glasses.

Rahn looked at it appreciatively; his head was swimming and the room was agreeably blurred. 'Remember that night in that Czechoslovakian pub? You vowed to be Sancho Panza to my Don Quixote . . . and that means you don't believe in devils, nor in Hell, because Sancho, the dear man, was a materialist!' He lifted the glass and took a swig.

La Dame nodded. 'Like Sancho Panza, I may not believe but I don't discount the power of belief. Haven't you heard of those Indians in America who go off to a mountain to die? They may be lunatics but they always die because they believe they will; that is the trouble with lunacy – sometimes your illusions can turn out to be real because you believe in them!'

Rahn said, 'The Countess P always said she would know the

day of her death. Now there is a regal woman, a true descendant of the Cathars! She hasn't returned any of my letters, you know. I think she's mad at me because of the way I left France. I'm hoping to see her while I'm here; perhaps she and I can go to the caves at Ornolac again in the Tourster, if she's feeling up to it. Do you remember how much she loved those caves?'

'You don't know, Rahn? Didn't Deodat get a hold of you?' La Dame said, all frowns.

'What are you talking about?'

'Bad news, I'm afraid.' He paused, trying to construct the words.

'Come out with it, La Dame.'

'The Countess P passed away about two months ago. The magistrate was looking for you . . . I assumed you knew.'

Rahn's heart sank. 'The last time I saw Deodat was three years ago, after we returned from the caves at Lombrives. I left France shortly after that. Two months, you say?'

'She had a stroke.'

'I can't believe it.'

'Well, the old buzz— I mean, the grand madame, was right about knowing when she was going to die. Apparently Deodat made a visit a week or so before the fatal day. She seemed perfectly well, in top form, enjoying the best of health, but she told him she had ordered a coffin because she had a sense she was going to meet her maker.' He fixed Rahn with a significant look. 'A week later she was cold and in the ground, just like that! You see what a devil of a thing belief is? It can kill you!'

But Rahn wasn't listening. He was recalling the last time he had seen the Countess. She had been standing, a tall figure dressed in yellow, in front of her old château in Toulouse, with its broken shutters and half-cracked pots brimming with flowers. Her voluminous hair framing a face still beautiful and unlined, her intelligent eyes half closed from the glare, and her mouth upturned in a smile that belied her sadness. She had not waved goodbye, nor had she said the words. She had always expected that he would return.

'Apparently she left something for you,' La Dame said, breaking into his thoughts.

'What?'

'A box. Don't ask me what's in it, nobody knows. Apparently it's sealed – the instructions were that you alone should open it. She was always a mysterious old crone. Do you remember those séances? And her eyes; I swear she was strange! Not to mention all that talk about being the reincarnation of Esclarmonde de Foix!'

'I believed it,' Rahn said, feeling miserable. 'She could have been that great Cathar dame, the guardian of the Cathar Grail.'

'I don't know about the Grail but I can imagine the Countess P giving the Inquisitors a run for their money.'

'Let's make a toast to our friend.' Rahn raised his glass. 'To the Countess P!'

'To the old buzzard, may she rest in peace!'

Rahn shot him a glance and La Dame shrugged. 'I mean it in the most affectionate way.'

They drank in silence, contemplating mortality. The café began to fill. Its interior grew noisy and full of smoke. Rahn turned to look for the commonplace man. He had his back to them.

'Well,' Rahn said, slurring his words, 'before I disappear, I guess I'll have to make a detour to Arques to see Deodat about that box the Countess left me. After that I'll go to Toulouse to pay my respects to the Countess. It's been good seeing you again, La Dame!'

'Listen, you know I would love to come with you, like old times,' he said. 'But all this business sounds, well, a tad on the risky side. In your absence I've discovered something rather perturbing about myself. I've found, to my great astonishment, that I'm quite fond of my boring little life. Don't look like that – it does have its advantages, you know! I am a valued member of the faculty and so I don't have to work too hard; being a professor of scientific methodology is not as boring as you might imagine; I get to pick and choose from an assortment of gorgeous young ladies working in the campus . . . and there are even one or two students nowadays. I have steady pay and an apartment not far from the Arc de Triomphe; I eat at Le Bouillon at least once a month; and last but certainly not least, I can afford to smoke Cuban cigars and drink a brandy that is better than passable. All these things please me. Pitiful I know, shocking I'll admit, but there it is: I'm a boring coward!'

'What happened to living in Morocco and travelling on a slow boat to South America?'

'Yes, but unfortunately there are realities that one must take into account sooner or later – I abhor the heat and have an aversion to water, and if that weren't enough, my morbid fear of snakes would not be well served in South America where, I'm told, one very often finds snakes in one's bed!' He sighed a defeated sigh. 'Besides, I have my children to think of. How could I desert them?'

'You don't have children, La Dame.'

'Not that I know of, of course, but one can never be certain!' The smile was wide behind that beard.

Rahn nodded. 'Don't worry. I've involved you in this as far as I want to. I'll call you if I need you to find out anything else. You can be my man on the ground.'

'So be it! I'm at your beck and call. Bravura at a distance, that's my style. But I'll see you off at the station, at least.'

'Only because you're curious, La Dame!'

'Yes, it's a miracle, isn't it, that curiosity can survive a formal education.'

Rahn paid the bill and before they left the café, he took a glance around for the man with the forgettable face. His table was empty, a half-full glass and a cigarette paper the only evidence that he had been there at all.

8

A BIRD IN THE HAND

'Never look for birds of this year in the nests of the last.'
Miguel de Cervantes, Don Quixote

That night the desk clerk interrupted Rahn's dinner. There was a phone call for him and he decided to take it in his room.

He wondered if the call was from Weisthor and how he could possibly know where he was staying, since he hadn't called him yet. Walking up the stairs, he considered what he would say to the man. Was Weisthor part of that inner circle, one of Hitler's ritters? There was no way of knowing and so he decided to listen and say little.

In his room, Rahn picked up the receiver, expecting to hear Weisthor's rumbustious voice. Instead, the voice that greeted him was French, polished and courteous.

'Monsieur Rahn?'

Rahn paused. 'I am he.'

'I hope you are enjoying your stay in Paris?'

'To whom am I speaking?'

'This is just a courtesy call. We have a mutual friend whom you met on the train.'

Rahn swallowed. 'Yes, I remember him.'

'He asked me to call and see how you are getting on.'

'Just fine, thank you.'

'We know you have to . . . tie a few loose ends before your journey to the south and we just wanted to wish you well. Will you be keeping your appointment with Plantard tomorrow?'

Rahn hesitated. 'I expect so.'

'That is for the better, we think. It is important to have the right information, you know, to understand the lay of the land. Now, it may have occurred to you that you might just lose yourself in the south. I would advise you to think again. You are not travelling light. Running is quite difficult when you have a ball and chain attached to your legs.'

A ball and chain?

'Soon you will be hearing from us again. In the meantime we rely on you to follow your plans and to do what you do best. Just one word of warning: keep a lookout for wolves.'

'Who are you working for?' Rahn asked.

There was a long silence, then: 'The name is on the card. I bid you a good night and a safe journey.'

Rahn put the phone down, his limbs drained of blood. He had been followed, after all! He took out the card and read the name – Serinus. Whoever these people were, they weren't going to make it easy for him to disappear. A ball and chain! Yes indeed, he was shown, once again, that he was not free and he would have to make a decision. He sat on the bed and loosened his tie, and wished that he had a brandy.

9

PIERRE PLANTARD

'This is indeed a mystery,' I remarked.
'What do you imagine that it means?'
Sir Arthur Conan Doyle, 'A Scandal in Bohemia'.

The office of Alpha Galates was on the first floor of a rundown two-storey building, above a bookshop on a narrow and unfashionable street.

The rain had dried up that morning, leaving in its wake a cold autumnal day with clouds streaking the skies. The streets were busy and Rahn had slipped easily in and out of the crowds, though he guessed he was still being followed. In truth, he knew it was possibly dangerous to try to lose his 'tail'. After all, he had been warned that he had a ball and chain around his leg and everyone seemed to know his every move. Even so, he had stopped now and again to look through a shop window, hoping to catch a glimpse of whoever was following him in its reflection. He had seen nothing amiss – the man was obviously a professional.

He took a winding stairway to a dirty hallway and followed the numbers until he came to a battered door. He checked his pocket watch for the time; he only had two hours before his train. Waiting for him on the other side of the door could be another way to Hell, he didn't know. He knocked and waited. He heard shuffling sounds and the door opened a little, revealing one dark, hooded eye, a sunken cheek, half a long nose and a couple of full lips.

'C'est quoi?' the mouth said, annoyed.

'Vincent Varas?'

'Qui veut savoir?'

'Otto Rahn,' he said, 'I telephoned you yesterday?'

The door closed. Rahn heard the chain. It opened again to reveal the tall young man.

'Entrez . . . entrez . . .' he said, his eyes furtive and his manner nervous.

Rahn's first impression of the apartment was that it smelt of burnt toast and sardines. He imagined a kitchen full of dirty plates and half-drunk cups of coffee. He could also hear soft music coming through the walls and it lent an atmosphere of nostalgia and decadence. He was led to a sitting room that was largely empty except for a table burdened by a typewriter and wads of paper. More piles of paper littered the floor and Rahn had to step over them. The young man – long, gangling and wet-eyed – came to stand before the table, wearing a vaguely disconcerted frown on his oily face. The pale light coming through the window fell on his emaciated frame, catching the plume of cigarette smoke through which his little bloodshot eyes squinted. He removed a pile of papers from a torn armchair and gestured for Rahn to sit, and in the meantime dragged a stool closer.

'Well?' Rahn said to him, feeling the onset of a headache and the desire to be out of this place sooner rather than later. 'As I explained on the telephone, I don't have much time . . . my train leaves shortly and I must be on it.'

The young man stubbed out his cigarette in a cracked saucer full of old butts and ashes and looked at Rahn with a cursory frown. 'Forgive me, monsieur, but what exactly did De Mengel say to you about *Le Serpent Rouge?*'

'I didn't speak to De Mengel,' Rahn confessed, feeling suddenly on the back foot. 'My superiors tell me it's an important and rare grimoire and I am to acquire it for the Führer.'

There was a nod of consideration.

Rahn grew annoyed. He didn't know why he'd come here, and he was of the mind to leave soon if the man didn't reveal whatever he knew. 'De Mengel told my superiors that you have information on the grimoire.'

'Gaston De Mengel says many things,' the young man replied with an irritating arrogance. He offered Rahn a cigarette from a crushed packet. He was smoking Black Russians – expensive.

'I've given them up,' Rahn said.

'Pourquoi?'

'The superior race must keep itself healthy . . . Himmler's orders,' he said, but his sarcasm was lost on the boy, who nodded appreciatively.

Rahn shifted in his chair and tried to keep the impatience out of his voice. 'Look, can you help me or not?'

The young man struck a match, lit the end of the cigarette and puffed until it glowed. He was stretching the moment out, making resolves and breaking them in the space of seconds.

'That depends,' he said finally.

'On what? Do you want money?'

There was a wide smile. 'Money? Look around, do I look like the sort of man who covets material goods, Monsieur Rahn?'

Where did he get the money for those cigarettes?

Plantard leant in. 'Truth is, monsieur, what I know is more unhealthy than this.' He took a drag of the cigarette and let the smoke out, looking at Rahn. 'It is unhealthy not just for the body, but also for the soul.'

'You mean dangerous?'

'Dangerous?' he asked, his long face wrinkled in a mocking smile. 'Yes.'

'Are you speaking about what happened to your superior, Monti?'

The young man seemed surprised. 'If you know about that, then you understand my concern,' he said, and sat back, satisfied he had made his point.

'What about Savoire, does he know?'

'Savoire?'

'Look, let's not play games. I know that your name is not Vincent Varas but Pierre Plantard, and I know that Alpha Galates is just a front for another group started by Monti and De Mengel. I also know that after Monti's murder, this Dr Savoire took his place, and that now there are differences between Savoire and De Mengel, am I right?'

The young man made a considered nod. 'Yes, you are correct, and yes, there are always differences.'

'Ideological?'

'Ideological, esoteric, especially esoteric, monsieur . . . it is the way of the world that there are hierarchies! Those higher on the ladder wish to keep things secret in order to maintain their position, while those who are lower want things revealed so they can rise higher.' He smiled sardonically. 'But Monti didn't believe in ladders. That is to say, he believed he could do what he liked.' The man ashed his cigarette thoughtfully. 'And for the most part, he got away with it.'

'Does he have something to do with this *Le Serpent Rouge*?'

'Some years ago there was a rumour circulating about it. Apparently, a man in possession of the grimoire came to Paris looking for a buyer. Monti was intrigued and made some inquiries that came to nothing. Whoever it was, he had come and gone, perhaps he sold the text privately and then disappeared again. Years later Aleister Crowley hired Monti to find it. He told Monti he knew someone who would pay any amount for information. Any amount, do you understand?'

'Who's Aleister Crowley?'

'Aleister Crowley? Mon Dieu! He is the head of OTO – Ordo Templi Orientis, a conventicle of magicians. Everybody knows who he is!'

Rahn smiled coolly. 'You said he wasn't buying it for himself?'

'Oh no! In those days he was bankrupt, living off the good graces of his followers. No, he wanted it for someone else.'

'A collector of books?'

'A collector, yes, but not of books. You see, Monsieur Rahn . . .' Plantard paused. 'There are certain people in this world who collect secrets. Such people invariably need others, who are brokers of secrets, to supply them with what they crave. Monti was such a man, a trader of secrets, and he performed this task for Aleister Crowley and for others. To do this job, he had to belong to a number of groups; some might say he was a serial joiner of esoteric societies. Anyway, as you can imagine, these groups compete intensely for the really good secrets – those that can lure the most distinguished members. That is why he could do as he wished. To put it simply, Monti was good at his job and in high demand. Over the years, he devised ways of learning what other men knew and also ways of knowing what other men knew about what he knew. Despite his cleverness, however, he could not uncover any information about *Le Serpent Rouge*. So he decided to take a gamble – he whispered into the right ears that he had met the owner and that the man was willing to sell it. He was hoping to flush the real owner out of his hiding spot, for owners of things like that are always on the lookout for copies. Perhaps they are afraid that the copy they have is not the original and they must test it by comparison, or they may just be interested in buying the copy to increase the value of the original.'

'But in doing that he would also have flushed out those who wanted the book at all costs?' Rahn said.

'Yes, a difficult situation, as you can appreciate, considering Monti did not have the book, nor did he even know for certain that it existed.'

'And you think this led to his murder?'

'Officially, no. Unofficially, who could know?'

'And so, does it exist?'

'The truth is, it is no longer relevant, Monsieur Rahn. A man has been murdered for it and this has made the idea, the dream that it exists, a commodité. Even now, a dozen groups have circulated that they have knowledge of it. Some purport to have part of it, others to own the entire manuscript.'

'So why did De Mengel send me to you? Didn't he know about Monti's game?'

'De Mengel? Of course not! De Mengel and Monti may have been behind Alpha Galates but they walked in different circles. Monti was a man of many faces and gave his loyalty to no group, while De Mengel was, and still is, a member of the Société Alchimique in France and this society is closely affiliated with a sister society in England called the Society for the Study of Alchemy and Early Chemistry. You see, Monsieur Rahn, De Mengel, one could say, is working with those English Lodges who are in no way desirous to have anything to do with Aleister Crowley. They see themselves as legitimate scientists, while they see men like Aleister Crowley as cheap magicians – Satanists. No, De Mengel did not know anything about what Monti was doing.'

Rahn was surprised that De Mengel had English connections and he wondered if Weisthor knew.

'So how much did De Mengel know about *Le Serpent Rouge*?'

'De Mengel only knew what I told him,' Plantard said.

'What do you mean?'

'It is complicated, monsieur. Monti knew of your book Crusade Against the Grail. You see, he wrote your name in a notebook he kept with him always. After his death, I found the notebook and when I saw that he had written your name in it I had to contact you. You can't imagine my surprise when I found out you're a member of the SS! After that I spoke to De Mengel. I knew he was having dealings with your superiors and so I told him about *Le Serpent Rouge* and suggested that he ask for you.'

'And you're not afraid of winding up like Monti?'

He smiled. 'I am nobody. Who would expect that an eighteen-nyear-old errand boy would know anything?'

'But here I am, because of an errand boy, one who wants me to find *Le Serpent Rouge*. My question to you is why?'

'Look, De Mengel is my superior but I don't have to like what he's doing!' Plantard said, sitting forwards.

'What is he doing exactly?'

'He is working for the English Lodges and using the Nazis, you see? But I am of a different mind, monsieur.'

'A different mind?'

'One could say I am sympathetic to the aims of the Nazis. One could say that I understand that the unification of our two countries under one national socialist government would be something mutually beneficial.' He motioned for Rahn to lean in. 'I have heard about Hitler from the occult circles that I frequent. I know that those who groomed him recognise in him the reincarnation of a powerful magician. So you see, if this grimoire does exist, then only such a man as Hitler can use it to its fullest potential.' He smiled wetly and his little eyes gleamed. 'You will tell him this when you see him – that I recognise his genius? He may be interested to know that I am of the lineage of Saint-Clair, and therefore, of Merovingian descent. He will understand that this is the lineage of magicians and the rightful heirs to the throne of France. You will tell him this also?'

'At the earliest opportunity,' Rahn lied, feeling an intense dislike for the impertinent and conceited youth.

Plantard nodded, stupidly satisfied, Rahn thought, and searched under the myriad of papers on his desk. 'If you want to hide something it is best to leave it in plain view, don't you agree? Here it is!' He brandished a small book covered in a dark leather binding. The cover was embossed with a gold sigil, or magic symbol: a pentagram inside a heptagon inside a six-pointed star inside another heptagon inside a circle.

'In the notebook,' Plantard said, 'Monti has written down

some references to *Le Serpent Rouge*. Also, he writes that the grimoire was not complete, that there was something missing – a key. Do you know much about grimoires, Monsieur Rahn?'

'A little. In a grimoire, keys are really formulas one uses to summon demons. The formulas can be in the form of a word, or a sign or sigil.'

'That's right, and you see, Monti seemed to think there was one very important key missing from all the grimoires. It looks like he thought you would know where to find it because he has your name in his notebook and a page number from one of your books in reference to it. Monsieur Rahn, one word of advice,' Plantard said, before handing the notebook to Rahn. 'Should you decide to go after this *Le Serpent Rouge*, I would urge you to beware not only physical enemies but also metaphysical ones.'

Rahn laughed. 'What do you mean, ghosts?'

The man closed his eyes and shook his head. 'If that were all . . . No. Shortly before Monti died, he took a trip to a small town in Languedoc to see a priest. You will see it says something in the notebook about an abbé, but there is no name. I don't know where he went exactly but he was gone only a few days. When he returned he was afraid for his soul.' His lips pulled at the cigarette and he let the smoke out with his words. 'Whatever the dangers associated with this book, they must be horrible.'

Rahn longed to be gone from the apartment; underlying the smell of sardines and burnt toast was the burgeoning stench of death and decay. He took the notebook and, after some cordial words, saw himself out, feeling intensely disconcerted. In the corridor, pausing to wipe his brow, he noticed a cheap print of a woodcut by Dürer. He had not seen it before because it had been obscured by the door. It was the Apocalyptic Angel, holding the key to the bottomless pit. Rahn paused. Was the Angel in the woodcut banishing a demon to the bowels of Hell or was he setting it loose on humanity? Rahn felt a crawling shiver and left quickly.

He returned to his hotel with Pierre Plantard's words weighing on his mind. He packed his bags, paid his bill and left by the back entrance to take a taxi to the station where he was due to meet La Dame. As the taxi passed the front of the hotel, Rahn saw a man standing on the pavement smoking a cigarette and looking out at the street. He couldn't tell if he was the same man he had seen at the café the day before, but something about him looked familiar: he was just an average man, average height, average build.

He found La Dame waiting for him in Le Train Bleu restaurant at Gare de Lyon station, wearing a bored expression. After a moment's complaint for the lateness of the hour he ordered Rahn a drink and sat back smoking his Cuban cigar with a tense impassivity.

'Are you going to tell me what happened?' La Dame said finally.

Rahn realised that La Dame knew almost everything now. What would it hurt for him to know a little more? 'Apparently Monti was a broker of secrets and he was working to find out something about *Le Serpent Rouge* for a man called Aleister Crowley—'

'The beast himself? Surely you know who he is?' He smiled from ear to ear. 'He is the notorious magician! A terrible dresser but charismatic – they say he signs all his correspondence with the numbers six-six-six!'

Rahn took a sip. 'Well, apparently Monti wasn't getting anywhere in his search for the grimoire and so he decided to mention it discreetly, here and there, hoping to flush out anyone who knew anything about it.'

'Not discreetly enough, by the sound of it.'

'So it seems. Anyway, this Pierre Plantard says that Monti made a visit to a town in Languedoc to hunt around and while he was there he met with an abbé. Whatever the abbé told him, it must have caused him to draw the conclusion that the grimoire was incomplete.'

'Really?'

'Apparently there is a key missing.'

'A key?'

'A formula.'

'Go on.'

'Apparently Monti thought this key could be found in Languedoc.'

'Where did he get that idea?'

'From me, so it seems.'

'You?'

'Yes, from *Crusade Against the Grail*. Did you ever read it?'

'Of course!' La Dame said, seemingly indignant at the accusatory tone in Rahn's voice.

Rahn put down the brandy to look at him.

A hangdog grin spread over La Dame's bearded face. 'To be honest, I only managed the acknowledgements. I wanted to see if you'd mentioned my name – you can't imagine my disappointment!'

'I was mindful of your reputation,' Rahn said.

'But I haven't got one.'

'You illustrate my point quite exactly, dear La Dame!'

La Dame gave him a laconic eye. 'And what would you say if I told you you're an opportunist?'

'I rarely give anyone the opportunity to say such things, except for you, of course, and now that you have, I will respond by saying that I find myself in esteemed and august company!' He raised his glass.

There was a nod from La Dame, to acknowledge the acknowledgement.

'So, what happened, did Monti find anything?' he said.

'No. After returning from Languedoc he grew afraid. Not long after that he was found dead, and you know the rest, but Plantard isn't certain who is responsible: rivals; the owner of the manuscript; or perhaps some metaphysical force.'

'Metaphysical! You mean like a curse?'

'I don't know exactly.'

'What else did he say?'

'He said De Mengel is working for the English Lodges.'

'English Masons! A nasty lot! Watch out for them, Rahn.' He grew thoughtful. 'So, that is why De Mengel wants you to find this *Le Serpent Rouge* – so he can deliver it to the English? The scoundrel!'

'Perhaps, perhaps not.'

'And what does Plantard say?'

'Plantard is the one who told De Mengel about me. It seems he is a fan of Hitler and used De Mengel to get me here so I could find it for him. The thing is, Monti never did set his eyes on the grimoire. For all I know, it may not even exist!'

He took out the notebook and gave it to La Dame.

'What's this?'

'It belonged to Monti. It's full of bits and pieces: appointments; notes to remember; this and that; a list of addresses; the usual sort of thing. But what interests me is what Monti's written towards the back – my name and references to the grimoire.'

Rahn watched La Dame's face change from frown to deeper frown.

> * 17th January
> Reference, Magic ceremonial.
> The Grimorium Verum once reprinted in the French language. Based on the Keys of Solomon. Of the Italian version there have been two modern editions, both poorly produced. The book of True Black Magic is known only by the edition of 1750. The Grand Grimoire reappeared at Nismes in 1823 and is, moreover, in all respects identical with the work entitled the Red Dragon or Le Dragon Rouge, of which there are several examples.
> The Grimoire of Pope Honorius is exceedingly rare in the original, but is better known by the reprints of 1660 and 1670, though these also are scarce. There is an edition dated 1760, and

*this commands a high price among collectors
(known as Le Serpent Rouge?).
Abbé d'Artigny was presented with an MS.
copy of this grimoire, which was much more
complete in all its keys than the printed
editions. Possibly it represented the transition
of the Sworn Book of the Theban Honorius
into the Spurious Papal Constitution, which
certainly reproduces the motive and moves in
the atmosphere of its prototype.
But all are incomplete (the last key still
missing).*

*Otto Rahn, Crusade Against the Grail,
page 93 — a skeleton key —*

* *Abbé knows!*

La Dame raised his brows. 'So which one of these are you looking for, the *Grimorium Verum*, the *Grimoire of Pope Honorius*, or this *Sworn Book*? And look at the cover of this notebook, Rahn! Positively diabolical!' He gave it back, appearing glad to be rid of it. 'As Sancho would say, *I have been considering how little is got or gained by going in search of these adventures that your worship seeks* — in other words, I don't see why you have to always find yourself mixed up in these things, but this time you've gone too far! Doesn't it bother you at all that your name is in a book owned by a man who was murdered looking for the same thing that you're hunting? If Sancho were here he'd suggest you follow your idea of finding a place to hide in the mountains!'

'But as Don Quixote would say, *it is requisite to roam the world, as it were, on probation, seeking adventures, in order that, by achieving some, name and fame may be acquired* — until today I would have agreed with you, but you've managed to miss the most important point.'

'What point? I didn't know there was a point!'

'There is always a point!' Rahn observed. 'When I mentioned a skeleton key in my book, it was in reference to the treasure of the Cathars.'

'You mean the *Apocalypse of Saint John*, or the Grail?'

'Both, but to be completely truthful, I was speaking metaphorically – it was a literary device. And now, because of it, Monti has linked *Le Serpent Rouge* to the Cathar treasure.'

'And how would it be linked, do you have a clue?'

'Not a one!'

'Well, you've done it,' La Dame said.

'Done what?'

'You've always wanted fame and grandeur! To have every man cry out the instant they saw you: "This is the Knight of the Serpent, who vanquished in single combat the gigantic Brocabruno of mighty strength!" You've become notorious.'

'One mention in a notebook hardly makes one notorious. And anyway, I think you're talking about yourself. Sancho Panza was the one who wanted material gain. Don Quixote didn't go into battles and adventures for opportunities and fame but for a higher gain – something Sancho Panza never understood.'

'That's because he always bore the brunt of those ill-fated adventures, being the only sane one of the two,' La Dame retorted.

'At any rate,' Rahn ignored him, 'I think Deodat will shed more light on it, considering his library has practically every heretical text known to mankind.' Rahn looked at his pocket watch. 'Time to go.'

He wanted to be away and was glad when they found the appropriate platform and a porter to take his bags.

'Give my regards to Deodat,' La Dame said, following the train's slow shuffle. 'Keep me posted and if you need anything, just call . . . and remember: *a clear escape is better than a good man's prayers!*'

Rahn watched his friend until he had disappeared from sight. A sense of freedom swept over him. Hopefully he had left the ordinary man behind, or for that matter anyone else who may have been following him. He nodded at this thought and went to find his carriage.

ISLAND OF THE DEAD

10

ONE MAN'S GRAVE IS ANOTHER MAN'S BED

'You have probably never heard of Professor Moriarty?' said he. 'Never.'
'Aye, there's the genius and the wonder of the thing!' he cried.
Sir Arthur Conan Doyle, 'The Final Problem'

Venice, 2012

The Writer of Letters paused and I realised that it was late. He insisted that I stay the night and soon I was being led to a frugal but not uncomfortable gues-troom. I didn't sleep well and woke early, just before dawn, lying awake for some time thinking. It was quite ludicrous that I didn't know anything about my host – a man with no name who lived in a cemetery in the middle of a lagoon. Moreover, I had no clue why he'd asked me here or what he wanted with me. I fancied that he was an admirer of Otto Rahn, perhaps even a distant relative, who needed a ghost writer to tell the adventurer's side of the story – as a form of literary redemption. But all this didn't explain the uncanny help he had given me over the years or the strange game he was playing with me now.

I dressed and ventured out to look at the cemetery in the day-light. It was cold and eerie at this early hour, with the sun rising and the fog lifting between the shadowed cypresses. As the light melted the night away it fell on monuments of astonishing variety: classical marble statues and headstones pointing the way Heavenward for the souls of the dead to follow. To my surprise, many plots were decorated with fresh bouquets of daisies and roses, carnations, gladiolus or chrysanthemums. On quite a few headstones there were even coloured photographs of the deceased behind glass or Perspex – strange disembodied pictures of life on dead stone. I stopped to read a few: a young dancer; a father of six; and a young man who died in a motorcycle accident. Every inscription a summary of a life lived all too briefly.

I followed the grassy track without aim. The cemetery was a labyrinth, divided into many parts, each with its own nationality and religion and character. The most humble section included long rows of tombs set into drawers stacked one on top of the other that were accessed by rolling ladders; a library of bones! What looked like the wealthier section was filled with large, stately, unattached family chapels adorned with neoclassical ornamentation. I saw some that were good examples of modernist architecture, and here and there caught a glimpse of freestanding sculptures by well-known artists. I passed into a section that housed a number of nineteenth century–style Gothic ruins hidden by a tangle of shrubs and trees. Overgrown paths almost indiscernible in the long grass led to cracked, fallen stones of famous residents. Among the neglected, the poet Ezra Pound was still lovingly remembered.

I paused to take in the wistful sadness of the place – after all, was there a happy way to die? It was cold and so I kept walking, the leaves crackling under my feet and the trees rustling in a stiff breeze. Without noticing it, I found myself in the French section, where I came upon an old monk sweeping a grave. It was hard to say who was more startled, he or I.

'*Proibito! Non permesso!*' he shouted. His ancient face was a tempest of wrinkles beneath the monkish cowl.

I told him in my best Italian that I was a guest, though I

couldn't give him the name of my host.

'It is forbidden for you to be here,' he said, waving. 'Go away! Go away! Do you hear? I won't tell you anything, nothing at all! I don't want anything to do with you!' He turned away and began walking hurriedly in the direction of the monastery, looking over his shoulder once or twice to make certain I wasn't following him.

The man was eccentric and no wonder, living on an island with only the dead for company. The grave he'd been cleaning was marked by the figure of a lion man carrying a staff and a key, and entwined by two serpents.

'This is his favourite grave.' The Writer of Letters was behind me, looking rested and calm but his eyes were penetrating. I wondered how long he had been standing there.

'Do you know what that figure is?' he asked me.

'It looks like a cross between a Hermetic and a Mithraic symbol. The staff of Hermes also has two snakes entwining it, and I think this figure, the lion man, is Mithraic, am I right?'

'It's a Leoncetophaline, the guardian of the World of the Dead, and you're right, it is both Mithraic and Hermetic.'

'There's no name and no date on this grave.'

'No. Do you see the inscription?'

I recognised it. It was part of an alchemical verse attributed to the famous alchemist Basil Valentinus. But before I could answer, the Writer of Letters appeared suddenly aware of the time and the fact that the cook had prepared breakfast and we should not delay. Obviously, he wanted the mystery of the grave to hang in the air between us, creating suspense, and he achieved his aim.

Later in the library, he took me to the shelves full of ancient books bound in leather. Some books were covered in studs; others had studs only on the bindings. One exquisite manuscript was decorated with a great rosette of gold over a large raised cross; its spine was covered in gilding and its fore page was emblazoned with the title written in impeccable calligraphy:

El Ingenioso Hidalgo
Don Quijote de la Mancha

Primera edición Mexicana Conforme a la de la
Real Academia Española, hecho en Madrid
en 1782. Además del análisis de dicha Academia, se han añadido las notas críticas y curiosas
del Señor Pellicer, con hermosas laminas...

'That's the Mexican edition that Rahn and La Dame were looking for when they first met,' the Writer of Letters said. 'I mentioned it yesterday. It is very rare – there are only three copies, one in the Biblioteca Nacional de Madrid, another in the Biblioteca Nacional de Mexico; and this one, of course.'

At this point the Irish monk entered with a tray on which sat two glasses of mineral water.

'Do you know,' the Writer of Letters said, 'many people fall into the pit of thinking that Parzifal, the Grail knight in Wolfram von Eschenbach's poem, was more important than Don Quixote to Rahn. But this is only because they didn't know him like I do.'

There was no need for a mental calculation. The Writer of Letters didn't look old enough to have known Rahn. Still, I decided I would play along. 'Are you saying you knew him?'

His grey eyes widened a little. 'I know him perhaps better than anyone else.'

'Do you mean he's still alive?'

He hesitated for just a moment. 'That depends on what you mean by "alive".'

I didn't know what to say to this oddity.

There was sudden amusement in his voice. 'You were wondering if I wanted you to ghost write his story, am I right? Don't be so surprised; it is a logical conclusion but an erroneous one. You see, logic is useless sometimes.'

'What am I doing here then?'

'I told you that this is for you to tell me. This is your story – remember? I'm just a character, your mouthpiece. Isn't that what characters do for their writers, answer their questions? Exorcise their demons? Writing books is better than psychoanalysis, and cheaper too if you ask me. Perhaps that's why the first natives who saw written words were terrified. They believed that letters were evil spirits dancing on the page and their primitive intuition was quite correct, for at times they are exactly that – the tormented soul content of writers! That is why I call this my garden of good and evil, my cemetery of thoughts, the angels and demons of men's souls,' he said, with a wave of the hand.

He was right about one thing: the library did remind me of the cemetery outside. Its atmosphere was weighed down by time and nostalgia. After all, the authors of these books were long dead, their words lying on shelves like the broken fountains and fallen angels of better days.

'So, what haunts an author like you?' he asked.

I found myself inarticulate. 'I don't know; failure, I suppose. Sometimes I feel life is just an endless attempt to remember something that is doomed to lay forgotten . . . like these books.'

'Well, the ancients knew how to open and close the door of memory,' he said, 'but the best we modern men can do is to try to pick the lock. Speaking of which, shall we?'

I looked at him questioningly.

'Shall we pick the lock?' He gestured to the two winged chairs.

Before sitting down he poked thoughtfully at the fire until it blazed. 'I hope you don't mind but I'm going to diverge for a moment,' he said.

'Are you taking me to one of those galleries you spoke of?'

'Yes, to that dimension where everything that has ever occurred in history, exists in space. You see, in order to understand

Rahn's predicament, his love of the Cathars, his attachment to the south of France, we have to look in the gallery called Matteu,' he said, and once again, with impeccable diction, he began.

11

BÉZIERS

'. . . there is nothing so subject to the inconstancy of fortune as war.'
Miguel de Cervantes, Don Quixote

Béziers, 1209

Matteu found himself in the city of Béziers on the eve of the Feast of Mary Magdalene. The boy, only twelve years old, belonged to the company of routiers, the mercenaries who were recruited from every low place for the Crusades against the Cathars of Languedoc. His master was known as the King of the Mercenaries, a Basque for whom all felt a repellent awe. He and his men had already entered the town of Béziers ahead of the armies of the northern knights, and the boy, having fallen behind, looked for him, walking the streets in the wake of his master's advance to observe, for the first time in his young life, men killing any living thing that crossed their path.

Fearful, he hid behind some wine barrels near the stables and watched the routiers drag the town's citizens into the streets.

Children were cut from their mother's arms; a small babe was skewered on the end of a sword and thrown a distance towards the walls to split open like a watermelon; an older one was struck in the back as he ran off; another was taken up to the saddle to have her small neck broken with a twist. Old men were run through or gutted or had their heads lopped off. The women, if they were old or ugly, had their faces beaten in or their throats cut from ear to ear.

The young pretty ones suffered more.

Near where Matteu hid, routiers brought forth two girls and held them down as they kicked and screamed. Matteu looked to see if these Cathars were the Devil's spawn: half calf and half goat, grotesque creatures, covered in boils, as the priests had said. After all, these were the dreaded heretics who thought the world was created by the Devil and who did not believe in the Holy Cross and the Resurrection. But he saw only plain girls, as plain as could be – girls who were terrified and hunted.

Matteu could barely watch as each man took his turn upon the girls. One was already dead from loss of blood; the other, who had fought and kicked and bit, had a boot stomped into her face and her head dashed onto the cobbles. Sated, the men moved on. Their festival of carnage and rape over, they now turned their business to plunder.

Matteu's mind was hollow – even his life in the violent hovels and bars of Barcelona had ill prepared him for the sight of so much blood and savagery, and he felt gall rise to his throat, which he tried, with all his might, to stifle.

The mercenaries were hauling great chests and barrels and trunks out of the houses to prise them open, overturning them and spilling out their contents: bolts of green silk shimmered in the sun; bags of grain, pepper or salt came open and overflowed onto the cobbles; parchments were scattered about. Clothing was ripped up and thrown around; furniture was broken to pieces; pots and pans and iron candlesticks were tossed onto the blood-soaked bodies of the dead. The routiers trampled over the carcasses, slipping on the blood and tripping over the dismembered parts to get at what they wanted. They beat at one another with fists or sword butts, fighting over the spoils. Pilgrims and camp followers, themselves looking for plunder, were run through if they happened to get in the way. The men were like wolves, their faces dark with war lust.

A thunder now came from the city gates: it was the sharp-edged hoofs of the great French warhorses. Upon them were the Crusaders who had by now bested the city garrison and were seeking their plunder with a fury, beating pilgrim and routier alike with their swords or boots or shields. After ordering the merce-naries to take anything of value to the French camp or face the sword, the Crusaders galloped away towards the upper parts of the city. The world was drowned out by the solemn 'Te Deum' they sang as they headed for the churches where the people of the city had fled in their desperation.

The routiers, angered by this insult, proceeded to put the city to the torch. After lighting the houses, they too moved closer to the upper city and now it seemed there was a moment of quiet, the only sounds the groans of the dying and the burning and crackling of the fires. Matteu came out from his hiding spot into the long, narrow street. It reeked of faeces and was buzzing with flies. He walked among the blood and brains, legs and arms and trunks ei-ther ripped up or stove in that lay in the infested gutters, littering the ground as though rained down from Heaven.

He looked about him at the tide of pain and misery and hous-es on fire, to the great panels of smoke that were blocking out the sun, attacking his dust-filled nostrils and snaking into his ach-ing lungs.

He realised he was standing near the corpses of the two girls, splayed out, naked, on the cobbles. He tried to look away but could not prevent his eyes from finding their faces. They were his age, he was sure of it, or a little older: fifteen, maybe sixteen. Their eyes lifeless, the soft milky parts of their young bodies stained red and blue with bruises, violated and exposed. To see it filled him with vacant loss. The mouldy bread he had eaten for breakfast began to turn cartwheels in his guts and the world made its rounds over his head and the buzzing grew louder in his ears. In a rush, a sour plug of gall rose up to his lips and he bent over, coughing and retching until the beast in his stomach unclenched its jaws and he stopped, his tongue a bed of fiery acid, more acid dripping from his nostrils.

He lay on the ground and waited for the world to stop spinning and for the misery of this new understanding of war to settle into his bones, where it might hurt less. Such was his state that he did not notice until too late that a knight on horseback was galloping in his direction with sword held high in one hand and a shield in the other bearing the device of the Temple. The knight was standing over him before he could get up and he pierced the skin on the back of Matteu's neck with the tip of his weapon.

'Who are you?' the great and awesome knight said loudly, letting the sword's tip draw blood. 'Well?'

Matteu trembled beneath that blade and found to his utter terror that he was unable to speak.

The tall knight told the boy to turn over and he put a foot to his chest. He pulled up his visor. 'Are you Cathar or Christian?'

Matteu's words, dammed up, came tumbling out like wine out of a barrel: 'My master is the captain of the Mercenaries . . . I came to see the war . . .'

Something flickered in the knight's pale eyes, a passing thought, perhaps an estimation of the boy's worth. The Templar sheathed his sword then and made for his horse. 'Now you have seen it,' he told Matteu, pulling himself into the saddle and looking about at the slaughter-ruined streets. As if he were speaking not to Matteu, but to some aspect of himself to which he must answer, he said, 'There is no glory in it.'

By now the fire in the city had taken hold of every building. Already the roofs were alight and he could hear the rafters letting go here and there. Matteu turned around to see that grey plumes were reaching upwards to the vaults of Heaven and a thunder of destruction came from every building.

'They will come looking for blood, boy!' the Templar said.

'Get on or join the carcasses in the streets!'

At that moment there was a splitting and crackling, a spurting and bursting of wood and rafters and beams giving way and collapsing, feeding the fire and causing the flames to rise higher, and the heat to grow in intensity. Matteu could see almost nothing except smoke and more smoke.

The stallion reared up but the Templar held firm; it made a dance of its terror and then calmed down. Matteu stood, uncertain. He caught a hold of the stirrups but began to cough and cough from the smoke. The inferno was spewing out the acrid smell of burning hair and incense and suddenly there were sounds of horn blasts rising above the roars of the falling timbers and the growling, bellowing sounds of the conflagration.

'What does that mean?' Matteu asked.

'The church is gone and likely all in it!' the Templar told him fiercely. 'The killing will go on for days. They believe that God will recognise who belongs to Him in heaven, for they do not know heretic from Catholic. If you do not hurry, it will be your fate as well, and I will run you through to save them the trouble.'

It was true. They would take him for a Cathar. He thought he could hear the rumble of the warhorses and the cries of the knights and routiers. His heart, his breath, his muscles, his thoughts, all of him grew terrified. He tried again to put a foot to the stirrup and with help from the knight he lifted himself behind the great man, barely managing to stay on the horse because of his fear.

The knight pulled down his visor and dug heels into the horse's flank. The animal left a trail of dust that mingled with the smoke all the way through the gate.

And so it was. His master would not miss him, there were plenty of boys to take his place. Likewise he would not miss the temperamental, violent ways of a man who liked to box him in the ear for sport. What this Templar wanted with him Matteu could not guess, and though this did not sit easy on his brow, he told himself that he had always been good at following his 'knowing'. This alone had saved him in the hovels of Barcelona after his mother's death; this knowing had taken his feet to that boat in the harbour and had showed him to hide in that French galley; and it was this knowing that directed him now, out of the howling pit that was the city of Béziers and into a future unknown.

He hugged the horse with his knees and held tight to the Templar as they rode over the bodies of the dead but before they reached the bridge, the Templar said to him, 'Take one last look, boy! The God of the church that you once knew is now dead for you!'

Matteu looked behind him: he saw nothing but a trail of smoke. Ash fell from above, like grey snow. He knew he would never be able to walk into a church again.

12

DEODAT

'You could not possibly have come at a better time, my dear Watson.'
Sir Arthur Conan Doyle, 'The Red-Headed League'

Arques, France, 1938

'She wanted you to have it, Rahn,' Deodat Roche said, puffing on his meerschaum pipe, which was shaped like a lion's head. 'She cared a great deal for you, as you know.' Rahn sat sprawled on a wicker chair in Deodat's drawing room before a great fire of oak. The train had arrived that afternoon and he had paid a local to take him to where Deodat lived – a place as far from Berlin as the moon, or so it seemed to Rahn. For here, in Arques, he felt like himself again.

He looked at the pleasant glow of the hearth that fell on the worn oriental rugs, the mahogany furniture and the dozens and dozens of books lining the walls of the sizeable library. He took in the faint perfume wafting from the rosemary and thyme bunches that hung from the blackened rafters, alongside sausages and ropes of garlic. Nothing had changed.

Rahn and Deodat sat together in an easy silence, broken momentarily by the housekeeper, a large woman with a severe face and a thick mass of greying hair that she tamed into a knot at the nape of her neck. Yes, a formidable woman was Madame Sabine, who in her prime had been the headmistress of an illustrious girl's school and whose ability to command, organise and control young and great minds alike had not faded in her waning years. She had a tray of coffee in her hands and a look on her face that would curdle milk. She set the tray down.

'I'll leave you to pour, but mind, don't spill it!' she snapped. Then to Rahn, 'Bed by ten o'clock! I'll hold you personally responsible if the magistrate's arthritis suffers because you've kept him up.' This was followed by a hard stare, which bespoke her expectations, whereupon she turned on her heel and stalked out of the room.

When she was quite gone, Deodat rubbed his face and sighed. 'There goes a demon fallen to Earth to harass me,' he murmured and poured the coffee, spilling a little on the tray in mischievous defiance. 'Oh dear!' he said merrily.

'Why don't you get rid of her?' Rahn asked, feeling warm and contented.

'What?' Deodat shot him a horrified stare. 'That woman is indispensable! She's the only one who can find things in the infernal order she's created. If I leave a book out, and turn around . . . *pff!* It's gone in a moment! You have no idea how many things can be irretrievably lost in a house the size of this one! If I were to let her go it would take me the rest of my life to find everything she's put away, and the old hag knows it too. She holds me by the collar like the Devil in Faust! Besides, the way she talks, one would think me near the end of the line!'

The truth was Deodat's age was impossible to tell — he was one of those men who seemed perennially youthful in his body and yet eternally old in his soul, so that what one saw on the surface never seemed to match what one discovered within. Nevertheless, Rahn guessed he must be somewhere between forty-five and fifty-five. His hair was not fully grey and his face was as yet unwrinkled, and his quirks of behaviour and speech signalled a fount of energy that far surpassed many men half his age. In fact, Rahn had met him caving, in the circles of Antonin Gadal, that great Cathar historian, and Rahn came to learn that Deodat was a prodigious speleologist, a man who would drop everything to go potholing in godforsaken places. Rahn respected his wisdom and sagacity and his deep knowledge of the Cathars, which long ago had earned him the nickname 'The Cathar Pope', and a position as the magistrate of the small town of Arques. This was a profession that suited him well since he was rather addicted to mysteries, be they the confounding disappearance of a neighbour's calf, or the perplexing theft of an old woman's heirloom. The truth was that many years ago, Deodat had met Sir Arthur Conan Doyle. The two men had hit it off and now Deodat told everyone that Doyle had modelled Sherlock Holmes after him – minus the sleuth's various addictions to certain intoxicating substances, of course. But Rahn knew this was impossible, for Deodat would have been no more than a child when Doyle's first story was published. Still, Rahn never contradicted him.

Deodat's most striking features were a prominent lower jaw and a fearsome forehead that hung over deep-set blue eyes that were so dark as to be almost black. The profundity of those eyes was disquieting and had undone more than one criminal, simply because one could never be certain what Deodat was really looking at – the body or the soul. In the final analysis it was just that Deodat, like Holmes, was a clever observer, a 'deducer' with a keen eye for the slightest detail, and it was under that eye that Rahn now unwrapped the package from the Countess P.

Inside the box, beneath several layers of newspaper, was an Empire Pendulum Clock. It had sat on the piano on which he had played many a tune for the countess. He realised now that he had never really studied it in detail. The clock stood no taller than two hands and was elaborately worked in bronze ormolu. He sat back to look at it. It was made in the image of a naked man with a lion's head. The body of the creature had four wings and two serpents entwined around it, and it sat on the globe of the world, which formed the bulk of the clock with its little Roman numerals. The creature held a key in one hand and a sceptre in the other. Upon closer scrutiny, Rahn observed the following words inscribed into the back of the clock:

THIS A TOMB THAT HAS NO BODY IN IT
THIS IS A BODY THAT HAS NO TOMB ROUND IT
BUT BODY AND TOMB ARE THE SAME

'Ugly, isn't it?' Deodat said, as Rahn set the clock down again on a small table. 'The countess was an unusual woman and she liked unusual things. She had a pertinacity that infuriated me, but I was rather fond of her, as you know. Do you remember the first time we all met?'

'It was at Montsegur on the night of the solstice.' Rahn smiled to think of it. 'All four of us were there: me, you, La Dame and the countess; all invited to observe that sunrise. We had to climb that mountain to the fortress in the dark.'

'And the poor countess in those shoes – highly impractical if you ask me!' Deodat exclaimed.

'The fire we built was so great it lit up the night.'

'And we sat by it eating bread dipped in fish ragout, my favourite dish,' Deodat said, relishing the memory. 'We listened to one another reciting poems for hours.'

'And we uncorked a battalion of bottles!' Rahn added.

'The finest wines of the region.' Deodat puffed on his pipe, contented. 'I recall that my first impression of you, dear Rahn, was that you seemed to me just like a troubadour.'

'And I thought you lived up to your nickname!'

'What nonsense! There was never any such thing as a Cathar pope.' Deodat waved a hand but Rahn sensed he was secretly delighted to hear it.

'What about La Dame? What did you think of him?' Rahn asked.

Deodat gave him a look. 'La Dame might imagine he shares a lineage with Nostradamus, but he hasn't a mystical bone in his body. The countess, on the other hand, was the last of the great mystics. One of a kind.' Deodat sighed. 'A fine woman, a fine woman . . .' He cleared his throat, obviously touched, and changed the subject. 'At any rate, she must have left the clock to you for some reason. I believe it is quite old . . . I would say, early nineteenth century. That figure on it is not unusual. They were generally decorated with mythological creatures.'

'I must admit that I never knew what it was,' Rahn said.

'The Leoncetophaline?' Deodat's dark eyes turned to Rahn. 'They're found in Mithraic initiation chambers all over Rome!

He is Arimanus, the demon king guardian of the Underworld.'

'And this inscription on the back of the clock?'

'It's a variation of an infamous riddle discovered in the sixteenth century on an old Roman tombstone near Bologna. I looked it up when the countess asked me to make certain I had it inscribed on the stone marking her grave. Apparently men have obsessed over its meaning. In fact, a large pamphlet on it was published in Venice, and later even Jung dedicated a full chapter to it in *Mysterium Conjunctionis*. But the important point is that no solution to it has ever been found.'

They both fell into a silent reflection. The Countess P had often talked about death. In fact, it had been her favourite subject.

Deodat puffed on his pipe and looked at Rahn with a peculiar mixture of vexation and affection that signalled his displeasure. Rahn had been waiting for it. He braced himself.

'Nearly four years, Rahn, without a word!'

Rahn drank down his coffee. It was hot and bitter. Yes, he had left France rather hastily, it was true, and had never found the right moment to write Deodat a letter of apology because he had not wanted to lie about whom he was working for and what he was doing – this was also true. On the train he had constructed eloquent reasons for his omissions, which now seemed to evaporate from his mind and so he looked at his friend and mentor, therefore, without the slightest notion of what to say. Deodat, being the man he was, saved him the trouble.

'I know what happened!' he thundered. 'There have to be some advantages to being a magistrate, we hear all sorts of things. If you had told me, perhaps I could have helped you. But you are stubborn – and petulant!'

'Well, I didn't want your help!' Rahn said, demonstrating his obstinacy nicely. 'It was my scandal! Bad enough I was being thrown out of town like some common criminal without having to advertise it. It was all rather undignified, as you can imagine, and you can't blame me for trying to salvage whatever scrap of dignity I had left.'

'Oh, let's forget the whole tiresome thing,' Deodat grumbled, getting up to pace before the fire, puffing away at his pipe. He took it out to say, 'The important point is that you're back, my boy, and, if I'm not mistaken, it isn't merely to collect a parcel from the countess. So.' He paused now to stare at Rahn with eagerness. 'I want straight answers, no dissimulation! Well?'

Rahn cleared his throat, feeling unbalanced. What should he say? He knew full well that he was a terrible liar, especially where Deodat was concerned.

Deodat looked at him in his singular fashion. 'You've come by some money by the look of you – new shoes, new coat. I sense a purposefulness in your manner. I think that you're ready to pick up where you left off, am I correct?'

Rahn cleared his throat. 'I'm not here to go potholing, per se . . . I'm afraid,' he let out.

'Why, in the devil, not?' Deodat couldn't hide his disappointment. He looked like a child robbed of a favoured toy by a trusted person. His expression moved from confusion to astonishment and settled finally into a wounded frown.

'I'm on rather a different hunt, though it might just turn out to be the same hunt, actually.'

The frown lifted a little. 'What are you hunting for?'

'I'm on an errand from my publisher. As it turns out he's a collector of books and he's heard of a very rare grimoire called *Le Serpent Rouge*. Have you heard of it?'

'*Le Serpent Rouge*?' The brow wrinkled and he puffed on the pipe vigorously. He was on the scent. 'Where did your publisher hear about it?'

'From a source in Paris.'

'Interesting . . .'

'Have you heard of it, Deodat?'

'Yes, but only as an alchemical substance – red mercuric oxide, which the Egyptians called Red Serpent. I've never heard of a book by that name.'

Rahn realised he would have to tell Deodat a little more, so he fished in the pocket of his jacket for Monti's notebook, opened it to the page in question, and handed it to Deodat.

Deodat peered at it through his thick lenses. 'What's this?' he said, looking up over their rim.

'It belonged to a man called George Monti.'

'George Monti?'

Rahn was surprised. 'Do you know him?'

'Yes, he's a rather shady fellow. He's dead now, I believe.'

'Apparently he came to Languedoc before he died in search of the grimoire. The notebook was found afterwards and for the most part it's completely dull, the usual sort of thing you'd find, until one looks in the back.'

Deodat took it, pushed back his reading glasses and read it out to himself picking out the important points, '*Magic ceremonial . . . known a*s Le Serpent Rouge *. . . the last key still missing . . . Otto Rahn,* Crusade Against the Grail, *page 93 – a skeleton key . . . Abbé knows.*'

Without another word, he got up. Rahn followed him to his library, which was dominated by a great table covered in marginalia. Deodat talked animatedly to himself as he perused his impressive collection. 'Damn that woman! Her idea of order in-furiates me. I know it's here somewhere. Ah! Joy! Here it is, a translation of *Magic Ceremonial* . . . let me see . . .' He found the book and flicked its pages. 'I think that note in your notebook is a reference taken from a footnote in this book. Here it is, in the part entitled *The Grimoire of Pope Honorius* . . .' He lapsed into thought and remained that way for quite some time, turning from one page to another. Rahn took one of the chairs grouped around the vast table and sat down.

After an interminable time Deodat spoke. 'I understand it.'

'What?'

'It seems, dear Rahn, that there are two grimoires of Hon-orius. The first is written by a Theban called Honorius and the second by a pope, Pope Honorius III to be exact. It's the latter that is known as *Le Serpent Rouge.*'

'You surprise me!' Rahn said. 'Two authors by the same name who both wrote grimoires, and to top it off one of them a pope, no less. How do you come to that conclusion?'

'I can't claim that it's due to any special sagacity, dear boy! It is all right here, in this book. Now, the first grimoire ever written was *King Solomon's Keys,* as you know, and every other grimoire seems to have been extrapolated from it. The Theban magician Honorius wrote his book a long time ago — no one knows ex-actly when. Apparently a number of magicians put the Theban in charge of compiling a grand grimoire of magic, containing all their keys, signs, symbols and seals, along with all the invo-cations, convocations and conjurations of their art. It looks like they were afraid that Rome was about to destroy all their books in order to keep control over the tenets of magic.'

'Rome?'

'The Roman Catholics, of course! It stands to reason, dear Rahn. Why do you think there are so many banned books in the Vatican archives? Why were so many witches strapped to pyres, not to mention the Templars and Cathars? The Roman caesars, starting with Augustus, took for themselves the title of high priest of all the mysteries, Pontifex Maximus. Later, the Catholic popes appropriated the title and that is why they are known as pontiffs – the bridge between Heaven and Earth. Now let me see here . . . The Theban was charged to make three books. The rules were that the books could only be passed on to males who were Christian and whose character had been confirmed for at least a year. These men were then sworn to keep the contents of the book a secret, and to protect the other initiates who possessed a copy of the book. If no person could be found worthy of the book then the owner, before dying, had to bury it in a hidden place, or ensure that it was placed in the coffin with him. These oaths, dear Rahn, are what led to the book being known as the Sworn Book.'

'So, how does this Theban's book connect to the pope's book, apart from the fact that they shared the same name, which in itself is odd?' Rahn asked.

'Edward Waite says here that the *Grimoire of Pope Honorius* is really nothing more than a distortion of the Theban's book. It may be that at some stage a copy of the book fell into the hands of a pope, and was passed down thereafter from pope to pope until hundreds of years later a certain pope called himself Honorius III, broke the oath and mixed those secrets of the Theban magician with Roman Catholic rituals, thereby creating a new grimoire, which he named *The Grimoire of Pope Honorius III.*'

'So he appropriated the Theban's book?'

'Yes, and by doing so, he has created a grimoire for priests, which is diabolical, because it not only brings demonology together with Christology, it also includes ritual sacrifice – on the altar, no less.'

'Wait a minute! Honorius III?' Rahn said pensively. 'He was the pope who continued the Cathar persecution after Innocent died.'

Deodat fell into amazement. 'I believe you're right.'

'I feel a strange synchronicity, Deodat!'

'Let's read on and see, shall we? The 1529 edition is entitled *Honorii Papæ, adversus tenebrarum Principem et ejus Angelos Conjurationes ex originale Romæ servato*, but it looks like it became known as *Le Serpent Rouge*, as this Monti fellow has in his note. The note also mentions that a key is missing – that is important.'

'Yes, that was also my estimation. So, what do you make of it?'

'Monti has hit on the truth, dear Rahn. It is well known in certain circles that *all* the grimoires are incomplete. Now he quotes a page from your own book in which you must mention a skeleton key. Let's see what you say, shall we?'

'Have you read my book?'

Deodat paused and raised one brow. 'I've been *trying* to read it ever since you gave it to me, but it is rather a muddled affair. You see, the crux is always missing from your work because you get lost in the peripherals. The crux needs an analytical mind. I've told you before it is not enough to have knowledge, you have to have *wisdom!*'

'I don't know what you mean, to my mind it's replete with wisdom!' Rahn retorted, a little hurt.

Ignoring Rahn's piqué, Deodat looked through the monumental pile of books on the table until he found a battered French edition. He flicked through the pages. 'It is very erudite, don't misunderstand me, but it is so full of marginalia that it makes one dizzy . . . Let's see: *The Caves of Trevrizent close to the fountain called La Salvaesche ... so on . .. so on ... in preceding pages we described why the Cathars built their hermitages and temples in the caves of Sabarthes . . . so on . . . little further on we will learn that according to Spanish ballads a skeleton key is hidden in the enchanted cave of Hercules, which resolves the mystery of the Grail . . .* There, you see?' He paused and took off his glasses to fix Rahn with a meaningful stare. 'You mention a key that will resolve the mystery of the Grail, and if we add that to what is in the rest of that man's note, we see that its author has connected the *Grimoire of Pope*

Honorius III, otherwise known as *Le Serpent Rouge*, to the treasure of the Cathars – through you! It's an interesting idea. If – among other things – the Cathars had possession of this missing key, it would explain why Pope Innocent set out to persecute them so vehemently, and why Honorius continued to do so after him. The popes may have been after the last missing key that could not be found in any grimoire.'

'What would it be – a sign, a word, a seal?' Rahn asked him.

'It could be any one of those,' he said. 'But there is something I can add to this.'

'What?'

'Since you've been away I've had moment to retrace our searches those years ago and I think I know why we didn't find the treasure of the Cathars inside those caves at Lombrives.'

'Really? I'm listening,' Rahn said.

Deodat smiled. 'I think it was moved.'

'By whom? The caves were inaccessible until recently.'

'Yes, we both know that the treasure was taken from Montsegur by four Cathars during the siege in the thirteenth century. We both have long suspected that it was taken to the caves at Lombrives. On this, most Cathar scholars agree, but what if the treasure was taken away from the caves? What if some time after the siege, and before the Catholics walled up all the exits out of those caves – condemning the last of those poor Cathars who were trapped inside to die a miserable death – someone escaped with it?'

Rahn was much struck by this. 'I see your point. After that, superstition and fear of the church would have prevented curious men from breaking down the seals to those caves to look for the treasure, until we decided to go there.'

'That's right. And the legend that it is buried in those caves has kept the treasure safe all these years. This is exciting, Rahn! Here, finally, is a scent we can work with!' He snapped the book shut.

'I had a sense for it, you know, and now your words are a confirmation.'

'Well, my boy! That Monti mentions an abbé . . . a priest . . .'

'Yes, he came here and saw a priest who knew something about the grimoire.'

'Interesting,' Deodat said, sitting down.

'Why?'

'Well, tomorrow I'm due to visit a priest myself, Abbé Cros.

He's retired and lives at Bugarach; we played chess once or twice a week for many years. He is a very erudite man but he's had a run of bad luck – a stroke left him paralysed very recently, and he isn't well. The point is, before he was paralysed he came to see me. From our conversation I gathered that he had been investigating something for the Vatican for a long time. He didn't want to tell me anything in detail. It sounded to me like he had found something untoward and that he seemed rather afraid. At any rate, I have seen him once or twice since and he has never mentioned it again. Only two days ago, his niece called saying that he has asked to see me urgently and I said I would visit him at the earliest opportunity, which is tomorrow. Why don't you come with me? We could ask him if he knows anything about this grimoire – perhaps he is the priest Monti saw when he came here. Stranger coincidences have been known to happen.'

Rahn agreed, though at the time he couldn't know that he was taking another fork in the path of his destiny.

13

OF FISH AND MEN

'In the pool where you least expect it, there will be fish.'
Ovid

That night Rahn slept fitfully. Dreams of screaming children woke him early, covered in sweat. He got up and padded to the kitchen to make coffee, feeling a little unnerved. The wood-fired stove hummed lazily and he threw two good logs in and sat at the table. He tried to keep warm while he read Monti's notebook. Now and again he paused to watch the world outside the window coming to life. The sun was rising and as a child full of night terrors he had always associated it with the return of normality. But were nightmares the reality and normality just a dream?

In that little kitchen with only the sounds of the fire and the pendulum clock for company, he thought things through. He wondered what Deodat would say if he told him the whole truth: that he was working for a madman on whose whim he had travelled to France; that in the meantime one man was already dead because of the grimoire; and that he suspected he was being followed by agents of a certain Serinus, whose true identity he didn't know. He didn't want to contemplate what Deodat would say if he told him about Wewelsburg. Rahn would never forget that crypt of death and those poor wretched children. Had he placed his friend in harm's way by coming here? He was certain of it and he told himself the only honourable thing to do was to keep Deodat completely out of the picture and to leave Arques as soon as possible. After all, he knew the Pyrenees better than many French men and it would not be hard for him to find a good hiding hole in the mountains. But as he thought this he was also, quite paradoxically, thinking of reasons why he should stay put because he and Deodat shared one fault: they were like hunting dogs whose noses could not be prevented from following their prey once trained on the scent of a fox. The lust for the chase had seized them. He sighed. What to do, what to do?

Deodat came into the kitchen looking fresh in a casual suit with a blue silk handkerchief in the pocket and a tie to match, disturbing the flow of Rahn's thoughts. He was the sort of man who always dressed impeccably, except when potholing; at those times, one could easily mistake him for a vagabond.

The pendulum clock in the drawing room struck seven.

'The Countess P still controls time, even from beyond the grave,' Deodat said, in a jovial mood.

Rahn smiled. It was true, the old dame did like to have the world march to her rhythm and now he'd inherited the clock, every hour on the hour, she would command his thoughts!

As soon as they had finished breakfast, Deodat herded Rahn out of the house at an inelegant pace and led him out to the barn, where in a perfunctory fashion he unveiled the Tourster. The great animal had been slumbering beneath a grey dust sheet and was in perfect condition: gleaming black with a beige top; tyres painted white; and chrome wheels polished to a mirror finish. Rahn felt joy to see it but it was temporary, for the car had been the Countess's favourite toy and he felt sad to think she would never sit in it again.

'You know,' Deodat said, touching it with a fond air, 'the Countess never allowed her German driver near it after you were gone. Do you remember that unsightly golfing outfit and the half belt jacket he always wore? Your countrymen have no taste,' he said, looking at Rahn's attire with paternal fondness. 'I see you're still wearing that lucky fedora. The same you risked your life to rescue from that ravine?'

'Before you say what I know you are going to say, please let me remind you that were it not for this lucky fedora, we may never have got out of that cave!' Rahn remarked, rather wounded.

'But you'd have to admit, Rahn, it does look rather odd teamed with those loose beige pants, and that flying jacket that appears to have been stolen from a Pabst film set.'

But before Rahn could reply to his friend's audacious accusation Madame Sabine's shrill voice sounded from the house, telling the magistrate not to be late for dinner, since regular meals were better for his digestion.

'Damn that woman!' he cursed under his breath, before calling out in a sweet voice, 'Yes, Madame!' Then: 'Quickly, Rahn, my boy, get in that bloody automobile before she comes, or she'll find some reason for me to stay.'

They took the road to Couiza and not far from Serres, Deodat told him to make a left turn.

'I forgot to tell you, La Dame sends his best regards,' Rahn said.

This made not the slightest difference to Deodat's mood, but Rahn did notice him grumble something under his breath. It must have been something unflattering, even offensive, because he smiled.

'Will you ever forgive La Dame?'

'Never,' was Deodat's quick answer, his determined cheerfulness wavering a little. 'I told you before and I'll tell you again, that day in the cave, when he convinced you to chalk in those engravings just to get a better photo . . . well, that was the end of everything as far as I'm concerned.'

Rahn wanted to say there was no use taking pictures if the drawings were not going to come out, but he knew Deodat would never change his mind, so he looked out at the road and tried to think of something besides his own troubles.

The country they were passing through was imbued with a special sadness and Rahn knew the reason for it – it was the soil's memory of bloodshed. Long ago the Cathars of this area had taken refuge in deep caverns within those wild hills, and in those densely wooded forests and shadowed narrow valleys pierced by the snaking river Aude. They had run away from their homes fearing the inquisitors and their terrible tortures, tortures that either led to the stake or to the murus strictus – a form of imprisonment so terrible it not only resulted in the loss of one's sanity but also one's humanity. In this country many had died but not one had ever revealed the whereabouts of the treasure of their people.

This now brought to his mind the promise he had made to the Countess P one evening after he had played her favourite piece, an improvisation of Handel's suite, *Gods Go a-Begging*. She had said to him, 'I only ask one thing of you, my dear, I want you to promise me that you will remember. You must remember – will you do that for me?'

He had nodded, but what he had promised to remember he didn't know exactly. He had always meant to ask her, only now it was too late.

By the time they arrived at Bugarach the day had turned windy. The priest's residence was set deep in a short valley some way from the township, near a brooding volcano whose hidden fires fuelled the hot springs of Rennes-les-Bains. The Maison de Cros stood large and stately at the end of a long dirt road and as they arrived a young woman met them. Immediately, Rahn was struck by how much she looked like the actress Louise Brooks who played Lulu in the Pabst film *Pandora's Box:* dark hair cut short to accentuate the cheekbones; straight fringe to accentuate the eyes; red lipstick to bring out the mouth; somewhere between eighteen and twenty-five; long limbed and graceful in a pantsuit that flowed as she walked, smoking a cigarette held in one of those long filters. She introduced herself as Eva, the abbé's niece, and escorted them through several rooms, sparsely furnished and decorated in an old style. Rahn didn't like the house. It smelt of blocked drains and ashes and reminded him of a church. He did see a painting that interested him as he passed, a good reproduction of Poussin's *Les Bergers d'Arcardie* hanging on the wall of the study. In fact the study walls were covered with paintings and he would have liked to have taken a moment to look at them. In the meantime, Eva talked with Deodat and Rahn overheard that she was visiting from Paris.

'My uncle will be so happy to see you, magistrate, he's been asking for you; in fact, he's been a little anxious awaiting your arrival. He's in the garden. These days he's taken to sitting there for hours. He seems to like the fish pond.'

The garden was dilapidated and its withered trees shivered occasioning a chorus of rustles in the late autumnal breeze. It was saved from gloom by its southerly orientation, which meant that it was mostly bathed in sun and it was in this sun that the old abbé sat, strapped to a wheelchair, with his knees covered in a thick red blanket and his head adorned with a black wool cap. Someone had placed him very near a large pond crowded with carp and ringing with frogs, and the old man stared into it with a vacant determination.

Rahn recognised the fountain that crowned the pond; it was fashioned into a boy riding a dolphin. He smiled for its aptness, considering the proximity of this house to the extinct volcano the Pic de Bugarach.

Eva noticed his smile. 'Do you like it? The monks had the infant made in Carcassonne.'

'The child hurled by Juno into the ocean from Mount Olympus,' Rahn said, realising that he was trying to impress her, 'before he became the god Vulcan. The god of volcanoes.'

She raised one brow but did not smile. 'That's right.'

'So this was once a monastery, that explains it,' he murmured.

'Explains what?' she said.

He wanted to say, *that explains why I don't like it*. Instead he smiled. 'It explains the architecture . . . thirteenth century?'

'Yes,' she said, but she didn't seem suitably impressed. 'It was deserted during the Revolution when most of the monasteries in the south were closed down. It was laid to waste for a time, but it has been brought back from the dead, so to speak.'

'Like a phoenix rising from the ashes, Mademoiselle Cros?' Deodat put in.

She smiled graciously at Deodat. 'Please, call me Eva.' She went to her uncle and said, 'You have visitors.'

Deodat approached the old man. The abbé's face was expressionless and there was dribble on his chin. Deodat shook one limp hand vigorously. 'You lazy old fool!' he said with fondness. 'I thought I'd find you sitting about doing nothing.'

The man's eyes focused on Deodat and were filled with a sudden, lucid intensity. Rahn had the sense that the man had something urgent on his mind and it would brook no delay. The abbé raised one hand slightly, led by an index finger that seemed to be pointing to the heavens.

Deodat didn't seem to notice anything amiss. He said, quite unperturbed, 'I have brought a friend: Otto Rahn. Do you recall that I spoke to you about him? He wrote that book I gave you on the Cathars.'

The man's sharp gaze moved over Rahn and returned to Deodat. He wanted to say something, but when he tried to speak, what came out sounded like garbled whispers. Deodat sat on the lip of the pond directly in front of him and tried to make some sense of it.

'You wanted to see me. Is it about what we spoke of before you fell ill?' Deodat asked.

The man's face moved barely a muscle but there was something strange playing about his eyes. He opened his mouth a little and Deodat leant in to hear.

'He wants to write something, I think,' Deodat said to Eva, and immediately she disappeared into the house. Meanwhile the old man began to make movements with his mouth again. He looked frustrated, worried – even afraid, Rahn thought.

When Eva returned, the abbé's anxiety seemed to grow. She placed a fountain pen in his hand and held a piece of writing paper over a book so that he could scribble down what he had to say. The effort agitated him and his breathing grew laboured, but he managed to write one word:

Sator

When he was finished his eyes, full of meaning, returned to Deodat. He shook his head, almost imperceptibly, and tried again to form words. Deodat leant in one more time. 'I think he's saying something about the church. Is there something in the church you want, Eugene?'

There was the slightest nod of the head.

'What is it?'

His eyes looked here and there, like a man seeking a place on which to lean his words. He glanced at his niece and Rahn saw something in the abbé's eyes he couldn't quite fathom. The girl bent to comfort him but the old man began silently weeping.

'Look,' Deodat said, patting the old man's knee, 'we can leave it for another time. We'll come back when you're feeling a little better.'

The abbé didn't look away from the pond and their polite exit was ignored.

'Please don't feel bad, magistrate,' Eva said, seeing them out. 'He's been like that since he was visited by a friend, another priest, a week or so ago. Afterwards, he was so anxious to see you . . . Perhaps he was just overwhelmed?'

Deodat turned to her. 'An old friend saw him? Who was it?'

'A priest, I think, from Saint-Paul-de-Fenouillet. But I don't know what my uncle could possibly want from the church, since all his possessions were brought here from the presbytery when he fell ill. As far as I know, there's nothing left at the church that belongs to him.'

'Is it possible to see the church today?' Deodat said. 'I wanted to show it to my friend while we were here.'

'I suppose so. It's Sunday but there isn't a priest there at the moment. Despite that the church is always open.' She looked thoughtful, then said, 'Would you like me to come with you?'

'What about Eugene, my dear, won't he need you?'

'Giselle is here,' she said, excited or so it seemed, at the prospect.

When she returned, she was dressed in a skirt and loose blouse, a cardigan hanging over her shoulders. On her feet were sensible shoes and on her face she wore the flush of adventure. Deodat sat graciously in the back, letting her have the front seat next to Rahn, who was disconcerted, since he found her perfume and those legs peeking out from beneath that long skirt rather distracting, but not enough to prevent him from noticing, as he pulled out of the driveway, that a black car was parked some way down the road.

He couldn't remember seeing it on their arrival. It looked like a Citroën but it was impossible to tell at this distance. He kept an eye on it as he drove on in case it pulled out to follow them, but it didn't.

'You said the church has no priest and yet it is always open?' Deodat asked Eva from the back.

'It's the tyranny of life in the country, I'm afraid, magistrate,' she said. 'The locksmith can't find the time to come all the way from Carcassonne to Bugarach just to change three or four locks.'

'Did something happen to the keys?'

'When my uncle was struck down by his illness the sacristan was given the keys to the church so that he could continue to do the ordinary things: open it, dust and mop and keep the various vessels of the sacrament clean. But the keys went missing.'

'Was he just careless?' Rahn asked.

'It's actually quite a sad affair,' she said, with a sigh. 'The sacristan committed suicide. He threw himself rather dramatically from the Pic de Bugarach. Things like that happen around here from time to time. Perhaps it was boredom or melancholy, who knows? You can't imagine how difficult it was to find him. There was an exhaustive search that took nearly a week. When the body was found, well, I won't go into it. It is too ghastly. At any rate, there was no sign of the keys on his person so it was assumed he must have put them away in a safe place before his demise. In the end the villagers nearly tore apart his small house but found nothing. So the church remains open until a new priest comes who can entice the locksmith here.'

The church was squat, old and worn out, with a cemetery and a scattering of ramshackle houses to keep it company. Rahn parked the car in its shadow and they got out. Even outside, he could feel that familiar dread come over him. He spoke now more out of a desire to calm his nerves than out of curiosity.

'Eighth or ninth century?'

'The fifth, the time of the Visigoths, actually,' she said, walking to the main entrance. 'I see you know your history.' There was a half smile. Was she mocking him? Her voice had that peculiar tone that left him unable to discern one way or the other.

'Rahn is a Cathar historian and a philologist,' Deodat informed her.

'I see,' she said. 'You'll be interested to know then, that this village was once a Gallo-Celtic fort. You wouldn't think so now, would you?' She opened the door with an air of irreverence. 'The town became a Cathar settlement somewhere along the line.'

Rahn hung back. He couldn't remember a time when he hadn't felt a morbid fear of Roman churches. As a child, whenever his mother had forced him to go to church it had been a wretched trial. Bargains had been offered and refused, tears had been shed and punishments meted out, but he had remained obdurate. The black cross, the dead, contorted Jesus, the effigies of saints, the sarcophagi – all things that may have inspired another child to pious reverence – generated panic and horror in Rahn. And it had remained so. It was, therefore, with great effort that he entered the cold, damp, silent space whose acrid smell of smoke from the votive candles and whose pungent scent of laurel made him feel ill. He loosened his collar, feeling a cold sweat on his brow, and there was that familiar tremor in his hands. He steeled himself like a man about to go into a field of battle from which no man had ever returned unscathed.

'The church was dedicated to Stella Maris, Our Lady of the Seas,' Eva said, walking along the nave, her disembodied voice echoing from the short vaults. 'But originally it was consecrated to Saint Anthony, the hermit.'

'Why Saint Anthony?' Rahn asked, keeping his mind on his feet, moving them one after the other.

'There's a hermitage of his not far from here. In Bugarach on Ash Wednesday there's a procession led by a man dressed like a hermit wearing a horse collar around his neck with bells on it and carrying a cross that has pork sausages hanging from its arms. All rather rustic.'

Eva looked at Rahn enquiringly. 'You don't look well, Monsieur Rahn.'

'I don't like churches,' he said, rather sharply.

Deodat took Eva's arm and confided, 'Our friend can walk into a cave without fear of crevices or lakes. He has no concern for bats, snakes or spiders and even rats are nothing to him, but put him in a church and he turns pale like this and looks like he's seen a ghost!' He laughed a small clipped laugh. 'Imagine!'

'That's very interesting,' she said to Rahn. 'Have you seen a psychiatrist?'

'Freud would say,' Deodat continued, in his element, 'that a fear such as this displays the psychodynamic conflict between desire for and repulsion of the mother on the one hand, represented by the mother church, and the idealisation and fear of the father – who is really God on the other.'

Rahn mustered his sarcasm and said, 'Oedipus, of course! Nothing new in that.'

Deodat, having had his fun, now appointed himself Rahn's defence counsel. 'The truth is, my dear, when one knows history, one cannot walk into a church unperturbed. In the final analysis, thousands were killed in a church not far from here at Béziers during the Cathar wars.

Rahn continued Deodat's line. 'Roman churches are not places of asylum, nor are they holy. They are nothing more than prisons and execution chambers; traps for the unwary.' He paused then, realising to his concern that he had unwittingly walked through the iron enclosures to the altar. But before his fear could take hold he noticed two plaques that seized his attention: one to the left of the crucifix, the other to the right. Both showed the Book of the Seven Seals.

'Ah! You've found the chief reason I brought you here, Rahn,' Deodat said at his shoulder. 'It isn't often one sees the Book of the Seven Seals so well depicted on plaques.' Deodat then pointed to a third plaque over a door on the right, leading to what might be the sacristy.

Rahn smiled, despite himself. 'For Heaven's sake, it's the Grail!'

'There's another one over there, too,' Deodat said, pointing to a fourth plaque over an identical door on the left wall. 'So you see, this may not be a Roman church after all.'

'This is very significant,' Rahn said, to himself. 'The Book of the Seven Seals and the Holy Grail together in the same church implies some knowledge of the Cathar treasure.'

'That's right,' Deodat said.

'What do you mean?' Eva came over to see, suddenly interested.

'The treasure is purported to include both,' Rahn explained. 'Apparently they were brought here to the South of France for safekeeping, and the Cathars are thought to have been their guardians.'

'What's this statue, my dear?' Deodat asked Eva.

'That's Saint Roch, patron of those afflicted by plagues. Apparently, he was saved from starvation in the wilderness by a hunting dog with a loaf of bread in its mouth, and so he is mostly portrayed with a dog.'

Rahn turned to see. 'Cerberus?'

'Look at him,' Deodat said, nodding towards Rahn. 'See how he comes to life as soon as there is an allusion to the myths!'

Eva smiled. 'Myths?'

Rahn went to the badly cast statue and looked it over. 'The dog Cerberus is the guardian of the world of the dead. It was Hercules' last labour to fetch the dog and to return it to the Underworld. Some say it's a symbol for a guarded secret. There is an effigy of Cerberus as large as a house in the caves of Lombrives.'

'Really?' Eva didn't seem suitably impressed.

'I can attest to that,' Deodat said. 'Now as far as this one's concerned, the bread in its mouth is likely to be an allusion to the manna that kept the Jews alive in the wilderness. And manna is also the same as the substance contained in the Grail, which fed the inhabitants of Montsalvache, the *panem supersubstanialem*, otherwise known as the bread of life. Now, look at this, Rahn!' Deodat took himself to a side chapel. Above a little altar, there was a stained-glass window depicting two men turning a wheel in the sky, in which sat a crescent moon illuminating an ocean and a boat sailing away from a rising sun.

'The symbol of destiny,' Rahn said, wiping his brow. 'The wheel of fortune in the tarot deck – this is quite extraordinary.'

'Symbols are interesting.' Eva came to take a look. 'My uncle's stroke has affected the speech centre in his brain, which not only disturbs his speech . . .'

But Rahn wasn't listening, he was thinking.

The boat of Hercules travels to the Underworld towards the rising sun . . . the Underworld is the realm of death . . . the wheel of fortune represents each man's destiny which ends in death . . . but this boat is travelling away from the rising sun, it's moving away from death.

' ... it also affects his ability to understand the meaning of things.'

The wheel . . . turns one way . . . and it reverses . . .

'For instance, he would not know what a toothbrush is, and would just as likely use it to comb his hair – he can't connect the item with its purpose, so I guess he wouldn't know symbols either, even words can come out back to front.' She looked around. 'I can't think what my uncle could want from the church. What was that word he wrote down – Sator? Do you know what it means?'

'Sator means sower, creator, reaper,' Rahn said automatically, still thinking.

'It's Latin,' Deodat informed her. 'But I may have to look up what other meanings there are, then we may understand what Eugene was trying to tell us.'

'My uncle told me about your library. Apparently it's full of heretical texts, the most comprehensive in all of the Languedoc. You know, he does think very highly of you, despite what he calls your strange leanings.'

'And I think fondly of him too, despite him being as stubborn as an old goat. Speaking of him, I think we should get you back. We've kept you from him long enough.'

Rahn was grateful to follow the others out of the church and once outside felt as if he had surfaced from a near drowning. But on the drive back to Maison de Cros he had the strangest sensation that he had missed something important in the church, and this caused him to drive in silence all the way to the turn-off, trying to think of what it might be. By then it was late afternoon and the sun was tilting its light over the unforgiving land-scape, creating ominous shadows in various shades of purple. He looked for the black car but it was gone.

When they arrived at the house there were a number of parked cars in the driveway and the housekeeper came bursting out of the great double doors in tears. After that Rahn and the others were swept up in a concert of cries, lamentations, imprecations and gesticulations that had no meaning whatsoever until they came to the garden, where they found the source of the mayhem – and, oh, what a frightful sight it was!

14

MURDER MOST FOUL

'My God!' stammered he, unable to control his emotion,
'What do you say – a crime?'
Emile Gaboriau, The Mystery of Orcival

The old abbé was lying on the grass. His clothes were saturated, his hair was plastered over a bloated face turned to one side, and his milky eyes stared wide and horrified, as if they had seen the face of the Devil himself. Rahn wondered if it was true that one could glimpse the image of the murderer frozen forever in the eyes of the murdered. He staggered a little to think on it, he had seen more death in one week than many men see in a lifetime and he was realising that his nature was a delicate one when it came to such things.

There were several gendarmes walking around and in a moment two ambulance men arrived to place the old abbé on a stretcher and take him away. A sad sight, Rahn thought. The girl seemed in shock as she accompanied her uncle's body into the house. At this point a short, pale little man walked towards them. He had thick brows and a wiry moustache that cut across his long pock-marked face like a dash.

He lifted his crumpled Panama hat with the tip of a finger in greeting and said, 'Good afternoon, messieurs, Inspecteur Guillaume Beliere, of the Brigade Spéciale of the Parisian Police Judiciaire.' He took a crushed packet of cigarettes from the inside pocket of his jacket, revealing the gun at his belt. He shook one out and lit it without taking his eyes off Rahn. Rahn held the gaze and tried to hide his disquiet. The man seemed to be the antithesis of those detectives in the novels that he loved, like Gaboriau's detective Monsieur Lecoq. Such a man analysed clues, employed the marvels of modern science and solved crimes by using logic and reason. Such a man, he imagined, never wore crumpled suits, and his sensitive probing fingers would be popping peppermint lozenges into his mouth, not holding a cigarette with a nicotine-stained thumb and forefinger, looking as if he had slept with an empty bottle of rum under one arm.

'You knew the deceased?' the inspector said after a perfunctory cough, looking from Deodat to Rahn.

'The abbé was more than an acquaintance, he was a friend, actually,' Deodat said, officious and annoyed. 'He asked to see me and we came today but he was unwell. We were gone only a couple of hours.'

The head tilted again and the brows arched slightly. He took a moment to think on it, while he let his entire weight rest on his heels. 'Gone?'

'To Bugarach, to visit the old church,' Rahn put in.

Those wet eyes fell on Rahn. The inspector smiled without showing his teeth. 'For religious reasons?'

'Not in the strictest sense,' Rahn said.

'No?' The man squinted through the smoke, holding the cigarette in the corner of his mouth.

'Can you tell us, inspector, what has happened here?' Deodat brought his authority as a magistrate to bear on the moment.

'A terrible accident, I'm afraid.' But the flat tone suggested he didn't find it quite so terrible. Perhaps he had seen worse ways to die. 'The maid was inside answering the phone. When she returned, she found the abbé in the pond. He must have tipped the wheelchair over. No one knows how it happened. The poor woman couldn't get him out. He was strapped to the chair and too heavy for her, you see,' he said, taking a long drag of his cigarette. 'A dead weight.'

Rahn felt Deodat bristle beside him.

'How in the devil could he have tipped the wheelchair?' Deodat said. 'The man was paralysed – he could hardly move his lips!'

The inspector gave an uninterested sigh. 'Who knows? Perhaps it was a fit or an involuntary spasm? The maid said he was a stroke victim, so this may have been another stroke. The clinical autopsy will reveal more. I will need to take your names.' He turned to Rahn. 'You, monsieur, you are a foreigner?' Rahn felt the burning interest in those eyes. 'Can I see your papers, your passport?'

Rahn searched his jacket and brought them out of his wallet, dropping a card.

The inspector picked it up and read it before giving it back. 'Serinus?' he said.

The blood rushed from Rahn's head. 'A business associate.'

'Serinus is the genus name of the canary, isn't that so?' The skin around those bloodshot eyes wrinkled.

Rahn hadn't thought about it and now he hesitated. 'I believe you're right, inspector.'

'May I?' He reached for Rahn's papers.

'Of course.'

'So, from Berlin, is that right?'

'Yes.'

'I see, and you are staying here in the south for how long?'

'A week or two.'

'And your accommodation?'

'He's staying with me,' Deodat put in, about to lose his formidable temper.

'And you might be?'

'Deodat Roche, Magistrate of Arques, that's who I am! And I'd like to know, inspector, what you are doing here, so far from Paris and in my jurisdiction?'

Inspecteur Beliere lifted that brow again, not at all perturbed. He touched his hat in deference and said, 'Forgive me, magistrate, I did not know who you were. I am staying at Carcassonne for a small time, investigating something in connection to a group called La Cagoule. Have you heard of them?'

'Of course,' Deodat said, 'everyone has heard of them.'

'Yes, the journalists have made certain of that,' the inspector said, blinking. He took a drag of his cigarette and let it sit a thoughtful moment in his lungs before spilling it out in a cloud around his face. He looked as if he was about to turn philosophical but instead he continued with a certain hesitation, 'We have information that has led us here. In fact, it was by sheer coincidence that I was at the gendarmerie at Carcassonne when the call came in about the deceased. I had nothing else to do . . .' He showed small, yellowed teeth. ' . . . so here I am!' He looked at Rahn. 'Are you Monsieur Rahn, the celebrated author? I think I have read your book!'

This struck Rahn. 'Really?'

'Yes,' the other man said, with a concentrated frown. 'The Sons of Belessina, the Troubadours, Esclarmonde de Foix – the great Cathar Perfecta, and Montsegur.' He took one last drag, threw the cigarette down and stepped on it. 'I'm rather fond of the Cathars and the Templars, it's a little hobby of mine. I read in my spare time. There is more to us police than making arrests and filing reports, you know. I thought when reading your book that only a strange twist of fate could lead a German to know more than the French about their own history.'

'One could look at it that way.'

'You say in your introduction, if I'm not mistaken, that it was Péladan who inspired you? I find that very interesting. Wasn't he a Rosicrucian, an occultist?'

Rahn's book had only sold five thousand copies and so, the fact that this man had read it, in itself, was an oddity. Moreover, out of all the things mentioned in his book, the inspector chose to touch on Péladan, for whom Monti had once worked. Rahn felt Monti's notebook burning a hole in his pocket. This had to be the inspector's calculated way of letting him know that he was aware of his visit to Pierre Plantard.

'I should let you go now,' the inspector said forestalling Rahn's answer, 'I must see to some . . . formalities, as you no doubt appreciate, magistrate.'

'Thank you, inspector, I would like to be kept informed of anything you find in relation to this unfortunate accident,' Deodat said.

'Of course. In fact you can expect that I will call in on you soon, to notify you of my progress.'

'That would be desirable,' Deodat answered tersely.

The man tipped his hat and lingered a little before turning to go. He paused then, as if he had just remembered something of great importance, and spun around wearing an enquiring face.

'Might I ask why the deceased wanted to see you?'

'I don't really know,' Deodat answered. 'But I have a suspicion that it was in relation to an investigation.'

'An investigation?'

'It was before his illness. He was investigating the priests of this area – he had the sanction of the Vatican; I don't know the particular details.'

'I see. And he said nothing to you today?'

'Nothing intelligible; all we could ascertain was that he wanted us to find something in the church. That's why we went there.'

'And did you find anything?' His raised brows were expectant, his wet mouth open slightly; he appeared to be hanging on Deodat's next words.

'No. I'm afraid not.'

Rahn couldn't tell if he saw relief or disappointment on the man's inscrutable face. 'I see . . . Well, I bid you a good evening.'

And with these words the inspector walked away, leaving them alone in that miserable garden, with the shadow cast by the dormant volcano pouring its gloom over them.

15

ENIGMAS AND CONUNDRUMS

The analytical power should not be confounded with simple ingenuity;
for while the analyst is necessarily ingenious, the ingenious man
is often remarkably incapable of analysis.'
Edgar Allan Poe, 'The Murders in the Rue Morgue'

The drive home was silent. At the house, Madame Sabine, havinheard from Rahn of the abbé's death, kept out of the way and refrained from complaining about the late hour of their arrival. She heated their dinner without saying a word and they ate the beans and potatoes in garlic in the kitchen, without appetite. The wood crackling in the stove and the wind brushing the tangled limbs against the window were the only sounds in the stillness between them.

For Rahn's part, what he had not told Deodat now troubled him. He wondered about the black car at Bugarach, about the strangeness of the abbé's demeanour before his terrible death, and about a police inspector who was supposedly here to investigate a group called La Cagoule but who just happened to know his book intimately.

Later, in the drawing room, drinking a much-needed brandy before the fire, Rahn resolved to do the inevitable.

'Look, Deodat, I'm afraid I haven't been totally honest with you. I have to tell you something.'

'What is it?' Deodat said from behind his pipe.

'It's a rather long and sordid story and you may not like me much afterwards, but . . .' He told Deodat everything – with the exception of those events at Wewelsburg, as he saw no reason to tarnish his own character more than he had to. Meanwhile, Deodat sat quietly through the long and painful confession, his face neutral – the mask of a wise, introspective judge. When it was over, however, he seemed unable to hold in his dismay.

'What in the devil, Rahn? What were you thinking?'

Rahn passed a hand over his hair, trying to find the right words. 'How on Earth was I to know who would be waiting at the end of that telegram? Do you think I would have gone there? Once in that apartment, what was I to do? I had to go along with things for a while until I could get away – and here I am.'

'Well, now that I'm piecing it all together it begins to make sense. It's elementary! This elucidates what that inspector is doing at Bugarach and why he knows so much about you.'

'It has something to do with Monti, doesn't it?'

'Yes, of course.'

'How?'

'La Cagoule, that group he mentioned, is known to recruit its members from another group called Action Francais. Action Francais is connected to Alpha Galates – the group run by Pierre Plantard, whom you saw in Paris.'

Rahn paused. 'And Alpha Galates is connected to Monti.'

'That's right. This La Cagoule is responsible for terrorist acts all over Europe,' Deodat said, 'and the Paris police have been after them for a while. If they were watching Plantard and they observed you going into his apartment they may have followed you here, suspecting that you are somehow connected to them.'

'What?' Rahn said, alarmed.

'Well, that's one conclusion!' Deodat grew introspective once more. 'Something bothers me though – did you notice the inspector's gun? I haven't seen one of those used by the police before, and did you see his shoes? Awfully shiny for a detective whose clothes look as though they've been slept in. Very peculiar . . . I don't know what it means but I'm certain it will reveal itself.' He got up to fetch a bottle of brandy. 'I think you have stumbled onto a viper's nest.'

'What do you mean?'

'In France, everywhere one turns these days, one is likely to bump into a society for this or for that.' He refilled Rahn's glass, sat down and stared into the fire a moment. 'Right-wing Fascist groups, like Action Francais and Alpha Galates, want to bring back the rule of the French kings. They have strong connections to the church, which lost its power when the Catholic lineage of kings was exterminated. Opposing them are the Freemasons – the republican capitalists and industrialists – men who exercise their influence on the markets. So you see, Rahn, you have a religious power opposing an economic power. Having said that, these opposing groups do have something in common – their hatred of the Communists and the Jews. But if you dig deeper, you begin to realise that these seemingly opposing groups are thoroughly interconnected.' He took out his pipe, filled it with tobacco and lit it.

Rahn sat forwards, incredulous. 'Let me see if I understand you. You are saying that the Fascists, Freemasons, Communists, Jews and the church are all intertwined? But they hate each other.'

'Only outwardly. I believe there is one central authority that rules them all; one body whose goal is political, economic and spiritual supremacy; a circle composed of representatives from every group. I call it the Cénacle.'

'But Pierre Plantard told me these societies are all competing with one another for secrets,' Rahn said, rather perplexed.

'Yes, that's true on one level: they fight wars on opposite sides, they assassinate one another, steal from one another, all of that.

But it's all an illusion, a smoke screen.' He puffed away thoughtfully. 'Every now and again, something surfaces which points to the Cénacle, but it is in such a veiled way that only the astute observer would ever recognise it.'

'This is extraordinary – a circle of men who rule Europe?'

'Yes,' Deodat said, 'a circle funded by powerful banks; banks like Barings, the Bank of Moscow and the most powerful of them all – the bank owned by the Rothschilds. But these aren't just any men.'

'What do you mean?'

'I mean they are esotericists, but not just that, they are black esotericists. You see, in the public eye you may have the black occultists, the attention-seeking braggarts like Hitler, Stalin and Mussolini, but these men are just chess pieces. Behind them, you have the hands that move the chess pieces.'

'The Cénacle?' Rahn said.

'Yes, and I fear they are grooming Hitler to become their supreme black occultist.'

Rahn recalled the people that had come and gone from Weisthor's office: Englishmen, Russians, clergymen, Tibetans. He remembered all the reports on different occult traditions and Himmler's desire for the grimoire. Things were beginning to make sense. 'They want war,' he said. 'And Hitler will give it to them. Is that it?'

'Yes; a war will destroy Germany and give them Russia.'

'I quite follow you, but the only point that I don't understand is this business with Russia. What do they want with Russia?'

'Russia is a sought-after jewel, destined to be the location of the New Jerusalem spoken of in Saint John's Apocalypse. Those who understand this know that whoever rules Russia will, in future times, control the world.'

'And Germany?'

'Germany is the middle, and it was destined to be the spiritual centre of a free Europe in preparation for Russia. Now that it has fallen into the hands of the Cénacle, it will be destroyed.'

'What?' Rahn sat up.

'I'm afraid so.'

'For what reason?'

'Because the Cénacle desires no spirit, no middle that might come between it and Russia.'

'You astound me, Deodat!' Rahn had to think this through. 'Did the Countess P know about these things?'

'I shouldn't imagine so. She was a theosophist, as you know, and theosophy is affiliated with various groups, but she was like you. She didn't belong to this time. She did know De Mengel, however, and I met him once at her château, that's how I came to know about Monti.'

'Why didn't you mention earlier that you knew so much about him?'

'I didn't know how deeply you were involved in all of it. He was a dangerous man, he was watching the anthroposophists in Paris very closely, and I believe he had something to do with Rudolf Steiner's assassination.'

Rahn knew that Deodat's fondness for anthroposophy had brought about the awkwardness between him and the countess, since she was a theosophist, because Rudolf Steiner, the leader of anthroposophy, had broken away from theosophy in quite a spectacular way.

'Why was Monti watching the anthroposophists?' Rahn said.

'Because anthroposophists are "white" esotericists.'

'So there are "white" and "black" esotericists?'

'Of course, and grey ones too — those who can't make up their minds! When Rudolf Steiner formed his own group, he made certain that it was completely independent from all the other groups and, as a result, he was hated by them all. I believe this to be the reason he was poisoned, and that Monti had a hand in it.' Deodat leant forwards. 'Now, let's assume that the key to completing *Le Serpent Rouge* does exist, Rahn. It would be a powerful tool of magic in the hands of a black occultist like Hitler and, therefore, in the hands of those black esotericists in the Cénacle who control him.'

Rahn looked up to the rafters, blackened by the smoke from the fire; he felt completely out of his depth. What had he got himself into?

'What should we do? If we don't try to find it they'll only send someone else.'

Deodat puffed on his pipe intensely and said nothing.

Rahn was filled with a singular restlessness. 'Is it possible that, as you said before, the abbé was a part of it somehow?'

'What?'

'Well, doesn't it strike you as interesting that Cros was investigating priests? Doesn't it strike you as strange that after he falls ill, the very person in charge of the keys to the church commits suicide, and when they find his body there is no sign of the keys anywhere? Next, the abbé himself dies, drowned a short time after asking you to get something from the church. And as if that's not enough, an inspector turns up, quick as a flash, looking like a dishevelled Professor Moriarty, not only knowing everything about my book but also looking for a group connected to Pierre Plantard in Paris? There are too many coincidences, Deodat!'

'As I said before, I think Inspecteur Beliere was following you, Rahn.'

'Perhaps, but are you telling me the abbé's death and the missing keys mean nothing?'

'Let me remind you that we must work a posteriori – that is, we must reason from observed facts.'

'Well then, let's do so. What was Cros doing spying on priests for the Vatican?' Rahn asked.

'It was probably some small matter, a misappropriation of funds or something of that sort. Things like that happen all the time in these small towns.'

Rahn was in no way convinced. 'I think the abbé was desperate. He wanted you to find something. What did he mean by Sator – the sower, creator or planter?'

'That usually refers to Christ.'

'Perhaps, usually, but in this case it sounds to me like a code.'

'A code?'

'Yes. Did you have something you shared apart from playing chess, some inside joke, anything?'

Deodat sighed and rubbed his chin. 'Well, sometimes, in the days when he was well, he was fond of puzzles. Actually, he rather liked Roman puzzles.'

'What are they?'

'Latin riddles, chronograms, palindromes, that sort of thing. For instance, one time a letter arrived by mail from him and in it I found a rebus: Ego sum principium, mundi et finis, saeculorum attamen non sum Deus.'

Rahn translated it: *'I am the beginning of the world and the end of the ages, but I am not God.* And? Did you solve it?'

'It took me some time. The solution was elementary: it was M.'

'M? Ah . . . yes!' Rahn's face brightened. 'The letter M is the beginning of the Latin word "mundi", which means world; and it is also at the end of the word "saeculorum", which means ages. Very amusing!'

'Yes,' Deodat said, although he didn't seem the least bit amused. He frowned, thinking about it.

Rahn had a sudden thought. 'Do you have a Latin dictionary?'

Deodat looked at him as if he had just asked him if the Earth was round. 'Of course.'

'We need to look up "Sator".' There was a large tome on the table in Deodat's library.

Rahn stood beside him as he pushed his glasses onto the bridge of his nose and flicked the pages until he found it.

'"Sator" . . . Well, well,' he said. 'Here it is. Apparently it forms part of a famous palindrome, that is, it reads the same up and down, backwards and forwards, and so it's sometimes called a magic square.'

He showed Rahn.

S	A	T	O	R
A	R	E	P	O
T	E	N	E	T
O	P	E	R	A
R	O	T	A	S

I've seen something like this before,' Rahn said, intrigued.

'Here it says that it means: The sower, Arepo, holds the wheels of work.'

"'Arepo"? That's not Latin?'

'No, according to this book, that word has never been deciphered.' Deodat continued reading: 'Magic squares have been found in Italy dating back to the first centuries, both in Rome and in Lucca.' He looked up. 'You know, quite a few have been found here, in the south, as well. At any rate, the book says that it was once a code used by the early Christians to denote places of sanctuary, but it must predate Christianity because one was found in the city of Pompeii, in an engraving preserved by the volcanic ash of Vesuvius. It also says here that many believe it forms a kind of esoteric puzzle.'

'What have you got on ancient puzzles in your library?' Rahn asked.

'Look under A, for ancient, or R for Roman, or P for puzzles . . . take your pick. That damned woman!' he murmured with exasperation.

After some digging about, Rahn found that Madame Sabine had placed a book under the first name of the author, a certain Pitois. 'Look, here's a reference,' Rahn said. 'The Sator Square is also found in *Solomon's Keys.*'

Deodat's ears pricked up. 'The first grimoire ever written?' He returned to his shelves again, tapping on his chin as he looked over them.

Rahn smiled. 'Don't tell me you have a copy of it?'

'Well, I've got two, actually,' Deodat said over his shoulder, with a certain smugness. 'One in French and one in English – doesn't everybody have at least one?' He took *Les Clavicules de Rabbi Salomon* from the bookshelf with particular reverence, blew the dust from it and turned the pages. 'Here it is. What in the devil . . . !'

'What is it?' Rahn joined him by the shelf.

'Look for yourself!' He gave Rahn the book.

'It's the Sator Square, but now it's in Hebrew.'

'Yes.' Deodat took the book back. 'This means that the Sator Square not only has connections to the Roman and Christian mysteries but the Hebrew ones as well. Now, here in this grimoire, the Pentacle of Saturn displays the magic square, which Solomon relates to the Alpha and Omega, or Christ as He is known in Saint John's Apocalypse.

'It also says here that the magic square can be used not only for warding off adversaries, as a conjuration to repel Satan – Retro Satan; but that one can also, by making a slight variation in the words, use it as a prayer to invoke Satan – Satan, Oro Te. You see, this is the interesting thing about grimoires – they can be used for good or for evil.'

Clearly this thought prompted another because he took himself to his bookshelves again, looking about feverishly.

'What now?' Rahn asked.

'I have a book written by Éliphas Lévi, a man you could call a "grey" occultist. It's a book on magic rituals and it's somewhere in this infernal disorder.'

It took some time but he eventually found it.

'Look, do you see this? Lévi speaks of the word rotas, which is sator back to front. He says it's connected to the tarot and to cut a long story short, the tarot is connected to the Alpha and Omega and Saint John's Apocalypse. Over and over we are seeing a connection between grimoires and the Apocalypse.' He paused. 'You know, Abbé Cros asked me for thebook years ago. He wanted to know something about the pope card. He kept the book for many months.'

But Rahn wasn't listening – inside his mind two things were colliding to make a third. 'So, Cros knew you would understand what sator meant, that is obvious to me, and he must have wanted you to find something connected to the grimoires and to the Apocalypse in the church. Now it all makes sense. The church was full of symbols: plaques depicting the Book of the Seven Seals – Saint John's Apocalypse, on either side of the altar; the Grail over the doors; and to top it all off, a wheel of fortune in the stained-glass window, which is straight out of the tarot. The wheel is a symbol for life and death, it turns one way towards death and another towards a reversal of death.'

Deodat nodded. 'The one who holds the wheel of fortune is Christ, sator, the sower, or the cultivator. The crux, or tenet, "what holds", is the middle word, and it forms a cross at the centre of the magic square. Do you see it?' He pointed it out to Rahn.

S	A	T	O	R
A	R	E	P	O
T	E	N	E	T
O	P	E	R	A
R	O	T	A	S

So what in the church could be related to the transformation of life and death and also to Christ, who died on the cross?' Rahn asked.

'Don't you know, Rahn? The *dead* bread and wine are brought to *life* magically by the priest who turns them into the *living* body and blood of Christ. The sacrament is the result of a transformation of matter into spirit and spirit into matter.'

'Birth and death, the wheel! So, Deodat, where are the transformed bread and wine kept in a church?'

'What isn't consumed during the mass is kept in—' He looked at Rahn. 'Do you think he wanted us to find the tabernacle?'

Rahn picked up the scent. 'Where is it?'

'In the altar, usually, but it's no doubt locked, and without a key . . .'

'And yet, what better place could a priest find to hide something?'

'Yes, but Eva said that the sacristan had the job of cleaning all the items used in the mass, and they are kept in the tabernacle. Surely the abbé knew the sacristan might see it,' Deodat said. 'That is, before he committed suicide.'

'I'd wager the sacristan didn't jump from the Pic de Bugarach, Deodat. I think he was pushed!'

'Now you're the one who is jumping – jumping to conclusions. You know what they say about the ingenious: they are often incapable of analysis because they get caught up in their own cleverness.'

'And do you have any better ideas?' Rahn said, suddenly annoyed.

Deodat walked away, tapping his chin. Eventually he turned around. 'I'm afraid there's only one way to test this hypothesis: we have to go there and see for ourselves.'

'Go where?'

'To the church, to see if you're right about the tabernacle.' He put his glasses in his pocket.

'What? Now?' Rahn was suddenly faced with the consequences of his own cleverness.

'If we're going to break into the tabernacle, it might as well be at night. Besides, it's easier at night to detect whether you're being followed. I read that in a detective story. Come on, dear boy, tempus fugit!'

'But how do you propose to get into the tabernacle without waking the entire township of Bugarach? Really, Deodat, it doesn't seem very practical to me, and I can see the papers now: "Respected magistrate to appear in his own courthouse after being caught breaking into the tabernacle of Bugarach church".'

'Nonsense! I could say I was conducting an examination in relation to a suspicious case, as any magistrate has a right to do.'

Rahn knew that once Deodat had made up his obstinate mind there was no stopping him. And so he watched helplessly as his friend slapped his black wool hat onto his head and put on his coat.

'I don't know what's more fun,' he said, 'going off to do some hole-and-corner work in the night like a thief, or watching your face pale when we go in and out of churches.'

16

TO HIT THE NAIL ON THE HEAD

'. . . he dashed into the midst of the flock of sheep and began to spear them
with as much courage and fury as if he were fighting his mortal enemies.'
Miguel de Cervantes, Don Quixote

R ahn drove back to Bugarach. The night was cold and
the moon that came out from behind the clouds to
light the narrow road was almost full.

He contemplated his mistake. He had allowed himself
to be seduced by the mystery and its connection to the Cathar
treasure and, in the fever of intellectual abandon, had forgotten
the resolve he had made earlier in the day – the consequences of
which were now quite plain to him: Deodat was becoming more
deeply involved in this dangerous affair; and he was not on his
way to a hiding spot in the Pyrenees but on his way to a church
at night to break into a tabernacle.

It didn't help that a part of him was enjoying the hunt. To the
contrary, his own excitement made that other part of him, the
sensible part, vexed because it knew that such a hunt would not
end well for either of them. And his mood was not lightened in
any way by their arrival at Bugarach. For if it seemed sad and ominous in the day, it was so many times more foreboding now, with

its silent houses and abandoned streets dominated by the old volcano swathed in moon glow. Bugarach was no ordinary church,
there was something decidedly pagan and mysterious about it. It
recalled to his mind stories of those ancient sibyls who foretold
the future by drinking in the sulphurous fumes of volcanoes.

Rahn parked the car discreetly on a dirt shoulder behind some
low-lying bushes and together he and Deodat made their quiet
way to the church, past the graveyard, which on this cold night
looked windblown and secretive. Rahn steeled his heart as he
made to open the door and nearly jumped out of his skin when
the rusty hinges groaned.

Deodat was in his ear. 'Could you be louder, Rahn? After all,
not everyone in the township heard your announcement: Here
is the magistrate of Arques come to steal something from the
church, wake up sleepy-heads or you will miss it!'

'Very funny, Deodat!'

Rahn concentrated on keeping calm and stepped inside. Once
across the threshold all his symptoms returned: his mouth was
dry; his hands trembled; sweat formed on his brow; and his
knees weakened. He looked about. The church seemed redolent
of decay, the flickering candles made shadows loom over the
walls. Shadows and shadows of shadows created sinister demons
of those saints upon their high stations. His mother's words rang
in his ears.

Don't be afraid, Otto, there are only angels in churches.

'Yes, but are they good angels?' he whispered out loud, making Deodat turn around.

They had made it to the choir enclosures without Rahn passing out, which was a relief to him, and now Deodat showed him
the tabernacle. Rahn forced his mind to turn away from imponderables and focused his thinking to the moment. The bronze
box was built into the front of the altar directly beneath the
crucifix, whose hideousness was lit by a perpetual flame. Rahn
tried the lock. It wouldn't give. He took a candle behind the altar,

which to him seemed less sinister than the front. He thought that the sacristan or the abbé may have left a key here for convenience but he found nothing more than a little bottle of oil, a box of matches and a couple of dirty rags. He opened the matchbox – it was full of matches but no key.

Deodat whispered his name and Rahn placed the matchbox absently in the pocket of his pants and went to him. Deodat was trying to open the sacristy door under the Grail plaque but it was also locked. Rahn went to the opposite door but he too had no luck.

'What now?' Deodat whispered harshly.

'We have to break into it.'

'How?'

Before Rahn could reply, they were interrupted by a noise.

'What in the devil is that?' Deodat whispered.

Rahn, who was facing the length of the nave towards the west, paused. The door was groaning. He brought out his old Swiss Army knife, knowing it would be no use at all against a man holding a gun. Without another thought he gestured for them to move behind the altar.

The footsteps were slow, light and deliberate.

A small man, Rahn thought, was headed in their direction. Whoever it was had already come past the enclosures. Rahn's breathing grew rapid. His heart was pounding. Had they been followed? Perhaps it was the same person who had killed the sacristan, perhaps one of Serinus's men, or the inspector, or worst still the Gestapo . . . Who knew how many people were after him by now? Another noise pierced the gloom – the sound of metal against metal and a click that reverberated a little in the church.

Rahn understood. Whoever it was had opened the tabernacle, not having yet reckoned their presence. He had to act now. The element of surprise would give him an advantage. He figured he would come from behind the altar, allowing the moment to dictate his actions and whatever came after that, he did not dare contemplate. He looked at Deodat and pointed in the direction of the altar, suggesting that they move to attack.

He sprang vigorously from his position in the darkness into the space in front of the altar, his every muscle and sinew straining into action. What came next was a blur of images and sounds: he saw a figure in black, he heard a gasp and then something heavy came down and turned night into day in a spray of stars. The ground then opened up beneath him and he felt himself falling . . .

. . . he was falling into a fissure in the volcano of Bugarach, redolent of sulphur and crowded with sibyls.

ISLAND OF THE DEAD

17

PROSPERO

'Who?' replied Don Quixote.
'Who can it be but some malignant enchanter . . .'
Miguel de Cervantes, Don Quixote

Venice, 2012

There was a pause. I was suddenly no longer in the church of Bugarach with Rahn; I was in the library on the Island of the Dead with the Writer of Letters, who seemed to me like a modern version of Shakespeare's Prospero.

'So, what do you think of it?' he said, sitting forwards, looking at me probingly.

'It has the makings of a decent mystery, so far. I like the way you've interpolated the inscription into your plot.'

'My plot?'

'Yes.'

He smiled. 'This is *your* story, remember?'

'Right.' I nodded, returning his smile. 'So, does the church in Bugarach exist?'

'Of course! All of those things that Rahn saw are there. You could see them today if you wanted to; not much changes in little villages like that.'

'All those clues?'

'Indeed. The interesting thing about clues is that you can find them everywhere – but are they an illusion? For instance, one can add two and two to make four, but four of what? You see, you have to know what you are adding before it can make practical sense. Sometimes knowing the number is not enough.'

He stood, then. 'Lunch?'

I followed him out to the garden to a table set for two. Prosciutto crudo, pane di casa and bresaola, with a bottle of recoaro.

'Before,' I ventured as we sat down, 'you said you knew Otto Rahn.'

'Did I?' He seemed surprised.

'Yes, you said that you knew him, but you didn't reveal how you knew him.'

'There are many ways of knowing an individual.' The Writer of Letters placed a linen napkin over his lap. 'I am an objective observer . . . and he has interested me for a long time. Just as you have.'

'You keep speaking of him as though he were still alive.'

'Do I? How remiss of me. They say he took his own life.'

'And did he?'

'We won't know that until we finish the story. If I were your character, would you have me disclose something crucial to the plot so soon in the narrative?'

'No, I suppose not.'

'Then again, you could always edit it out, if it turned out not to be true.'

'Is it true or not?'

'Perhaps the answer to the riddle you came here to solve, the inscription about death, is related to the mystery of Rahn's life?' he said, as enigmatic as ever.

'How so?'

'To write about the Grail is to write about eternal life. To know the meaning of life, one has to understand death and to understand death, one has to know the meaning of evil. You see they are interdependent. The idea of a Grail chalice is really quite old. Priests used to drink from a chalice long before Christ. That was how He *revealed* Himself to His priests in the old mysteries. When He came to Earth, He was a revelation of the mysteries and drank from the cup, that is, He died so that He could rescue *life* from *death* . . . *good* from *evil* – that is the secret of the blood in the chalice – the secret of the Holy Grail.

'But I'm not writing about the Grail . . . I want to write a book about the *Apocalypse of Saint John.*'

'Oh, I know what you're writing about . . . but what is the Apocalypse if not a *revelation* of the Grail – and what is the Grail if not a vessel of *revelation?* You see, the two always go together. In fact, Rahn's last book was about this very mystery – but I'm not talking about Rahn's little travel diary that Himmler had printed and bound in calfskin; the one he made compulsory reading for the SS. That book, *Lucifer's Court,* was just something Rahn patched together in a hurry. No, Rahn's last book has not been published yet.'

'What are you suggesting?'

'I don't know.' His eyes were full of jocularity and it annoyed me. 'You're the one writing the story. I'm just one of your characters. What would you have me suggest?'

I sat back in the pale sun. 'A character only comes to life when he starts to disobey the writer.'

'Well countered! In that case I shall divulge that what Rahn found in the south of France was not what anyone had expected. Perhaps it is not even what you expect.'

'So where do we go to from here?'

'Imagine we are once again in that universe consisting of endless interlocking galleries. Let us turn away from Rahn, who is lying in a stupor in that church at Bugarach, to another aspect of the past. We need only find the gallery marked 1238.'

'That's exactly seven hundred years before Rahn's time.'

'Yes. Rahn was living seven hundred years after a very significant happening, you might say, an event which cast both its light
and its shadow into the future, seven hundred years forward in
time.'

'But as you stated earlier: in a room full of galleries, time is
one with space. So what does time matter anyhow?' I tried to trip
him up.

'It is true that time is significant only in the world of the living,
in the world in which history happens. But insofar as these things
occurred in the world of *time*, their *timing* is of great importance.
Do you remember that young boy, Matteu, who was saved by the
Templar knight in Béziers? Well, by now he is a Templar troubadour. He has been to the East crusading against the infidel; he
has sat with Sufi poets in the courts of Frederick II; and he has
cheated death countless times. Now his task is to run messages
from the Temple to the Cathars during the war of religion and
sometimes to escort important Cathars to safety.'

'So they were affiliated, the Cathars and Templars?'

'Of course, the Templars called the Cathars their cousins and
they did what they could, in a "quiet way", to help them during
those years of Catholic persecution. If you read Rahn's books,
you will see how he is trying to remember something of that
time, in fact, he's trying to keep his promise to the Countess P.'

'Which was?' I asked.

'To be a guardian . . .'

18

ISOBEL

'To that I may reply,' said Don Quixote,
'that Dulcinea is the daughter of her own works . . .'
Miguel de Cervantes, Don Quixote

Montsegur, 1238

The red valley gouged out by giants was already in shadow when Isobel and her mistresses, Rosamunda and Blanche, came to the base of Montsegur. Ahead of them the Templar troubadour, Matteu, led the way – a man already past his prime and yet eternally youthful. She had always felt safe with him and she did so now despite the dangers of this journey. In truth, they had been walking for days in fear of being caught, and despite their exhaustion they would have to climb that steep narrow path to the château before dark.

Yes, Isobel was tired, so tired she could barely feel her feet, and to add to everything else the dark clouds above were scudding across the coppering sky and threatening a downpour. She felt she must soon collapse from the weight of the belongings she carried added to that of the child in her belly. For they had been forced to leave the animals below in the township, since the way to the château could only be scaled on foot and a perilous way it was, with its narrow path and smooth stones. She dared not look down, forcing her eyes to stare ahead to the straight backs of her mistresses who led the way, pausing now and then to lend her a hand.

She had never seen the mistresses tired, nor had she ever seen them afraid. They had made this pilgrimage each year for as long as she could remember and she recalled them walking just as they were doing now, alongside one another, both with their black dresses flapping, each moving one leg after the other in a rhythm that matched the rhythm of their prayers.

Soon, she told herself, they would reach those walls – and safety – but now, through the trees, she could hear the herdsmen gathering the goats before the storm broke. In the distance, bells clanged their discordant resonance and the sky grew closer. Such sounds made her want to hide behind a clump of hazel bushes fearing danger, for she was a child of war.

She couldn't remember a time without it, nor the fear of the Dominicans or their familiars. She knew the stories back to front. A papal legate had excommunicated the Count of Toulouse for protecting the Cathars and he was, in turn, murdered by one of the count's officers, causing the pope to call for a Crusade against the heretics. She would not be here if her mother, just a bundle at the time, had not been spirited away from Béziers by the two sisters on the eve of the Feast of Magdalene. They had taken the small child and the treasure that had once belonged to Mary Magdalene herself – the Cathar treasure, which must be handed down from woman to woman. From that time on, the sacred treasure in its pouch had been safely hidden beneath the folds of Rosamunda's dress, and it was there now.

Isobel looked up to see the clouds gathering in counsel and preparing to drizzle their concerns over the valley floor. A low rumble made the Earth tremble and she pulled the shawl over her shoulders and recalled the stories. After the fall of Béziers in 1209 and the terrible massacre of all its citizens, the world turned over into a hell pit. Siege after siege, battle after battle. Those were terrible years. War in the Corbieres, war in the Minverois and in the Razés, war in Foix and in Toulouse. The land was laid to waste, and villages and towns were destroyed. Who would want to tend crops that would surely be trampled to dust? Who would want to repair a stable door or to fix a leaking roof when at any moment everything might be put to the torch? Insecurity and chaos ruled the land, and the nobles, despoiled of their inheritance, went into hiding, striking out at the Crusaders from their high strongholds. In the meantime a vast network of secret agents, troubadours like Matteu, had brought news of planned attacks, sieges and skirmishes. Her mother had been seventeen and pregnant with Isobel when the young Count Raymond, having returned from exile with an army, took over the city of Toulouse against the foreign enemy. Alongside the other women her mother dug walls, hauled rubble through the streets and worked the siege engines. For three weeks they waited for Simon de Montfort, the leader of the Crusade, to come to rescue his wife from the Château de Nabornnais. Isobel's mother was among the women recruited to fire the heavy blocks of masonry from a trebuchet and they had been firing at random into a confused mass of soldiers when Simon de Montfort was struck on the head and killed. That same hour her mother collapsed and some time later died giving birth to Isobel.

Isobel could see the walls of the château of Montsegur rising up out of the trees and she paused to catch her breath. She wondered if the good Cathar bishop would be waiting for her with his smiling eyes at the summit.

After her mother died the twin sisters Rosamunda and Blanche took over her rearing and she had travelled with them whenever they visited the good Bishop Guilhabert de Castres, usually nearing Easter and the Festival of Bema. They said the bishop had lived for twelve years as a hermit in a cave to make penance for the sins of the world. Some said he was given to drink from the cup called the Holy Grail in that cave; the cup from which the

Lord Himself had drunk at the Last Supper. There were many tales about him, but Isobel knew him as a teacher. He came to Montsegur now and again to teach and to counsel and to prepare for a momentous occasion he had seen in his visions, which he referred to as an Apocalypse – the end of the world.

The wind swirled the brambles and bracken now and shook their wiry arms. Ignoring the temper of nature Isobel followed her mistresses up the steep-edged path holding on to the trunks of the boxwood trees that grew all around. Isobel knew that this journey to Montsegur had something to do with the Apocalypse the good bishop was expecting. After all, they had come here to prepare for it and to safeguard the treasure that Rosamunda had carried under her skirt all these years. Yes, the world was darkening and war was once again upon them. That is why the bishop had asked the noble Raymond de Parella to donate Montsegur to the cause, so that it could be made ready for the dark time, when the dragon of the church would come to steal the Holy Grail. She also sensed excitement in those around her for the child she was carrying, the child of the gallant young noble she had married when she was seventeen. She had known her husband only two months before he died at the hands of the inquisitors, and now she would soon have his child. She was afraid.

Her thinking had taken her to the top of the mountain, tearful and breathless. At the gate built into the great wall she turned around to see the mountains, mist laden and quiet, before her. She wondered if this would be the last time she would see them and was afraid for what would become of her child in a world that was soon to end. The painful thought made a tremble pass through her body and a strange and unwelcome wetness moved downwards over her legs. 'My child?' she said, making the sisters turn around to look at her. A terrible cramping pain now seized her and the thoughts for her child and the world came together with the thoughts of God and snapped shut on her mind like two opposing blades making a final cut. When she looked down she saw blood on the earth at her feet and she gave a sob of fear.

The sisters were at her side, each taking her by an arm and carrying her to Bishop Guilhabert, who was then instructing the children. When the bishop saw her he knew what to do. He took Isobel to the keep and ordered the women to get some hot water. And so it was that upon a bed of straw, Isobel strained for all her life's worth to give birth to the child. She knew she must be screaming and yet she did not hear anything except her child's heart beating in her ears. The world was a confusion of sounds and light. The only face she recognised was Bishop Guilhabert's when he came to her and said, 'It is a boy, my dear, a beautiful boy. Listen, child, you have done a good thing. He is our master born again . . . he will live!'

She felt herself smile, but all her strength had gone out from her, leaving her feeling like a naked limb in winter, trembling with the slightest breeze; she was the breeze that shook it and the sun that made it grow and the water that fed it. A voice whispered in her ear that her name Isobel meant 'Beautiful Isis'. Somehow she knew what this meant.

For a moment the troubadour Matteu's face stared down into hers. She heard the voice calling in the distance . . . the blackness came.

19

A KEY, A LIST, AND A SIGN

'However that may be, the young lady was very decidedly carried away.'
Sir Arthur Conan Doyle, 'A Case of Identity'

Bugarach, 1938

When Rahn came to his senses he found a face staring down into his. He remembered words . . . something to do with a book, an author and a master . . . but nothing more.

He sensed he was being spoken to but this was just a distant murmur. He felt a gentle slapping on his cheek. His shoulder ached and his head felt like a bowl of jelly.

He heard Deodat say, 'Wake up, Rahn!' and then someone was trying to lift him to a sitting position. He could see a face. He put two and two together and made five – five beautiful faces.

What is Louise Brooks doing here? Am I on a film set?

'You were coming at me like a maniac!' Louise Brooks kindly informed him.

He thought he sensed a note of humour in her voice.

What an actress!

The five faces became one and he held his skull to prevent them from separating again.

'What happened?' he said to her.

'I'm afraid I had to hit you,' she answered.

He muttered, 'Of course. What did you use, a train?'

'A candlestick, actually.' The grin was somewhat proud.

This isn't Louise Brooks; it's the abbé's niece!

'But I didn't hit you as hard as I *could* have.'

He gave a perfunctory nod of his head, which made his temples creak. 'I'm very glad of that, I'm sure.' He sat up and was helped to his feet by Deodat while the world spun, a jumble of light and mirrors. They sat him down on a pew and he nursed his wounds, feeling now altogether like the highest grade of fool.

'What are you doing here anyway?' he said to her, taking her in, her helmet haircut and the deep brown eyes that showed no sympathy. She was dressed like a man, in pants, flat shoes and a black beret to match.

'I came to open the tabernacle,' she said.

It took a moment for Rahn to reason this through. How had she figured it out?

'When they took my uncle away,' she continued, 'I had the pond drained.'

'What pond?'

'The pond in the garden – I had it drained. Actually, we only had to drain it partially because we found it.'

'Found what?' He delicately touched the throbbing lump on his head.

'I had a hunch about my uncle's obsession with those fish. I wondered if it wasn't the fish he was obsessed with at all, but something else in that pond. It did seem to me as if he might have fallen in looking for something. I found this.' She showed them a key in the shape of a cross. 'I knew that it belonged to the tabernacle, so I came here to see what might be inside it.'

Rahn looked at her expressionless face. She was smart and he didn't know exactly why he was annoyed by it, but he was. Apart from the fact that she had occasioned the dull thumping at his temples, she had a way of making him feel like a pimply-faced schoolboy, standing before a headmistress. 'So the key was at the bottom of the pond all this time?' He cleared his throat. 'How did you find it? It must have been covered in scum and algae.'

'Not at the bottom, it was in a box placed on an inner ledge set into the stonework. It looks like the sacristan never had it on his ring of keys. Monsieur Roche told me how you figured it out, and I am impressed! But what I don't understand is why my uncle didn't just write "tabernacle" on that piece of paper if he wanted you to look there.'

She appeared so vulnerable, so lovely – and yet there was that lump on his head. He winced. No, the girl was vicious, and at the same time, terribly beautiful – a vicious beauty, a beautiful terror. His mind was spinning and he contrived to make it stop.

'So, did you find anything in the tabernacle?' he said, after a moment.

'That is the interesting part,' Deodat replied, sounding vexed. 'There appears to be nothing in it out of the ordinary.'

'Impossible!' Rahn cried, irritated in the extreme. 'Let me see!' He got up and made his way to the altar, passing the candlestick that Eva had so discourteously used as a weapon to assault him. Luckily, it wasn't made of solid brass and the brunt of the blow had been taken by his shoulder and arm, which were both aching and no doubt bruised.

'There's a monstrance and a chalice,' Deodat said behind him, 'a little box for the wafers, a spoon and a little bottle of conse-crated wine . . . some oil, but nothing else, I'm afraid.'

Rahn paused a moment to let his head settle. It felt like one of those snow globes with an Eiffel Tower inside it. Someone had shaken the globe, causing the tower to be obscured by snow, and moreover there was a peculiar buzzing sound – as if a bee had found its way into it and was having a hard time finding a way out. He took a candle from the altar and peered inside the tab-ernacle, trying to concentrate, but his intermittent double vision

was disconcerting. He brought the chalice out towards the candle.
It was nothing special, made of bronze, as was the monstrance.
It was a poor church, after all. He removed the wine bottle and
the spoon and a bottle of oil as well as the box of consecrated
wafers, which looked to be made from wood. He then inspected
the inside of the tabernacle and found something strange: there
was a symbol scratched and burnt onto the base of it. He could
just make it out. It looked like a double pentagram.

'What's this, Deodat, do you know?'

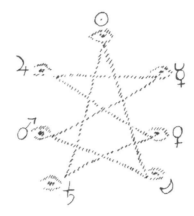

Deodat put on his reading glasses and came over to take a
look and said, 'What in the devil? It's the sign of the lamb – the
intelligence of the sun!'

'What do you mean?'

'This seven-pointed star is found in the Book of the Seven
Seals in Saint John's Apocalypse. At each point there is an eye and
a sign which denotes a planetary intelligence: Saturn, Sun, Moon,
Mars, Mercury, Jupiter, Venus; all together they stand for the Cos-
mic Christ. I've seen it before in the work of Rudolf Steiner; it
can be used as a talisman to ward off evil, like the evil eye. The
Templars also used it on their secret seal.'

Eva came to take a look.

'Why would the abbé feel a need to scratch that symbol into

a place that is holy anyway?' Rahn said, unconsciously taking a swipe at the bee which now seemed to be somewhere beyond his line of vision. He searched the tabernacle, checking for a false compartment, and felt something at the top of it: it was a piece of paper stuck with tape. He worked at it carefully until it came away without tearing. It was a list of names and places.

He showed the others. 'Do either of you recognise any of these?'

> *Jean-Louis Verger – Paris*
> *Antoine Bigou – Rennes-le-Château*
>
> ~
>
> *A J Grassaud – Saint-Paul-de-Fenouillet*
> *A C Saunière – Rennes-le-Château*
> *A K Boudet – Rennes-les-Bains A*
> *A Gélis – Coustassa*
> *A L Rivière – Espéraza*

'Wait a minute! That's the abbé I told you about,' Eva said, 'the one who visited my uncle a short while back, the Abbé Grassaud, from Saint-Paul-de-Fenouillet.'

'Do you think these might be the priests he was investigating?' Rahn asked Deodat.

Eva raised her beautiful brows and turned to Deodat. 'What is he talking about?'

'Your uncle was investigating a number of priests in this area for the Vatican,' Deodat informed her. 'I don't know exactly why, he talked in generalities about the church and the laws of the state. He seemed anxious to keep things quiet, so I complied. When he asked for me this week I thought he wanted to raise the matter again. Anyway, whatever it is, this list must have been important for him to hide it like that.'

'I don't understand,' the girl said.

'If you're right and your uncle died trying to get the key to this tabernacle, it must have mattered a great deal to him,' Rahn said, pointing out the obvious. It had the desired effect: Eva frowned and said nothing more.

Rahn looked about him. 'We had better leave. It won't be long before daybreak and it would be better if we weren't found here like this.'

'You're right, dear Rahn, we would have to explain our actions and I think for the time being we should keep what we've found to ourselves – no sense in creating a scandal precipitously.'

Once outside, Rahn felt a great relief wash over him. The gibbous moon had set and the world was a playground of fog and damp vapours and shadows but there were too many thoughts running through his mind for him to notice it.

'Go home, my dear, and rest,' Deodat said, taking Eva to her car. 'You will have a lot to do in the coming days, organising your uncle's funeral . . .'

She got into the car as if she didn't have a care in the world and said, through the open window, 'There's really not much to do. He arranged everything with his lawyers a long time ago; his body is to be interred somewhere secret, he didn't want anyone to know where, not even me, and there is to be no funeral, nothing at all.'

Rahn thought this exceedingly strange but said nothing. He stood beside Deodat and said his goodbyes, watching the taillights of Eva's car die away on the ribbon of road with a strange wistfulness in his heart. *A vicious, terrible beauty!*

He wiped his hands of dust and of the girl too. He had neither the time nor the inclination for girls, for as Sherlock Holmes would say, they were inscrutable – their most trivial actions could mean volumes and their extraordinary conduct could depend on a hairpin.

It was still dark and very cold when they climbed into the Tourster for the long drive back. Like the miners whose lives depend on it, years of potholing in the Lombrives had developed in Rahn an ability to sense danger and he could smell it now – there was certainly something fishy in this entire business.

20

MUCH ADO ABOUT NOTHING?

'Between ingenuity and the analytic ability there exists a difference far greater, indeed, than that between the fancy and the imagination.'
Edgar Allan Poe, 'The Murders in the Rue Morgue'

The sun was tinting the sky in watered hues by the time they finally arrived back at Deodat's house at Arques. Madame Sabine was not home. On Thursdays she left early for the markets at Espéraza but she had left them breakfast, a freshly baked brioche and a pot of jam that tasted like heaven. They ate in the kitchen and at the same time tried to reason through their findings.

'It's strange,' Deodat said. 'I wonder what he was investigating and why he went to such lengths to conceal the list?'

'It must have been controversial, perhaps even dangerous; after all, someone wanted it enough to kill the sacristan.'

'But, my dear Rahn, we don't know that for certain! It is a capital mistake to theorise without all the details because one begins to twist the facts to suit theories, instead of twisting theories to suit facts.'

'You can quote Sherlock Holmes all you want, but if he were here, I'm certain he would connect the sacristan's death to that list of priests the abbé was investigating.'

'What makes you so certain of that?'

'Well, my theory is this: I think someone wanted that list, someone the abbé had confided in – like he confided in you. That person knew the list was hidden somewhere in the church and when the abbé fell ill he saw his chance. He accosted the only person who might know, the one who had the keys to the church and knew it intimately – the sacristan.'

'And what if he didn't know anything?'

'In his desperation he may have handed the keys to his assailant, hoping it would suffice. But the die was cast, his tormentor had to kill him or risk being exposed.'

'Yes, but why not go directly to the abbé and make him divulge the location of the list? He was vulnerable, after all.'

'I don't know, but don't forget the abbé couldn't even string a sentence together and had trouble even writing down one word, not to mention the fact that there's always someone with him because of his condition. Perhaps whoever did it, didn't want to threaten a priest. I haven't figured it all out yet.'

Deodat looked at Rahn and sighed. 'As I said, you're simply twisting a few meagre facts to suit your theory.'

'You might be right. But all that aside, you have to admit, carving the sign of the lamb into a tabernacle is an unusual thing for a priest to do.'

'Yes, I agree with you on that score. Especially considering that it's an esoteric symbol, something most priests would call heretical, even witchcraft.'

'And is it?'

'In a way, yes, but it is white magic – a protection from evil.'

'Well, it appears that the abbé was no ordinary priest.'

'No, perhaps not, you might be right,' Deodat said. 'My guess is, he was trying to protect the contents of the tabernacle from something.'

Rahn drank down the last of his coffee. He was pensive but it hurt his head to think. He felt for the lump and winced – it was hot and angry. 'Perhaps the sign of the lamb means the list is somehow connected to the grimoire I'm looking for.' He looked at Deodat. 'I know it's too much of a coincidence, but maybe it isn't a coincidence at all, but a design. It might be a bit jumbled but there is some sense in it. Hear me out.

'I was sent to France to meet Pierre Plantard about a grimoire. I then find out that a man called Monti had come here to see a priest about a grimoire. After that I meet a friend of yours who is a priest, and his last word before he dies is connected to grimoires. The inspector, who just happens to turn up to the scene of the abbé's death, is searching for Le Cagoule, a group connected to Alpha Galates and Pierre Plantard – through whom I found out about the grimoire in the first place. It's a snake biting its tail. So, if you ask me, there are two common denominators in these strange and seemingly disparate events – a priest and a grimoire.'

Deodat sat back to think on it. 'No. Actually, there is another common denominator: *you*, Rahn.'

'Me?'

'Yes, of course. In all your reasoning you've missed the most important link. You are the lead character, you are in every scene!'

Rahn was struck by the truth in this and though he had no idea what it meant, it gave him pause.

'Don't worry, Rahn, sometimes there's a simple explanation. Perhaps we are adding two and two together to make twenty-two?'

'But if we are making too much of it and this has nothing at all to do with grimoires, why did Cros write sator? Why not just write tabernacle, as Eva pointed out? After all, sator is not an everyday word. No, I think he wanted you to know where the list was *kept,* but not just that, he also wanted you to know what the list was *for,* that it had something to do with grimoires. That's why he gave you that word. I surmise, therefore, that the list has something to do with a grimoire – *my* grimoire!'

'I think we should pay a visit to the Abbé Grassaud, from Saint-Paul-de-Fenouillet. After all, he is not only on our list, but he also saw Abbé Cros recently.'

'Where is that town?'

'South of here, a couple of hours away . . . Can I see that list again?' Deodat said, reaching for it. 'Cros may have told Grassaud about the list and what it means. At this stage he is our best lead.'

He took a pad and a pencil and set about copying the list. 'It doesn't hurt to have more than one copy. Put this copy in your pocket, Rahn, and come with me.'

He followed Deodat to his library where he slipped the other list into the pages of Éliphas Levi's book. 'We will leave our friend here to guard the original.' He replaced the book under E.

'No one will think to look for it there, except for Madame Sabine, perhaps.'

Rahn sighed. 'You know, I feel rather strange, like a puppet or a character in someone's crazy plot.'

'Your head has taken a good knock, dear Rahn, and I'm not as young as I look. So I suggest before anything else, we should get some sleep. After that, we'll go to see Abbé Grassaud. What do you say?'

And so it was decided. Rahn went to his room and closed the curtains to block out the early sun. He lay down feeling drained. The bee was quiet now, but his head was thumping in time to his thoughts on secret brotherhoods, magic squares, the names on that list, the symbol of the lamb . . . until he fell into an uneasy sleep.

He dreamt he was in a tomb. It was impenetrably dark, the cold went right to the bones and he was running out of oxygen.

21

GONE

*'– and yet it was dark – all dark – the intense and utter
raylessness of the night that endureth for evermore.'*
Edgar Allan Poe, 'The Premature Burial'

Rahn woke with a gasp but when he tried to sit up he
hit his head on a solid surface. He almost sank into a
double blackness but he bit his lip and concentrated
on coming out of it. There was a cramp in his right
calf but he couldn't extend his legs. He was on his back in a foetal
position. He opened his eyes. Darkness.

He was in an undersized coffin or a tomb!

He panicked.

What has happened?

He tried to calm his nerves and piece together those events
prior to this nightmare but they were trapped behind a mist at
the back of his head. Where was he? Was this a dream? Would
he wake up at any moment? He remembered the church, the
altar, the tabernacle . . . the blackness. Was he still in the church?
Something occurred to him and he felt in his pocket. The box
of matches from behind the altar was still there. That much of
it at least was real. He took the matches out and struck one in
front of his face. He was in a strangely shaped box made from

some sort of metal. He was lying on a number of cold, hard objects that were digging into his back. He realised he could smell gasoline and blew the match out. He listened for sounds. The darkness filled him with panic but the smell of gasoline made him nervous about lighting another match. He then remembered his pocket watch. It took him a moment to retrieve it but he had to chance lighting another match to see it.

Nine o'clock.

But was it morning or night, today or tomorrow? He didn't know.

He blew out the match again.

It was hot.

He needed air.

He loosened his collar and tried not to let the panic take hold. He pushed up on the lid and it moved slightly allowing a blinding light to enter the box for a moment. He was filled with hope. The lid seemed to be caught on something, a latch perhaps? Maybe he could use those metal shapes that were digging into his back to break the latch, or at least to make enough noise to bring notice to himself — wherever he was. As he contrived to reach behind his back, however, a scream tore into his dark captivity. Startled, he involuntarily jerked his knees against the lid and it flew open.

His eyes were assaulted by the light then but he was breathing fresh air. He sat up carefully and waited for his head to stop taking turns at thumping and spinning and for his eyes to adjust to the glare. He realised where he was. He was sitting in the trunk of the Tourster. The car was in the barn and the door was slightly ajar allowing the sun to slant into his eyes. He took out one leg after the other and flung them over the edge of the trunk where they touched something soft. He looked down and saw a man sprawled out on the ground. The shock of it nearly made him pass out again and he sat still for a time until he was ready to look again. Yes, a man. He got out of the trunk and forced himself to roll the body over. It was lying in a pool of blood mixed with gasoline. An empty fuel can lay nearby. Rahn shivered. It looked like this man had been about to set the car on fire with him in it when someone cut his throat from ear to ear, nearly severing his head. The killer had pulled the man's tongue through the gash in his throat. Rahn put a hand to his own mouth and fought down a rising revulsion while he searched the man's pockets. He found an old train ticket and nothing more, no wallet, nothing to identify him.

Who goes about with nothing in their pockets?

He inspected the hands looking for an SS ring, or any evidence that he belonged to the Gestapo, but all he found was a small tattoo on the right wrist – an upside down anchor with a snake coiling around it in the shape of an S. He stood up straight, looking about. He didn't know what any of it meant. The whole place smelt of congealed blood combined with urine and gasoline, and the smell caused a sudden rush and he barely made it outside before emptying the contents of his stomach onto the grass. He sat in the garden then, feeling dismal and confused, trying to get his bearings. He realised he was shaking from head to toe and got up to steady himself. He remembered now lying on the bed upstairs. He and Deodat had resolved to do something.

What was it?

Deodat! Where was Deodat?

He made his way back to the house, treading carefully, fearful that the murderer might be lurking somewhere inside. He took a furtive peek through the front door and saw that the place was a shambles: books, papers and cushions had been strewn over the Persian rugs; furniture lay overturned; and every drawer had been emptied of its contents by the look of it. Nothing was untouched. Rahn's heart pounded, his head pounded, his ears pounded and his mouth was as dry as kindling and the bee was back, trying to find a way out of his head. A strange urge came over him then – he wanted to lie down. So what if there was a dead man in the barn, a murderer lying in wait in a ransacked house and he didn't know where Deodat was? This was a dream and nothing more! Surely to sleep in a dream was to wake up in real life! He almost had himself believing it when he heard a noise.

At this point he remembered the scream – how could he have forgotten it? It sobered him, lifting the fog long enough for him to realise that someone was in the house. Perhaps Madame Sabine had come home? He edged his way to the kitchen. It was topsy-turvy but there seemed to be no one in it. He entered cautiously, looking this way and that. Something caught his leg then and tripped him, causing him to fall flat on his face.

He heard something drop and a gasp.

'Monsieur Rahn!'

The world spun around itself, making the bee in his head angry. He felt someone turning him onto his back. 'What are you . . . ?' he began but forgot what he was going to say. 'I'm so relieved to see you, I thought you were—' It was Eva and she was helping him to sit up.

'You thought I was . . . ?' He looked at her, trying to focus. Her eyes expressed their concern in browns and golds.

'Dead,' she said, 'or gone.'

'Gone where?'

She helped him to a chair then found a glass that wasn't broken and brought him water. He sipped at it but it made him nauseous. He paused a moment; that bee was in his ear now and the Eiffel Tower was still snowed under. He looked at the girl; she was in the same clothes from the night before. Her face was pale. She was obviously in shock for the second time in as many days and he knew he had to come to grips with himself – no good both of them being hors de combat. This thought seemed suddenly ludicrous and he nearly let go a nervous laugh – something completely inappropriate, he realised, given that there was a man in the barn wearing his tongue for a necktie.

'My uncle's house is like this too,' she said, looking around.

'When I got there this morning the whole thing had been turned inside out. I'm glad that I sent Giselle to stay with her family yesterday. I didn't know what to do, so—' she looked at him with those rounded eyes, '—I just drove around. At first I thought I might go to the gendarmerie at Carcassonne but last night the magistrate said to keep this between us for the time being. I remembered I had the magistrate's phone number and address in my handbag so I tried to call but there was no answer. I resolved to come here. When I arrived I thought you were taken too.'

'Taken where?'

'I don't know. I looked through the house before I looked in the barn. He's not here. I found this – a note – in the kitchen.'

Rahn tried to read it but couldn't bring his eyes together. Eva read it for him: *They are coming. Find it – don't trust anyone.*

'They're coming!' he said to Eva. 'Who are *they*? Where have *they* taken him?'

'I have no idea.'

Rahn paused to let this sink in. 'I was passed out.' He probed his head appreciatively. 'I must have slept through the whole thing!'

'You were concussed.'

'You don't say?'

'No need to be sarcastic,' she said.

He sensed an inappropriate hint of humour in her tone. He looked at the double image of her face and choosing one, he said to it, 'I've been hit on the head with a candlestick and locked in the trunk of a car in which I was very nearly cremated. Then, having escaped what was to be my funeral pyre, I happen upon the body of a man whose head is hanging by a thread, and now I find out that my good friend is missing, that his house is ransacked and that his life may be in peril . . . I beg your pardon if I sound a little indisposé.'

'You were in the trunk of the Tourster?' she said, ignoring his various misfortunes and concentrating on what interested her.

'Yes, and rather an undignified end it would have been too if someone hadn't done-in the man who was about to cremate me!' he said with passion, seeing an image of it before his eyes.

'I saw the dead man,' she said.

'And you screamed, I know.'

'The dead man was going to kill you?'

'I don't know but there was a can of gasoline on the floor not far from the body. Lucky for me someone came along and stopped him with a knife to the throat. I dare say I might have ended up the same way, had I not been in the trunk.'

Rahn felt for his jacket and realised he wasn't wearing it. He had taken it off before lying down. He got up and the world was a plaything of his vertigo. He had to wait for it to stop before he could pick his slow way through the mess and up the stairs with Eva following him.

The bed had been overturned and Eva helped him to move it. Underneath, he found his jacket but the pockets were empty. Monti's notebook was gone and so was the list. He looked about and found his wallet. It was untouched and his papers were still in it, together with something else, the card the Russian Grigol Robakidze had given him at the Schloss on Lake Malchow. There had been something about *Black Swans* and if he was ever in any trouble he was to call the number on that card. But he remembered Deodat's note: *Don't trust anyone!*

He found his lucky fedora — it was badly out of shape but he put it on his head, glad to have it back. He took a change of clothes, stuffed them into a small leather bag and went to Deodat's room. It had been similarly treated. He told Eva they should go but through the miasma in his head he remembered something and took himself to the library. Some of the books had been tossed out of their comfortable beds, quite a few looked to be missing, but not Éliphas Lévi's book. He found the original list, still tucked away inside it.

He put the list in his pocket and went looking for the pendulum clock. There it was, the ugly thing. For some reason he was glad to see it.

'So, are you going to tell me what this is all about?' Eva asked.

'It's rather complicated and you'll have to hear it along the way, I'm afraid.'

'Along the way to where?' she said.

He put the clock under his arm and his mind fell into a palsy. What was he to do? Eva was watching him warily. He must look and sound quite mad. He drew himself together and said, 'My dear Mademoiselle Cros, might I ask you to drive me to Saint-Paul-de-Fenouillet, if you will be so kind? I'm really not up to it as you can see.'

'Of course, are we going to see Abbé Grassaud?'

'Yes, I believe he may know quite a lot about this entire loathsome affair.'

Once they were well on the way, he told Eva what she didn't know. She listened to all of it heavily, driving a long time in silence; thinking things through, he supposed.

'So, you are a Nazi, *Monsieur* Rahn!'

The look in her eye made him sigh. He hated unpleasantness, but he was sick of being judged by all and sundry. 'I'm an author and a historian but I'm *not* a Nazi!' he snapped. 'I admit I was seduced by the possibility of having the means to continue my work, but that's all. I despise everything they stand for!'

'You said you came here to look for something?'

'It's a long story, but in short the SS want me to find a grimoire, a book of black magic written by Pope Honorius called *Le Serpent Rouge*. I saw a man in Paris who knew something about it and he gave me a notebook that belonged to another man, a man who visited a priest here in Languedoc some months ago. The notebook contained information that has led me to surmise that he wasn't only looking for the grimoire, but also for a key missing from it. It's all rather sketchy and complex.'

'A key? You mean like the key to the tabernacle?' 'No, in grimoires a key is something that unlocks a secret – that enables one to conjure a spirit. It can be a *verbum dimissum*, that is, a magic word, or it can be a sign.'

'What sort of pope writes a grimoire of black magic?'

Rahn nodded. 'A diabolical one! Can you see now why I don't like churches?' He put a hand over one eye and then over the other to see if his vision had improved. 'You don't happen to know the symptoms of a brain haemorrhage, do you?'

'What?'

'A brain haemorrhage, when it bleeds in the brain – the symptoms, do you know them?'

She shrugged. 'Headache, dizziness . . .' She didn't seem particularly interested.

'I know there's something about the eyes – the pupils. They either contract or dilate . . .'

She wasn't listening. 'I still don't understand how this has anything to do with my uncle.'

'I think that your uncle is the priest this man Monti came to see and I also think that the list of priests has something to do with the missing key. On his return to Paris, Monti—'

'The man with the notebook?'

'Yes. Monti grew afraid and for good reason, since he was soon murdered. I think that Inspecteur Beliere turned up so promptly, miles from his jurisdiction, because he was watching your uncle.'

'How do you know that?'

'I saw a car parked on the road nearby the Maison de Cros when we left for Bugarach and it didn't follow us. I'll wager that was an unmarked police car.'

'You think my uncle was involved with this Monti fellow?

That's absurd!'

'But the list isn't all that connects your uncle to the grimoires. Don't forget the last word he wrote was sator. He gave that to Deodat as a clue to finding the list.'

'What does it mean?'

'It's part of a very old magic square used in certain grimoires.'

She raised both brows. 'Magic square?'

Rahn took a pencil from his bag and drew the square on the back of the paper with the list.

She glanced at it.

'The words are the same up and down, backwards and forwards.'

'I see, and that is why it has magical properties?'

'I don't know. I think your uncle knew that if he gave Deodat that one word, Deodat would be able to figure out not only where the list was kept but also that it was connected to the grimoires. Deodat's house and your uncle's house were both ransacked because someone was after this list and they wanted it enough to kill for it.'

'Do you have any idea who that dead man in the barn was?'

His conversation with Deodat about the various groups floated in his head. 'Who knows?' he said. 'Yesterday Deodat mentioned a number of secret brotherhoods, societies and groups that are at cross-purposes though they sometimes work together without knowing it. I noticed that the man in the barn had a tattoo. I've seen something like it before but I don't remember where exactly.'

'Do you have any idea what nationality or group he may have belonged to?'

'No . . . there were no papers in his pockets but the tattoo was unusual – a snake entwining an anchor. It could be a Hermetic symbol, possibly the symbol of some order, but who knows? I know I've been followed. Before I left Paris, a man who called himself Serinus contacted me. He also wanted me to find *Le Serpent Rouge* but he wanted me to keep it out of Himmler's hands.'

'Who is he working for?'

'I don't know, but *Inspecteur* Beliere saw a card from Serinus when it fell out of my wallet and he said something that I should have known . . . serinus is the Latin genus name for the canary.'

'The bird?'

'Yes, but I think it's a codename. There is a man called Canaris, he is the head of Military Intelligence at Gestapo headquarters. Everyone is afraid of him, including Himmler. He has files on everyone. He may be the one who contacted me.'

'So he's working for Hitler?'

'Somehow I don't think so.'

'But . . . why would he be working against his own government?'

'I don't know.' Rahn felt nauseated and opened the window to let the cold air wash over his face. He should have left Arques yesterday, now it was too late and things were well out of hand. If this was a script then he wanted to register his complaint: not only was he the most unlikely protagonist but also the plot was also too complex to be believable! He rubbed his face, feeling anxious and overwhelmed.

'You don't look so good, why don't you try to get some sleep?'

He sighed, realising that she was right. He put his head back and his hat over his face and tried to clear his mind of his worries, allowing the motion of the car to lull him to sleep.

ISLAND OF THE DEAD

22

THE LIVING DEAD

'Strange destiny, That deals with life and death as with a play!'
Miguel de Cervantes, Don Quixote

Venice, 2012

The light was descending now behind the cypresses.
'So, this is true about *Le Serpent Rouge*?' I asked.
'Of course,' the Writer of Letters answered. 'We should move inside, it is getting rather cold.'
At this point I saw a figure. It was the old monk I had met earlier, the one who warned me to leave, walking towards the cemetery in the twilight. He looked askance in our direction and continued on his way hurriedly.

'He seems frightened,' I said.

The Writer of Letters observed this with a nod and said, 'He's always afraid.'

'What does he fear?'

'I think he has been among the dead so long he fears the living. Have you heard of the living dead?'

'No.'

'They are souls caught between two worlds . . . vulnerable souls.'

'In what way are they vulnerable?'

'There is a mystery about those who in life either died violently or too early, or those who were connected to particular groups and had sworn oaths while alive. The living can use these souls because they retain certain abilities after death, one could say the future is open to them. This means they can inspire the living in scientific and artistic endeavours that are ahead of their time, but unfortunately these souls are also susceptible to being used by evil-minded men during séances or black magic rituals. Himmler was one of those who sought to use the dead – he understood the enormous power that could be harnessed through them. That is why he wanted *Le Serpent Rouge*.'

'The old monk told me no one stays in the monastery anymore. He said it is prohibited. Is this true?' I ventured.

'Of course. To his mind only the dead should have intercourse with the dead. He sees this intercourse between the living and the dead and he flees from it.'

'Why doesn't he leave here and go somewhere more . . . alive?'

'It is too late for him, I'm afraid,' the man replied. 'He has nowhere else to go. In a way, he has condemned himself to this place, it is his choice, his particular destiny.' He stood then. 'Tomorrow is All Saints' Day and the day after that is All Souls' Day, the Day of the Dead. Two particularly difficult days for him,' he explained. 'On the Day of the Dead, the dead are said to return to visit their families. All day the priests in Venice wear black, inside the churches the altars are similarly draped and the faithful pray for the souls of their departed, in the hope of shortening their time in Purgatory. Our monk usually goes into his cell until it is over. But we should be going inside, as I said, it is getting cold.'

He led the way back to the library and our seats before the fire.

'This brings us to the next gallery,' he said, when we were comfortable.

'The middle ages again?'

'Yes, we've seen the galleries of Matteu and Isobel, and now it is time to see the gallery of Bertrand Marty. This is now six years later, 1244, and Matteu is at Montsegur during the siege. He must safeguard the Cathar treasure and also a child – the child of Isobel. Shall we begin?'

23

THE TREASURE

'The treasure is lost,' said Miss Morstan, calmly.
Sir Arthur Conan Doyle, 'The Treasure of Agra'

Montsegur, 1244

The siege of Montsegur lasted eleven difficult months and during it, Matteu had come and gone by the secret route, either bringing them news of the outside world or escorting soldiery to help them fend off the Catholics. When their last defence, the eastern Barbican, was taken, it was decided by the lords of Montsegur to surrender; the Catholics gave them fifteen days to make their preparations to leave the mountain. Some would choose life in prison and some would choose death on the pyre. Matteu's destiny was a different one. He had the task of taking the Cathar treasure and Isobel's child by way of the secret passage out of the fortress to a safe haven. It would be an onerous and dangerous task in a country full of spies and Crusaders. The fate of the Cathar religion was in his hands and still it did not sit well with him to leave his friends. Many of them had decided not to recant their faith and would rather walk with courage into that great pyre which the Crusaders were constructing for them.

The afternoon before his leave-taking he came across Bertrand Marty. Over the years he had come to know the shy bishop a little. He was younger than Matteu by one or two years, and yet he had always seemed older and wiser. He had often wondered what it must be like to be such a man, full of the wisdom and the power of grace. When he saw him now he fell to his knees before him, waiting for his blessing, but Bishop Marty asked him to rise and told him he was not worthy of his adoration.

'But you are a Cathar Bishop, a *perfect!*' Matteu said to him.

'Who in the world can call himself perfect?' The bishop answered and asked that Matteu follow him to the gate, which these days stood open to the expanse of the mountains. He gestured for him to sit down on a rock, and there they remained side-by-side, quiet, staring out for a long time, until the bishop spoke. He told Matteu he would say something to him about his songs and Matteu, knowing that the bishop had never liked songs of the Grail, braced himself for one of his invectives.

'No . . . no,' Marty said with a laugh, noticing Matteu's face. 'I am not going to rebuke you! I wanted to say that I have grown some sense of these songs of the Grail that you troubadours sing.'

Matteu couldn't believe it; his face opened up in a smile. 'You do?'

'Yes, I think I know what it is, this thing called the Grail.'

'Well then: is it a stone or a cup?'

'I think it may mean many things,' he said. 'One might say it was Jesus, who came to Earth to be the vessel for the Lord; or the soul of every man, the soul full of faith in Christ; or the Earth and all its creatures, for the Earth has taken up the body and the blood of Christ.'

Matteu fell silent and thoughtful, looking at it for a long time with his face to the dying sun. These were good answers.

'Do you know, I dream that it is a woman,' Matteu said. 'A woman holding her dead son. Sometimes I think I see it when the moon is only a sickle. Sometimes, it looks like that to me as well, like a vessel.'

Bishop Marty nodded as if he were privy to some knowledge he was not going to share with him. 'Yes,' he said, 'that is a good likeness.'

Matteu grew full of enthusiasm. 'You know, I think after this I shall sing a new song – I shall sing of how once upon a time a castle of the Grail was threatened by the Devil's armies. I will tell how at the time of the greatest danger a dove flew down from the Heavens to split open the summit of Bidorta with its beak so that Esclarmonde de Foix, the angel keeper of the Grail, could throw the Grail into the heart of that mountain to keep it safe! Do you think they will look for it a long time, thinking that it is in the mountains?'

He smiled. 'Yes, I think they will.'

'They may burn all the pure ones,' Matteu said, 'but no one will forget them because of my songs. I will sing how Esclarmonde turned into a dove and flew from the very top of the keep, towards the mountains of the land of Prester John. And that is why her grave will never be found, because she never died.'

The bishop looked at Matteu. 'But Esclarmonde has been dead many years . . .'

'Yes, of course,' he said, 'but just between you and me, I feel her presence every now and again, in the night. Sometimes I think she whispers songs into my ears – she is so beautiful!' He remembered something then. 'Do you recall how you once told me that when you were a child you escaped from the Crusaders? How a beautiful woman woke you in the night and told you to hide in the forest?'

The bishop paused. 'Yes, I remember it.'

'Perhaps that was the Goddess herself?'

He smiled. 'Yes, perhaps it was.'

They sat for a time like that. They could hear the sounds of the army making revelry below. Matteu realised he must soon go.

'Matteu, I wondered if I could ask you to take something else away with you?'

'What is it?'

'This.' He handed Matteu a roll of parchments. 'It is a wisdom I have learnt while I have been on this mountain. It belongs with the child.'

Matteu took the roll and put it inside his pouch.

'Go with God, Matteu,' Bishop Marty said.

Matteu nodded full of sadness. 'And you, Bishop!'

Afterwards, Matteu took the quiet child and the treasure and together with four perfects made his way through the Porteil Chimney to the secret track. They travelled all night over that path with nothing to guide them but the waning moon, and came to the summit of Bidorta before sunrise.

While the child rested, Matteu and the others made a great fire, big enough to be seen from the field below. When the sun rose over the world, casting its rays over the spines of the dragon mountains, he went to look to the valley below. He could see one great pyre on which many of his friends would soon meet their death. He remembered Bertrand Marty and a deep sadness overwhelmed him. He knew that the bishop would be looking up to the summit seeking the sign that the child and the treasure were safe and that when he saw it he would be thankful. Matteu was weary. He had seen too much death. He would not wait for the Catholics to light the pyre; he did not want to hear the screams of his friends.

He said, 'We go!'

24

MAGIC SQUARES

'Not far from here,' said the cousin,
'is a hermitage where a hermit has his residence.'
Miguel de Cervantes, Don Quixote

En route to Saint-Paul-de-Fenouillet, 1938

Rahn was woken by a sudden jolt and opened his eyes. He was in the Tourster with Eva driving along a narrow road, perilously close to a low stone wall, the only thing between them and the gorges below.

'Something is happening to the car!' Eva said.

Rahn turned around and tried to focus his eyes. There was nothing behind them, nothing beside them. Ahead, the narrow road seemed to wind its way around one bend after the other. He felt another great thump then, which sent the Tourster rumbling towards the precipice. Eva pushed down on the brakes with all her might but the car had a mind of its own.

'I've got no brakes. Do something!' she shouted at Rahn. As she finished her words, however, a sharp corner sent the car skating over the gravel. Rahn braced himself, certain the car was going to mount that low stone wall, or break through it. Either way, they would be finished. But the wall held them and there was a crunching and scraping and tearing at the body and tyres of the car before the curve reversed and the Tourster left the wall and careered towards the mountainside.

'Change to a lower gear, for God's sake,' he told Eva.

'Can't you see I've been trying to. It's stuck!'

The collision with the wall had caused the Tourster to wobble for a time on its wheels like a drunk running out of steam. Eva seemed to have regained some control until another jolt sent them hurtling towards an approaching bend. She put her foot down on the brakes again as hard as she could but they remained useless.

Rahn had an idea.

'Steer along the rock wall – stay away from the edge.' He grabbed hold of the hand brake and pulled on it with all his might. The back wheels locked up and the car began to slide, scraping along the hillside with a terrible screech until the engine stalled, bringing the Tourster to a noisy and unhealthy-sounding stop.

Eva got out of the car with an air of calm annoyance. She had a bruise on her forehead and scratches here and there but she was essentially unhurt. She helped Rahn climb out. His many aches and pains seemed to have cancelled each other out and he stood beside Eva, who seemed to be looking at the mangled Tourster in disbelief.

'Something took hold of that auto-car!' Eva said. 'I had no control! Someone or something was driving us straight into those walls. Black magic perhaps?' she said sarcastically, but Rahn thought there might be an element of truth in it.

'Well?' She was staring at him from under that straight-cut fringe with a look of expectation.

Rahn liked her for not being hysterical; at this point he couldn't have coped with a panic-stricken woman since he was feeling rather frenetic himself. But there was something singularly annoying about her unruffled attitude and her calculated audacity.

'If Sancho Panza were here,' Rahn gave back, 'he would say:

"whether the pitcher hits the stone or the stone hits the pitcher, it's bad luck for the pitcher . . . " and it was bad luck for the Tourster, I'm afraid.'

'And are you going to take a look at it?'

He straightened his aching shoulders and, feeling put on the spot, walked to the car. It looked as if some great beast had clawed it. He resolved that it was irreparably damaged, at least for the time being. He opened the hood and peered inside. Everything seemed to be in order, as far as he could see, but in truth he knew almost nothing about cars and the gesture was in the spirit of creating the illusion that he was in control of things, as any man should be. He closed the hood again and wiped the grease from his hands with an air of authority. He was about to deliver his diagnosis when she cut through the entire charade with her sharp, sarcastic tone; hands on waist, eyebrows raised.

'You don't know anything about auto-cars, do you?'

'As a matter of fact . . .' he began, and was saved from a complete loss of face by the sound of a horse and cart coming around the hairpin bend. He brightened and said, 'As a matter of fact I can hear our taxi now!'

He waved the man down and asked if he could take them to Saint-Paul-de-Fenouillet.

'Are you just going to leave the car here?' the girl interjected.

'What else shall we do with it, Mademoiselle Cros? Perhaps you feel like getting behind the wheel again?'

She huffed, defeated, and Rahn repressed a smile, feeling he'd redressed the imbalance.

The man asked them what business they had in Saint-Paul-de-Fenouillet and Rahn told him they were on their way to see the priest.

'No, you're not,' the man said. 'At this time of the year, Abbé Grassaud is not at his presbytery but at the hermitage. I am more than glad to take you there—' he paused, '—for a fee.'

It was with a whistle then that he set off with Rahn and Eva in the back, bouncing among baskets full of produce. But it was only a short ride before the road widened and they saw a small sign and a level area. The man let them down and told Rahn to ring the bell. He said someone from the hermitage would hear it and come to greet them.

The bell's clang resonated over the gorges and it seemed a long moment before they saw a monk in a coarse grey cassock making his way along the overgrown path to them. When he arrived, puffing for his efforts, he revealed himself to be young and friendly and when Rahn told him whom they had come to see, he smiled.

'Ah yes, the abbé is here. But it will soon be time for the service, and if you want to talk to him we had better hurry.' He looked at the girl fleetingly, fearfully, and bent his eyes to his sandals. 'I'm afraid it isn't possible for a woman to enter. I'm sorry, but women are welcome during Easter and the time of pilgrimage only.'

Rahn looked at the young man gravely. 'It is a delicate matter – the mademoiselle is Abbé Cros's niece. Unfortunately, he died yesterday and she has come to tell Abbé Grassaud the news. You see, they were good friends.'

The monk looked a little embarrassed. 'How sad. I'm sorry for your loss, but it does not change things – we must abide by our rules.'

'Go on, I'll be all right,' Eva said, emphatically. 'I'll just wait here.'

Rahn hesitated. 'You'd better stay out of sight then, mademoiselle. I won't be long.' He didn't like leaving her; so many strange things had happened these last hours and no matter how annoying she was, she was still only a woman and therefore vulnerable. Seeing no other way around it he relented, following the monk over the narrow rocky path while looking over his shoulder now and again until they reached a series of buildings that seemed to be built into the mountain, penetrating deep into the natural caves behind them. Rahn needed a brandy, his head hurt and the bee was resting, but he thought that now and again he could hear the occasional buzzing through the novice's commentary on the history of the hermitage.

'We believe that a hermit found these caves in the seventh century,' the man was saying, 'he saw that they had everything he needed to survive: shelter, water from a spring, vegetation, roots and herbs and quiet from the world. Eventually others joined him. The original grotto is dedicated to Mary Magdalene, who was also a hermit. We Franciscans only came here in the fifteenth century. A long time later, in the eighteenth century, an epidemic struck the town of Saint-Paul-de-Fenouillet, so the townsfolk placed themselves under the protection of Saint Anthony, the patron saint of hermits, and there was a miracle.

The epidemic was cut short. The townspeople, full of gratitude, built the chapel inside the large cave.'

'So that's why a hermit leads the procession during Ash Wednesday at Bugarach?'

'Yes,' the man said. 'Saint Anthony is revered in these parts.'

They descended further until they entered a building in which a large vaulted grotto had been converted into a chapel formed out of the existing rock. It was cool, and sparsely lit by votive and altar candles. The monk gestured for Rahn to take off his hat, which he did, reluctantly. The chapel was essentially a cave and so when Rahn made his way down the nave to the altar he felt no anxiety at all; in fact, the fog was lifting and behind it his instincts were becoming sharper. On the left near the steps that led upwards to the sacred space there was a sculpture of Saint Anthony but when Rahn looked to the right he was stopped in his tracks. A stone tablet like a large grave marker stood against the grotto wall. Inscribed into the stone he was surprised to see the Sator Square. Above it the sculpted head of a man screamed in terrible pain, his jaws open wide.

'Oh!' the novice said. 'Do you like it? No one knows how

old it is. We think it may even be older than the original hermit who lived here. Some say it is older than a thousand years. The inscription, Sator Arepo Tenet Opera Rotas, means the Great Sower holds in His hand all works – and all works the Great Sower holds in His hand. In other words, God is the sower and He inspires all the creative work of man. Man should not think himself greater than God. In fact even here in this hermitage we have an example of how small we are in the presence of God's designs. The cavities in this mountain go deep into the Earth and there is another gallery even larger than this whose access, in the grotto of Mary Magdalene, is now forbidden. There was a priest who decided to explore these cavities—'

'That's right.' An old monk entered the chapel now. Rahn guessed he must be somewhere in the vicinity of eighty years. His face was a landscape of wrinkles whose folds had overcome what had once been a cleft chin and nearly buried those squinting eyes whose gaze was suspicious and wary. 'It was Albert Fonçay,' he said. 'He ventured into our network of tunnels . . . they say he was accompanied by a nun, Marie-Bernard Brauge. No one knows what happened to the nun but Albert Fonçay was discovered coming out of the grotto three days later, gravely injured. He had no recall of the events. He lapsed in and out of consciousness and when he woke he could only manage to utter incoherent phrases. He died three weeks after his ordeal, delirious and in terror for his soul. Since then the entrance has been closed. The sub-earthly ethers,' he said, 'are dangerous. In the Earth lies the potential for the greatest evil and this tablet is placed here to remind us of this. Now, who are you and what do you want?'

'I've come about Abbé Cros . . .'

'Eugene?' he said.

'I'm afraid he is dead,' Rahn said.

'What?' The old man frowned, squinting.

'Yes, unfortunately.'

'Cros is dead?' The news having sunk in, he took himself to a pew to sit down. 'But how?'

'He drowned yesterday, in the small pond in his garden.'

The old man paused. He told the other monk to leave them alone and when he was sure the young man had gone, he stared upwards at Rahn with unreserved distrust. 'What was he doing in the pond?'

'I think he was trying to find something – a key he had hidden there,' Rahn told him.

'The key was in the pond?' The man looked down; many thoughts were apparently crossing his venerable mind.

'So, you know what it was for?'

'What?' he said, coming out of his contemplation.

'The key?'

'No . . . I . . . well . . .' The abbé seemed at a loss.

'The key opened the tabernacle at Bugarach – in it we found a list of names,' Rahn said.

'You have the list? Let me see it!' Grassaud ordered.

'Do you know what it's for, Abbé Grassaud?'

'How should I know?'

'Because your name is on it.'

The old man started to wheeze. 'My name . . . on the list?'

'Yes, and so is your church, along with a number of other churches and their priests.'

'A number – how many?'

'You saw Abbé Cros a week ago, is that so?'

'Well, yes . . .'

'After you left he was somewhat upset,' Rahn said.

The old man faltered. 'I don't know what you are getting at with these questions—'

'What did you want with him, Abbé?'

'It was just a visit to an old friend.' He shrugged it off, but Rahn could see an underlying anxiety.

'Did he tell you anything about the list?'

'Go away and leave me alone! I don't know anything! My advice to you is to go, throw that list out and forget you ever saw it!'

'But I'm afraid it's too late for that,' Rahn said.

'Too late?'

'The magistrate of Arques has disappeared, there are two men dead and a policeman involved – an inspector from Paris.'

This must have made an impression on the abbé because he sat back with a look of defeat on his face. 'An inspector from Paris? What does he want?'

'He happened to be at Carcassonne when the call came in about the abbé's unfortunate accident, and now he's investigating it in connection to a group called La Cagoule. Have you heard of them?'

The old abbé wavered. 'No.'

Rahn knew he was lying. 'In fact, I believe the inspector may be arriving here very soon to make further enquiries.'

'Mon dieu!' The abbé cupped his bearded chin, like a man faced with an insurmountable conundrum.

'Do you have any idea why your name might be on that list?'

'I won't know until I see it,' he said, looking up with a duplicitous eye. 'I have to see who else is on it.'

Rahn took it out and showed it to him and the old man's eyes widened as he read the names. Rahn put it back in his jacket pocket then and the man looked disappointed, as if he had not extracted everything he could from it.

'So?' Rahn said.

There was a moment of the greatest hesitation and then it seemed as if the abbé had come to a decision; he nodded. 'Yes, I am on that list because I was something of a friend to Bérenger Saunière, the abbé of Rennes-le-Château, who was being investigated by Cros for the Bishop of Carcassonne but that was many years ago; if my mind serves me, it was in 1910. You see, Saunière moved here in 1885 but I met him in 1886. In those days we saw each other from time to time because he was interested in the history of this area and I had a good library in my sacristy. He was a bit of an amateur archaeologist, or so he said, and he showed me some things – artefacts he found when he was renovating his church. There was a goblet from the Knights of Malta, some coins, and various semiprecious things. I only heard later that he had found something else, something he was very secretive about. I don't know what it was but it must have interested Bishop Billard because he paid for Saunière to go to Paris to have whatever it was appraised.'

'Was this the same bishop who was investigating him?'

'Oh no! At that time Abbé Cros was Bishop Billard's secretary, actually, but later when the new Bishop of Carcassonne, a man called De Beauséjour, was appointed he also worked for him. It was the Bishop De Beauséjour who started investigating Saunière. You see, De Beauséjour was nothing like Billard.'

'Why not?'

'Well, Billard was of the old school. Look, after the revolution and especially after Napoleon, the government had complete control of the clergy. It could withhold the wages of any priest opposed to the republic and could even prohibit contact between a priest and the Vatican. The government also controlled which priests were selected for positions in episcopal vacancies. Billard and Saunière were both staunchly anti-republican. In fact, speaking out against the government is what got Saunière into hot water on several occasions. The truth is, he was a restless, ambitious man, and Rennes-le-Château was a backwater. He didn't like living like the rest of us, from hand to mouth, on whatever scraps were thrown to us; preaching to heretics in churches that were falling to bits. He was soon to learn that what kept many of us alive was our healthy friendship with the nobles, who often opened their purses in exchange for a mass here and there. These same nobles also belonged to Masonic Lodges. Bishop Billard condoned these delicate but lucrative relationships . . .'

'Are you saying Saunière and Billard were involved with Freemasons?'

'Yes, of course! Many priests were, including myself. But that was before the pope put a stop to it.'

'So was Saunière being investigated by Cros because of his connection to the Freemasons?'

'He was being investigated, so they say, because he was selling masses for the dead.'

'How can you sell masses to the dead?' Rahn asked.

'You don't sell masses to them,' Grassaud said this as if he wanted to add *you imbecile*. 'One pays for a mass to shorten the time of a dead loved one in Purgatory. The nobles paid highly to have masses said for their relatives. As I said, it was what kept many of us alive in those days – what we got for the dead. Ironic, don't you think?' He leant forwards. 'They say Germans have had to learn the meaning of irony the hard way.'

Rahn held back his chagrin, though inwardly he was prickling.

Having secured higher ground, the old man now spoke with a certain arrogance: 'But the masses were just an excuse because De Beauséjour had an ulterior motive for filing that suit against Saunière.'

'Another reason besides weeding out corruption?' Rahn said, making his point.

'Look, Billard himself had taken money from nobles for things such as the odd appointment of a relative to a certain parish. In truth, in those days there were not many bishops who would have cared less if a mass was said here or there for a loved one . . . no, there was another reason.'

'What was the other reason?'

'There was a rumour,' the other man wheezed, 'only a rumour mind you.'

'Rumour of what?'

'Of treasure . . . This is not so unusual, you know, there's treasure hidden everywhere in caves and holes and churches all over the south. Some of it may have once belonged to the aristocracy fleeing the revolution; the rest could have belonged to the Visigoths or even the Cathars. Perhaps Saunière found something valuable? I don't know, perhaps something heretical? I don't know that either.'

'You said he took what he found to Paris. Whom did he take it to?' Rahn said.

'From what I've heard he went to the seminary of Saint-Sulpice, and then somewhere else, to an order named the Society for the Reparation of Souls.'

'Who are they?'

'I don't wish to speak of them!' he said abruptly. 'Except to say, you should look into the Abbé Louis Verger, the man on the top of your list, then you will know more. The only other thing I can tell you concerns another priest on the list, Abbé Rivière of Espéraza. Some time before Saunière died, he confessed everything to Rivière. But when Rivière heard his confession he didn't give Saunière the sacrament until after he was dead.'

'Is that normal?' Rahn said.

'No! I've never heard of it before!' the old man said. 'Whatever Saunière told him must have upset Rivière so much that he couldn't bring himself to absolve him. Afterwards he was never the same, poor man – they say he never smiled.'

There was the intonation of the great bell. It woke the bee in Rahn's head.

Monks began to arrive for the canonical hour and the abbé got up. 'You will leave now,' he said, with authority. 'But before you go I will tell you this – apparently, days before Rivière died, he told a friend that Saunière had sold his soul to the Devil.'

Rahn left the hermitage and returned to the flat area but he found no Mademoiselle Cros waiting for him. She was missing and the contretemps completely baffled his head, causing him to stand there looking around like an abandoned orphan. He called her name but there was no sign of her – she had completely vanished. He decided the only recourse left to him was to walk to

Saint-Paul-de-Fenouillet. As it turned out, it was a considerable walk and by the time he reached the small township he was both exceedingly annoyed and frightfully concerned, in equal measure.

He found Eva sitting in a small café looking calm and composed, completely oblivious to his vexations and his obvious sufferings. He had blisters on his feet, and the worry had given him palpitations.

She explained that she had found a ride in an auto-car headed for the town and had taken the liberty of ordering herself lunch. She had a hunch he would find her.

What a nerve!

Not at all mollified, he told her of his conversation with Grassaud.

'So, Saunière sold his soul?' she said.

'According to Rivière . . . Now, I have to make a phone call and perhaps you can ask around if there's anyone headed in the direction of Rennes-le-Château.'

'Rennes-le-Château?'

'Saunière's village.'

He paid for her meal, asked to use the telephone and was directed to the post office where he called La Dame in Paris. The phone rang several times and Rahn was about to hang up when his friend answered, with a voice full of sleep.

'Are you still in bed? For God's sake!'

'Is that you, Rahn?'

Rahn heard a female voice and he imagined his friend lying next to a blonde student or a brunette secretary trying to wake up after a long night of soft battles in the bed. For some reason this vexed him.

'Time to get up.'

'What time is it?'

Rahn sighed. 'The sun's out.'

'Perhaps in the south, but in the north the sun's not out until I pull the blinds.'

'I have a job for you.'

He yawned. 'And it couldn't wait until my first brandy? What is it?'

'No time to explain now, except to say it's very important. I want you to find out anything you can about a certain Jean-Louis Verger and the Society for the Reparation of Souls.'

'Wait a minute, let me write this down.' Rahn heard him scrounging about for paper and a fountain pen. 'What's all this about anyway? Has it got something to do with that book, what was it called?'

The female voice purred his name and La Dame seemed to disappear for a moment.

'Bastard!' Rahn said, but he couldn't help smiling.

'Sorry, Rahn, here I am . . . what was that name again?'

'Jean-Louis Verger and the Society for the Reparation of Souls. And, La Dame, this is important, for God's sake! Will you get me the information as soon as possible?'

'Dear Rahn, are you all right? You sound terribly odd!'

Rahn took a deep breath of calm. 'I've got more than one lump on my head and I've been trying to maintain an outward show of imperturbability amid terrible and chaotic events the likes of which I'd rather not describe, lest I involve you more than I need to – so don't ask questions. Also, find out what you can about a symbol, an anchor entwined with a snake, would you? It may have something to do with a Masonic order of some kind, or that terrorist group, La Cagoule.'

'Sounds like you're in some trouble? What does Deodat think of all this?'

'I can assure you that right now he's not very happy about it.'

'So, you've done something to put him off side, and now you run to me! Meanwhile, you have all the adventures while I sit in the Bibliothèque Nationale looking up information. Somehow it doesn't seem fair!'

'What happened to your love for the boring life? Your creature comforts?'

'Well, these creatures of comfort do have their advantages.'

There was a squeal.

Rahn rubbed his unshaven jaw. 'I assure you, you've made the right decision. This adventure is not fun; it is rather a terrible exercise which, should you learn of it someday, you will be very happy to have missed. Why don't you take your lady friend with you to the library to keep you company?'

'I'm afraid she's not the . . . literary type, if you catch my meaning.'

'Say no more, La Dame, please! I'll call you in the next few hours.'

There was the unmistakeable sound of stretching and another yawn. Finally La Dame said, quoting Don Quixote, 'I shall not open my lips to make fun of your worship's doings, but only to honour you as my master and natural lord!'

Rahn sighed. La Dame was his only true friend besides Deodat. This thought filled him with apprehension for the whereabouts of his friend. He put the phone down, and resolving not to lose his spirits, went to find Eva.

25

RENNES-LE-CHÂTEAU

'The devil's agents may be of flesh and blood, may they not?'
Sir Arthur Conan Doyle, The Hound of the Baskervilles

They caught a ride in an old truck full of flour headed for the markets at Espéraza. Inside, Rahn sat nursing his head next to the driver, while Eva sat in silence at the window watching the landscape pass. He knew things were moving fast for her and she was no doubt perplexed. No wonder! There seemed to be no end to the complications and number of deaths: first the sacristan, then Abbé Cros, then the man in the barn. He was worried for Deodat's safety. There were people obviously willing to kill, but kill for what? Was it *Le Serpent Rouge* or was it the key to complete it, which seemed to somehow be connected to the treasure of the Cathars? Perhaps as Plantard had said, it didn't matter anymore if the grimoire existed or not, the mere *idea* that it existed had become a commodity and they were now caught in the middle. But Deodat's note was clear: he wanted Rahn to find *it*, whatever it was, even though he knew *they* were coming for him . . . But who *they* were and what *they* were going to do with him, he couldn't know.

He was confused. He tried not to think of what Deodat might be suffering. Perhaps whoever *they* were, they didn't want him to find *whatever it was* and he was placing Deodat's life in peril just by going around asking questions. On the other hand, if they wanted it, they might kill Deodat if it turned out to be a hoax, or Rahn couldn't find it. They might cut off a finger or a toe as he had seen in the movies – or do more than that . . .

'Hey, are the two of you hungry?' the truck driver said, interrupting his thoughts. 'In that bag, mademoiselle, behind you there, I have a baguette stuffed with sheep's kidneys and mustard. You're welcome to some of it.'

Rahn was nauseated and gestured for Eva to open her window so he could get some air.

The girl answered the driver with a casual voice: 'Thank you, but we've just had a most satisfying lunch.'

'Mais oui,' he said around the cigarette which sat in its reserved place at the corner of his mouth. He changed gears with one sinewy, tattooed arm and said, 'So, you are going to Rennes-le-Château to visit family?'

'No, we would like to see it for . . . for its historical significance,' Rahn said.

'You like history?' The driver smiled broadly. 'Well, Rennes-le-Château has history!' He laughed but said nothing more.

For a few francs he took them over the serpentine dirt road leading to the town but he dropped them off at the bottom of the hill saying, 'I won't go further, I will leave you here,' he said firmly.

Rahn observed the steep walk. 'Why?'

'The town smells of death, and if I were you I would not stay there long,' he said, touching his nose. He turned his truck around with haste and disappeared in a trail of dust.

The sun was still high and Rahn took off his coat as they toiled up the hill without speaking. Eva seemed to be quite fit compared to Rahn's abused self and walked ahead with a stride that would impress a Teuton. The air was crisp and thin and from this altitude one could see clearly for miles, but Rahn was in no mood for sightseeing. His head felt like it was caught in a vice and he badly needed a comfortable chair and a brandy, but at least for now the snow in the globe of his head had settled and the bee was quiet.

When they reached the top he realised that Rennes-le-Château hardly looked promising. It was a cluster of some forty rundown houses set on an ancient chalky outcrop rising up out of a vast landscape. Rahn guessed there could be no more than two hundred or so souls living on the small piece of land that was dominated by the old ramshackle castle of the Hautpouls.

As they walked into the shade of those frowning buildings Eva threw him an amused glance. 'Do you think that truck driver is right about this place?'

'I agree with him. I don't like it either, there's something sinister in the air.'

'Well, I suggest we go to the church; usually in these small towns the main road leads straight to it. The priest will know something about Saunière, no doubt.'

'No doubt,' Rahn said, feeling on the back foot.

They passed a woman sweeping the steps outside her door. Her form was large and her eyes were keen. 'Who are you?' she said, holding her broom in front of her like a weapon.

Rahn put out both hands, his nerves frayed. 'I beg your pardon, madame. We didn't mean to startle you. We've come to see the priest.'

'The priest?' She raised one brow, deeply suspicious. 'Why do you want to see *him*?'

In the corner of a little garden not far from the door sat an ancient woman bent over a bowl. Her gnarled hands shelled peas with lightning speed in an exercise that defied the eyes.

'Good morning, madame!' Rahn called over to her, trying to fend off the question.

'Oh, she can't answer you, she's mute,' the woman said dismissively, leaning on her broom. Apparently, having decided that the two strangers were not dangerous, she now made them her confidantes. 'She's my husband's mother and this is her house. A modest home, but we do let the rooms now and again to visitors – are you visitors?'

The old woman in the corner was staring at Rahn with unreserved intensity, making him falter.

Seeing this exchange, the buxom woman said, 'Stop that, Maman!' The madame leant in, her voluminous décolletage straining the buttons of her floral dress. 'The peasant has no manners. Now, what do you want with the priest?'

'We were hoping he might tell us something about Marie Blanchefort,' Eva said out of the blue.

'Blanchefort? You mean the Hautpouls? Why do you want to know about her?'

Eva did the strangest thing then – she grabbed Rahn affectionately by the arm. 'We're looking for family connections, that sort of thing.'

The woman's face was full of knowing. 'Looking for family connections?' She smoothed her floral dress over her bosom.

'I'd say looking for treasure more like it! That's why people come here generally, for gold and silver, not family connections! They're always disappointed though. Anyway, it's none of my business. Just follow this street all the way to the end, it'll take you directly to the church. The priest is there every day, poor man. They say he has a condition and was sent here to calm his nerves. Imagine that! Will you be staying the night? The Autan's getting ready to blow.'

'The what?' Rahn said.

'The Autan . . .' she repeated, gesticulating as if informing a child or an imbecile. 'Haven't you noticed how calm it is?' She raised both brows and leant on her broom again, rather like a witch, Rahn fancied, and it made him smile a little. 'Do you smell how fine the air is? That is how it always starts with the Autan . . . the calm before the storm. You don't want to get caught up in the middle of that devil! Once, you know, they found an auto in the fork of a tree after the Autan! I will reserve a room for the monsieur and madame; you are married of course?'

'Newly,' Eva answered quickly, to Rahn's surprise.

'Look, Maman, love birds!' the woman said, with a wistfulness that lingered only a moment before vanishing in light of practicalities. 'Well, that's settled then! Mind you don't fall on those cobbles! Dinner is at six, on the dot. If you're late I feed your portions to the pig.'

As they walked Rahn asked, 'Why did you tell her we're married?'

Eva came disquietingly close and whispered. 'If someone comes here looking for you, they will not be looking for a married couple, will they?'

Rahn couldn't argue with her logic. Her quick thinking impressed him but he didn't know how it would go at night when he would have to sleep on a chair, or worse still, on the floor. The thought of it didn't sound the least bit appealing.

They hadn't walked long before a short wall defined the path to the door of the church. The path cut through a garden, which on one side was crowned by a crucifix and on the other by a statue of Mary on a pillar of sandstone. Rahn could tell it was of Visigoth design.

Standing outside the door to the church, Eva pointed to the inscription over the lintel:

'*Terribilis est locus iste*!' she said.

'This place is terrible . . .' he translated.

'Interesting words to put over the door to a church!'

Rahn couldn't agree more because he felt that familiar nausea come over him and had to brace himself as she pushed the door open, allowing the light to fall on an old water stoup directly in front of them. It made him pause in amazement for the second time that day, for it was held up by a red devil with horrible eyes.

'Asmodeus . . .' he said, his breathing deliberate and slow. 'The king of the Underworld.'

'A handsome devil!' Eva said, walking in. 'I've always wondered why so many churches have him at the front door.'

'I wouldn't know. But if pressed I might venture to say that it could have something to do with Solomon.'

'The king?' She turned around, boyish, tall and as calm as a cold lake.

'Yes, he invoked Asmodeus to help him to build his temple in Jerusalem. See how the devil holds the stoup of holy water as a symbol that he's bound, like a servant, to the elemental beings and the angels above him? Solomon wrote the first grimoire and men have used it to bind devils for holy purposes ever since.'

'So the book written by this Pope Honorius wasn't the first one?'

'No. Solomon was the first, centuries before Christ. After that came the book by the Theban who was also called Honorius, and then later Pope Honorius appropriated it. It is complicated. Look do you see those griffins and salamanders on the water stoup?' Rahn pointed to them. 'They're guardians of treasure. And the initials BS?'

'Bérenger Saunière,' Eva said to herself. 'Not a modest man!'

'Perhaps not, but BS also stands for something else in Black Magic: Baron Samadi – the lord of graveyards and death. Asmodeus by another name is still Asmodeus.'

She gave him a shiver of a white smile. 'How nice. I like this place more and more. Who are those four angels?'

'That's also in the grimoires. The invocation of the spirits of the four directions: Michael, Gabriel, Uriel and Raphael. And see this inscription on the water stoup: *By this sign you will vanquish him . . . ?* This is usually attributed to Constantine, who was converted to Christianity after he saw the sign of the cross in a dream. It's supposed to mean that by virtue of the sign of the cross one conquers one's enemies, but here it says you will vanquish him, which is an aberration of the initial inscription.'

'Does it mean with the sign one conquers the Devil?'

'Yes.' He looked at her. 'The sign of the cross . . . The interesting thing is that in the magic square, the word tenet forms a cross; tenet means to hold. The one who holds the cross, or in this case the sign – the key that is missing from the grimoires – can vanquish or become the master of Satan himself . . . just a conjecture.'

'I see.'

The church wasn't large. Directly ahead on the west wall there was a confessional, above it a striking relief of the Sermon on the Mount. Running west to east the nave was tiled in black and white leading to the altar. On either side there were pews and on the walls representations of the Stations of the Cross, as well as the obligatory saints. There was a pulpit to the left, stained-glass windows high up, and the vaulted ceiling was painted blue and studded with stars.

'Can I help you?'

Rahn saw the shape of a priest in the glare of the doorway.

'I heard we had visitors in town,' he said. 'I'm the curator – Abbé Lucien.' He came forwards out of the light and Rahn noted that his face was so youthful it looked like it had never seen a razor. His hand showed the slightest tremor as they shook hands.

'News travels fast,' Rahn said to him.

'Well, I saw Madame Corfu on the way back from my walk.' He glanced furtively at Eva and blushed violently. To cover it he bent his head, touching the tip of his black hat.

Eva smiled in answer.

'We don't often see . . . people. It seems that you are a cause célèbre. I hear that you are interested in the Hautpoul family.'

'Yes,' Rahn said.

'I'm not an expert but I know a thing or two.'

'We were enjoying looking around your church,' Rahn said.

'Quite unusual, isn't it? The man who renovated it was a rather interesting priest.'

'Interesting, in what way?'

'Oh he was quite . . . uncommon . . . if you know my meaning.' He leant in. 'I'm not supposed to talk about him!' There was a nervous chuckle.

'No?'

'No, orders from above.' He indicated the ribbed vaults of the church with a finger, like a young, unbearded John the Baptist.

'From God?' Rahn asked.

'What?'

'Your orders?'

'Oh no!' The young priest blushed again and laughed it off as best he could. 'No, dear me, no! From the bishop at Carcassonne. But I could tell you something about the church, and if he comes into it—' he lowered his voice, '—well, one can't help that, can one? A little tour perhaps?'

'We would be delighted,' Eva said ingratiatingly. 'If you don't have more pressing matters to attend to, that is.'

'Oh, no, not at all.' A sad expression entered his cow-like brown eyes. 'I'm really very free – the people haven't grown accustomed to me yet, I'm afraid. They keep very much to themselves. Bitten once, you see, twice shy.'

'Surely they come to church on Sundays?' Rahn said.

'Yes, but not all of them, there are some who have fallen away from the flock. But that's not your concern, is it? Alright.' He rubbed his hands together. 'Let's see, shall we? What can I tell you . . . first, a little history . . . what do you know so far?'

'Next to nothing,' Rahn said.

'Well, where shall we start? This village was a large Visigoth centre in its day. You wouldn't know it now but thousands of people lived here. When the Franks defeated the Visigoths they sold the village and eventually it came into the hands of the Trencavel family. You may have heard of Roger Trencavel, the great Cathar.'

'This town belonged to the Cathars?'

'Indeed, and they, in turn, were conquered by the Catholic Crusader, Simon de Montfort. Perhaps the heretics cursed the town because after that it was bedevilled by the plague and under constant attack from mercenaries – until it was almost completely destroyed. So, to cut a long story short, the village eventually came under the governorship of the Hautpoul-Blancheforts. Marie de Nègre d'Ables Hautpoul-Blanchefort was the last in their line. Her castle is fallen into ruin as you no doubt have seen.'

'Blanchefort?' Rahn said. 'Isn't that the name of one of the Grand Masters of the Templar order?'

'Indeed. The Blancheforts were Cathars but they also belonged to the Temple. This place is dotted with Templar castles because it formed a part of the pilgrim route to Santiago de Compostela.'

'And what about the church?' Eva asked.

'When Saunière came here around 1885 this church was falling to bits, and he decided to renovate it. That's how it has become what it is. Shall we start at the entrance? I suppose you've noticed our devil, Asmodeus?'

'Yes. What interests me,' Rahn said, 'is the inscription. It reads, "Par ce signe tu le vaincras," that is, "With this sign you will vanquish *him*", instead of "Par ce signe, tu vaincras" – "With this sign, you will vanquish".'

'Why, I believe you are right!' the priest said, enlightened. 'Fancy that! Perhaps it was a mistake? Yes.' The priest seemed at a loss for words and turned his attention to the church again. 'You see there, above the confessional, there is a relief of the Sermon on the Mount and the inscription "Come to me all those who suffer and I will ease your pain" . . . And as we walk down the central nave, we see along the walls the Stations of the Cross. Now, behind us, as you can see, opposite the entrance, is the baptismal and a statue of Jesus with John the Baptist.'

'John looks rather large?' the girl said.

'Yes, but after the baptism it is well known that Jesus increases while John the Baptist decreases. Quite a clever man was our Abbé Saunière. Now, if we move along, on your right we see a statue of Saint Germaine, the shepherdess who was disfigured and gave away all her possessions, and to your left Saint Roche, and then Saint Anthony the Hermit, who was tempted by devils.'

'The same saints that are found in the Bugarach church,' Rahn remarked.

'Bugarach?' the priest said, suddenly attentive.

'The abbé of Bugarach was my uncle,' the girl said.

He looked at her with a questioning expression, as if he were trying to fit a piece to a puzzle. 'I didn't think he had a niece?'

'Did you know him?' Rahn asked.

'What do you mean, "did"? Has something happened to him?' There was a sudden intensity in his voice.

'My uncle had an accident,' Eva said.

'Oh, I'm sorry to hear that. May I ask, what sort of accident?' He leant in.

'He drowned,' she said in a matter-of-fact voice.

'Drowned? I thought he'd had a stroke. Strangely enough, I had a choice of coming here or going to Bugarach—'

'Really?' Rahn said. 'What made you choose Rennes-le-Château?'

Abbé Lucien looked at Rahn. His blond eyelashes shivered like wings and he smiled a nervous smile, wrinkling that young face. 'I don't like volcanoes.' He nodded his head and touched the tip of his black cap again. 'My condolences, mademoiselle.'

Eva had charmed him!

The young priest continued with an awkward, self-conscious tone that made Rahn feel like a third wheel: 'Well . . . here on the right we have Mary Magdalene, for whom this church is dedicated. Further along on the left we have the pulpit and opposite that, Saint Anthony of Padua, the patron saint of lost items. Behind the altar, one sees the Holy Virgin holding her child on the right, and on the left, Joseph is also holding Jesus.'

Eva turned to the priest with a frown. 'Two Jesus babies in one church, how remarkable!'

'I did say he was an interesting man!' He laughed a little, embarrassed and delighted.

The altar drew Rahn's attention. He pointed to it. 'Can we get closer?'

'Well . . .' The abbé seemed uncertain. 'I suppose that would be permissible . . .' He took a step and opened the gate leading to the enclosure.

Rahn paused on the threshold to quell the anxiety he was feeling, before following the other two. He wiped his brow and tried to look calm but he glimpsed something that immediately took his eye. It was a slab of engraved stone sitting against the wall. 'What is that, Abbé?' he said, going down on one knee to look at it.

'Oh, that is the knight's flagstone. I don't know where to put it.'

'It reminds me of a Templar Seal,' Rahn said as he looked closely, 'two knights on one horse . . .'

'It was placed here by the Blancheforts, I believe.'

'I see.' But Rahn's mind was now on the altar. 'This looks quite modern.'

'Yes, the entire renovation began when Saunière replaced the old altar, which was really just one great slab of stone sitting on two ancient pillars of the Visigoth period.'

They drew closer to look at the painted relief of Mary Magdalene praying in a grotto some distance from a township; she was depicted with a book by her side and a skull nearby.

'What is that book?' Eva asked.

'Some say, mademoiselle, it's the original Apocalypse of John – the Book of Revelation in the New Testament. There is a Cathar legend that Mary Magdalene was the sister of Saint John and that she was the guardian of his book. The Cathars called it the Book of the Seven Seals.'

Rahn's mind was running through the connections. 'What's that town behind Magdalene?'

'Ah! Well, that is purported to be the New Jerusalem, but some believe it looks like Rennes-le-Château. Have you seen the Tour Magdala? It looks like the tower in the relief. Saunière painted the entire thing himself, with the help of another priest.'

'And this inscription is not correct either.' Rahn read it out, *'Jesu Medela Vulnerum Spes Una Poenitentium. Per Magdalenae Lacrymas Peccata Nostra Diluas* – Jesus you remedy against our pains and only hope for our repentance. It is by way of Magdalene's tears that you wash our sins away. The word "paenitentium" is not only spelt incorrectly, he has also added the word "per" unnecessarily.'

The abbé nodded. 'Once again, yes, I see your point.'

By way of . . . per . . . tenet . . . Rahn set this aside for later digestion and looked around, feeling hot under the collar. He concentrated, swallowing down his fear. The wallpaper around the altar drew his attention. Something looked familiar . . . and then he was struck suddenly and he saw it, and it was all he could do to keep himself from crying out. There were hundreds of small upside-down anchors entwined with snakes. His head pounded the significance into him. That was the symbol tattooed on the dead man's wrist!

'Now, over here, there was once an entrance to the tomb of Sigebert IV,' the abbé continued.

But Rahn had to take a moment to digest his insight and only managed to say, 'That's very interesting.' He could feel his hands shaking and put them in his pockets.

'Yes, he was Dagobert II's son,' the priest said.

'A Visigoth tomb – is it possible to see it?' Eva said, unable to hide the excitement in her voice.

'I'm afraid no one knows where the entrance is since the renovations.'

'What a shame,' Eva said, looking at him with her brown-gold eyes.

'Oh, but Saunière's housekeeper is still alive!' he said brightly, completely under her spell. 'She might know something. She doesn't usually talk to anyone but it won't hurt to ask. In the afternoons she is usually in the conservatory. I will see if she's available. In the meantime you can have a look in the cemetery — you might find something to interest you there.'

The graveyard lay on the south side of the church and was sequestered behind a wall. To reach it they had to traverse the garden with the Cavalry cross they had seen on their arrival. Rahn breathed in a sigh of relief to be out of that church and welcomed going into the cemetery with a lustful enthusiasm.

'Did Saunière build this garden too?' Rahn asked.

'Oh yes, to commemorate the end of his building works. Bishop Billard himself came to bless the church. In fact, his name is engraved on that plaque below the crucifix.' The priest led them to an arched portal dominated by a relief of a skull and bones, and unlocked the gate covered in verdigris. Rahn noted that there was a rounded protrusion on this side of the church with a little window high above. It looked like a recent addition. 'Is that a storeroom?' he asked the priest.

'Oh, that's just the sacristy,' he said, fumbling for his keys.

Eva frowned. 'Do you always keep the cemetery locked? What about those who want to visit their relatives?'

'There are not many who want to, but I'm glad to open the gate for anyone who asks.'

'But why lock it at all?'

'To prevent people from . . . digging up the graves.'

She laughed, incredulous. 'What?'

The abbé gave a sigh. 'Yes, unbelievable, isn't it? The lengths to which we must go to prevent the desecration of graves! When it comes to treasure, nothing is sacred.'

'What treasure are they looking for?' Rahn asked.

'Visigoth treasure . . . not far from here, a shepherd fell into a hole in the ground and found a casket of coins dating to the time of the Visigoths. Since then it's been rather difficult to keep people out of this cemetery because beneath it lies the crypt of the dames.'

'So, beneath the church were buried the males and beneath this cemetery the females?' Eva said.

'That is what the church records say.'

They stood a moment inside the gates, looking over graves that were less than well cared for. Above, the sky was as hard as enamel and below, the weeds grew everywhere, headstones looked to be crumbling and some had even toppled over.

'The cemetery needs some work, as you can see, but I can't get anyone to do it.'

'Why not?' Rahn said.

'We can't keep tourists and riffraff from tearing the gates down and yet the residents of the town won't venture beyond them!'

'Really?' Eva remarked.

'They are afraid.'

Eva looked about her. 'Of what? Their dead?'

'So it seems.'

Rahn listened to this while he glanced down a long avenue of graves. Towering above it, beyond the wall of stone, he could see what looked like a glass conservatory.

'Abbé Saunière is buried there, at the end of this avenue,' the priest said, noticing his interest. 'I'll go and see if the madame will speak to you.'

He excused himself with a tip of his hat and a bat of his eyelashes and left with his long black cassock rustling between his legs.

It was eerily quiet now and Eva took Rahn's arm again, sending an electric shock to his abused head. 'I agree with you, I don't like it here,' she confided.

'That's why I think it is exactly the right place,' he said to her as they walked to Saunière's grave. He had not had a woman's arm in his since Etienne, and it felt disconcerting.

The grave was nothing special, almost conspicuously so, just a simple horizontal stone slab with the usual inscriptions. They turned around again and walked back looking at other graves. Rahn noticed an ossuary on the far left and Eva went to a place set apart for the burial of unbaptised children.

'Isn't this sad?' she said. 'Some people say unbaptised babies become angels . . . others say they live in limbo. Apparently they are always buried where the rainfall from the church can run off onto their little plots – to baptise them with Holy Water.'

Rahn came over to her and took a look at the miserable patch of ground. 'Well, Dante depicts limbo as the first circle of Hell but the pagans see it as a brightly lit castle, like the Elysium. Apparently, you can be in limbo and not know it—'

Rahn was interrupted by the priest who had returned wearing a triumphant smile.

'Madame Dénarnaud has agreed to see you!' he said. A moment later they were leaving the gloomy cemetery and retracing their steps past the church. Eventually they came to a small garden that led to a larger one shaded by tall trees.

'Once,' the priest said, walking briskly, 'this was a magnificent paradise. Saunière planted rare, exotic species of trees and orchards bearing fruits never seen in these parts. All nurtured by subterranean aqueducts and cisterns. Quite ingenious!' He paused a moment to orient them. 'That large building is the Villa Bethany.'

'Interesting name,' Eva commented, still hanging onto Rahn's arm.

'Well, I suggest it has some connection to the church. Bethany being the home of Mary Magdalene and Lazarus, her brother, the one who was raised from the dead by Christ and became Saint John because of it.'

To Rahn the villa looked rather austere. 'Did the priest build that too?'

'Oh yes. These days it's where the madame lives. She used to live in the vicarage, until I came. Ahead is the tower of Magdala – it once had a wonderful library.' Rahn grew attentive. 'You say it once had, what happened to it?'

'Unfortunately for me, an antiquarian bookseller from London came shortly after the abbé's death to buy all his books. I would have liked to have seen them.'

Looking for *Le Serpent Rouge*, the *Grimoire of Honorius III,* perhaps? Rahn wanted to ask. But instead he trailed behind, glancing about at the decrepit garden, trying to imagine how it must have looked in its glory days.

'All sorts of celebrities came here, apparently,' the priest said, looking over his shoulder. 'They ate and drank till all hours, even royalty, so I hear.'

'Royalty?'

'Yes, this village was graced by a visit from the Tuscan, Johann Salvator, of the Austrian Imperial family, who was also as it happens the nephew of Countess de Chambord who lived nearby. Actually, the Countess de Chambord was actively involved in trying to unite the exiled French Royal family with the House of Austria. There were some who wanted her husband, the Count de Chambord, to lead a new monarchy, but he died before it could be realised. Her donations helped to build these buildings and this garden. At any rate, her nephew, Johann Salvator, one day renounced his title and privileges and assumed the name John Orth, upon which he married a commoner, purchased a ship called the *Santa Margareta* and sailed for South America. They say his ship was lost and he was never heard from again, that is, until he came here to visit Abbé Saunière.'

'Perhaps it was true love?' Eva said.

'More like he got a whiff of what was to befall the Hapsburgs and wanted to distance himself,' Rahn answered.

'Yes, suicide, assassinations, war and eventually their downfall.'

The priest climbed the steps to the semicircular walkway that overlooked the vast, mountainous footfalls of the Pyrenees. The walkway connected the Tour Magdala on the left with the conservatory on the right. This was the glasshouse Rahn had seen from the cemetery a moment before. It had seemed far grander from below. As they neared, Rahn realised it was rather a shabby place. The floor was littered with rotting leaves and dead snails and the corners were hung with cobwebs. Above, bird droppings clung to the broken glass panes that allowed the filtered light to fall over a wicker chair in which dozed an old woman. She was dressed in black like a nun, with a black shawl over her head that accentuated the paleness of her withered face. She was resting her chin on her chest and making low snoring sounds as they approached.

'Madame Dénarnaud,' the priest said tentatively, giving her a little shake. 'These are the people who wanted to see you.'

She opened both eyes sharply and lifted her head to survey the abbé with contempt. She turned her slow and penetrating eyes to the strangers standing before her and said, 'Who are you, and what do you want?'

26

MADAME DÉNARNAUD

'Then I cursed the elements with the curse of tumult;
and a frightful tempest gathered in the Heaven where,
before, there had been no wind.'
Edgar Allan Poe, 'Silence, A Fable'

'These are the visitors I told you about. They would like to ask you some questions,' the abbé said, the perfect model of politeness and decorum.

Madame Dénarnaud turned to the abbé and spat, 'Get out!'

This abruptness caused a violent blush to flower on the priest's face and a few words of apology were followed by a hasty exit.

When he was gone she addressed Rahn and Eva: 'Strangers usually want one thing from me, and if that is what you're seeking you will not be satisfied.'

Rahn ventured to ask, 'And what do they usually want?'

'They want to know about the treasure, of course,' she said, with a wily smile and narrowed eyes.

'Is there treasure?'

'I knew it!' she shouted. 'Take your carcasses out of here!'

'We're not here about treasure,' Eva hurried to say.

'I read the cards this morning. I pulled out the Tower – destruction – mayhem – death! The planet Mars!' Madame Dénarnaud punctuated each word with a jab of her finger.

'The Tower can also mean a blessing in disguise,' Rahn countered.

There was a reluctant grunt. 'You know the cards?'

'Of course. There's a wealth of knowledge locked in each one that can only be mined by those who are wise.'

She was soothed, but only a little. 'What do you want to know?'

Rahn decided to take advantage of her momentary good humour to get to the point. 'We're looking for any information on something called *Le Serpent Rouge* – a grimoire written by Pope Honorius.'

'A grimoire?' she said with raised brows.

'A book of black magic,' Rahn said.

'Why would I know about such a thing?'

'We wondered if Abbé Saunière had known about it.'

'And if I did know, why would I tell you anything?'

'Because a priest has died and I think his death is connected to the grimoire.'

This made her stop. 'What? What did you say? Who is dead?'

'The Abbé Cros from Bugarach.'

She paused to think about it, and Rahn could see that Madame Dénarnaud was a good actress, for the addled exterior fell away and what surfaced now was a fiercely lucid intelligence. 'Bugarach?' She looked at Rahn, the whites of her eyes as yellow and dry as medieval parchment. 'How did he die?'

'His wheelchair tipped into a fish pond and he drowned,' Eva said, without expression.

The old woman frowned. 'What?'

'He was paralysed,' Eva answered.

The old woman pursed her puckered lips. 'But he wasn't—' She looked at Rahn sharply, ignoring Eva. 'What do you know about that book?'

. 'I know that Saunière must have found something to do with it, and whatever it was he took it around to certain societies in Paris,' Rahn informed her.

'Look,' the old woman said, pointedly, 'I was only a young girl when he came to this village. I was beautiful, you wouldn't think so now, but I was. I worked at Espéraza making hats but it wasn't a good living, we were poor. My mother took him in as a boarder. Oh, he was a handsome man all right, in his broad hat and cassock! He won the hearts of the people of this township, that's for certain. He even won my heart . . . a little. He had a wonderful humour and he was full of emotion when he spoke. The church was falling to bits and he found some money, not much mind you, but with the help of his congregation he fixed the foundations that were falling down because of the water, that is all. Now leave me alone.'

'If you don't tell us what you know, I'll be forced to go to the gendarmes at Carcassonne,' Rahn bluffed. 'I know a certain inspector who'll be very interested to know about Abbé Cros's investigation into the priests and their involvement with certain brotherhoods. I might even show him a list of priests in which one finds the name Bérenger Saunière. I'm certain he'll find it most enlightening, since he's already looking into the death of Abbé Cros. A death that occurred shortly after the abbé informed us of where the list was kept.'

'A list you say? An inspector? What is his name?'

'Beliere.'

'Beliere . . .' she said, a light seeming to blink on and off behind that old façade. 'Look, all I know is that when Abbé Saunière moved the altar, he found something in the Visigoth pillar. I never saw it. That pillar is now outside the church. He had it placed there, upside down, and had an image of Mary of Lourdes sat on it. It is there for all to see.'

'Why upside down?'

'How should I know?' she spat.

'What did he find?' Rahn pressed, trying to keep calm, though he could hardly forget that time was ticking away and that his friend was still missing and possibly in grave danger.

She looked at him squarely as if she could read his thoughts. 'Do you dare to go to Hell?'

He held her stare, defiantly. He wasn't going to let the old hag get the better of him. 'If there exists a way towards Heaven and it crosses Hell, then, yes – I dare!'

'You may recite Faust, but you don't know the meaning of it! Heaven?' she scoffed. 'There is no Heaven!' Then her face changed into a look of terror. 'Listen!' She sat stock-still. 'It comes – le Autan, le Autan is coming! Do you hear it? It's the Devil's wind!' Her face was full of alarm. 'I told you! Disaster. The cards never lie. We have to go!'

To Rahn the sky was no different. 'I don't hear anything,' he said.

'God help us! Lift me up, you idiot!' She made a grab at Eva's arm and used it to pull herself out of the chair. 'Can't you hear the snapping of the trees? It's here!'

Now Rahn could hear a faint whirring sound, like a large motor, perhaps a plane, echoing in the valley.

'Take me out of here, now!' The woman was suddenly frantic.

It took only a moment for it to be upon them. From out of nowhere it came, shaking the old glasshouse and rattling its loose windowpanes so that they came crashing to the ground. The wind fetched the glass door then and swung it open and then shut it again with such force it shattered a number of old panels, spraying the three of them with glass splinters.

'You idiots! I told you!' the old woman wailed.

Rahn tried to open the iron-framed door but it was jammed. Glass was falling all around them and the entire conservatory was rattling now as if the wind's hands were about to shake it loose and take it away. He eventually managed to rattle the door open and, leaving the wreckage of the glasshouse behind them they ventured out into the gale. The wind was an animal, roaring over the trees and loosening their limbs. Dust flew into their eyes and Rahn could hardly see to take the old woman down the precarious steps to the garden. Eva went ahead to fetch the priest and Rahn toiled to get the old madame over the debris, while leaves and dead twigs fell over them, littering their path and making every step dangerous. The old woman's dress flapped and caught around her legs and she stumbled on a twig but Rahn managed to catch her before she fell.

Up ahead the priest was gesturing with his hat and shouting something he couldn't hear, his cassock fluttering and ballooning. He pointed to the villa.

By the time they reached the house the woman was exhausted to the point of being limp, and Rahn and the priest had to half carry her through an annex that looked like it had been converted into a chapel and down a corridor to a sitting room.

Together they sat her in a large chair. She was shivering and the priest directed Eva to a flight of stairs.

'There are bedrooms up there,' he told her. 'I'm sure you'll find a blanket for the madame in one of the cupboards. I'll go and fetch her some water.'

Rahn could smell sewage, old pipes and damp. The shutters knocked at the windows and the wind whistled through cracks. He took in the room; there was a crucifix on the wall; a good reproduction of the Shepherds of Arcadia; a cold hearth; expensive carpets on the floor; and floral wallpaper. The décor was opulent for a small town like Rennes-le-Château and he thought that the house must have caused quite a stir among the citizens of the town when it was built.

The old woman sat forward and grabbed at his arm so suddenly he jumped. She looked furtively to the door; her eyes were as sharp as nails. 'Quickly! Before he comes back. You are German, are you sent by Hitler?'

'I—' Rahn began but she didn't let him finish.

'Watch out for that raven!' she said, and paused, listening.

Rahn could hear the sound of footsteps in the hallway. 'Penitence, penitence – remember that!' she said, in a quick whisper. She lay back in the chair then and closed her eyes one moment before the priest returned.

The room had fallen into a gloom. The abbé put down the glass of water and tried the light switch. The lights came on, shivered a moment and died away. He looked a sight: cassock dishevelled and his thin hair, uncovered now, matted with sticks and dirt and leaves. He said, 'It looks like tonight we are in darkness!'

They placed a lit candle by the old woman and the priest promised to send someone to light a fire and to look in on her, and they left. Once in the hallway Rahn asked if there was a phone in the town. 'Of course, we are not so old-fashioned, you know! I have one in the presbytery that you can use, if the lines aren't down.' And with these words he led them out into the awful afternoon.

27

A FRIEND IN NEED

'Hell is paved with priests' skulls'
Miguel de Cervantes, Don Quixote

L a Dame it's me! I don't have much time and I can't talk
openly,' Rahn whispered into the phone in the hall of
the presbytery while Eva kept the young priest distracted in conversation in the sitting room.

'Rahn!' La Dame sounded excited. 'Burn my beard! Listen,
you won't believe what I've found out about Jean-Louis Verger!
Simply the most incredulous and odd things!'

'What?'

'Apparently he was an interdicted priest. Do you know what
that means?'

'No.'

'He was under investigation by the Inquisition. That was back
in 1856, but here's the clincher: a year later he murdered the
Archbishop of Paris, one Marie Auguste Dominique Sibur, in
broad daylight!'

'What?'

'Yes indeed! According to reports it was the only murder of its
kind. It looks like Verger was an opponent of the doctrine of the
Immaculate Conception and also wanted to put an end to celibacy
for the clergy – a cause any man in his right mind can understand.

But as you might guess it did not go down too well with his peers. The story goes that on the first afternoon of the novena of Saint Genevieve in January 1857, he entered a church while it was full of worshippers, and boldly walked up to the archbishop to thrust a rather long knife into his gut, crying out "Down with the goddesses!" He was found guilty, of course, but here's the important point – the verdict was pronounced on the seventeenth of January.'

'The seventeenth of January?'

'Odd, isn't it? That's the same day as the feast day of Saint Sulpice.'

'I don't know what you're getting at, La Dame.'

'Well isn't that the same date that's on the notebook of that Monti fellow?'

'Of course! Yes!' Rahn remembered.

'Well, at any rate he was sentenced to death but right to the end he was convinced that Napoleon was going to pardon him. I guess he was convinced that the sun rises in the west too. Now, here's another interesting thing: have you heard of Éliphas Lévi; they called him the Magus?'

'Yes, I know of him.'

Deodat had hidden Cros's list of priests in a book written by Éliphas Lévi.

'Well, Verger met with him a year before he killed the Archbishop of Paris.'

'What?'

'Yes, he went to see Lévi looking for – wait for it, Rahn, are you ready? A grimoire. Yes! He wanted to conduct a magic ritual apparently, and needed one.'

'Don't tell me . . .'

'I think you've guessed it. He was looking for *The Grimoire of Pope Honorius III – Le Serpent Rouge!*'

Rahn was speechless.

'Lévi couldn't help him but Verger didn't give up. He must have continued asking around because he found one at a bookseller in Paris.'

'How do you know that?'

'Well, Lévi wrote a book called *The Key of the Mysteries,* in which the entire affair is discussed. In that book he says he discovered, long after Verger was executed, that the man had found and obtained a copy of the grimoire from an antiquarian bookseller that Lévi knew. Interestingly, the grimoire was never seen after Verger was executed, it simply disappeared. Lévi assumed that Verger must have used the grimoire to conjure demons of protection so that he could do the dastardly deed of killing the archbishop. But there's another possibility. He may have been afraid for his life. At his trial, Verger stated that the Inquisition was out to destroy him because of something that he had in his possession and that certain people, whom he could name, were responsible for the machinations against him. Could the Church have been after that grimoire, Rahn?'

'Oh, this is astounding, La Dame!'

'And it gets more astounding. You know that society you asked about, the Society for the Reparation of Souls? Well, apparently Verger belonged to them . . . some refer to them as the penitents.'

'What?' Rahn caught his breath. 'This is just too fantastic to be true!'

'Yes. They were a nasty lot, dabbled in the cult of the dead – you know, graveyard services, masses for the dead, that sort of thing. Their cry was "Penitence, Penitence!" It was an order founded by a man called Joseph-Antoine Boullan, apparently a brilliant theologian. I don't know many details except to say that Boullan began to experiment with new methods of exorcising demons. He prepared concoctions out of Eucharistic wafers mixed with excrement and urine.'

Rahn paused: *The consecrated wafers in the tabernacle . . . the Sign of the Lamb . . . so Cros had been protecting the wafers from black magic!*

'It's also rumoured that Boullan made a nun pregnant and that she subsequently gave birth to a child in secret, a child Boullan is said to have summarily sacrificed on the high altar.'

Rahn gasped. 'A priest! Sacrificing his own child on an altar!'

'Yes, diabolical, isn't it? Anyway, the child was never found, nor was any incriminating evidence, but the black masses continued. To cut a long story short, Boullan was publicly disavowed during an ecclesiastical trial but His Holiness Pope Pius eventually pardoned him – after which he simply started a new order and continued as before.'

Rahn thought this through, touching the lumps on his head as if a little delicate prodding might make his thinking clearer. 'Saunière was involved with this order of penitents.'

'Who is Saunière?'

'Never mind. It looks like Monti, Crowley, the Church, the Freemasons, Lévi – everyone was after this grimoire.'

'Perhaps it would be easier, Rahn, if you just told me who wasn't after it!'

'Good work, La Dame. Listen, why don't you take a room in a little hotel outside Paris and lay low; the bill's on me – and keep your head down.'

'What for? What's going on?'

'Look, I didn't want to tell you – something terrible has happened. Deodat was kidnapped early this morning, I think . . . at least I hope, because he has just disappeared, his house was ransacked and a man tried to kill me but someone killed him before he could finish the job. This is becoming dangerous and I would feel better if I knew you were somewhere out of the way.'

'What? Are you joking? Someone tried to kill you? This isn't funny, Rahn!'

'I wish I were joking, La Dame, but to put it mildly, I'm deadly serious.'

'Where are you?'

'In a strange little backwater called Rennes-le-Château.'

'What are you doing there?'

'This is Saunière's village and I believe I'll get to the bottom of this tiresome thing soon. At least I hope so – for Deodat's sake, not to mention my own.'

The voice at the other end of the line was nervous. 'All right, I'll take a room at the university, you know the number . . . call me there in a couple of hours, by then I should have an answer for you about that sign. You know what, Rahn? Seems like Cervantes was right after all.'

'What do you mean?'

'Hell *must* be paved with priests' skulls!'

28

ANOTHER TO ADD
TO THE LIST

'What the devil's the matter now?'
Edgar Allan Poe, 'The Premature Burial'

They made their way back to Madame Corfu's house, with the winbeating its fists into their faces, both of them grateful to have a place to stay for the night. Rahn indulged in an overdue wash, a shave and a change of clothes. Afterwards, he met Eva at Madame Corfu's table and he had to admit that she looked rather more than fetching.

For her part, Madame Corfu was dressed in her best blue dress and fake pearls, and presided over the table, opposite her sour-faced, unshaven and scruffily clad husband. The mood was sombre and they ate in silence – a surprisingly tasty plate of mushrooms à la Languedocienne followed by a *cassoulet* washed down with a bottle of Carignan. Afterwards the madame served a dessert cake made of wine and they savoured it, while outside the wind whipped up a frenzy, thrashing the limbs of the trees whose woody fingernails scratched at the shuttered windows.

The madame broke the silence. 'This is the way it is. Some

days before it blows, it is calm just like you saw today. The air is clear, dry as a stick, a dryness that makes the palms itch, and then from nowhere – it comes! And you know, it stays for days. The noise of it is so incessant it drives people mad, that's why some call it Les Vent des Fous. Around these parts, they call it the Devil's Wind, but I call it the Wind of Death because there is a legend that when the wind blows, someone will die,' she said this, as if it pleased her immensely. 'And if it storms . . . well.' She left the rest open to their interpretation.

Monsieur Corfu grunted. The old woman who sat opposite Rahn chewed her food with her gums, making the occasional sucking sound and drooling over her chin.

'I hear that you saw Madame Dénarnaud, Saunière's old housekeeper, this afternoon?' the mistress broached. 'Did she tell you anything of interest?'

'Not very much, I'm afraid,' Rahn answered evasively, rubbing a stain from his knife with a serviette.

'That cagey old bird!' She could hardly contain the malice in her voice. 'I thought as much.'

'What does she have to be cagey about?' Eva asked, open faced, sweet.

She is good at this, Rahn observed.

'Oh! There is much! Isn't there, Marcel?'

'Just gossip!' Monsieur Corfu dismissed, between spooning food into his mouth and chewing.

Madame Corfu ignored him and considered her guests. There was a raised brow. 'Did she tell you that she was the priest's lover? Of course she didn't . . . but it's true. She lived with him for years. Everybody knows what they got up to, the two of them in that presbytery – together!'

'In the presbytery – didn't he live in the villa?' Eva asked.

'What? No, the villa was meant to be a home for retired priests – his circle of *friends.*'

'Who in particular?' Rahn asked.

Madame Corfu regarded Rahn with a pregnant smile, full of teeth and gossip. 'Did the old woman mention the renovations to the church?'

'A little,' Rahn said.

'Did she say what the bell-ringer found?'

'No.'

'Well, he hated the renovations and fussed like an old woman, tidying up after the workmen and telling them to be careful. Anyway, apparently one night he was descending the stairs from the bell room and found that one of the wooden pillars that held up the pulpit had been moved a little and that he could see inside it. There was something hidden there.'

'Madame Dénarnaud told us that Saunière found something in a stone pillar under the altar,' Rahn countered.

'Oh yes, but that comes after,' she said with relish. 'The bell-ringer found something in one of the wooden balusters, which he handed over to Abbé Saunière. In any event, whatever it was it must have made Saunière curious because he asked the bell-ringer to help him look around the rest of the church — something about removing the altar and, as the story goes, upon doing so they found bones and other things, perhaps coins glinting in the hollow beneath the stones. Treasure? Who could say?'

'But doesn't the bell-ringer know what they found?' Rahn asked.

She leant forward. 'He was immediately sent away and told to lock the church doors behind him.' She gave a significant nod as if to say, *you see?*

'All he found were Lourdes medallions, completely worthless, woman!' her husband pointed out, wiping his dripping chin with his wrist. 'You're making a temple out of an outhouse!'

She straightened her back, smoothing down her ample décolletage. 'Well, Saunière may have said that what he found was worthless . . . But if so why did he continue to dig?' She looked down at her nails. 'Night after night.' She stretched out her hand.

'Knee-deep in the graveyard, digging up graves, moving the head-stones, *grave robbing*.' She looked at Rahn. 'And it didn't end until the mayor finally demanded that the Bishop of Carcassonne do something to put a stop to him and that diabolical madame.'

'Madame Dénarnaud was digging in the graveyard?' Eva asked.

Madame Corfu drank down her wine imperiously and dabbed at her mouth with a napkin. She held their eyes, a master of suspense. Rahn had to prevent himself from smiling.

'She did *everything* with him, if you know what I mean! Except that she didn't go with him when he travelled – and he did a lot of travelling too! The word is, he didn't understand what he had found and took it to some trusted friends, men of learning: Abbé Gélis of Coustassa; and Abbé Boudet of Rennes-les-Bains.'

Rahn sat up. If he was not mistaken, these were both on Abbé Cros's list!

The husband glared at his wife, and waving a piece of bread at her, said, 'Don't go talking nonsense!'

Defiance shone in her eyes and she raised her double chin and pursed her lips. 'Shut up! I'll speak as I please!' She turned now to her guests with a pleasant smile.'Do you want to know what happened to Abbé Antoine Gélis?'

Rahn felt a shiver at what her tone implied and, just like in a horror film, at that very moment, the wind howled and shook the shuttered windows, making the fire flap its arms in the hearth like a dying man.

'They found him on the Day of the Dead – tomorrow it marks forty-one years. It happened in 1897.' She leant her corpulence over her plate and looked at her audience. 'He never left the door of the presbytery open and he only let people he knew into the house. So, whoever it was that did it, knew him.'

The mother-in-law with no teeth burst into silent tears and reached for a napkin to dry her eyes but this only made Madame Corfu perversely determined to finish the story.

'Whoever it was that did what?' Eva asked, those dark eyes staring from beneath that fringe. It was amazing to Rahn how easily she moved from detached to vulnerable, from disinterested to full of awe.

'Whoever it was that killed him of course, my dear! I know, because my aunt lives in Coustassa. She was a young woman when it happened. Apparently, he was frightened by something and took to being a hermit, refusing to leave his presbytery and barring the door to all.'

'What was he afraid of?' Rahn pushed aside his plate.

'For a long time,' she continued, 'he was obsessed by something, he didn't tell his family what it was but when they found his diary they saw that he had written over and over in it about having discovered something valuable. At any rate, on that fateful night someone broke into the presbytery – it was somewhere around midnight, on the cusp between All Saints' Day and All Souls' Day. There was not a thing stolen, there was even money in the house left undisturbed.' She crossed her arms. 'The police said it was a mystery.'

'How was he killed?' the girl dared to ask.

Madame Corfu bent back that large head. She had been waiting for that very question. She was poised and ready, sharpening her words on the tip of her tongue before looking at them again with brilliant eyes. 'He was butchered with an axe!'

'Good God!' The words escaped from Eva unbidden and she immediately put a hand to her mouth.

The old woman with no teeth sobbed into her cake and the husband made a frown that would have withered a weed.

The madame smiled a red smudge and shrugged. 'Well, some say it was a fire poker, but there was no murder weapon found. Whatever the murderer used, it did the job and it made a big mess! *Bang! Bang! Bang!*' She thumped her closed fist three times on the table so suddenly and with such vigour that it made every person jump. The old woman got up and took herself out, crying.

Monsieur Corfu threw his hands up in the air. 'I've had enough!' he said, and hurled his napkin onto the table before leaving the dining room.

The madame calmly watched her husband leave but Rahn knew she would not stop now, not while she still had an audience. 'He was struck thirteen times in the back of the head!' she continued with a fiery eye. 'There were bits of brain all over the stove and on the floor – even on the walls! Apparently there was so much blood that the gendarmes were slipping about. Anyway, the interesting thing is what they *found.*'

'What did they find?' Rahn took a breath in, engrossed.

'His slippers were placed next to his head, his arms were crossed over his chest and one leg was bent under him. A tidy fellow, whoever did it! And the only evidence he left was a packet of Tzar cigarette papers beside the body. On the packet, the murderer wrote two words: *Viva Angelina,*' the madame ended, triumphantly.

29

MORE WATSON THAN HOLMES

'You suspect someone?'
'I suspect myself.'
'What!'
'Of coming to conclusions too rapidly.'
Sir Arthur Conan Doyle, 'The Adventure of the Naval Treaty'

In the bedroom Rahn paced up and down like a caged lion in front of the small hearth. The fire glowed but its warmth was meagre against the draughts spawned by the Devil's Wind outside.

'What do you make of it?' Eva said to him.

'Your uncle's list has something to do with the book of Pope Honorius or, as they call it, *Le Serpent Rouge*. As Deodat would say, it is *elementary*.'

'Really? Are you certain you're not jumping to conclusions?'

He told her the phone call to Paris had been to a friend whom he had asked to look into Jean-Louis Verger. He informed her of what La Dame had found out about the connection between *Le Serpent Rouge* and the murder of an archbishop. He told her about the group Abbé Grassaud had mentioned at the hermitage, which was known as the penitents; and that Verger was rumoured to have belonged to this group at the time he committed the murder.

'And now I'm quite certain that Saunière also had something to do with that group.'

'What makes you think that?'

He stopped his pacing to look at her. 'Because when I was alone with Madame Dénarnaud, she said these words: "Penitence, penitence – remember that!"'

'I see . . .' Eva said, from her chair near the bed. 'Who are these penitents?'

'They're a group of Jesuit priests who dabble in rituals of black magic and human sacrifice. The interesting thing is, that the sacrament had a special part to play in these rituals. All sorts of terrible things were done to it, like mixing it with urine and excrement and forcing people to consume it to rid them of evil spirits . . . or perhaps to do the opposite.'

'To inoculate them with evil spirits – to possess them!' she said.

'Yes, that is what I have learnt.'

'So, do you think that's why my uncle scratched that symbol into the tabernacle, to protect it?'

'I think so.'

Her paleness made her lips look all the more red. 'He was afraid,' she said.

'Perhaps he wanted to make certain that when his time came he would have a sacrament that was untainted.'

She turned to the hearth and fell quiet. 'So, you think the priests on the list formed a kind of—'

'Conventicle?' Rahn prompted.

'Yes.'

'Perhaps – let's look at the list again and go through what we know, shall we?' He took the list out of his pocket along with the pencil and gave them to her. 'If you would be so kind as to write down what I tell you, it may help me to get some perspective.' He resumed his pacing. 'Verger was executed in 1857 . . . can you add that date? Antoine Bigou, we know nothing about yet except that he was a contemporary of Saunière's. Now, the next abbé, Grassaud, met Saunière in 1886 when he came to Saint-Paul-de-Fenouillet. I think he has a lot more to do with this than he admitted. Saunière came here to this village in 1885 and sometime later he found something; something so interesting that the Bishop of Carcassonne paid for him to take it to Paris.' He continued to pace. 'We also know that Saunière told two other priests of his discoveries: Abbé Boudet and Abbé Gélis. Gélis wrote something in his diary about treasure and shortly after that he was brutally murdered, in 1897. The next abbé is . . . ?'

'Rivière,' Eva said.

'That's right. He outlived Saunière. He's the one who refused to give him his last sacrament in 1915. He refused because of something he'd apparently heard in Saunière's confession and before he died he told someone that Saunière had gone over to the Devil. What does that mean and what did he hear?' He paused to look at her. 'All of these priests were connected and they all seem to gravitate around Saunière – like the rings of Saturn.'

He went to Eva to look at the list again.

> *Jean-Louis Verger – Paris* 1857
> *Antoine Bigou – Rennes-le-Château*
>
> ~
>
> *A J Grassaud – Saint-Paul-de-Fenouillet* 1886
> *A C Saunière – Rennes-le-Château* 1885
> *A K Boudet – Rennes-les-Bains*
> *A A Gélis – Coustaussa murdered* 1897
> *A L Rivière – Espéraza refused last sacrament* 1915

'These five priests were contemporaries and are set apart from the other two. Why? Perhaps they had a different significance for Abbé Cros.'

'Or perhaps those are the priests my uncle was investigating?'

she said.

'We don't know that with any certainty yet.'

'Do you think Saunière found the Pope's grimoire, *Le Serpent Rouge*?' she asked.

'Or else he found the missing key that we spoke about before, the formula that is missing from the grimoires.'

She watched him take up his pacing again, with a puzzled expression. 'Do you know what this key is?'

'I haven't a clue, but everything we've heard points to it having something to do with the Cathar treasure.'

'If it's been left out of the grimoires intentionally, perhaps it is too evil?'

'That is a very good assumption. I have a sense things will be clearer when we learn something about this Abbé Bigou, the man who sits at the top of the list with Verger. It seems to me that he had a very important part to play in the mystery surrounding these priests.'

But Eva wasn't listening. She was taken by her own thoughts and he had a moment to observe her more closely. She was taller than most women and thinner than was generally considered the ideal, but there was no angularity in her frame and it gave her a look that was almost elf-like. Her face was fine boned and symmetrical, her eyes large and widely spaced, her short hair reflected the firelight in reds and golds. She needed protection, someone who knew what he was doing, and right now Rahn felt more like Sancho Panza than Don Quixote, more like Watson than Holmes. Deodat was right – what good was knowledge without the wisdom to use it? Maybe Satan knew him too well and had surmised that he was good when it came to imponderables but a poor detective when it came to real life.

Eva sighed. 'I need to sleep.'

She was right, there was nothing they could do until morning.

She took the bed and he settled down valiantly in the lumpy, uncomfortable chair. She blew out the candle and he heard her undress in the darkness and get into bed. To be so near to a woman reminded him of his last night with Etienne.

Etienne had always been her nom de guerre. They had met in the circles of Antonin Gadal and thereafter had seen one another occasionally, but it had been four years or more since she had vanished without a trace, and he had stopped thinking about her until recently. Once again, he thought how the motives of women were inscrutable and he wondered how a man could build on such quicksand.

The last time he saw Etienne it was in Berlin where she had come to write an editorial on National Socialism for *La République*. They had celebrated the New Year in grand fashion by going to The Femina Club on Nurnberger Strasse; a club usually frequented by men looking for feminine company. Etienne, true to form, had hung on his arm dressed in a suit and tie like Marlene Dietrich, her hair combed through with pomade. Dressed this way, she hadn't made too many heads turn when they sat down to order a bottle of Sekt, and to conspire about which girl they would invite to the table. There were pneumatic tubes that crisscrossed the room and carried messages, or presents, from patrons on one side, to girls on the other side – all one needed was money and good eyesight. But it had been nothing more than a bit of harmless fun, and they had laughed afterwards. Towards the night's end, as they were walking back to the hotel, Etienne paused to look at him, and Rahn thought she looked almost vulnerable, a strange androgynous creature with the round blue eyes of a hunted doe. She had said to him, 'One day I will leave and you will never see me again . . . You will forgive me, Otto, won't you?'

At the time he had laughed it off and later they had made love affectionately, tenderly. In the morning, however, he woke to find he was alone. He never saw her again.

The Countess P's clock on the table chimed ten times. He sighed and brought his mind to the present. If he was to be of any use to Deodat he had to sleep. Tomorrow he would think about the Rotas wheel, Pierre Plantard, Monti, De Mengel, Abbé Cros, the church, the fish pond, the key to the tabernacle, a symbol to ward off evil, a list of priests, Abbé Grassaud, Gélis bludgeoned to death and the only evidence being a packet of cigarette papers . . . cigarette papers . . . Etienne had been involved with Marxists and she had smoked Russian cigarettes . . . like Pierre Plantard. He remembered the cigarette paper left beside Gélis's body, a Russian brand? He wondered who had killed Gélis and why, and then he remembered the inspector, Beliere. Madame Sabine must have arrived home by now to find the house a shambles, a dead man in the barn and he and Deodat gone! Surely she would have called the gendarmerie at Carcassonne and that meant that to-morrow the inspector, who reminded him of Professor Moriarty, would be on their trail like a bloodhound on a scent. Then again, for whom was the inspector really working?

His eyes grew heavy . . . He thought of the satanic grimoire of Pope Honorius and the missing key sought by a shadowy circle of powerful men – those bankers Deodat had mentioned– sitting in an underground room, smoking Russian cigarettes, making decisions about the fate of the world. He saw their faces: Englishmen, Frenchmen, Russians, Freemasons, Jesuit priests, black magicians . . .

Outside the wind howled, and the trees rapped on the windows in time to the old woman's words: *Penitence – remember that!'*

ISLAND OF THE DEAD

30

NOTHING IS WHAT IT SEEMS

'You do not comprehend?' he said.
'Not I,' I replied.
'Then you are not of the brotherhood.'
Edgar Allan Poe, 'The Cask of Amontillado'

Venice, 2012

'Is it true about those brotherhoods?' I interrupted the Writer of Letters.

He contemplated the fire a moment, tenting his fingers, his face striated by shadow and light. Something about that face, the singular angle of the nose, the mouth and chin, struck me as deeply familiar. I had the sudden sense that he was a miror and that I was looking at myself. The feeling vanished the moment he spoke.

'The first Lodge in Paris, the French Grand Lodge, wasn't started by Frenchmen, it was founded by British merchants. Did you know that?'

I told him that no, I had not heard of it.

'It is interesting, isn't it? In fact, the British founded Lodges all over Europe in the eighteenth century, weaving a web capable of disseminating occult and political impulses. Of course, once a web like this has been spun, it takes only the whisper of one word to set everything in motion.' He threw a log into the fire and gave it a poke. 'For instance, who do you think was behind secretive revolutionary groups like the Carbonari and the Jacobins?'

'Are you suggesting the English were behind the French Revolution?' I was incredulous.

'Would that be so preposterous?'

'For one thing, it would rewrite history.'

'And would you consider that a bad thing?'

I smiled. 'Who knows?'

'The truth is—' he looked at me pointedly, '—the English Lodges were also behind the American Revolution.'

'But that doesn't make sense,' I told him. 'It wasn't in the interest of the English to lose America.'

'Who said they lost anything?' The fire in the hearth blazed now as if he had conjured the flames. He then said, quite fittingly, 'From the ashes was born the phoenix – the replacement of a physical aristocracy with a spiritual one: an aristocracy of the Lodges working behind the façade of democracy. In other words, the Lodges were the puppet masters of the new world. It is well known that Benjamin Franklin was a Mason, as were most of the founding fathers. Now . . . many of these men had fine intentions but there were also those whose intentions were not fine; those who wanted to gain power over the many on behalf of the few by using a means that lies hidden in the Lodges.'

'What *means*?'

'The power of magic.'

I considered this.

'Why do you look so amazed?' He laughed, but it was cold and cheerless. 'Every time you go into a church you are exposed to ceremonial magic: incense, song, mantras; they're all magical, any priest will admit it, and so are the rites and rituals of the Masons. Now, I'm not suggesting they're all the same. There are white, grey and black ceremonies.'

'And the book of Pope Honorius?'

'It is the blackest, in some respects.'

'Because it mixes the rituals of the Catholic mass with the rituals of black magic?' I asked.

'What you have to understand is that white magic doesn't trespass on human freedom – it is based upon the premise that human will is free, but because the will lies asleep in the human being, it can be seized, pulled out and manipulated by the black magician – an example of this is hypnotism. Now, this will in the human being is also a form of energy – a form of magnetism. A similar type of magnetism is found in the Earth. Have you heard of kundalini?'

'The yogis achieved enlightenment through it, am I right?'

'That's right, they called it the fire that works upwards from the base of the human spine to the head – like a fiery snake. A similar fire, or magnetism, runs upwards from the centre of the Earth and becomes trapped within those great mountain ranges that are aligned towards the magnetic north. Rahn was working on a report written by De Mengel about grid lines and ley lines of energy – places where magnetic forces become exceptionally strong. Black magic rituals connect these forces in the Earth with the same forces in the human being, and you can't imagine the untold power this gives to the magician capable of manipulating it.'

'I remember something about the Templars and the building of churches . . .'

'The Templars built their churches on locations they knew were potent, magnetically, hoping to redeem the rising forces of the Black Mother.'

I sat forward, amazed. *The Black Mother* . . . is that why there are so many churches devoted to the Black Madonna – Chartres for instance?'

'Yes, didn't you know that?'

'You are opening up a universe to me,' I admitted.

'Those who built these churches understood that the Black Mother is the Earth's kundalini – this is what makes a place like Wewelsburg powerful.'

I was speechless, breathless. I wanted to laugh out loud like Rahn. At least to shout 'Aha!' I didn't, of course.

'Even Matteu didn't realise how close he had come with his *Song of the Grail,* which portrays how Esclarmonde de Foix sealed the Grail inside a mountain. But to understand that we have to move onto another gallery, and this one is called The Abbot. The abbot of the monastery of Saint Lazarus.'

I sat up, surprised and puzzled. 'I know that monastery! I've written a novel about it!'

'Yes . . . of course you have,' he said, with raised brows. 'You also had the Grail locked in a mountain, didn't you?'

'I don't understand where this is going.'

'You will.'

31

THE ABBOT

'Death on the summit of the hills struck from the sky:
The abbot will die when he will see ruined
Those of the wreck wishing to seize the rock.'
Nostradamus, Century II Quatrain 56

Monastery of Saint Lazarus, 1244

The monastery was hung with low cloud and stood sequestered in the bosom of the mountains like a creature grown from out of the snow. So hidden was it from the world of ordinary men and so protected by false paths that, even with a guide, it took the four men and the child all day to reach the foot of it; and then it was long past compline before they knocked at the great gate.

The gatekeeper, having sat hours in the gatehouse awaiting their arrival, took no time in allowing them passage. The stable hand took the horses and a monk was fetched to lead them over the white-covered grounds towards the edificium, whose tall shape loomed under that low sky like a reproach from Heaven.

They entered through a portal leading into dark cloisters and the sound of their footfalls over those damp stones made a resonance that appeared to stir the sleeping creature of the monastery to wakefulness: with each step a candle was lit in the upper rooms and the sound of one more hushed voice was added to the hum of other voices coming from unseen corners.

Matteu walked behind the monk, hugging his cloak to him to keep out the bitter air, until they came to a large apartment warmed by a great fire. The flames yawned and spat and roared at the darkness.

A number of cowled shapes were grouped around a canopied bed; their shadows danced on the walls and ceiling to the sound of a low and mystic chant. When Matteu approached the bed, the monks parted like a black sea, allowing him access to a man whose bony frame was overwhelmed by coverlets and sheepskins. Numerous candles barely illuminated the head drowned beneath a skullcap, the face bloated and red with fever, the eyes closed and sunk deep into the lines around them.

Time passed. Matteu thought he had come too late. The old abbot would not return from his journey towards Heaven and Matteu's heart gave a lurch then, rent by the weight of responsibility.

The infirmarian looked at Matteu and shook his head. There was nothing he could do, his face told him. He gestured for the priest to resume his prayers.

At that moment the soul of the old man made his eyes come open and an expression of recognition passed over the fever-worn face. 'Matteu? Is that you?' he said then. 'Come . . . closer!' He tried to raise his head and the exertion caused a strangled cough to erupt from his parched throat, leaving a streak of blood over the pale lips.

Matteu bent his head close, and when those infirm eyes focused on the form before them, they welled with tears and a gasp escaped from the feverish mouth. The old man raised a hand. The brothers, knowing the signal, gathered to them their prayers and moved out of the room in single file.

'Tell it to me quickly — this carcass is impatient and will not last.'

Matteu leant close and his lips almost touched that hot ear. 'He is here.'

'Where, where?' the dying man said, looking about with milky eyes.

Matteu went to fetch the boy and brought him to the bedside.

The abbot reached out a hand to touch the boy's cheek. 'Praise our Lord! This is Isobel's child? Oh! He once stood beneath the cross! The reincarnation of Saint John!'

Matteu led the child back to the others.

'You've done well, Matteu. Now, tell me of our cousins?'

'They are all dead.' Matteu found the words hard to say.

'All? And cousin Marty?'

'In one great pyre . . . at the foot of the château.'

The old man closed his eyes and began a quiet weeping. He looked away from Matteu and said, 'Who are these others who have come with you?'

'Four perfects, the guardians, the last of those taught by Marty.'

He nodded and lay back, exhausted. 'They have a home here, if they wish it,' he said.

'I have something for safekeeping.' Matteu reached into the sack he carried over his shoulder and brought out the scrolls Marty had given him.

The old man reached out a hand to grasp Matteu's arm. 'What is this?'

'Written by brother Marty.' He reached in again and brought out the treasure.

'Is this . . .?' The old man looked up and his eyes were full of fear. 'But you must take it away from here!' he cried.

Matteu was surprised. 'I don't understand. Where shall I take it?'

But the old man coughed so hard that he lost his grip on Matteu's arm. He seemed to lose his breath and his eyes widened and loosened and took one last hold of Matteu's own.

A moment later, the old man lay still.

Matteu waited. His heart fluttered in his chest like that of a frightened hare, his breathing stopped and the blood threaded through his veins in small degrees.

The old man said nothing more.

He put a hand to the centenarian's mouth – no coming and going of breath. His head went into a fog. He must gather his thoughts together. He said a pater noster and took himself to the door of the chamber to call for the infirmarian.

By the time the bells tolled the abbot's death, the gates were opening to allow Matteu's passage out of the monastery. He hesitated a moment. Where was it safe to take it? Where should he go?

A thought came to him then: his song of Esclarmonde de Foix, and the Grail that fell into the bosom of the mountains for safekeeping. He pointed his horse away from the monastery, towards the mountains and the caves of Lombrives.

32

UNDERWORLD

*'Of the dungeons there had been strange things narrated, fables
I had always deemed them, but yet strange,
and too ghastly to repeat, save in a whisper.'*
Edgar Allan Poe, 'The Pit and the Pendulum'

Rennes-le-Château, 1938

Rahn slept fitfully. He dreamt that Deodat was inside a dark place. He could hear people weeping, some were reciting prayers. He sensed they were all doomed to die and that Deodat would die with them. Into his dream came these words:

Jesus, you remedy against our pains and only hope for our repentance . . .

He woke in a cold sweat. The uncomfortable chair had taken its toll on his muscles. He could hear Eva sleeping soundly in her bed and looked about in the shadows, trying to remember the dream. There was something about a monastery, and a cave . . .

Deodat was in peril!

Years ago, he and Deodat had been to the caves of Lombrives. They had seen the bones of the Cathars who had died in those caves. Some skeletons were arranged like the spokes of a wheel, their heads to the centre and their feet raying out like a sun.

He sighed. He had to get up and return to that awful church

despite his revulsion. He suspected that Deodat's life depended on his finding out whatever it was that Saunière had discovered, and he wanted to see if the answer lay in the word penitence. He had to find out now – while the village slept and he could look about undisturbed.

Outside the world was windblown and angry, lit now and again by a waxing gibbous moon peeking out from behind thick clouds. Branches had fallen along the path and leaves crackled under his feet and the elements seemed alive. A feeling of dread passed over him, this was the second time he would be going into a church at night in as many days. Moreover, this time he would be alone; even so, he would have to find the strength . . . for Deodat's sake.

It took him a time to reach the church and a part of him wasn't at all relieved to find it unlocked. Once inside, the feeling of dread was multiplied. The desire to sneeze was overwhelming and, as he passed Asmodeus in the shadows, he was unable to contain it. The sound reverberated around the room as if a bomb had struck it. He paused, his every nerve raw and prickling. The wind whistled. He shivered with cold, he was tired and foggy from a lack of sleep, his eyes watered and there was a pounding in his head.

Penitence . . . penitence . . .

He made his way down the nave to the choir enclosures, sniffling. Taking a candlestick from the altar, he bent its light to the relief of the Magdalene. He wanted to see the inscription.

Jesus, you remedy against our pains and only hope for our repentance, it is by means of Magdalene's tears that you wash our sins away.

His dream!

He tried to reason: repentance . . . a sinner goes to confession to repent and to ask for forgiveness, thereby he becomes a penitent; a penitent by means of Magdalene's tears. Through these tears, sins are washed away. He looked up. The stained-glass window above the altar had Mary Magdalene anointing Christ's feet.

Magdalene had washed Christ's feet with her tears, and anointed them because she was the Magdala or the tower that connected Heaven with Earth; she had possessed the power of service. Christ also washed the feet of his disciples to make them clean . . . like the soul is clean after confession . . . confessional – the confessional!

He turned around and looked down the nave to the confessional. It was directly opposite the altar – was this significant? Trying to think of nothing else, he made his way to it. It was a large structure made of oak and above it he could barely see the large coloured bas-relief of the Sermon on the Mount. There were three cubicles: the middle cubicle for the priest and those for the penitents on either side. He let the light of the candle illuminate the small space inside the left cubicle; it was wide enough for a person to kneel on a fixed padded step. There seemed to be nothing here of interest. The other penitent's cubicle was the same. The old woman had said penitence and the entire church seemed to be devoted to Magdalene and to penitence, but perhaps he shouldn't be looking for the one who performs penitence but for the one who remedies sins. The priest was the representative of Christ and he took His place during a confession. He was tenet – he was crucial.

Rahn entered the middle cubicle. On the floor was a worn rug nailed in place. Rahn lifted its edge and it came away enough for him to see that a hatch had been cut out of the floorboards. He tore the rest of the rug away to reveal the entire hatch. He lifted the lid and this released a rush of damp, stale air into his face. He lowered the candle through the opening. He could barely see the curve of a narrow flight of stone steps leading down. He smiled and, setting the hatch lid to one side, squeezed through the opening.

The steps were slippery with moss and he half stumbled to the bottom step. Still holding his candle, he stood in a large natural cavity beneath the church, only just high enough in places for a grown man to stand without stooping. In the flickering light he glimpsed open tombs, partly submerged in water, their covering slabs discarded. The crypt seemed to follow the dimensions of the church above it. As above, so is below – the old Hermetic maxim came to his mind. He could hear an echo of water dripping. When he stepped into it the water was high enough to cover his shoes and as it seeped into his feet he cringed from cold. He walked, mindful of his step and invisible submerged debris, until he came to more steps – the hatch in the confessional wasn't the only way into the crypt. He guessed this access must come out somewhere near the pulpit. He continued, feeling in his element, moving with confidence over tree roots and rotted wood beams until he came to another set of steps leading up to the church. These steps must come out somewhere near the sacristy. There were three entrances!

He also noticed a stain on the wood columns supporting the floor of the church; this crypt was subject to flooding and he could see that the water had reached as high as his shoulder. The old madame told him earlier that Saunière had done some work to shore up the foundations of the church because of the water, now he understood. It also made sense of the network of cisterns that fed the gardens above, as the abbé had mentioned.

Returning, he approached an open tomb and looked into it; it was full of old bones, dirt and debris. As he inspected it he heard something, a whisper of a sound. A voice. He listened but all was still again. His nerves were on edge – was he hearing things? No, there it was again!

He put out his candle and crouched down behind the tomb.

Someone had entered through the hatch and was coming down the stairs!

He tried not to breathe because in the cold his breath formed clouds of condensation around him – a giveaway.

He heard a stumble and then a splash.

'Where are you?'

Eva!

He relaxed and in a moment his fear was replaced by annoyance. 'What are you doing here?' he said, stepping out from behind the tomb, feeling less than the courageous hero. 'Well?'

She had slipped but luckily her candle had not gone out. Her hair was wet and her cheeks were flushed. She looked exhilarated.

'I heard you leave the room. How do you expect me to sleep? You were calling out "penitence" all night long! I knew you would come back to the church, so when I saw the door to the confessional open . . .' She looked about her. 'This is remarkable! How did you figure it out? Is this the tomb of the Visigoth – Sigisbert?'

'I haven't found anything yet to prove it,' he said curtly, 'one way or the other. But if there's ever been any treasure here it's gone now, ransacked. See the pickaxes and shovels resting against those walls? There's been a lot of digging and I suspect it wasn't all just to shore up the church. It looks like Saunière wasn't only grave robbing above, but also below.'

'Looking for what? Hadn't he already found something in the church?'

'I don't know.'

'All this water – where does it come from?'

'There's an underground spring. I suspect this place is practically floating on water.'

'So what now?'

'Again, I don't know.'

Rahn lit his candle from hers and in doing so noticed something he hadn't seen when he had descended those steps. Some distance from the steps leading to the confessional the wall grew darker at one point. He walked through the water to it and discovered a narrow tunnel. He figured it must lead under the church and away from the crypt in the direction, he guessed, of the cemetery. He looked down. The water seemed deeper here and this made him cautious. He couldn't imagine why it would be deeper. Every potholer knows that rainfall above can end up inundating a cave below in a matter of minutes. But it had been utterly dry when he'd left the house to come to the church, so he surmised that he was standing in a natural depression in the floor of the crypt.

He resolved to see where this tunnel led and began to make his way into it.

'Wait, I'm coming with you!' Eva said.

He turned around, irritated. 'Certainly not! I forbid it.'

She laughed. 'You *what*?'

'I mean, I beg you to go back up where it's safe to wait for me. If I don't come back in an hour send a search party.' He turned around again, but was halted by her insistent voice.

'No matter what you say, I'm coming.'

'I won't allow it,' he said, but it sounded feeble. 'It's far too dangerous.'

She met his look with an unruffled mien. 'I'm coming!'

'This shaft is likely to lead to another crypt as singularly unfruitful as this one and it's important that I have someone who can call for help should I run into trouble,' he said, but something told him that logic would get him nowhere at all.

'I have a hunch you'll need me.'

'You and your hunches!'

He wasn't used to women, let alone potholing with women, and he doubted that their sex was capable of it, considering most of them lacked any sense of direction and had an abhorrence of things that liked to have their abodes in holes. But he sensed she was going to hold her ground and he didn't have time to argue with her, so he entered the tunnel with her following close behind and hoped for the best.

'Why are the two crypts so far apart? It doesn't make sense,' she said, behind him.

'Noble women were never buried with their men, for obvious

reasons.'

'I can well imagine that being holed up for eternity with controlling, egotistic, ignorant men would have sounded as unappealing to the dames of yesteryear as it does to the women of today.'

He paused in his tracks. 'Are you certain you wouldn't like to go back and stand guard?'

'Absolutely not! I'm enjoying being your partner in crime.'

He grunted.

The ground was drier here and seemed to rise a little. Eva stumbled on something and gasped. It was a skull. Rahn picked it up. It had a gash on the temple. 'An ossarium!' he said with glee, showing her.

It seemed to fascinate her and she took it from his hand for closer inspection. 'Alas, poor Yorick,' she said. 'It looks old.'

'Yes, I think this place is ancient. The Visigoths liked to bury their dead in underground places. Look!' The flickering candle-light illuminated more skulls and bones, heaped one over the other, lining the walls of the tunnel. 'Just like the catacombs of Paris! A lot of people died here during the war with the Franks, not to mention the Cathar wars and the Great War. They had to store the bones somewhere.'

At this point the shaft narrowed abruptly and they had to walk in single file, sometimes having to squeeze through a tight opening. He predicted that they would soon come to a dead end and have to track back since the air was stagnant and oppressively humid. He took off his jacket and carried it in his hands, moving ahead with caution. Above them, the roots of trees and other vegetation poked through the dirt, catching in their hair and clothes. Below, the rocks and debris made their progress slow and tedious.

Rahn came to an abrupt stop.

'What is it?' Eva said.

'Look for yourself!' he said happily, shining the light of his candle on the matter at hand. The girl did not gasp as he had expected and this disconcerted him. The low ceiling and the sides of the shaft were completely covered in a black mass that consisted of a tangle of legs and hairy bodies. Some of the creatures dangled and dropped at their feet, while above whole clusters sat on lacy webs.

'It's a large nest of spiders, see the egg sacks?' Rahn said.

'What are you going to do?' He thought he could hear a smile in her voice and it irritated him.

'Here,' he said, 'back up, and give me your candle.'

'Why?'

'Mademoiselle, you can turn around and go back if you like but I intend to go on and I need your candle for just one moment. If you please.'

'As you wish,' she said. 'But you haven't told me what you're going to do.'

'I'm going to burn them.'

'You're going to cremate them?'

'Would you rather walk through them and have them crawling all over you? I assure you that their bite is quite painful.'

She gave him the candle and he placed a candle to each wall simultaneously. It was not a pleasant scene. The mass of bodies caught alight creating an arch of fire. Rahn braced himself for the sound.

'Do they always squeal like that?' she said, unperturbed.

'Yes.'

There was a frenzy and those spiders that had not been consumed by the conflagration moved off almost magically, leaving only an acrid smell.

He gave Eva her candle. 'That was easy,' he said merrily. 'Far easier than a nest of snakes, or rats. Why, I remember there was a cave at Ornolac that—'

She was looking at him with a singular expression.

'What?'

'You have one on your head,' she said.

259

He scrambled to get it off and stomped on it until it was nothing more than a brown stain.

'Yes, frightening indeed!' she said, and walked ahead.

Rahn gathered what pride he had to him and followed. *This girl is something else!*

As Rahn had foreseen, the tunnel came to an end. It looked like someone had tried to wall up what might have once been an entrance to another chamber. When he inspected it further, he found a short, narrow opening in the wall at head height. He managed to pull down some rocks, and shone his candle into it. He had been right, there was another chamber behind it. He was in his element: his heart pounded with excitement and this made his head throb. He looked around but there was nothing on which he could stand.

'I'll give you a hoist,' the girl said.

'What? Nonsense!' he answered. He tried to lift himself up but it was too hard.

'Like this – just put one foot here and I'll hoist you up. I said you would need me.' She was smiling as she held out her laced hands for him. 'Am I going to wait all day?'

With Eva's help he was soon scrambling through the aperture. He told her to wait for him and fell into a round chamber for his efforts. He walked about the perimeter, looking to the centre and couldn't believe his eyes. A circular depression had been cut into the floor of the rock that looked just like the one at Wewelsburg, only half the size. He was filled with a nauseating memory: the man pleading for the life of his children; Himmler grimacing; the sounds of shots.

'Are you alright?' Eva said, behind him.

'I thought I told you . . . wait a minute, how on Earth did you get here?'

'I'm very athletic. Look,' she said, pointing to the walls. 'What are these?'

Still vexed, he took his candle to the symbols drawn on the

walls. 'I've seen them before, in grimoires. This is proof that we're on the right track! This crypt has been used for black magic rituals.'

'But why here, in the tombs of the dames?'

'Remember, the Order of penitents that Saunière and Jean-Louis Verger belonged to supposedly had a copy of *Le Serpent Rouge*, the pope's grimoire; this same order was involved in saying masses for the dead and the sacrament . . . the sacrament given to the dying. The pagans conducted their funerary rites near tombs or underground and I'll bet the penitents did too. Black magicians, you see, don't only use demons, phantoms, ghosts and elemental beings for their infernal ends. I'm beginning to think they also use the dead.'

She was silent, perhaps horror-struck.

He continued, 'They invoke the spirits of the dead, or those who are in limbo, the living dead.'

'Like in séances?'

'I think so. I'm afraid this is not my line of expertise, but I'm learning fast.' He looked about for another exit. 'Saunière must have tried to get to this crypt through the graveyard. That would explain all the digging.'

'But why not just come through the other crypt?'

'Did you see all the water? That crypt must fill up when it rains. That's what the young Abbé Lucien told us yesterday. This town is riddled with tunnels and cisterns – a catchment that supplies water to the residents.'

Eve looked into the circular depression. 'What's that? Is that stained with what I think it is?'

'It's a ceremonial pit and yes, that's blood.' But when he shone the candle into it he was taken aback by what he saw.

'What is it?' she asked.

'Look for yourself!'

The stone in the depression had been carved to depict a circular version of the Sator Square:

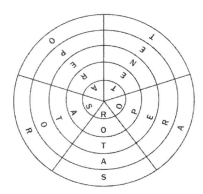

'They've circled the square,' Rahn said. 'But that's not all. See the floor up here? It's been marked in the shape of a penta-gram and a hexagram inside a square. Outside that a larger cir-cle completes it.' He showed her. The smaller circle is the soul; the square represents water, fire, earth, air; the pentagram points to the etheric forces, the forces the alchemists say are related to warmth, light, sound and life. These forces run through the hands, feet and head, just like Leonardo da Vinci drew in his Vit-ruvian Man, but they are also found in the Earth; and the hexa-gram represents the astral forces, the forces of thinking, feeling, and willing. These signs all form a *protection* for the one perform-ing the ritual sacrifice.'

'I just had a thought. That little patch in the cemetery for un-baptised children—'

'Don't think about that,' he said quickly. 'They use mostly ani-mals: goats or kids, chickens, sheep; that sort of thing.' But in his heart he felt a tremble. *'Kids' in grimoires actually meant children . . .*

They both heard something and paused.

'What's that?' she said.

He knew what it was, he'd heard it before and it had nearly cost him his life. He looked at her. 'When you came to the church was it raining?'

262

'Yes, it was falling down like buckets!'

'In that case we had better go, and now!'

'What's wrong?'

'A flash flood. This chamber is protected by the wall.'

'You mean we'll be trapped?'

Finally — the girl sounds ill at ease! 'Not if we hurry. Come on!' he said, grabbing her arm.

He led the way out of the crypt and waited for Eva to climb down through the opening first. By the time they were halfway through the first part of the tunnel, the water had reached Rahn's knees. It was unbearably cold. Rahn could hardly feel his feet and he was trembling. Eva followed, stumbling in the near dark.

'How does it happen so quickly?' she said.

'I was caught in the caves of Ornolac during a rainstorm. I hit my head,' he said, between breaths, 'and I only survived because a Senegalese friend, a man who is almost a giant, carried me on his shoulder through the channels swollen with water. He carried me for miles! Hard to believe, but true.'

Eventually, they emerged from the tunnel and found the steps that led to the confessional. The water was waist-high here, too close for comfort, Rahn thought, but when the opening above became visible, he made an awful discovery.

'Someone has locked the hatch!' he said.

'What?'

'The hatch! The hatch is locked! But I saw two more exits. Wait here. And don't worry, as I said, I'm used to things like this.' He left her shivering on the topmost steps, encroached upon by the rising water.

Moving through floating bones and other debris, with the candlestick held high over the water in one hand and his jacket in the other, he took an eternity to make his way to the other steps he had seen earlier. No luck! These only led to a boarded-up sub-floor. Immersing his shivering limbs back into the water he looked for the third set of steps. If he found that boarded-up as well, then things were not going to work out in their favour. To his great relief these steps led upwards in a spiral to a small room full of bric-a-brac.

He descended again quickly. 'I've found it!' he called out, and made a hasty journey across the flooded crypt holding the candle out before him.

His return with Eva was difficult because the water was now nearly at the level of his chest and he had to help her through the mud and debris, bones and swimming rats and floating spiders. All this while trying not to trip on submerged obstacles, keeping his candle lit and, most importantly, his coat dry. By the time they reached those steps, however, Rahn had dropped his candle into the water, and Eva's had gone out, leaving them in utter darkness. His legs and hands were numb and he had to find fresh reserves of strength in order to drag Eva, who was now listless, up the steps and into the room.

The room felt narrow and smelt stuffy. He could see almost nothing except that the walls appeared to be whitewashed and the floor underfoot felt like compacted dirt. There was a small window, which was hardly sufficient for ventilation or light. The only way out was what looked like a door or hatch at the top of another set of steps.

'Where are we?' Her voice sounded sleepy and drugged, and this alarmed him. He placed his jacket over her shoulders.

'That way must lead into the sacristy.' Rahn pointed to a door. 'This must be a second secret way in and out of the crypt.'

He was mentally prepared for it to be locked and so when he found that it opened easily into a small closet, he was so relieved he nearly fainted. He had to get past a number of musty priest's robes in order to find a second door, through which he emerged into the sacristy. He returned to help the poor shaking girl.

The door leading to the sacristy from the church opened out into the area between the statue of Saint Anthony of Padua and the altar enclosure. The priest had said that the tomb of Sigisbert lay somewhere beyond it, perhaps because he knew that, behind that false wall in the sacristy closet, there was a way to the crypt.

The church seemed to be bursting with light compared to the darkness of the sacristy. Rahn made certain there was no one in sight. Someone had locked the hatch and they might still be in the church. Luckily for them, whoever it was either didn't know about the second entrance or didn't think he and Eva would be able to find it. Peering down the nave, he realised the pulpit had been built over the second entrance. Perhaps by Saunière, wishing to keep it secret? These thoughts ran through his mind in the time it took for him to blink. He felt his old fear rising up. He tried to calm himself. There was sweat forming over his brow. Having survived being trapped and nearly drowned in a crypt hadn't made him any braver when it came to churches. But he could hear his teeth chattering and he knew he had to get out of his wet clothes, or he would succumb to the cold himself.

'What are you waiting for?' Eva shivered next to him.

Rahn took her arm and the two of them made their way out of the church and into the awful night, frozen to the bone, toiling through the wind and rain back to the house. Rahn helped her up the stairs, got the fire going in the little hearth and gently helped her out of her soaking clothes and into the bed. He took off his own wet things and found a spare blanket, which he swung over his shoulders, moving the chair closer to the fire for warmth.

'Please, get on the bed, won't you?' Eva said, surprising him. She held out her hand, long and slender like the rest of her.

He hesitated. *She isn't in her right mind and might regret this in the morning.*

'I'm afraid I—'

'Please!' she said. 'I'm so cold!'

Falteringly, he lay on the bed over the covers. He lay there rather stiffly, not knowing what to do. Arousal was the furthest thing from his mind; after all, she was under a score of blankets and besides, Rahn's body had taken a battering these last few hours and he doubted that it would obey him, even if he could stop thinking for a moment to sense the stirring of desire. Also, he felt enormously guilty for having dragged her and Deodat into this mess and he was not about to compound it by taking advantage of her when she wasn't in her right mind.

'Do you believe in the Devil?' Eva said to him.

'The Devil . . . you mean Lucifer, the one that was cast out of Heaven? Well . . . yes, I do believe in him.'

'Lucifer,' she said sleepily. 'Isn't he the one who absconded with Isis, the keeper of God's wisdom?'

'Yes, you see it in fables and fairy tales – the damsel in distress who is eventually rescued from the dragon by a hero; the damsel is a symbol, she represents a man's soul.'

'Really? And the dragon?'

'The Cathars told a story to their children – would you like to hear it?'

'Mmm.' She drew near to him, he could feel her warm breath on his cheek.

'It went like this,' he said, softly. 'The good gods of light created human beings and sent them to Earth, where lived the dark dragon of matter. When the dragon swallowed mankind whole, a seed was planted in it for its redemption because inside it now there was not merely darkness, but light as well.'

'I see, so, to redeem the dragon you have to get inside it, you have to enter into its belly . . . is that what the story means?' She yawned.

'Yes, before you can find Heaven you have to go through Hell, because Hell tests the nature of a man.'

Eva said, almost inaudibly, drifting off, 'And if you were to save me from the dragon, you'd be saving yourself, because I am really your soul . . .'

'I would be saving all that was holy and beautiful and virginal in me, do you see?'

But no answer came, Eva was asleep.

He waited for her breathing to become regular and more rhythmic before allowing fatigue to overtake him. Soon he was dreaming that Etienne was in his arms, thin and angular and beautiful. It was once more their last night together. She moved away from him and lit a Russian cigarette and looked at him through the velvet darkness and her face melted away a moment, revealing the deformed grimace of a devil whose mouth opened wide in a terrible screech – *Viva Angelina!*

Rahn woke with a start. Eva was not in the bed but he had no time to think on this particular strangeness because there was a clanging of the church bells that tore through the birthing day like a cataclysm. With his nerves still raw and on alert from his dream, he jumped out of bed and changed into his only dry clothes. Soon he was out in the streets meeting the confused faces of others, who, like him, had come to see what the noise was about. Something was wrong, terribly wrong. Where was Eva? He pushed his way to the church just in time to see the young priest stepping out, looking pale and out of sorts.

The sun was rising now and a faint light came through the windblown trees.

'What is it?' Rahn said to the stunned abbé.

'In the church,' he managed to say. 'It is horrible!'

Rahn hurried through the door, past the devil's stoup and, with the confessional and the grand relief of the Sermon on the Mount behind him, he paused to look down the central nave. Breathless, cold, anxious, exhausted, he tried to see but it took a moment to adjust his eyes. His fear of churches momentarily forgotten, he hurried over the chequered tiles to the enclosure, seeing a little more and then a little more, until he paused.

What he saw made the old woman's words return to his mind. *Beware of that raven!*

33

BLOOD ON THE ALTAR

'It's devilish Mr Holmes, devilish!' cried Mortimer Tregennis.
'It is not of this world.'
Sir Arthur Conan Doyle, 'The Adventure of the Devil's Foot'

A man approached, announcing in a tedious and perfunctory manner that he was the mayor and wanted to know what was going on.

When he saw what Rahn could see he cried, 'Mon Dieu! Wicked priests! Wicked priests are born again as ravens! Saunière!' He sank to his knees, crossing himself.

Rahn ignored him and concentrated on the scene before him. A black raven had been sliced open and its carcass was hanging from the crucifix by a cord tied around its neck. Below, on the altar, someone had placed a white cloth on which a symbol, a circle and a cross, had been drawn in blood. In each quadrant letters were drawn that when read clockwise formed the word AGLA

Beside him, the mayor awoke to his civic duty and sent all the townspeople to their homes, commandeering two men to take down the bird and the white sheet and its contents and to burn them outside the town gates.

In the meantime Rahn looked for Abbé Lucien and found him at his presbytery, keeping company with the last person Rahn would have expected. It was Eva, looking spritely and, for all intents and purposes, not at all touched by their shared nocturnal ordeal.

'Hello Otto, I woke earlier and went for a walk. I returned immediately when I heard the bells. What a terrible upset!' she said, taking the kettle off the hob to make tea.

The abbé looked distraught and gestured for Rahn to sit at the table with him, perhaps the same table at which Saunière had once sat before his fire. Rahn acquiesced and, pushing aside his suspicions, tried to formulate his thoughts into questions.

'She went too far this time! To desecrate a church on All Saints' Day! Pure evil,' the abbé said, shaking his head, his blond eyelashes batting nervously.

'Who do you mean?' Rahn said to him.

'Madame Dénarnaud of course, who else?' He blushed with anger. 'I saw her last night. I was coming back from the mayor's house on my way to the presbytery and I saw her at the church.'

'What time was that?' Eva sat down, her good-natured domesticity disappearing in the wake of a cool detached curiosity that made her brown eyes brilliant, like two burning coals.

'Quite late; you see I ate at the mayor's house, as I do every week. We usually play cards, a bit of harmless fun. It must have been well past midnight. It was raining and the wind was wild, as you know, and the woman looked wet through and I thought she might be sleepwalking because she is known for it. She told me she had been praying in the church but I doubted it. I offered to help her to the villa but she told me to go to Hell!' He shrugged.

'I would have locked the church, as I usually do before going to bed but I realised I didn't have the keys, so I decided to leave it. The mayor is trying to call the police but the telephone lines came down in the storm.'

Rahn sat forward. 'I doubt if Madame Dénarnaud could reach as high as the crucifix to hang the raven without help.' But Rahn remembered the madame's words: *Beware of that raven.* And he couldn't deny that it all sounded suspicious. He rubbed his sore head. 'Do you know why the mayor's first impression on seeing the bird was to say that it was Saunière?'

The young abbé shrugged. 'Why don't you ask him?'

'Abbé, what did Saunière find in that church?'

He looked up. 'What has that to do with anything?'

'All I know is, two men are dead in as many days and now this sign in the church—'

'Two men?'

'The Abbé Cros and another man.'

'What connection could there be between the death of the Abbé Cros at Bugarach and this horrible desecration?' He frowned then and something must have occurred to him, because he looked at both of them and said, 'Who are you? Why are you here?'

'We want to know what Saunière found,' Eva said.

'Treasure hunters! I should have known.'

'Listen,' Rahn said, 'some years ago Cros was investigating Saunière and a number of priests here in the Roussillon. He left a list of names. We think the investigation had something to do with what Saunière found here.'

'I'll tell you nothing at all!' The abbé crossed his arms, as stubborn as a child.

'But Abbé, if you don't help us, a third man may die. A good friend of mine, the magistrate of Arques, and it will be on your head.'

The abbé put a shaking hand to his brow and seemed on the

verge of tears. 'Can I see the list?'

'In a moment, but first you must tell us what you know.'

'All I know is what everybody knows, that Saunière found something when the workers moved the Visigoth pillar to replace the altar during the church renovations—'

'Not the wooden baluster?' Rahn asked.

'Look, whatever he found, it made him rich. Pillar, baluster, it makes no difference! I told you before, the villa, the tower, the church – he built all of it and also renovated the presbytery and the gardens. How could a priest afford to do all this with what he earned from selling masses for the dead, which is what he was accused of doing? How much can one make in a village this size, with no more than a hundred people? He couldn't have made so much money – unless he had made a pact with the Devil.'

Rahn raised his brow.

'You might think this unbelievable, but I think it is true.' The abbé looked down into his cooling tea. 'In fact, this rumour has saved me from boredom, God forgive me! You can imagine, this is not a stimulating place to live, even for a priest, and so when I first arrived here I passed the time sorting through the files left behind by previous abbés, looking for clues. I came across a diary belonging to Abbé Saunière. When I asked Madame Dénarnaud about it, she turned wild. She demanded that I give it to her immediately but I refused and she has behaved rather abominably towards me ever since. The old hag thinks everything that once belonged to Saunière is hers for the taking, just because she inherited everything else. I told her, the diary belongs to the church archives and I refused to part with it. Do you know what she said? She said she would put a curse on me! Some say she and Saunière were lovers but I don't believe it; I think there was a far more sinister union, which I dare not mention for staining my soul.'

'Where's the diary?' Rahn said, leaning forward slightly.

'If I show you that, will you show me the list?'

Rahn nodded, wary.

When he was gone, Rahn looked at Eva, expecting to see some shared warmth, some conspiratorial acknowledgement of their intimacy, but there seemed to be no trace of that vulnerable girl of the night before. Her eyes betrayed nothing at all, as if the memory of it had been erased from her mind.

She said, 'You don't honestly think it was the madame who did that to the church. The old woman can hardly walk!'

Rahn shook his head and whispered: 'She's not as feeble, nor as stupid, as she looks. Yesterday, when you went to fetch her a blanket, while the abbé was out of earshot, she said to me, "Beware of that raven" – referring to the abbé. What happens next? We find a raven hanging on the altar, with its bowels cut out!'

He could say nothing more because the young abbé returned, carrying a small book in his hands and a blush over his cheeks.

'All is made clear,' he said, 'once you know the chronology in this diary. Saunière spent an incredible sum and wrote a timeline for all his renovations from the start, which was 1886, until the finish, 1891. It all begins when he visits Abbé Boudet. Here he says, "*The abbé encouraged my desire to commence renovations as soon as possible.*"

'After that he finds something hidden in the church and then removes the altar, whereupon a short time later he begins to work on the foundations of the church. He writes: "Discovered a tomb in the evening. Rain."

'He then makes a number of entries. He travels to Carcassonne, to Rennes-les-Bains and to Coustassa. Here, he says, he met with some priests: "*Saw the curé of Névian, Gélis and Carrière: saw Cros and Secret—*"

'See? He mentions a priest from Névian, though I don't know who he was, as well as Abbé Gélis of Coustassa and a certain Carrière. At this time, Abbé Cros was the vicar-general of this diocese. It wasn't until later, in his near retirement, that he became the abbé of Bugarach.'

'From vicar-general to just an abbé, do you mean he was de-moted?' Rahn asked.

The other man smiled, weakly. 'Who can say? At any rate, a certain Pierre Pradel was the secretary-general, I believe the word secret was no doubt an abbreviation for secrétaire.'

'Unless it means *secret*,' Eva pointed out.

'Yes,' he said, perhaps surprised that this had not occurred to him. 'Saunière goes to Paris in 1892 to Saint Sulpice,' he contin-ued, 'where he visits with a certain Abbé Bieil and Abbé Hoffat. Then he goes to Lyon, where he meets with Abbé Boulle.

The penitents!

'When he comes back, he digs about in the graveyard like a fox looking for a carcass and the mayor at the time complains to the Bishop of Carcassonne – who is now one Monsignor Beauséjour – that he is moving the graves about. This is a rumour, but it is substantiated by the fact that soon Saunière erects a fence around the graveyard with an iron gate, to which he alone holds the key. Now, some time afterwards, Abbé Gélis is murdered and the po-lice find a fortune secreted in his house, thirteen thousand gold francs! Where did it come from? Who knows? In the meantime, Saunière travels more and more, only returning to keep an eye on his restoration works: the tower, the belvedere, the Villa Bethany. Next, Monsignor Beauséjour suspends him, because he can't ex-plain where he got his money but that doesn't prevent him from celebrating the mass at the Villa Bethany. Did you see the chapel in the annex yesterday?'

'Yes, when we brought the madame in out of the storm,' Rahn said.

'The parishioners were so mesmerised by Saunière that they continued to go to him for mass even after the Bishop of Car-cassonne sent another priest to this town. At any rate, getting back to the diary: after his suspension, Saunière continued his renovation work, as if nothing had happened. He constructed his conservatory and here, you see, there is a map of the church and his relocation of tombs, including the cavalry cross. He was a wealthy man until the day he died.'

'When did he die?' Eva asked.

'He had a stroke on the seventeenth of January 1915. The feast day of Saint Sulpice.'

Rahn sat stock-still. 'He died of a stroke?'

'Yes.'

'On that date?'

'Yes.'

Rahn was thinking that the Countess P, the Abbé Cros and now Saunière had all suffered strokes. A coincidence? He didn't think so, but that date – the seventeenth of January – again! First he finds that date in Monti's notebook; then he discovers Verger had been sentenced to death on that date; and now he learns that Saunière had also died on that *same* date.

'In the church register,' the priest continued, showing him the page whose topmost part was torn away, 'Abbé Bigou, Saunière's predecessor, writes the following line twelve times.' He showed them.

Jesus of Galilee is not here.

Rahn paused. Bigou was the only priest they knew nothing about on the list.

'Jesus of Galilee is not here . . . in Rennes-le-Château?' Rahn asked.

'Why would he write that?' Eva leant in to look.

'Perhaps it means the Devil lives here, because of whatever Marie Blanchefort gave him. You see, the page has been torn out and interpolated in the register on the date of her death.'

'Which was?' Rahn said with expectation.

'The seventeenth of January,' the priest announced.

Rahn was dumbfounded.

'Do you know what she gave Abbé Bigou?' Eva asked.

'There are rumours that she gave him something on her deathbed but no one knows what it was, however the consensus is that it was some impious treasure which he then hid in the church and which Saunière found during his renovation. Perhaps he never found it and it is still buried somewhere beneath the church, who knows?'

'We were in the crypt last night,' Rahn blurted out.

'You went there? But how did you . . . ?'

'Through a hatch in the confessional.' He observed the abbé with a steady eye. 'We found the crypt under the graveyard. Someone has been using it as a den of black magic.'

'What? Black magic?' He blushed and immediately crossed himself.

'It has been sealed up a long time, by the look of it. That was probably what Saunière was looking for in the cemetery – a way into it. And there's something else. Someone closed the hatch in the confessional knowing we were down there. We only just managed to escape with our lives. The heavy rain flooded the crypt very quickly. Luckily for us we found a way out through the sacristy.'

'The sacristy?'

'Didn't you know there was a way into the crypt through the closet?'

'Me? Well . . . no.' He looked flustered. 'It must have been Madame Dénarnaud! She must have closed the hatch! She would have known about it from Saunière. Can you show me the list now?' The man could hardly conceal his interest.

Rahn took it out.

'Where did you get it?'

'From the tabernacle at the church of Bugarach.'

The abbé looked at Rahn. 'The tabernacle?'

'We think Abbé Cros hid it there to safeguard it. See that priest at the top of the list? He was the priest who murdered the Archbishop of Paris eighty-one years ago. He is alleged to have possessed a copy of the *Grimoire of Pope Honorius*, after that we don't know what happened to it.'

'Grimoire of Pope Honorius?' he said.

'Yes, it's a long story.'

'Five priests?' he said, looking at the list. 'Espéraza, Coustassa, Rennes-le-Château, Saint-Paul-de-Fenouillet, Rennes-les-Bains . . .' He seemed to be committing them to memory and Rahn whisked the list away from him. The priest's demeanour altered suddenly.

'Rennes-le-Château,' Rahn said, 'seems to be at the centre of everything. All those priests knew Saunière personally, except two, who are listed separately, at the top of the list – Abbé Bigou and Abbé Verger.'

'There is not much more I can tell you, I'm afraid,' the priest said, brusquely. 'I suggest you go and have another conversation with Madame Dénarnaud. Perhaps you should ask her why she closed the hatch and left you there to die!'

Rahn was reluctant to leave him, but something told him he would get no further with the man.

Before they went in search of Madame Dénarnaud, they took themselves to the Corfu house to collect their things and were grateful to realise that Madame Corfu was not in. Like many townspeople, she was no doubt bothering the long-suffering mayor about the events of the morning. They found the mute grandmother, however, peeling potatoes in the kitchen. She looked at both of them with fear in her eyes and crossed herself and gestured for them to stay. She left and returned a moment later with a piece of paper, folded over, which she put in Rahn's pocket.

He left the money for the rooms with her, they said their goodbyes and made their hasty exit. As soon as they left the house and were on their way to Villa Bethany, Eva asked what was on the note. Rahn opened it and what he saw alarmed him. He looked at Eva. The note said:

Sauvez vos âmes!

Eva's great brown eyes searched his. *'Save your souls?'*
Rahn nodded.

'Does she mean – because of this morning, or something else?'

'Who knows?'

When they finally found Madame Dénarnaud, she was not at the villa as they had expected but in the Tour Magdala, sitting on a window seat near a small hearth ablaze with logs. The room was surrounded by empty bookshelves, silent behind their glass doors. She had what looked like a bible in her hands from which she appeared to be reading when they burst in, interrupting her.

'You certainly took your time,' she said, looking up calmly.

ISLAND OF THE DEAD

34

SHE READS
TO THE DEAD

'In fact, the dead live elsewhere, nor is it known where.'
Girolamo Cardano, 'Somniorum Synesiorum'

Venice, 2012

It was All Saints' Day, and I was walking about the cemetery again after breakfast. The Writer of Letters said he would be busy preparing for the following day's festival and I was to keep my own company for a couple of hours. I spent some time in the library reading Rahn's book *Lucifer's Court*. A passage near the end caught my attention:

> I know a way through the forest that is overshadowed by huge conifer trees . . .the path is called the Thief's Path . . . I am carrying a Dietrich with me . . .

A 'Dietrich' was a skeleton key! I wondered if he had found the missing key after all and what he meant by 'the Thief's Path'?

Afterwards, I walked out into the cold day with Rahn's story on my mind, hugging my coat for warmth. I didn't really know what to believe at this point but I had to admit I had been swept along by a story that seemed too fantastical to be true. A grimoire written by a pope, black magic among a conventicle of priests, Freemasons, Nazis and a Cathar treasure handed down over the centuries. I smiled. If I wrote it – who would believe it?

The cemetery on the island was quiet this day. There were only a few people scattered about, as the bulk would arrive to-morrow. For some reason, I felt like visiting the French section again and I was surprised to see a woman sitting by that strange grave without a name. She was young, with straight brown hair and large eyes that seemed to pool the stark light. She had some books on her lap and she was reading from one. I was intrigued so I stood nearby. She must have sensed my presence, because she looked up and paused.

'Hello,' she said.

'I see this grave is remembered, at least by you.'

She seemed embarrassed. 'Yes.'

'What are you reading?'

'Poems mainly. I go from grave to grave. My mother taught me how to do it. She also read to the dead, as did my grand-mother before her. You could say it's a vocation that runs in our family.' She closed the book and made a slight frown. 'They are so close at this time one can almost touch them.'

'The dead?'

'Yes.'

'But I thought that the Day of the Dead was the time to visit the graves?'

'I know, but I prefer coming today, All Saints' Day. Tomorrow will be so busy and noisy. It's far more peaceful today.'

'May I ask why you read to the dead?'

She blinked at me. 'Why not?'

'I suppose I don't know,' I said, rather stupidly.

'You're not from here, are you?'

'No, I'm sorry, my Italian is a little rusty.'

She smiled and looked down just a little. 'You're visiting?'

'I'm writing a novel. I guess one could call this . . . my research.'

She gave a slight nod of understanding. 'Many writers were fascinated by Venice. Ezra Pound . . . Henry James, he's also here. Did you see his grave?'

'Yes.'

'Do you like it here?'

I looked around. 'Venice is a beautiful city.'

'No, I mean, do you like the Island of the Dead?'

I paused. 'I've never been to a more intriguing place.'

'Are you interested in the dead?'

'I suppose I must be.'

'They are in need of communication.'

'Is that what you're doing? Communicating with them?'

'I'm not a medium, if that's what you mean. I don't do that!' she said, hurriedly. 'Communication with the dead has to be a conscious experience. But it's usually very difficult because when we speak to them everything is reversed.'

'How do you mean?'

'You know, here you ask a question and I answer it . . . that's how we communicate. But across the threshold, when you put a question to the dead, it should be a statement and the answer comes to you as a question.'

'And so the dead can think?'

'One's awareness, one's consciousness still exists, even without a body. One can still have awareness without it, if one develops it in life. If one does not, one enters a realm of shades.'

'As the Greeks feared?'

She smiled. *Better to be a beggar on Earth, than a king in the realm of shades!*

I nodded. There was something old-fashioned about her, something I couldn't pinpoint. 'So what does reading do for them?'

'It informs them.'

'But aren't they all-knowing?'

'The dead can't know anything they didn't know in life, unless . . . well, there are extenuating circumstances, but in the natural course of events if while alive they spent all their time learning only about the material world, they're lost when they enter the world of the spirit. This is the tragedy, you see? What I do for them gives them comfort; my reading warms the cold they feel and cools the heat. It is a gesture of love.'

'But what is love to them?'

'Love is the bridge that unites the dead with the living. Love, to the dead, is a consciousness of life.'

She put the book down and looked about her furtively, seeming fearful suddenly. 'Soon, terrible things are going to happen. I don't know that I can help so many young souls who are going to pass across the threshold.'

'What do you think is going to happen?'

'Don't you know?' she said, wide-eyed.

'No.'

'War, of course! A war unlike any other war; so many will die and they will not know they are dead. Then there are others who may have made pacts, all sorts of rituals, promises . . . They will remain tethered to life, even in death, which constitutes a kind of torment. But then you already know that, don't you?'

I had no idea what she was talking about.

'You don't remember me, do you? That's all right, as long as you don't forget the solution to the riddle of this grave.'

'What solution?'

'Don't you remember? Oh, dear! You should leave. These places have a way of growing on you until you can't distinguish whether you're alive or dead. Look over there, see that?' She pointed to a tall palm growing out of a grave. 'That was once a seed, floating free in the wind, now it's a part of this place. You don't want to end up like that. Not all of the dead rest easy.'

I looked at her more closely and realised that she was dressed as a woman would have dressed in the 1930s.

She leant forward. 'You have to come back in 2012.'

'But we are in 2012.'

'No! That's still seventy-four years away!'

I gave a nervous laugh, completely thrown. I could see that she was either an excellent actress or entirely serious. I didn't know which would be more disturbing. 'Has someone paid you to say these things?'

'What?'

'Look, it's about time someone was honest with me and it might as well be you!'

'I don't know what you mean . . .'

'You're an actress, and someone's hired you to play this part. Your costume, reading to the dead, all of it.'

She seemed disconcerted and began gathering her books. 'I don't know what you're talking about. I've given you what you want. Now you have to take the vaporetto out of here. You should slip out tomorrow, when there are many people here. You can go unnoticed . . . They are after you!'

'What? Who are after me?'

'They haven't forgotten you – they know!'

'Know what?'

She stood and looked at me with what I thought was pity. 'I have to go now. Don't forget what I said to you: tomorrow, when the place is busy . . .' she said this and left, not looking back.

A moment later I was alone and it seemed as if she had never been there at all. When I returned to the monastery, the Writer of Letters was nowhere to be seen. Feeling puzzled and disconcerted I went to the library and sat down before the fire. This game had gone on for long enough. Then again, maybe that was what he wanted me to believe: that he was playing a game. No doubt he'd been standing in the distance, smiling and gauging my reaction. I resolved that to leave would be akin to a writer becoming manipulated by his own characters. I would leave when I wanted to, and I really didn't want to. I was becoming consumed by the story and I needed to hear the rest of it. In that sense, I realised, I was not so different from Otto Rahn.

I was so lost in my thoughts that I didn't hear the Irish monk until he was already standing beside the chair.

'Can I get you something?' he asked. I must have had a strange look on my face because he frowned a little. 'Are you alright?'

I nodded. 'Just jet lag, you know.'

'I see. Well, enjoy the quiet. Things are going to turn upside down tomorrow.'

'I wonder, before you go, could you tell me something about my host?'

He paused, a strange veil falling over his features. 'Your host?'

'Yes.'

'What do you want to know?' he said.

'What a commotion!'

I turned in my winged chair to see the Writer of Letters walking towards us. I felt as though I had been caught in flagrante delicto – like a thief with his hand in the safe.

'I hope you haven't been too bored while I was detained?' he said, with perfect urbane calm.

The monk slipped out and we were alone.

'Not at all, in fact I met a woman who reads to the dead,' I said to him, ready for a showdown.

'Really?'

'Yes, she warned that I should leave – that someone was after me.'

He sighed. 'Was she wearing clothes from the last war?'

'Yes, in fact she was and, I have to say, she was very good. She had me believing her for a moment.'

'Very good?'

'A good actress.'

'I don't know that she's an actress. She comes here every year and reads at the graves. When one lives on this island, one gets used to such things.'

I measured my words. 'And so you didn't put her up to this?'

'Me? No. I think your writer's imagination is carrying you away.'

I didn't know what to say.

'The fact is,' he said, settling into his chair, 'most people are in constant contact with the dead only they know nothing of it because it lies in the subconscious. For most of us, the time of going to sleep and waking is most propitious for communicating with them. You see, they have no past; they live in that world of galleries, like those that Borges spoke of – where everything is present. They have no concept of yesterday or tomorrow or, for that matter, time itself.' He looked at me expectantly. 'I would like us now to turn to something else. I want to tell you about the symbol of the snake and the anchor in Rahn's story. You've seen it before, haven't you, on those letters from me? Do you recall?'

The watermarked paper he used for his letters! He had planned everything down to the very smallest detail – why? Perhaps reason didn't come into it at all? The Writer of Letters might be seriously deranged; he could be a brilliant psychopath. I searched his face a moment and looked away to the fire. Then again, I could be making too much of it, allowing the story to affect me, reading into things. I tried to calm down. This thought immediately called to mind Rahn, travelling to Wewelsburg on that train, splashing water on his face and telling himself the same thing. Perhaps this had been the intention of the Writer of Letters: to show me first-hand what it was like to be Rahn. If so, he was cleverly achieving it by degrees.

The Writer of Letters looked at me quizzically a moment, perhaps trying to discern the tenor of my thoughts. With a smooth voice he said, 'That watermark was used by Aldus Manutius, one of the great printers of Venice.

'You must imagine it is 1515 and the famous Venetian printer is working amid the dust and heat of his printing shop when a visitor is announced. The visitor is a stranger but the moment the man shows him the tattoo on his wrist, Manutius knows the importance of the visit. Manutius likewise shows him his own tattoo, which depicts the same symbol, and the man is satisfied.

'The visitor removes a book from a velvet pouch and hands it to him. Manutius holds it tentatively in his hands. He knows what it is, you see, because of the embossed gold letter H on the front cover.

'Manutius opens it and begins reading the German words:

> The Holy Apostolic Chair, unto which the keys
> of the Kingdom of Heaven were given by those
> words that Christ Jesus addressed to Saint Peter: I
> give unto thee the Keys of the Kingdom of Heav-
> en, and unto thee alone the Power of commanding
> the Prince of Darkness and his angels, who, as
> slaves of their Master, do owe him honour, glory
> and obedience, by those other words of Christ
> Jesus: Thou shalt worship the Lord thy God, and
> Him only shalt thou serve – hence by the Power
> of these Keys the Head of the Church has been
> made the Lord of Hell . . .

'The first time Manutius had heard mention of this book had been from his pupil and friend, Pico della Mirandola, the young humanist who had worked for Lorenzo the Magnificent in Florence. He had whispered to him something of a terrible book, which had come into his hands and which he would one day translate into Italian; a book spoken of only in whispers. By chance, or maleficent providence, the book had somehow escaped the purifying flames of that infamous monk, Savoranola, who inspired the people of Florence to throw into the Bonfires of the Vanities many heretical books, jewellery, and even works of art. Now, Manutius cannot believe what he holds in his hands. He looks up to the man who has brought it. "Is this . . . *Le Serpent Rouge?*"

'"Yes, the original penned by Pope Honorius himself, with an interpolation added at a later date."

'"Dear Lord . . . what shall I do with it?"

'"Lock it up and guard it with your life. Do not read further than you have. You will soon hear from us again."'

I looked at the Writer of Letters. 'Let me see if I have it right. There are three copies of the Theban magician Honorius's book, and one fell into the hands of a pope, who called himself Pope Honorius – is this the one that fell into the hands of Manutius, *Le Serpent Rouge*, the book Rahn is looking for?'

'Indeed.' His eyes gleamed.

'But I'm confused – what about the treasure of the Cathars?'

'There are two aspects to this mystery: *Le Serpent Rouge* and the treasure of the Cathars, in which Rahn suspects he will find the missing key that completes it. To know what happened when the key of the Cathars and *Le Serpent Rouge* came together at the same time and in the same space, we need to go to the gallery called Chavigny. There we shall find those happenings at the court of Francis, son of Catherine de Medici . . .'

35

CHAVIGNY

'In the world there will be made a king who
will have little peace and a short life.'
Nostradamus, Century I Quatrain 4

Blois Castle, France, 1556

The night was tempestuous. The moon was in Scorpio and it was a terrible omen, but Chavigny, drenched to the bone, did not know this and so he walked into the grand apartment panelled in oak unperturbed.

Neither the torches nor the light of a hundred candles flickering in their silver stands could pierce the darkness of this room. Nor could they cheer the mood, for screams and moans could be heard coming from a four-posted bed canopied in black silk.

A number of men stood around the bed, arguing. The air reeked of incense mingled with the smoke from a monstrous fire and the sickly smell of corrupted flesh. Chavigny had to stifle a cough. He looked to his master, whose face was silhouetted beneath his physician's cap, and noted that his features betrayed no disgust or concern. This did not surprise Chavigny, for in the past ten years he had come to know the most foundational aspect of his master's character – that he could be expected never to behave in a way one expected, even if one expected the unexpected.

'The king dies?' he asked into his master's ear.

'You realise this only now, and you want to be a physician?' his master said, staring at a woman standing among various physicians and monks. She was dressed in black and her pale, round face was like the reflection of a moon cast upon the waters of a dark lake.

'No, I will not allow it.' Her tone was emphatic and regal.

'Who is she?' Chavigny whispered again.

'The Queen Mother.'

'Madame . . .' said one of the doctors unrolling his sleeves. 'My mind is decided – this is the only course.'

'Why do you prolong my husband's suffering?' another woman spoke now. She was seated by the bed, her back to them. Chavigny guessed that she was Mary, Queen of Scotland and France.

'It is only a device to relieve the pressure,' the doctor offered. 'Without it, your son will die, madame!'

'Maitre Pare,' replied the Queen Mother, 'it seems to me that to cut into my son's head will only relieve him of his life.'

'Madame!' The physician was affronted. 'As the master of the king's wellbeing, I will take charge of his health as I see fit!'

'You want to cut into my son's skull as if it were a watermelon – I will not allow it! As a member of the council of the regency, I order you to stop. For I have requested the attendance of another physician. A man of great reputation and worthy accomplishments . . . And he is just arrived,' she said, pointing to Chavigny's master.

The room erupted in a shiver of whispers.

'Maître Michel de Notre Dame, come into the light,' she said, with a welcoming hand.

In a moment, Chavigny's master was standing before the Queen Mother and was taking off his physician's cap. Chavigny observed him with affection: a gnome-like man, with a flat, unwrinkled face framed by white hair cropped short, and a beard that grew long over his chest. His nose was straight, his cheeks ruddy, and his expression taciturn, even when he smiled.

'Your servant has come as requested, your majesty. Nostradamus at your service,' he said.

Her face seemed to soften at the sight of him; she offered her hand and he kissed it. Her tone turned grave. 'This is our son, monsieur, you have met him before, in better days.'

'I remember it, your majesty,' he said.

'He is gravely ill, and we are, as you can see, at your disposal.'

Nostradamus looked at the Queen Mother, and Chavigny could see he was thinking. 'May I speak plainly, your majesty?' he said, finally.

'I expect it, Master Nostradamus.'

'If we are to do anything——' he looked about him, '——we must have fresh air. No more candles, no incense and all men and women, priests and doctors must go. They suck the goodness out of the air.'

Another round of indignant whispers circulated the room.

A cardinal standing nearby said, 'Madame, this man's work has been called into question by the Holy Inquisition on numerous occasions. He is a sorcerer, a necromancer . . . a——'

Catherine, the Queen Mother, raised a hand and cut in with an imperious tenor: 'Nostradamus is a doctor who saved thousands from the plague in many diverse places. He is renowned for his remedies and for bringing the near dead back to life. I have summoned him and he has come in haste. If he says all men should leave for the king's sake . . .' She paused, fixing this man with her pointed eyes. 'Then, Monsignor Cardinal de Lorraine, how could those of us who love France do otherwise?'

Ambroise Paré, the surgeon, flew into a rage. 'I will not allow a charlatan maker of jams to touch the king! I am master of this room!'

Another man countered, saying, 'I say all of you have had ample time to perform a miracle, and you have not done so! It will not hurt to add another voice to your choir of physicians.'

Ambroise Paré moved his incredulous and angered gaze from the Queen Mother to this man. 'Monsieur de l'Hospital, you do not know anything about medicine!'

Another now stepped into the light. This had to be the Duke of Guise, for Chavigny had heard tell of the scar on his face, received at the siege of Calais, which had earned him the nickname Le Balafre, the scarred. Catholic to the marrow, he was tall and dark of eye and when he spoke his voice made inroads into the heart. 'The king dies, madame. Will you give orders to arrest the Prince of Navarre? He will dethrone your son before he is yet cold.'

'I know,' she said.

'Will you give the order, then, madame?'

'No, I will not,' came her firm reply.

'Then I must surmise,' the duke said, 'that you are an enemy of the crown and that the king is in this bed by your own doing because you are in league with the Protestant princes of the blood.'

'How dare you! The King of France is first and foremost my own son! In any case, why would I need to arrest the Prince of Navarre? I have another son waiting to take the king's place if he dies,' Catherine said, with utter calm.

'Charles is too young,' said the Duke of Guise, smiling affectedly. 'You know this yourself. Your behaviour forces us to consider that you have become infected with the heresy of the Huguenots and that you now wish to see your son, who was a loyal Catholic, dead, and replaced by a heretic.'

Catherine's face grew blank, studied and hard. 'Us? When you say us, you mean yourself and the cardinal, your brother! It is well known that both of you have something to gain from my son's death, namely the throne, which the house of Lorraine covets through an ill-conceived notion that it is the rightful heir of the house of Charlemagne! I warn you, you had best take care that the court does not hear how it is in this room! For how many are faithful to you? How many will run to the princes of the blood when they learn that Orleans is arming itself against you and your brother? You might find yourselves stepping onto the scaffold that you have so hastily prepared for Louis of Conde!'

A tremble seemed to pass through the entire party. The doctors and nobles left the room one by one, and this meant that Chavigny and his master were alone with the Queen Mother, Catherine de Medici. When she noticed Chavigny hanging in the shadows, she said to Nostradamus, 'Who is that young man? Is he yours?'

'Oh!' His master turned around, as if Chavigny were an afterthought. 'That is my secretary Jean-Aymes de Chavigny of Beaune. Chavigny, come, let the queen get a look at you!' Nostradamus waved an impatient hand in his direction, and Chavigny walked reluctantly into the light and dropped down to his knees before the Queen Mother. He realised that he was shaking a little, for his heart was pounding. He was conscious of his road-soiled attire, of his unruly hair dripping rainwater on the flags at his feet, his possibly bleary eyes and undoubtedly scrubby jaw.

'Your majesty,' he said.

'Get up, sir! You look pale from your long and arduous journey. The question is,' she said to Nostradamus, 'is he discreet?'

Nostradamus nodded. 'He has a doctor's degree in law and theology and his small time as the Mayor of Beaune, in Burgundy, was salubrious. He is learned and vain like all young men and stubborn-minded at times. I tell him he should drink more to loosen himself and I do what I can to encourage him to enjoy life a little, for he is far too serious. He has a good hand for writing though – and, I think, a heart to match. He thinks he is a poet, but his poems are clumsy.'

Thus was his life summarised for the Queen Mother in five easy sentences. Chavigny made the best of it and bowed his head even lower. *His poems were clumsy?*

But the Queen Mother had already turned away from him and returned to her son's bedside. 'You heard what Ambroise Paré proposes,' she said. 'He means to cut my son's head open.'

'This is often done in battle, madame, when there is fluid in the brain. But if I may, it will do nothing to prevent the course of this disease.'

She passed a hand over her rounded face, over those bulging eyes. She was not a beautiful woman and yet she was graceful in her gestures and this affected an image of beauty. 'I think I read it in one of your quatrains.' She looked at him with a sudden frailty. *The first son of the widow of an unhappy marriage . . . before the age of eighteen will die.* Tell me, were you speaking of my son, the king? Tell me plainly.' She cried suddenly, 'Do not spare me!'

Nostradamus shook his head and made a squint, for his eyes were bad. 'The future is not set like . . . like quince jam, your majesty. I only see one possible outcome out of many alternatives. Like a garden where there are many divergent paths . . .'

She turned away, thoughtful. It was long before she spoke again, and when she did, her words were quiet. 'When my son dies, France will hang in the balance. He fell to the charms of the Catholic Guises and married that woman, but the Cardinal de Lorraine, her uncle, uses black magic to kill him because he wants the throne. I know this because Cosimo Ruggieri, my own sorcerer, has turned against me. He is in possession of a copy of the book of Pope Honorius, which he brought with him out of Florence.' She looked at Nostradamus with a significant eye. 'Surely you must know what this means?'

Nostradamus faltered. He put a hand to his chest absently, as if such a thought had seized his heart and made it pause. 'The grimoire, written by that black pope, the pope who made a pact with the Devil?'

'Yes. I need not tell you that there is no hope for my son. But Francis must not die before de Montmorency arrives, do you hear me? Did you not see how keen the Guises are to put me in a dungeon? It was I, you see, who alerted de Montmorency of my son's condition and of his Protestant nephew's imprisonment.

When he arrives to fetch him from the dungeon,' she said, her eyes shining, 'all will be put to rights. That is why I pray that you delay my son's dying as long as possible . . . Use the magic in the grimoire of King Solomon to counteract the poison of Pope Honorius.'

Chavigny's master was long quiet. 'If I am successful in using white magic against black it will only work for a time. The king will suffer, your majesty: terrible headaches; vomiting; fevers; diarrhoea; convulsions — all of these will visit him before the madness takes him. It is a horrible thing to behold. Not even the plague makes a man suffer more.'

She observed his words. 'And yet, he is a king,' she said, looking at Nostradamus a little too dispassionately, 'and kings are born to suffer, is this not so? Do what you can to keep him alive.' She considered her words and nodded. 'Tonight we celebrate his improving health. After all, he is sitting up and is eating a bowl of gruel . . .' She looked about her as if she had misplaced something of herself in this conversation. 'Tonight, Master Nostradamus, you must use all your powers and I pray that your magic works.' She left the royal chamber in a rustle of black silk.

Nostradamus rolled up his sleeves. He put a hand to the king's brow.

'What will you do?'

The old man squinted to look at Chavigny. 'Do?'

'Will you prolong the king's agony with magic?'

He shook his head. 'It is not always successful, and we must retire to our chamber to consult the books.'

Later, in the apartment provided for them, Nostradamus sat down, impassive, anxious. Chavigny had never seen him like this.

'What was that book the Queen Mother mentioned, master?'

Nostradamus looked up from his thoughts. 'What? Oh, yes,

that book. It is the most infamous of all grimoires. Now, be quiet and unpack those bags. Perhaps you can prevent yourself from disturbing my thoughts.'

Chastened, Chavigny went to the great trunk and took from it firstly the great brass astrolabe by which one could calculate the position of celestial bodies, some charts, and those Arabian instruments used for mathematical calculations, which he lay carefully one beside the other on a table. There was a great collection of simples in small bottles that were stoppered with wax, as well as glass ampoules for alchemical experiments, and his master had not forgotten his mirouer ardent, nor that other treasure he never spoke of, which Chavigny knew lived inside a red velvet bag encased in a box of polished wood.

'How long have you been with me now, Chavigny?' his master said.

'Ten years or thereabouts,' Chavigny answered.

'How many hurdles did Dorat place in your way, when you said you wanted to be my pupil?'

'It took me near a year to convince him and then he gave me no letters of introduction.'

'That's right, and you made the two-month journey south to my home and arrived empty-handed at my door. And what did I tell you then?'

'That if I intended to become a student of the mystic arts, I would have to be prepared to do those tasks you set me.'

Nostradamus nodded.

'But in all this time you have set me no tasks and there has been no instruction!'

'Really?' Nostradamus raised one bushy brow. 'No tasks and no instructions? Well, you have not been very attentive, then. Bring me that box.'

Nostradamus opened it and took out the velvet pouch; what lay inside it looked ancient. 'When I was given this I was sworn to never divulge what I saw except to an acolyte who would one day replace me. Circumstances have now precipitated what should not have come so soon. And so, my dear Chavigny, I must ask you before all else, to take an oath.'

Chavigny, who had been listening without taking a breath, gasped. This was the moment he had been waiting for! But he told himself not to be hasty. The wrong answer could cost him his privilege.

'Perhaps I'm not ready. Perhaps I am, as you have said, too vain and unwise . . .'

Nostradamus raised a brow and looked at him serenely. 'Come now, Jean, will you have me believe that after ten years you are not ready for what I am offering to share with you? Will you not swear the oath to be my loyal student?'

Chavigny felt a momentary confusion, unsure if he was swearing an oath of silence or one of loyalty, and there was a very fine but important distinction. 'What exactly am I swearing I will do?'

'Listen to me, I don't have time now to go into all of it with you except to say that you will learn everything as we go along. Right now I need you to swear to me that you will not read it. I have not shown it to any man since I myself received it.'

A realisation struck Chavigny and he looked down a moment. Of course, he understood now. Nostradamus did indeed live in a forest of isolation, unsure of whom he could trust, looking around every corner. Chavigny would now be the only other living soul to know some of his innermost secrets. His heart swelled and he was about to say what this moment meant to him when the impulse was forestalled by his master's next words, which were short and sharp.

'Will you have me waiting all night?' His grey eyes were full of anxious glints as he prompted, 'Well?'

'Yes, of course,' Chavigny blurted out, 'I swear on my life not to read it.'

'Good,' he said. 'Now listen carefully. This book I hold in my hands once belonged to the secret library of a great man, a doctor and alchemist named Scaliger. Did you know that your old teacher Dorat and I studied together under Scaliger? I lived with Scaliger at Agen and we worked side by side to vanquish the plague. He taught me all he knew and initiated me into the secrets of the Rose Cross and after that allowed me to enter into his secret library, which was hidden by panelled walls. Those were happy days, sitting in the dark with a lighted candle and the world's thoughts in my hands. When he considered that I was ready he showed me this. Not long after that, his niece, who was also my first wife, died of the plague, as did all our children.' He sighed. 'The people rose up against me because I was not able to save my own family, you see? They accused me of sorcery and without their protection the Inquisition came knocking at Scaliger's door. That is why we pretended to quarrel publicly, so that he and his family would not suffer through our friendship. One stormy night he packed a wagon full of his books for me, handed me this treasure and wished me well. I left Agen and later settled in Salon, but the Inquisition has long arms and soon caught up with me. I was forced to burn most of the books one terrible night to save my new family from the Dominican priests.'

'And this?'

'This—' he caressed it, '—belonged to the Cathars. They had safeguarded it from the Church for many years in the caves of Lombrives. Before that it belonged to Mary Magdalene, Saint John's sister and the guardian of his Apocalypse. Days before the pope's men and the king's imperial guard blocked up every exit from the caves – condemning countless men, women and children to a slow and agonising death – an unknown man slipped out carrying this. I don't know how the book fell into the hands of the Rosicrucians who were the followers of Saint John, but through them it came into the possession of Scaliger. It has passed through many hands and must do so again. You see, if Cosimo Ruggieri has a copy of the book of Pope Honorius, there is no telling what he will do if this book falls into his hands.'

'I don't understand.'

'It is dangerous, Chavigny. That is why I have carried it with me all these years. Why I cannot trust to leave it in any place.' Tears welled in his eyes. 'I did not know whom I could trust . . . this is a heavy burden I have carried, Chavigny. But now, I can do nothing else. I must trust you. And you will take it from here.'

'I?'

'Yes, you! One day you will understand why this was your destiny. I have seen the future in the mirror. I have seen that we will be together again. In those far-off days you will still be as stubborn as you are now, you will still think yourself a poet and a writer and you will yet need my guidance.'

'You have seen my future?'

'Not now, Chavigny, you must leave. The Queen Mother will arrange it. I cannot go. I'm too old. Who knows what this night will bring? The mirror showed me nothing of it. You saw the township of Blois on the way here – Protestant reformers gathering with weapons. The guards had to beat them off with staves to let us pass. The Duke of Guise has arrested the Protestant Conde and his supporters are not merry about it. That Catholic Cosimo Ruggieri has turned against the Queen Mother because of her leanings for the Protestants. He has sided with the Cardinal of Lorraine, a necromancer who uses the Church for his own ends. Should they win out, I will be jailed for my loyalty to her and they will find the book. My dear Chavigny, I fear we are headed for a bloodbath!'

'What will happen if they find the book?'

'Pope Honorius had the keys or formulas which allowed him to summon all the demons one by one, for whatever purpose. But there was one key missing in his grimoire. If that key, which is contained in this book that once belonged to the Cathars, is united with the knowledge in the book of Pope Honorius, Ruggieri and the Catholic Cardinal of Lorraine will be able to bring about the end of the world – they will cause the Apocalypse that Saint John foretold, ahead of time.'

At that moment a bolt of lightning sent a silver vein across the night sky and lit the room with incandescence. Chavigny braced himself for what would come, since it seemed to him that Heaven itself had underscored his master's words.

'I am afraid,' Chavigny told him, truthfully. 'Where will I take it?'

'Go to the descendants of Raymond de Parella. Centuries ago this family owned Montsegur, the fortress of the Cathars, now they have become the lords of Perillos, in Roussillon. They are the only ones who can be trusted. They will hide it and I will secret the knowledge of it in one of my quatrains – it will say that the treasure can be found with the twin infants from the illustrious and ancient line of a warrior monk.'

'Twin infants?'

'The townships of Perillos and Opoul.'

'And the ancient line of a warrior monk?'

'Templars! Hurry – to Perillos!'

36

ONE MYSTERY REVEALS ANOTHER

'The facts that I am about to reveal to you are incredible!'
Emile Gaboriau, The Lerouge Case

Rennes-le-Château, 1938

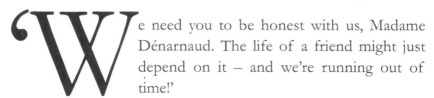e need you to be honest with us, Madame Dénarnaud. The life of a friend might just depend on it – and we're running out of time!'

She raised her brows but said nothing. She seemed to find his words amusing.

'Saunière found it, didn't he?' Rahn pressed. 'That's what those antiquarian booksellers from London were looking for when they came here to search his library after he died. But you made certain that it wasn't there!'

'Found what?'

'You tell us.'

'Me? You give me too much importance, monsieur, I was just a housekeeper.'

Eva cut in: 'But you were more than a housekeeper, madame!

You inherited everything . . . perhaps it is more accurate to call you an accomplice?'

The old face changed, almost imperceptibly – it became hard, cunning. 'Accomplice to what?'

'Rituals,' Rahn said.

'What rituals?'

'Rituals of black magic, right here beneath the church, in the crypt of Marie de Blanchefort.'

She laughed then, a guttural laugh. 'You have been reading too many mystery novels!'

'You warned me about ravens and then we find one hanging in the church this morning. Did you do it?' Rahn said.

'Did I hang the raven from the crucifix? Of course not!'

'But you were in the church last night – the abbé saw you,' Eva remarked.

'Are you asking me who tried to kill you? Why don't you go look for him – you will find that he's long gone, with whatever you told him tucked away in his heart!'

'What?' Rahn said.

'Monsieur Rahn, for a lover of mysteries you've not done well in figuring out this plot, have you? You've played right into that priest's hands. I suppose his blushing did it. He looks like such an innocent – those fair eyes! But he is an innocent with the heart of a devil.'

'What do you mean?' Rahn said.

The old woman looked at him with a smug expression that annoyed him. 'Well, who do you think locked the hatch leading to the crypt last night? I suppose he told you I did it, didn't he? The truth is, if I hadn't *unlocked* the door to the sacristy you wouldn't be here now. He did not know about that door, you see. And so, what did you tell him? Did you show him something you had found perhaps? Was it that list of names you mentioned?'

Rahn blinked.

Madame Dénarnaud gestured to a seat and said with a sudden

affectation of motherly concern, 'Sit down, my dear, you look pale. I think it's time I told you some things, and you are free to do whatever you want with them.' She composed herself and began: 'It all started, in many ways, with Marie de Nègre d'Ables, Dame d'Hautpoul, Marquise de Blanchefort. She was the last in her line and the last to live in the castle of the Hautpouls, the one that is deserted now and fallen to ruin on the hill in this village. On the eve of her death, she called for her confessor. Quite naturally, he was the priest of Rennes-le-Château, the Abbé Antoine Bigou. I believe he is on your list?'

'How do you know that?'

'Never mind, just listen,' she said to him, ignoring Eva.

Eva watched them from her seat opposite with an aloof detachment, apparently unperturbed by the other woman's rudeness.

'On her deathbed,' the woman continued, 'Madame Blanchefort gave Abbé Bigou something that had been in her husband's family for many years. Something that came into her husband's possession through the lords of Perillos – at least that's what Saunière managed to find out.'

'The lords of Perillos?'

'No one knows how the house of Perillos came to have the treasure, but the house of Perillos and the house of Blanchefort have had close ties since the Crusade against the Cathars.

The Blancheforts were a Cathar family with Templar affiliations, and the lords of Perillos were connected to the Cathars through Raymond de Parella, the master of Montsegur. They were united, if not by blood, by loyalty. So it was natural that when the Perillos family became diminished the treasure passed into the hands of the Blancheforts for safekeeping. Knowledge of it and information about its whereabouts eventually reached François d'Hautpoul when he took for himself the lands and the titles of the lords of Blanchefort. François then married a nineteen-year-old orphan, Marie de Nègre. On his deathbed he bequeathed knowledge of the whereabouts of the hidden treasure to Marie, and on her deathbed, having no male heirs and fearing instability in the land, she in turn passed the information to the only man she could trust – her priest.'

'You say there were no heirs?' Eva said coldly.

The woman glanced sharply at Eva. 'I said no *male* heirs.'

'So there *were* female heirs?'

That glance was full of contempt. 'Yes, but perhaps she did not consider them suitable. Women were just chattels, to be disposed of at will, they held no power in society and were quite defenceless. This information was a perilous thing, after all,' she said, and smiled at her little pun. 'Marie then died. Do you know the date?'

Rahn nodded. 'The seventeenth of January 1781.'

She smiled and raised one brow. 'As it happens, her confessor, Abbé Bigou, was himself affiliated with a circle, a brotherhood that had inherited the knowledge of a *secret*. To be precise, they were called the Compagnie du Saint Sacrament. The order was formed in Toulouse sometime around 1630 but was based at Saint Sulpice whose feast day is—'

'The seventeenth of January,' Rahn said.

She sat forward. 'Saint Vincent de Paul was a member of this order, as was Richelieu, who was not only a cardinal of the Church but also King Louis XIII's prime minister. Now, after Marie de Nègre died in 1781, we find that the old Abbé Bigou, a member of the Compagnie, which now calls itself Association Angelica, is in possession of the information that relates to the whereabouts of the inheritance of the Hautpoul-Blancheforts – not the treasure itself, but the information pertaining to where it had been hidden by the family Perillos. Of course he had a sense for its significance in relation to the *secret*, but he couldn't take it to anyone more senior, since the order by now consisted of a network of provincial branches that were forbidden contact with one another. Moreover, France was erupting in a revolution inspired by the Freemasons and everything was falling into chaos; he did not know whom he could trust.

'It was a difficult time for the Catholic Church. Many priests were killed and their churches ransacked or put to the torch. This meant that Association Angelica was in disarray and those clergy who did survive chose to leave the country rather than swear an oath of fidelity to the revolutionaries. Abbé Bigou and a certain Abbé Caunielle, of Rennes-les-Bains, decided to head for exile in Spain together. But before Bigou left for Spain he hid the information somewhere in the church here at Rennes-le-Château, as he'd been told to do by Marie Blanchefort before she died. Fearing for his own health and to ensure that it would not be forgotten, he confided that he had hidden it, but not its whereabouts, to the younger Abbé Caunielle of Rennes-les-Bains. He encouraged him to tell his successors what he had done if ever the young abbé returned to France. When Abbé Caunielle finally made his way back to Rennes-les-Bains some years later, he mentioned it to his successor and the information came, finally, to the attention of Abbé Boudet – who became a friend of Abbé Saunière's.'

'This Boudet is on the list,' Rahn said, under his breath.

'Of course! Abbé Boudet was a very knowledgeable man, a historian of the Celtic past of this area. It was Boudet who encouraged Saunière to begin his modest renovations. He even supplied him with the funds he needed from donations made by the Countess of Chambord and others. These renovations bore fruit with the discovery of that parchment that Marie de Blanchefort had given to Bigou before she died. Bigou had hidden it inside the baluster that supported the pulpit.'

Madame Dénarnaud took out a small, weathered parchment from inside the pages of the bible and gave it to Rahn.

He looked at it:

*Jevousle que cetindice dutres or qui apparti
entaux seign
eursderen nes etce stlam ort.
Lefeur evele*

XOTDQTKWZIGSDGZPQUCAESJ
XSJWOFVLPSGGGGJAZ
MQTGYDCAFZVYMFUAQBUWPNDGZRLEURZ
MQTGYDCAXSXSDRZWZRLVQAFFPSDAPW
POEKXSXDUGVVQXLKFSVLXSSWLI
PSIJUSIWXSMGUZVVQZRVQSJKQQYWDQYWL

'It's a cipher!' Rahn said.

'It was a simple cipher, at least the first part of the parchment. Still, it took Saunière some months to work it out, but once he found one word, seigneur, the rest began to form a recognisable pattern, and each word he picked out revealed other words in French, until he had deciphered the entire first part. It read: *I bequeath to my successor this clue to the treasure that belongs to the lords of Rennes. It is death. Fire reveals it.*

'Saunière was an ambitious man, and the thought of treasure was enticing, but he could not understand the jumble of letters in the rest of the cipher. It vexed him terribly and he became obsessed with decoding it, without luck. Finally, he resolved to ignore the cipher entirely, convinced that the treasure had to be hidden somewhere else in the church. He took note of the words "It is death" and searched in the niche created at the foot of the altar wherein he suspected were buried relics as was customary in churches. When the niche was opened, he was emboldened by the fact that on the underside of the stone cap there was a depiction of the knightly lords of Rennes, however he found nothing except a few scraps hardly worth his trouble. He then took to the altar itself because altars are traditionally places of sacrifice. He looked in the pillars that held it up and again he found nothing, so he began to tear the church apart, under the guise of renovation.

'Despite months of searching he failed to find anything, and yet he continued, for he had come too far. He then turned his attention to the ancient crypt, which he knew held the sepulchre of the lords of Rennes. Telling his parishioners that he wanted to shore up the foundations of the church, he began looking for a way down. He was convinced that the treasure was hidden in the crypt below the church and that there must be a hidden way to it. He did find the crypt eventually, but it had been ransacked, and was empty of anything valuable. Even this did not dissuade him. He continued his search and discovered a tunnel and at the end of it a wall. This, he was certain, led to the crypt of the dames of Rennes. The night he began to dismantle the wall, there was a downpour and the crypt flooded with water, as it no doubt did last night. He only just managed to escape with his life. After that, one could say, Saunière became slightly mad. Rather than wait for the floodwater to recede, he began looking in the cemetery late in the night for another entry into the crypt.'

'Did he find it?' Eva asked.

'Yes, there was an entry near the church concealed by a gravestone inscribed with the words *Et in Arcadia Ego.*'

'So he did use the crypt for magic rituals?' Eva asked.

The woman gave her a whisk of a glance. 'That is not important. What is important is that he never found what he wanted in that crypt and it ate away at him until finally, at his wits' end, he decided to tell his friend about the parchment.'

'Abbé Boudet?' Rahn said.

'Yes, of course.' She smiled as if he were an orphan and she had just adopted him. 'Boudet suggested that Saunière go to the Bishop of Carcassonne, a certain Billard. The Bishop was very interested in what Saunière had to say and he even gave him money to travel to Paris, to see if someone could solve the cipher.'

'To whom did he take it?' Rahn asked.

'Why, to Association Angelica, of course, who are based at

Saint Sulpice.' She sat back, with narrowed eyes. 'You see, Bishop Billard also belonged to the same order that Boudet belonged to – and Bigou before him. Billard understood clearly the significance of the parchment and he told Saunière to go to Saint Sulpice, to see Abbé Hoffat who was a senior member of that same order, and whose knowledge of all things occult was unsurpassed. The man realised instantly that the note was related to the secret their order had been safeguarding for many years and he set about trying to decipher it. He worked out that in the second part of the note he was dealing with *le chiffre indéchiffrable* – a Vigenère cipher. Do you know what that is?'

Rahn nodded, thinking that he wasn't going to tell her how many reports on ciphers he had written for Himmler.

'Then you will know, Monsieur Rahn, why the Vigenère cipher is called indecipherable. Without the master word, it was impossible to unscramble the message and therefore find the treasure. And they did not have the master word. They tried every word in the first part of the cipher and a number of combinations of words but even with his vast knowledge, Hoffat failed to find the solution! After that, Saunière contacted those with whom he had a special connection from his early days in Narbonne, thinking they might be able to help him.'

Rahn felt an excitement rising to his throat. Things were coming together. He was intoxicated by the complexity of the puzzle. He was tense and alert.

The old woman noted his eagerness. She smiled and continued, 'Saunière visited with a certain Boulle, leader of the penitents, and showed him what he had found. Boulle was immediately excited because, you see, the penitents were in the possession of a book . . .'

'*Le Serpent Rouge*, the Grimoire of Pope Honorius?' Rahn blurted out.

'Yes, not the original but a copy of it that they had acquired through the murderous priest, Jean-Louis Verger.'

'So, did Association Angelica also have a copy of it? Is that what you meant when you said they were also in possession of a secret?'

'Very well surmised. They held the original.'

'And Saunière knew about the grimoire?'

'No, he wanted the Cathar treasure, or what he imagined it might be: gold coins, precious jewels.' She half smiled, nodding mysteriously. 'Saunière was playing a dangerous game. He was a very audacious, if not a stupid man. Now, this Boulle offered Saunière money to continue his search, having by now heard that Association Angelica were also involved.'

'So now there are two orders that know about the treasure,' Rahn said, 'Association Angelica and the penitents. Both were in possession of Pope Honorius's grimoire, *Le Serpent Rouge*, one the original and the other a copy, and now they suspected that Saunière had found the key to completing it.'

'Yes! You catch on fast, Monsieur Rahn. Saunière began travelling to Paris and Lyon and Toulouse regularly, courting the good favours of a number of groups – who were all vying for the treasure. He soon became a celebrity, giving parties here at the villa and drawing to himself the attention of the most illustrious people; people like the opera singer Emma Calve, the Countess of Chambord and any number of disaffected members of the Austrian Hapsburg family.'

'Was he party to some intrigue to bring France into the Austrian empire?'

'Yes, better the empire than the government! At any rate, his entertaining drew the attention of his friend from the nearby village of Coustassa, Abbé Antoine Gélis, who became suspicious of Saunière's newfound wealth and celebrity. When he asked Saunière about it, the braggart, thinking himself invulnerable, could not resist. He told him, "I have found something of great value, and so far I have made it work for me – and I will hold on to it! Do you want to know what it is?"

'Thus was Antoine Gélis added to the ring of priests who now knew about the treasure, and a lot of good it did him, as you no doubt already know. At the same time, through the renewed influence of the penitents, Saunière became interested in the "Cult of the Dead", saying more and more masses – since he needed money to continue his search. In the meantime Saunière's confidante, Bishop Billard, died of a stroke. A new bishop, a man called De Beauséjour, was appointed to Carcassonne, a man who was dedicated to the Church's reconciliation with the government of France; in other words, a Freemason. Having heard rumours of Saunière's renovations and his parties with movie stars, singers and royalty, De Beauséjour sent his right-hand man, the Abbé Cros, to investigate. Subsequently, Abbé Cros and his underlings arranged a meeting with Saunière, Boudet and Gélis at Coustassa. I remember the night quite well because on his return home, Saunière was laughing at how frustrated Abbé Cros had been that they wouldn't tell him anything. As it turned out, they were to suffer at the bishop's hands. Saunière was sued and Boudet was hounded. Perhaps Cros, knowing Abbé Gélis's weakness for money and desire for the grand life, offered him a large sum to divulge what he knew. Perhaps that is why he was killed so brutally? Did you hear how they found him? The killers took pains to place his limbs in a certain pattern, both hands on his chest and one leg bent behind him. What in the tarot reminds you of that, Monsieur Rahn?'

'The hanged man!' Rahn said, suddenly illuminated.

'Yes, the betrayer of secrets!' she hissed with glee. Her eyes twinkled. 'You see, none of them, not Saunière, nor the Bishop of Carcassonne or even Cros understood the dangerous game they were playing. They did not realise it until Gélis was killed. The hanged man was Association Angelica's calling card; they also left their catchcry, "Viva Angelina", on a packet of Russian cigarette papers at the murder scene.'

'So Saunière and Gélis were not members of AA?'

'What? Do you think they would allow men like that to enter their fold? Of course not! After that, Cros fell silent and Bishop Beauséjour let things die down. But Saunière did not stop. Sometime later he went to Abbé Grassaud at Saint-Paulde-Fenouillet because he had a good library. He told Grassaud that he was interested in the Blancheforts and the man gave him access to his files. That is when he discovered records pertaining to the transfer of a painting, a Poussin – *Les Bergers d'Arcadie* – the Shepherds of Arcadia, perhaps you have heard of it? It was transferred from the family of Perillos to the Blancheforts. When he returned to the village he searched the old castle of the Hautpouls but he found nothing. On his next visit to Paris he bought a reproduction and it sits now in the study. Perhaps you saw it yesterday?'

Rahn was struck then – two things colliding! Yes, he had seen it and now he remembered that Abbé Cros also had the same painting in his study! Why?

'What has that painting to do with anything?' he asked.

'Perhaps something.' She shrugged. 'Perhaps nothing.' She snapped the bible shut and looked at Rahn. 'Now, if you want my advice, you had best watch yourself. You have entered into a field of war and you are in no-man's-land. I asked you yesterday if you were prepared to enter Hell and you answered in the affirmative. That is how I knew you were the one to whom I could tell these things. I hope you are ready for the consequences.' She said this and her face changed before his eyes: the hardness softened, the eyes became vague and the mouth drooped. Once again the master of deception adopted the mien of a fragile, arthritic old woman. 'I am tired, I must rest,' she said, settling herself into the role of old Madame Dénarnaud.

Rahn was not about to be dismissed. 'Not so fast, madame! You weren't just Saunière's housekeeper! You were watching Saunière for someone else – who was it? Who was paying you to watch him? Was it Boudet? Was it Association Angelica? Or was it the penitents?'

'Paying me?' she said and her eyes became pinpoints without a speck of humour or humanity. 'I am not for sale, to any order, or to any man, Monsieur Rahn! Our time is now over. I have nothing more to say to you.' She turned her attention to Eva with a certain removed amusement. 'So, you say you're Cros's niece? But who are you really, mademoiselle?'

The two women glared at one another. A momentary flash of recognition passed over the old woman, occasioning a strange battle of wills between the two of them: one old and a space from death, and the other replete in youthful vitality. Rahn observed it helplessly, without understanding, having been left quite out of the loop created by that silent battle.

When it was over the old woman broke off first, a little breathless. She gave Rahn a wisp of a glance.

'If I were you, Monsieur Rahn, it is to this young lady that I would be directing my questions.' But she could say no more because a voice disturbed them.

'Well, burn my beard, there you are!'

Rahn couldn't believe his ears until he turned around and looked to the doorway and saw La Dame's dishevelled shape.

'La Dame, what on Earth—?'

'Never mind that! The police are right behind me!' La Dame shrieked.

The sound of distant sirens reached them at that very moment. Feeling wretched, tired, frustrated and confused, Rahn turned to the old woman. 'Is there another way out of this tower?'

'At the bottom of those.' The madame pointed to steps that led in a spiral downwards into darkness. 'There is a room below that leads out in the direction of the old water tower; once you reach it, you can circle the town.'

Rahn got up to go but the old woman stopped him with a gnarled hand. 'Don't forget this.' She gave him Bigou's parchment, and in a moment she was a memory.

37

DATA, DATA, DATA

'It is a capital mistake to theorise before one has data.'
Sir Arthur Conan Doyle, 'A Scandal in Bohemia'

ollowing Madame Dénarnaud's instructions, they skirted Saunière's garden and picked their way down side lanes. Luckily for them, most of the citizens had gathered at the church and, taking advantage of the chaos, they kept out of sight and slipped out of the town. They found La Dame's Peugeot and were soon leaving Rennes-le-Château behind them. They drove in silence to Couiza, watching for police cars. Rahn had too much to think about and now he wasn't certain he could trust Eva. Just as Deodat had written: *trust no one!*

It was only later, as they sat in the shabby interior of a boulangerie that Rahn began to relax a little. Eva had gone to freshen up and La Dame was dunking his croissant into his coffee and eating with relish, dribbling it over his blond beard.

'Do you know how long it's been since I tasted croissant like this?' he said, as happy as a child.

Now they were alone, Rahn asked La Dame the burning question, 'What *are* you doing here, La Dame?'

'Firstly,' he said, wiping his mouth with a napkin and leaning forward, 'before she comes back, you simply have to tell me. Are you and she . . . you know . . . ?'

'What do you mean?' Rahn said.

'Are you and the mademoiselle . . . amoureux . . . perhaps even intimately involved?' He smiled.

'Eva and I?'

'Is that her name? But of course! It suits her. Eva, the temptress from the garden of good and evil, with the eyes of an angel. I have to say, dear Rahn, she's terribly like an actress. I'm trying to place her . . . dark, large eyes, slender . . .'

'Louise Brooks,' Rahn said, tapping his fingers nervously on the table.

'That's it! Louise Brooks exactly, in that Pabst film. What was it called?' He bit at his croissant as if both the idea of the actress and the reality of the croissant were closely matched, in his estimation.

'*Pandora's Box,*' Rahn said, about to lose his temper.

'Yes!' La Dame said cheerfully, oblivious to Rahn's escalating vexation. 'That's it! *Pandora's Box*! So, if you're not, you know . . . do you mind . . . if I . . . um . . . partake of the apples of Hesperides?'

'If you what?'

'If I were to . . . take a bite from that apple, so to speak!'

Rahn lost his temper and thumped the table. 'La Dame! Will you get your mind out of those London Cut pants and concentrate on what matters, for God's sake! What are you doing here?'

'I came looking for you,' he said, a little taken aback, 'and you might treat me with a little kindness considering I have that information you wanted. I couldn't get a hold of you on the number you gave me, so I came here. You told me you were at Rennes-le-Château. Besides, I really had no choice in the matter . . . because of an *unfortunate event*.'

The boulangerie was quiet. There were only two other patrons. La Dame called the waiter over and ordered another pot of coffee.

Rahn leant in. 'What unfortunate event?'

La Dame bit into his last mouthful of croissant, licked his fingers and rubbed his hands together before saying, between chews, 'I spent most of yesterday looking up Masonic emblems at the university library and when I returned to my dormitory I found something rather distasteful.'

'I dread to think,' Rahn said, sarcastically.

'Well, your mind is in the gutter, Rahn! No, I found that a colleague had been murdered in my absence.'

Rahn blinked these words in. 'Murdered?'

La Dame nodded, satisfied, as if the mere act of speaking had released the genie from the bottle and had made him someone else's concern.

'Murdered, by whom?'

'I don't know but whoever did it they certainly know how to slice a throat from ear to ear.' He grimaced. 'Disconcerting – not to mention messy. But the point is, dear Rahn, it could have been me. So much for my comfortable life!' he said. 'Please remind me not to help you again.'

The waiter brought a new pot of coffee. La Dame took a silver flask from his pocket and poured some brandy into his cup. 'I can kiss my life goodbye now,' he said sourly, offering the flask to Rahn, who nodded in commiseration and poured two nips into his own cup.

'I am now, as they say, a hunted man!' La Dame said theatrically.

'Sorry, La Dame,' Rahn said, dejected, worried. 'I wonder if I could have made a bigger mess of things if I'd tried.'

'I'll drink to that!' La Dame replied and the two of them clinked cups.

Rahn had a thought. 'Wait a minute, how do you know the murder is related to me?'

'Well, it's like this, Rahn.' La Dame paused for effect. 'The poor wretch couldn't stand the noise of the music master's snoring – which, like a discordant instrument, comes right through the walls – so he asked me if I would swap rooms with him. As you know, I sleep like a log.' La Dame took a good sip of his brandied coffee and gave a silent *ahh!* before continuing: 'Charity does have its advantages. Luckily for me I didn't have time to change our names in the register before they had closed for the night.' He looked at Rahn with bleary eyes and croissant crumbs on his moustache and beard, more crumbs on his suit. 'Are you going to tell me what's going on?'

Rahn swirled the brandy and coffee grounds around and around, hoping to mine some wisdom from them. He saw only coffee grounds. 'Well, corpses are piling up, La Dame. Four in total if you count Monti, and who in Heaven knows what they're doing to Deodat right now, as we speak.'

'Who do you think has him?'

'I haven't a clue,' Rahn sighed. 'There are several who are after this treasure, I think, whatever it is.'

'*Treasure?* You mean the grimoire, don't you?' La Dame said, his mouth full again.

'A great deal of water has flowed under that bridge since we last spoke.' Rahn poured another coffee from the pot, applying the last contents of the flask liberally before taking a good sip. Everything went a little out of focus and the world seemed a better place. 'I suppose I should fill you in.'

'What?' La Dame said.

Rahn realised by the look of him that he had been more focused on the contents of the flask than in what Rahn was telling him. 'Will you pay attention, for God's sake!'

By the time he'd finished giving La Dame an update on current events, Eva had returned. She had changed her blouse, and was wearing a red sweater that left little to a man's imagination. She had also applied lipstick and was wearing a hat over her short hair. She looked rather à la mode. She ordered a tea and sat down, ignoring La Dame.

'So, let me see if I have it,' La Dame said, giving her a smile. 'You are in possession of a list of priests who were being investigated by this Cros fellow, you think in connection with the treasure of the Cathars – am I right so far?'

Rahn nodded, gesturing for the waiter to bring another pot.

La Dame added contemplatively, 'And this treasure of the Cathars, you and Deodat have ascertained, contains something you call a key, which makes this *Le Serpent Rouge* or *Grimoire of Pope Honorius III* more potent. But you don't know what it is.'

'You've got it in a nutshell.'

The pot arrived and was set down on the table.

'This sounds completely absurd, you know,' La Dame said, filling his cup again, plunging three teaspoons of sugar into it and taking the time to extract any last drops from his flask before taking an audible gulp. 'Surprisingly good! Amazing how danger amplifies the senses. You know, Rahn, nothing makes one feel more alive than having a close shave with death!' He threw an appreciative glance at Eva. Rahn rolled his eyes.

'Now, as I was saying,' La Dame went on, 'a clue to the whereabouts of this key or treasure, had fallen into the hands of a priest at Rennes-le-Château, a certain Bigou. It was an encrypted parchment which no one has been able to decipher because the master word has been lost, right?'

'So far so good.'

'So who was it that made the parchment in the first place?'

'It looks like it was the lords of Perillos, the most recent guardians of the Cathar treasure.'

'And the parchment was then inherited by the Blancheforts and that is how it came into the hands of this Marie Hautpoul-Blanchefort?'

'That's right. By the look of it, the Hautpoul-Blancheforts were never able to decipher it.'

La Dame paused to light a Cuban, taking the time to smile

again at Eva, who behaved as if the chair he was sitting in was empty. 'My apologies, mademoiselle, but in all the commotion my friend has quite forgotten his manners. My name is Alexis La Dame . . . lovely to meet—'

'Not now, La Dame!'

'All right, dear Rahn, keep your shirt on! I was just being polite. So, you think the police are after you because of Deodat's disappearance and the dead man in the barn?'

'I don't know if the inspector heading the investigation into Abbé Cros's death is what he seems.'

'You think he's one of them?'

'I'm suspicious of him and the police.' He sighed, passing a hand over his face. 'What did you find out about the snake and the anchor?'

La Dame's smile was wide. 'This is where I come in, thank you for reminding me of the most important part! Apparently that sign is often used on graves, so it has something to do with death and resurrection. It also has some connection with the Masonic thirty-third degree, which ties in with this hanged man business – something about traitors. Anyway, that sign was also used as a watermark to denote the work of a printer from Venice, a certain Aldo Manutius. Sometimes he made the snake look like a dolphin, but most of the time it looked like a sea dragon, or a serpent from the sea. Now, if one digs down deep enough, one finds that Manutius was also member of a guild that used that same sign as its emblem and its members had that sign tattooed onto their right wrist, which would explain that man in the barn and his affiliations. I dug around a little and found a rare book entitled *AA Cléricale – its history, its statutes, its mysteries*. In it I learned that AA stands for Association Angelica and that supposedly they were the custodian angels, or one could say, the guardian angels of a *big secret* . . . this was the order behind the guild to which Manutius belonged.'

'Yes, Madame Dénarnaud mentioned them, a circle of royalists. Their big secret is that they have a copy of *Le Serpent Rouge*

– the Grimoire of Pope Honorius III.'

'Well then, there is another more obscure and highly secret group called AGLA that is related to them. Did you know *that*?'

Rahn sat back. 'The symbol in the church!'

'What?'

'In the church – along with the raven there was a sign drawn in blood. I forgot to mention that it spelt out AGLA.'

'But here's where your theory falls down,' La Dame said, smugly.

'What theory?'

'You told me just now in your account of events that you thought the young Abbé Lucien was a part of the desecration of that church. If he was, he doesn't belong to this group AGLA. You see, members of this order are like a Catholic mafia: they go right to the top. They are strictly forbidden to do anything to bring attention to themselves – on pain of death. So whoever made that sign in the church you described, could not have belonged to AGLA.'

'Wait a minute,' Rahn said. 'Perhaps that young abbé was warning us about AGLA – now it makes sense! He might be a member of the penitents and that's what Madame Dénarnaud was trying to tell me the night of the storm. *Penitence, penitence ... watch out for that raven!* But then how did I work out the way into the crypt by using that clue – was it just a coincidence?'

'Everything is connected, Rahn, as they say.' La Dame shrugged, grinning at Eva. 'Interestingly,' he continued with emphasis, 'Association Angelica allowed the admission of women and laymen into its ranks and that's how that printer Manutius got to be a member without being a Jesuit.'

Rahn took out the list and put it on the table for La Dame.

'See here? Abbé Bigou and Abbé Boudet of Rennes-les-Bains were members of Association Angelica.' He wrote the order's initials beside their names. 'The same order that safeguarded the *Grimoire of Pope Honorius III*, or *Le Serpent Rouge*, the book I was sent here to find and the same one Monti was looking for. Saunière wasn't a member and neither was Gélis. But the man in the barn had the tattoo of the anchor and the snake on his wrist so he was also a member. Jean-Louis Verger, on the other hand, belonged to the penitents.'

> *Jean-Louis Verger – Paris* 1857 *– Penitents*
> *Antoine Bigou – Rennes-le-Château –* 1781 *AA*
>
> ~
>
> *A J Grassaud – Saint-Paul-de-Fenouillet* 1886
> *A C Saunière – Rennes-le-Château* 1885
> *A K Boudet – Rennes-les-Bains* 1885 *– AA*
> *A A Gélis – Coustaussa murdered* 1897
> *A L Rivière – Espéraza refused last sacrament* 1915

'But the walls of the church at Rennes-le-Château are covered with that symbol?' Eva said.

'Isis the veiled goddess speaks!' La Dame cried jovially.

'That was no doubt Bigou's work,' Rahn said, ignoring him.

'So we know of at least two groups that have a copy of *Le Serpent Rouge* – Association Angelica and the Penitents,' Eva said. 'And now they want the key, the Cathar treasure whose secret location is encrypted in that parchment.'

'Yes.'

'I don't understand, old boy,' La Dame said, 'does Deodat's life depend on you finding *Le Serpent Rouge* or the treasure?'

'I don't know…perhaps both,' he answered.

At this moment a boy came into the *boulangerie* and walked towards them carrying a note. 'For you, messieurs,' he said.

Rahn opened it.

'What does it say?' La Dame asked.

Once more, Rahn felt the hairs stand up on the back of his head. He turned to look out of the window. Parked outside was a black car, a Citroën.

Eva frowned. 'What's wrong?'

'This is Deodat's handwriting! Don't look now, but there's a car parked outside. The same car, I think, that I saw at Bugarach near Maison de Cros. Something's been bothering me.' He formulated his thoughts. 'Why did Cros fall into the pond looking for the key, when he'd already told us the clue? We could have opened the tabernacle eventually, even without a key. We could have picked the lock or broken into it with enough time. What if he didn't fall into that pond at all? What if the man outside in that car killed him while we were at the church?' He gave them a significant look.

La Dame slipped his flask into his pocket and said, 'Perhaps the best recourse is to find the back door to this establishment.'

ISLAND OF THE DEAD

38

DEAD OR ALIVE?

'I secretly felt that I feared him, and could not help thinking the equality which he maintained so easily with myself, as proof of his true superiority'
Edgar Allan Poe, 'William Wilson'

Venice, 2012

'So, have you worked it out yet?' the Writer of Letters said, sitting back.

I smiled but he didn't smile in return. My earlier anxieties having been mollified by Rahn's troubles, I found myself turning congenial. 'What, precisely, should I have worked out?'

'The question of what you're doing here, of course. I believe that was the first question I put to you.'

I hesitated and he gestured with a hand. 'Please,' he said, 'I realise that you can't really answer that until you know something about me and I'm afraid I haven't been totally truthful with you. Now, I'm prepared to "come clean", as they say.'

He was coming clean? I wanted to trump him, to show him that I was one step ahead of his game. 'I do hate to spoil your plans, but I've already seen through the role you're playing.'

'You have?' he said, looking pleasantly surprised.

'Yes, I believe so.'

'Well, you can't spoil my plans because I don't have any plans. They are all yours – the plans – you see? But I'm comforted that you've started to see through me. It was what I'd hoped for.'

I held his eyes and they gleamed like pools.

'Why would you hope for that?'

'Because we are near the end and so by now you must be better acquainted with the character you've written for me. Am I right?'

He was playing the game again. He had no intention of coming clean. But I would play along, because in spite of my host's strange spirit of contradiction and the words of the woman at the grave earlier today, I liked the game more than I cared to admit. I looked at him with as much equanimity as I could muster. 'You don't give much away, but so far I imagine that it is an intelligent, somewhat eccentric character. I think you came here a long time ago, so long ago in fact, you've forgotten what it's like to live in the outside world. Perhaps you were banished to this place, perhaps you were running from something? Whatever the case, what's important is not why you are here, it is the fact that in the meantime you've had the opportunity to indulge in your first love, books. Erudition has always been dear to you and this library has become your labyrinth.'

The Writer of Letters nodded his appreciation. 'Go on.'

'However,' I continued, 'as time passed you became like that man in the library of galleries, moving from one gallery to the next, all alone, looking for meaning while surrounded by the marginalia of death. Here, you came across Rahn's story and because you have no story of your own, it became yours and you wanted to tell it. You thought that you could draw me here by promising to solve a puzzle, hoping that once I heard the story I would not be able to leave until it was finished.'

'And is this so?' the Writer of Letters asked.

'Well . . . yes – but the point is, you believe that somehow by telling me the story of Rahn you will also solve the puzzle of your life. Perhaps you will be allowed to leave this labyrinth then, because you have found a suitable replacement?'

'And who will that be?' The Writer of Letters sat forward, expectantly.

'Well . . . obviously me!'

'But how would I know you are suitable?'

'I would have to pass a test.'

'What test?'

'I haven't figured that out yet.'

The Writer of Letters kept me waiting a moment and somewhere beneath the look in his eyes there was a hint of irony. 'Perhaps I live only in your imagination. What do you think?'

'Let me answer you this way,' I said. '*Aulus Gellius* once asked, "When I lie and say I'm lying, am I lying or telling the truth?"'

'That's an unsolvable puzzle,' he said.

'And so is your question.'

He laughed a little and I believe he was amused. 'Have you heard of metatheatre?'

'Where there is a play within a play?'

'Yes, during the performance the actors allow the audience to see that they are playing roles. Shakespeare uses this device to create an illusion of reality, to make the audience draw closer to the play, to make them feel a part of its machinations.' His dark eyes wrinkled slightly. 'This collusion between audience and actor helps both to reach new heights because it suspends disbelief. To create a sense of reality based upon an illusion is an interesting paradox, don't you agree?' he asked.

'When you put it like that, I have to say yes. But when the audience walks out of the theatre they return to the true reality. As I will do, when I leave here,' I ventured to say.

'Ah, but will you return to reality or just the allusion, an insinuation of reality?'

I was confused. 'I don't know.'

'Well, perhaps this has to do with the riddle: *body and tomb are the same.* Have you worked it out yet?'

'I think you're insinuating that I'm dead,' I said.

He paused. 'On the contrary! Perhaps I'm alluding to the reality of your life.' He grinned without humour. 'We are very close to unveiling the reality. In metatheatre an unveiling usually precedes the final act of a catastrophe.'

I felt suddenly cold. *Catastrophe?*

'I want to show you something. Will you follow me once more?'

'Into that labyrinth of galleries – which one this time?'

'No doubt you know of Alexandre Dumas's work *The Man in the Iron Mask?'*

'Yes, of course.'

He paused. His face was more concentrated than I had seen it before. 'Well, you know, Dumas belonged to the Freemasons and in his books he was doing what many writers, painters and poets did in those days – he hid the truth behind allegory and colour. He wanted to show King Louis's duplicity, his double face; and so he depicted the man in the iron mask as Louis's twin brother. I will now reveal the true identity of the masked man and the secret that he held. A secret that a king was willing to do anything to gain.'

39

MORE THAN MEETS THE EYE

'The devil, devil, devil!' repeated La Fontaine; 'what can I do?'
Alexandre Dumas, The Man in the Iron Mask

Fortress of Pignerol, Italy, 1666

The bishop carried the lantern before him into the dungeons of the old jail. The night was silent. The sound of his own steps on the stone flags and the metallic clink of the keys that were held tightly in the jailer's calloused hands reverberated loudly in his ears. When the jailer came to a halt before a heavy oak door he seemed disconcerted and uncertain. He fumbled with those hands to find the one key among a score of identical keys that opened its lock. When the door finally came open with a screeching of rusty hinges, the Jesuit said to the jailer: 'You may not be present during a prisoner's confession.'

The man began to argue but he was silenced when the bishop raised a hand.

The Bishop said, 'Go!'

Chided the jailer nodded, allowing the Jesuit to enter the cell alone.

He closed the door and waited a time to hear the dying sound of the man's footsteps, ensuring that whatever passed between him and the prisoner would not be overheard. He turned his attention then to the man on the bed. He couldn't tell if he was asleep or awake. The man lay on his back unmoving. The Jesuit observed what he had already been told but it was still a shock to see the mask made of riveted iron.

It was said to be padded with silk but despite the assurances that it had been designed to fit the prisoner perfectly, the Jesuit didn't imagine that such a thing could be comfortable. The mask covered the prisoner's head rather like a helmet and was clasped at the neck with a large lock, the key to which was kept on the governor's key-ring. To attempt to remove the mask would doubtless cause injury to the skull, perhaps even death from a dislocation of the neck. There was sweat on the Jesuit's brow; he did not feel as calm as the man in the mask appeared to be.

The prisoner stirred. 'Confessor, is that you?'

'It is I, Aramis, Bishop of Vannes, at your service.'

'Please, make yourself comfortable. I have only meagre furnishings, but they will do to rest your legs.'

The bishop nodded, bowed and, placing the lantern on a table, sat in an old leather armchair near the bed. The mask reflected the light of the lantern in a glint of greys and yellows and oranges.

'Firstly, I want to say that I have no regrets,' the muffled voice said.

'Nothing at all?' Aramis was surprised.

The man sat up to cough, allowing his head to take the weight of the mask. 'No. I regret nothing,' he said finally. 'You will tell your friend D'Artagnan?'

'Yes.'

'He was a gentleman in his treatment of me.'

'Well.' The Bishop wiped absently at nothing on his regal lap. 'He was not happy to arrest you.'

'No,' the other man said. 'He graciously allowed me to burn papers that would have further incriminated our order. Pity my brother's letter did not burn as well!'

'Do you regret the loss of your liberty?'

There was a moment of contemplation. 'Perhaps in the beginning this concerned me, but I have long been free of desire and have passed my days in peace.'

'And the mask?'

'A Jesuit who wears a hair shirt and who uses the strap on his back knows what it is to master the will. A member of the Company knows how to control the snake!'

The Jesuit nodded, and although he had never truly been one of those men who liked to mortify the flesh – indeed indulging in it was more to his taste – he knew the signal well. The mention of the snake meant he must now show the sign. He rolled up his sleeve, sat forward and took the lantern from the table to illuminate the tattoo for the masked prisoner.

The prisoner did likewise.

'Who knows you have come here?' the masked man said.

'No one except your jailer and he has been well paid.'

'If you were found here, you would soon see the glint from the king's axe.'

Aramis smiled. 'I should like to see them try! But we were wise, I think, to wait until you were moved here, to Italy.'

'There is yet a musketeer in you, I see!'

'I never could make up my mind – monk or knight. It has always bothered my friends.' He paused a moment. 'I am glad to see you alive.'

'The king's judges would not condemn an innocent man to death, so Louis made certain that I would be tortured this way for the rest of my life and for this reason do I choose to be at peace. In this way, you see, I wrest from him his victory over me.'

'What will you tell me?'

The masked man gestured to the door and Aramis got up to

ensure that the hallway was empty.

When he returned the prisoner began: 'Poussin, the celebrated painter, has secreted something of import in his painting of the shepherds. When Louis asked me to send my own brother to Rome to speak with Poussin, I saw an opportunity to learn what it was that he had secreted. No doubt you know of the letter he sent me and that I am in this prison because I would not divulge its meaning. This is what I am to tell you, before I die.'

'Does it concern the treasure of the Cathars, which we have awaited?'

'Indeed. The painting tells the history of the treasure. In it there is a woman, Mary Magdalene, the first guardian of the treasure. After her death it was passed from woman to woman until the fall of Montsegur in 1244, whereupon it was passed to three known guardians: the man who took it from Montsegur, a troubadour; Nostradamus; and the family Perillos. These three guardians are the shepherds depicted in that painting by Poussin. But it does not only give the history, it also gives the solution to the cipher that was created by the family Perillos to guard its whereabouts.'

'How did Poussin learn of it?'

'The painting was commissioned by the family. You see, they could not have known that Poussin was one of us. At any rate the hidden clue is connected to a tomb in the painting on which is inscribed the words *Et In Arcadia Ego*. They mean: *and in the sacred box lies the ego* or the word – the master word.'

'The master word that reveals the cipher?' Aramis could hardly contain his excitement.

The masked man, Nicholas Fouquet, King Louis XIV's old minister of finance, wheezed in the darkness. 'Come closer, Aramis, and I shall tell you . . .'

The Bishop leant in until the iron of the mask touched his cheek.

'It is . . . Mo—'

But at that very moment the door burst open. It was the jailer flanked by a number of guards.

'Bishop!' The Captain of the Guard came into the room brandishing a blade. 'You are to come with us!'

40

A BOX, A TOMB, AND A WORD

'It came upon me like a flash of lightning. I had got the clue.
All you had to do to understand the document was to read it backwards.'
Jules Verne, Journey to the Centre of the Earth

Campagne-sur-Aude, France, 1938

The three of them sat in the Peugeot hugging their coats to keep out the cold. Earlier, they had left the *boulangerie* via the back exit and circled around to La Dame's auto, whereupon they had driven off, leaving the black Citroën behind them. La Dame's driving had been fast and jerky, and Rahn was glad when he stopped near a high overgrown patch alongside the old road near *Campagne-sur-Aude*, where they were afforded some cover. The wind had died down and a few scattered opalescent packets of mist drifted over the lowland fields but Rahn paid them no mind, he was turning it instead to the contents of the note.

MITTO TIBI
NAVEM
PRORA PVPPIQVE
CARENTEM
PALIM

'What does that mean?' La Dame said.

'It's Latin: I send you a ship without stern – or prow – backwards.

'Odd,' La Dame answered.

'It's a rebus, La Dame, a Roman puzzle. Deodat and Cros were fond of bewildering each other with them. Deodat and I had been talking about rebuses the day he was taken, that's how we came to the relevance of the word sator. Let me see . . . a ship . . . navem. Without stern or prow, without beginning or end . . . is navem without N or M . . . ave!'

'Ave?' La Dame said, popping an unlit Cuban into his mouth.

'It means greetings. I send you greetings . . . backwards . . . or back-to-front greetings.' 'Odd,' La Dame said again, stroking his beard. 'That's what it means!' Rahn said, suddenly illuminated.

'What?'

'Ave backwards is Eva.' He turned to her. 'You, mademoiselle!'

'Me?' she said.

'Yes, you! I suggest that whoever has Deodat has made him write something that I could recognise as having been written only by him, and Deodat, the crafty man that he is, has written me a warning in Latin. A warning against you! You must be in on it!' He formulated his theory as he spoke. 'Madame Dénarnaud intimated that you were not what you seemed. And now I realise why Abbé Cros appeared to act strangely around you. He was fearful, that's why he waited until you were out of earshot to whisper to Deodat that he wanted something from the church. That's why he wrote down sator, and not tabernacle, because he figured you wouldn't know what it meant. Everything you've told me has been a lie, isn't it true?' He was elated at having solved two mysteries with one stone – the mystery of the Latin note and the mystery of the girl – but at the same time he was also affronted for being treated like a fool. And then it struck him. 'You're just like *The Woman*!' he said, aghast.

La Dame began a solemn nod of agreement.

'What woman?' Eva said, indignantly.

'*The Woman*!' La Dame said to her. 'Irene Adler! "A Scandal in Bohemia"?'

'I don't know what you're talking about.'

La Dame leant in, savouring her attention. 'Well, she was the only woman, nay the only person, ever to have outwitted Sherlock Holmes. Whenever Sherlock spoke of Irene Adler it was always under the honourable title of *The Woman.*'

'Honourable! I wouldn't say that!' Rahn blurted out, annoyed. He proceeded then to take up the reins of the conversation. 'This leads me to ask two questions, mademoiselle: who are you, and whom are you working for?'

She paused, glanced at the two men calmly, and said, devoid of emotion, 'Don't go jumping to conclusions, Otto. It isn't what you think.'

'No?' Rahn said.

'No. You see, some time ago I moved into the house with Cros. He had no family because he was an orphan,' she said. 'He was also paralysed, couldn't speak and, to make matters all the more simple for me, he lived a long way from the township of Bugarach. No one asked questions and no one came to visit him, except for your friend Deodat Roche, and Abbé Grassaud. Who was to know that I was not his niece, returned from Paris to keep an eye on him?'

'I would appreciate it, mademoiselle, if you would just get to the point,' Rahn said, realising his feelings were hurt.

She raised one brow very high. 'Years ago, Abbé Cros came to Paris. At the time I was working temporarily for his lawyers as a secretary and so I knew everything there was to know about his affairs. He was very wealthy, you know, but his wealth was transient: large sums of money would appear and disappear in and out of his account, as if by magic, one might say. I was also terribly intrigued by his funeral arrangements and his elaborate design to keep anyone from knowing where he would be buried, even his lawyers. The more I looked into this priest, the more I was convinced that he had found a store of Visigoth treasure at Bugarach, and that he was planning to bury himself with it.'

'How do you know so much about the Visigoths?' La Dame said.

'I'm a student of archaeology, with a special interest in them. I was just earning some money working as a secretary, before coming here to work on my dissertation.'

'So that's why you knew so much about Bugarach and its history,' Rahn said.

'That's right. I've been studying it. I guessed that the abbé's wealth must have come from something he found, perhaps in the church. When he fell ill I saw an opportunity to quit my job and come to the south. Since he already knew me, it was easy for me to say that I had been sent to sort out some of his more mundane affairs, to settle his books and pay any outstanding bills. I fired his maid and hired a new one and from that time on I became his niece.'

'How did you know the key in the pond belonged to the tabernacle?' Rahn asked.

'Just a hunch.' She smiled. 'When Abbé Grassaud arrived unannounced to see Cros, I feared he might ask questions about me, so I hid in a room nearby. I overheard Grassaud tell Cros he wanted the list and if he didn't give it to him he had ways of getting it – sooner or later. Cros was very upset after Grassaud left and wanted to see Deodat.'

'So Grassaud knew about the list, that's why he was so anxious to look at it. Cros suspected you by the time of our visit, didn't he?' Rahn said. 'That's why he gave us the veiled clue.'

'I didn't need to know that word sator to find the key to the tabernacle,' she pointed out to his annoyance.

Irene Adler to the core!

'Wait a moment, mademoiselle,' Rahn said. 'Didn't Deodat know that Cros had no family?'

'No. Cros kept that to himself all those years in the seminary. Apparently he didn't like to be pitied,' she said.

Rahn seethed. 'So, you've had your eye on the treasure, haven't you?'

'Like you, perhaps?' she answered icily. 'But unlike you, I don't want it for myself. The Cathar treasure belongs in a museum. Not in the hands of a brotherhood of greedy priests.'

Rahn sat up. 'Which brotherhood?'

'You and Deodat think yourselves very astute but neither of you noticed one very important clue in the church at Bugarach. In fact it was staring you right in the face!'

Yes, he remembered having a feeling that he had missed something.

'What did we miss?' he said. 'Come – out with it!'

She smiled wider again. 'You didn't notice the walls?'

The realisation hit him like a candlestick. 'The anchor and the snake?'

'With one difference – the S in the anchor is entwined with an R and topped with a crown. The Royal Serpent Rouge, or Golden Crista, as some call it.'

Rahn stared.

Those eyes peeking out from their dark curtain were smiling.

'So Cros must have been a member of Association Angelica!' Rahn concluded. 'And that is why he had those symbols painted on the walls of his church!'

'Wait a minute!' La Dame's unlit cigar played at the corner of his mouth. 'You're both drawing rather a long bow. A symbol on the wall of a church doesn't automatically make its abbé a member of a secret order. The symbol could have been there long before he arrived at Bugarach.'

'That's true,' Rahn conceded, deflated, looking out to the trembling trees.

'All right, but what about that parchment the madame gave you?' Eva asked.

He took it out and looked at it. 'I'm convinced the master word is locked in the line that Saunière worked out.'

La Dame lit his cigar, took a puff and, gratified, said, 'Surely whoever encoded it wouldn't have been stupid enough to have placed the master word and the message in the same parchment?'

'I agree with you, La Dame, this is not how it's usually done, the master word or combination of words is usually kept separate from the cipher for obvious reasons. However in this case the family Perillos may have feared it would become lost or forgotten over time and so, they could have encrypted it in the cipher as insurance. That's what I would have done . . . Let's see if I'm right.

'Now, Saunière had deciphered this much:

Jevousle que cetindice dutres or qui apparti
entaux seign
eursderen nes etce stlam ort.
Lefeur evele

I bequeath to you this clue to the treasure that belongs to the lords of Rennes. It is death. Fire reveals it.

La Dame nodded. 'But, my dear Rahn, I thought you said that all those priests have already tried every word in that deciphered part to crack the code but to no avail. What do you propose to do?'

'It could be something very simple,' Rahn said, 'so simple it was overlooked. It is death . . . fire reveals it – that has to be a clue! But what kind of clue, I don't know. This is the rest:

XOTDQTKWZIGSDGZPQUCAESJ
XSJWOFVLPSGGGGJAZ
MQTGYDCAXSXSDRZWZRLVQAFFPSDAPW
MITMZSKWZHRLUCEHAIIMZPVJSSI
POEKXSXDUGVVQXLKFSVLXSSWLI
PSIJUSIWXSMGUZVVQZRVQSJKQQYWDQYWL

'It's getting desperately cold, Rahn, why don't we go to a hotel? You'll think better by a warm fire, I assure you.' La Dame was rubbing his hands together. 'The mademoiselle would like to go somewhere warm, wouldn't you, mademoiselle?'

'Not particularly' she replied.

'I know it's cold, La Dame, but you must steel yourself, we have to solve this puzzle,' Rahn said, obstinately, 'before something else happens.'

'Let me see if I understand you,' La Dame said. 'You, my friend, are going to attempt to solve a puzzle in the discomfort of a car with daylight dwindling and temperatures dropping; a puzzle that no one has solved in fifty years, even though they may have sat in comfortable rooms, in front of fires with entire libraries at their disposal? By the time you work out the frequency of the distribution of the letters in the cipher, we'll all be dead.'

'I know, so we have to work out the master word and fast.'

'If only Arthur Conan Doyle were here, now there's a genius,' La Dame said. 'Remember "The Adventure of the Dancing Men", Rahn? A cipher of stickmen, each representing a letter of the alphabet – quite brilliant!'

Rahn looked up from his calculations, feeling querulous. 'I still think Poe's "The Gold-Bug" is by far the finest piece of fictional literature written on the subject.'

'Totally improbable, dear Rahn.' La Dame shook his head. 'A gold bug that when suspended through a skull, points the way to treasure – ha ha!'

Rahn narrowed his eyes. 'It was quite scientific and you obviously missed the point.'

Eva cut in, with a degree of impatience: 'Are you going to argue all afternoon, or are you going to solve the cipher?'

'All right,' Rahn said. 'Look . . . Fire may not be the word but I think it's a clue. There is a fire trial in all Mithraic initiations, a candidate dies to the earth and is born to the spirit, which is fire. This was illustrated in the mysteries by jumping over fire, or running through a fire-lit forest, or over hot coals . . . fire . . . fire . . . fire . . . death . . .'

'But as I've already pointed out to you, the word fire was used by Saunière, and it didn't work,' La Dame repeated.

'What about the Pentecostal fire?' Eva offered.

'Or the fire of Hell and eternal damnation?' La Dame threw in.

'Wait a minute – death, Hell or Purgatory! That makes sense. Purgatory,' Rahn said, excited. He took the piece of paper with the list and a pencil he had in his pocket and began to write purgatoire, over and over without a break between words.

'The one good part of that story about the bug, mademoiselle,' La Dame said, 'was the bit about the chemical preparations . . .'

Meanwhile, Rahn drew a Vigenère Square.

'There are preparations,' La Dame went on, 'that are visible only when subjected to the action of fire. Remember, Rahn?'

'What?' Rahn said, annoyed at his interruption.

'The gold bug, dear fellow – the man draws the shape of a gold bug that he finds on an old parchment and later, when the parchment is placed near a fire, it reveals an invisible writing. You see, mademoiselle, the writing only appeared when the parchment was heated—'

'What did you say?' Rahn paused to look at La Dame, utterly taken aback. 'The gold bug!'

'The invisible ink – remember?' La Dame said.

Rahn blinked this in. 'It couldn't be that simple, surely? Give me your matches, La Dame!'

'What for?'

'I'm going to try it,' Rahn said, taking the packet from his hands.

'You're not serious!' La Dame laughed. 'That was just a tale.'

'It's worth a shot.'

'If you burn the parchment, that will be the end of it,' Eva warned.

Rahn lit the match, held it a long way from the parchment and passed it back and forth, allowing the flame to warm it only slightly. Something miraculously appeared before their eyes – an alchemical transformation.

XOTDQTKWZIGSDGZPQUCAESJ
X**S**JWOFVLPSGGGGJAZ
MQTGYDCAXSXSD**R**ZWZRLVQAFFPSDAPW
MITMZSKWZHRLUCEHAIIMZPVJSSI
P**O**EKXSXDUGVVQXLKFSVLXSSWLI
PSIJUSIWXS**M**GUZVVQZRVQSJKQQYWDQYWL

Four letters turned red. 'SROM–' Rahn said. 'I give up! What does that mean?'

La Dame shrugged, still puffing on his cigar, making the inside of the car feel like a chimney.

'You can't see the tree for the leaves, Otto!' Eva said. 'Look at it!'

Rahn sat up. 'You have to read it backwards – like the rebus, like in *Journey to the Centre of the Earth* . . . it's MORS – in Latin, that means death! The master word is death and fire reveals it!'

La Dame nodded and slapped both hands together. 'You see, I told you! It may be, dear Rahn, that you are not luminous, as Sherlock Holmes once said to Watson, but a conductor of light. Some people, without possessing genius, have a remarkable power of stimulating it.'

Rahn noted Eva's smile and it did not amuse him. 'Let's not have a party, La Dame, until we know it works.'

He set about writing the master word over and over in a table.

He then marked the horizontal lines on the Vigenère Square corresponding to the master word. Taking the first letter of the ciphertext, E, he picked out the letter E along the horizontal 'M' line in the Vigenère Square. From this point he read the corresponding letter at the top line of the square and found the letter S. He worked through the ciphertext until he had deciphered the whole line.

Master word	M	O	R	S	M	O	R	S	M	O	R	S	M	O	R	S	M	O	R	S	M	O	R	S

	a	b	c	d	e	f	g	h	i	j	k	l	m	n	o	p	q	r	s	t	u	v	w	x	y	z
1	B	C	D	E	F	G	H	I	J	K	L	M	N	O	P	Q	R	S	T	U	V	W	X	Y	Z	A
2	C	D	E	F	G	H	I	J	K	L	M	N	O	P	Q	R	S	T	U	V	W	X	Y	Z	A	B
3	D	E	F	G	H	I	J	K	L	M	N	O	P	Q	R	S	T	U	V	W	X	Y	Z	A	B	C
4	E	F	G	H	I	J	K	L	M	N	O	P	Q	R	S	T	U	V	W	X	Y	Z	A	B	C	D
5	F	G	H	I	J	K	L	M	N	O	P	Q	R	S	T	U	V	W	X	Y	Z	A	B	C	D	E
6	G	H	I	J	K	L	M	N	O	P	Q	R	S	T	U	V	W	X	Y	Z	A	B	C	D	E	F
7	H	I	J	K	L	M	N	O	P	Q	R	S	T	U	V	W	X	Y	Z	A	B	C	D	E	F	G
8	I	J	K	L	M	N	O	P	Q	R	S	T	U	V	W	X	Y	Z	A	B	C	D	E	F	G	H
9	J	K	L	M	N	O	P	Q	R	S	T	U	V	W	X	Y	Z	A	B	C	D	E	F	G	H	I
10	K	L	M	N	O	P	Q	R	S	T	U	V	W	X	Y	Z	A	B	C	D	E	F	G	H	I	J
11	L	M	N	O	P	Q	R	S	T	U	V	W	X	Y	Z	A	B	C	D	E	F	G	H	I	J	K
12	M	N	O	P	Q	R	S	T	U	V	W	X	Y	Z	A	B	C	D	E	F	G	H	I	J	K	L
13	N	O	P	Q	R	S	T	U	V	W	X	Y	Z	A	B	C	D	E	F	G	H	I	J	K	L	M
14	O	P	Q	R	S	T	U	V	W	X	Y	Z	A	B	C	D	E	F	G	H	I	J	K	L	M	N
15	P	Q	R	S	T	U	V	W	X	Y	Z	A	B	C	D	E	F	G	H	I	J	K	L	M	N	O
16	Q	R	S	T	U	V	W	X	Y	Z	A	B	C	D	E	F	G	H	I	J	K	L	M	N	O	P
17	R	S	T	U	V	W	X	Y	Z	A	B	C	D	E	F	G	H	I	J	K	L	M	N	O	P	Q
18	S	T	U	V	W	X	Y	Z	A	B	C	D	E	F	G	H	I	J	K	L	M	N	O	P	Q	R
19	T	U	V	W	X	Y	Z	A	B	C	D	E	F	G	H	I	J	K	L	M	N	O	P	Q	R	S
20	U	V	W	X	Y	Z	A	B	C	D	E	F	G	H	I	J	K	L	M	N	O	P	Q	R	S	T
21	V	W	X	Y	Z	A	B	C	D	E	F	G	H	I	J	K	L	M	N	O	P	Q	R	S	T	U
22	W	X	Y	Z	A	B	C	D	E	F	G	H	I	J	K	L	M	N	O	P	Q	R	S	T	U	V
23	X	Y	Z	A	B	C	D	E	F	G	H	I	J	K	L	M	N	O	P	Q	R	S	T	U	V	W
24	Y	Z	A	B	C	D	E	F	G	H	I	J	K	L	M	N	O	P	Q	R	S	T	U	V	W	X
25	Z	A	B	C	D	E	F	G	H	I	J	K	L	M	N	O	P	Q	R	S	T	U	V	W	X	Y
26	A	B	C	D	E	F	G	H	I	J	K	L	M	N	O	P	Q	R	S	T	U	V	W	X	Y	Z

word	M	O	R	S	M	O	R	S	M	O	R	S	M	O	R	S	M	O	R	S	M	O	R
Plain text	l	a	c	l	e	f	t	e	n	u	p	a	r	s	i	x	e	g	l	i	s	e	s
Cipher text	X	O	T	D	Q	T	K	W	Z	I	G	S	D	G	Z	P	Q	U	C	A	E	S	J

'Six churches hold the key . . .'
He continued with the second line:

XSJWOFVLPSGGGGJAZ

'The secret of Poussin . . .'
And the third line:

MQTGYDCAXSXSDRZWZRLVQAFFPSDAPW

'Completes the demon guardian of midday . . .'
He soon had the entire six lines deciphered in French:

La clef tenu pars six eglises
Le secret de Poussin
Accompli le gardien du démon de midi
Aucune tentation pour un berger
Dans l'église de juste et le bezu –
Derrière le voile de la Déesse cherchez

Six churches hold the key
The secret of Poussin
Completes the demon guardian of midday
No temptation for one shepherd
In the church of Just et le Bézu
Search beneath the veil of the Goddess

Rahn's face broke out in a wide smile of disbelief. 'We've done it!' he said. 'Look, the secret is hidden in six churches, so that no one priest would be tempted. Now I know why Cros and Saunière both had reproductions of Poussin's painting *Les Bergers d'Arcadie*. From memory there's a tomb and some shepherds and the goddess Venus. And there's a famous inscription, but I can't remember what it is.'

'Do you think Poussin belonged to one of the brotherhoods?' La Dame asked, blowing smoke rings in the already choked air of the Peugeot.

Rahn considered it. 'I don't know. Let's see what we know now: it looks like there are six churches and each one must have one part of the secret, whatever it is, and when one brings all the parts together one can complete the demon of midday, that is, one can find the treasure of the Cathars that completes *Le Serpent Rouge*. At least, this is my guess! So, the first church is Just-et-le-Bézu, where's that?'

'Saint-Just-et-le-Bézu . . . I know where that is,' said Eva.

'Well let us go then, we're losing light!' Rahn was single-minded and absorbed.

But La Dame must have seen something, because he said, 'Hold on!'

What happened next was so sudden that Rahn didn't so much think as act by instinct. He slipped the parchment and the note with his calculations into his left shoe a moment before La Dame's door was flung open and he was pulled savagely out of the car. In a blink Rahn himself was being dragged out and thrown onto the icy ground next to his friend.

41

THREE'S COMPANY AND FIVE'S A CROWD

'You look frightened out of your wits what's the matter?'
'A great misfortune I fear.'
Emile Gaboriau, The Clique of Gold

Rahn was sitting beside La Dame, who was nursing a broken lip. He looked up and saw a man standing over them, pointing a gun in their direction. Meanwhile, a second man was holding Eva, a gun to her temple.

She struggled. 'Let go of me, you brute!'

But the man's oily face was a mask. Obviously he wasn't the principal of the two because the other man was the first to speak. He was impeccably dressed in a double-breasted suit, and from this angle Rahn could see the sky reflected in his shoes.

'You're a difficult man to catch, Monsieur Rahn,' he said, a wry smile wrinkling his smooth face.

'You're Russians,' Rahn said, recognising the accent.

The grin widened. 'Serbians, actually.'

'Who are you?' Rahn was indignant.

The man leaning over Rahn drew his face into a concerned frown and shook his head. 'We are friends . . . and we are concerned for Deodat, just as you are.'

Trust no one!

'What do you know about Deodat?' Rahn said.

The man raised a hand to stop him. 'We were there at the house, but we didn't see you. Perhaps you were hiding?'

'Hiding! I don't like what you're suggesting! I was bashed unconscious and left in the trunk of the Tourster – I'm lucky to be alive.'

There was a momentary illumination and the man whistled. 'So, that's what that man was doing in the barn? He was going to set fire to it with you in it! You would have suffered the fate of your heroes, a purifying death in the flames . . .' He smiled a crooked smile. 'Had it not been for your friend Dragomir.'

Dragomir nodded his head in appreciation of his superior's acknowledgement.

Rahn said, 'Do you know who took Deodat?'

'I believe he is being held by some very ruthless people.' The man squatted, light on his toes, and pushed the hat back from his sizeable forehead with his gun, in a poor imitation of Humphrey Bogart in *Bullets or Ballots*.

Rahn felt a welling up of anger and impatience and disdain and he made to get up but the man aimed the gun at a place between his eyes and calmly said, 'I would like you to remain seated, if you please. Think of it this way, if you die . . . what will become of your friend? This will only take a moment.' He considered his next words as if he were choosing from a menu in which every item sounded as good as the next. Finally he settled on: 'The people who have your friend may be encouraging you to find—' he smiled again, '—let us call it, a dangerous and very powerful *article*. Perhaps Deodat is their insurance that you will do so with haste, am I right?'

Rahn was shaking from anger and from cold and exasperation because the following words were indeed the truth, 'I don't know!'

The man's smile turned sympathetic, an old friend commiserating with another. Rahn didn't know if a compassionate villain made things better or worse. 'Now as far as who has your friend,' the man continued, 'if it is the penitents, those Satan-worshipping Jesuits, then his soul is already lost; if it is Association Angelica . . . well, one cannot even imagine what those war-mongering royalists are doing to him.' He sighed, and scratched his cheek with the barrel of the gun pensively. It was the natural gesture of an artisan's familiarity with his tool of trade and it made Rahn nervous. 'If either of those brotherhoods have him – trust me, if he is not already dead, he will be praying for it. People like that can make death seem like a holiday.' He laughed, and turned around to his fellow, who made a smirk and a huff.

'Perhaps,' he said, 'if the penitents have him, they are saving him for midnight tonight, the beginning of *The Day of the Dead*. They'll use him in their ritual, that is, the one they hope they can enact when you find them the *article*. They will gut him while still alive, on a black onyx table with a knife shaped like an angled snake. That's the usual fare, isn't it, Dragomir?'

The man grunted, acknowledging the fair estimation.

'Dragomir should know – they cut out his tongue! That is what they usually do for minor infringements.'

Rahn's eyes widened.

The other man nodded sadly.

'On the other hand, if it is Association Angelica that has him, then there is no problem.'

Rahn raised a brow. *Was there a hope?*

'No problem,' the man continued, 'because he would be dead by now. So you see, handing over your *findings* to either of these groups, in the hopes of saving your friend's life, would not be profitable.'

Rahn felt a grey cloud overtake him and he was terrified he was going to faint. He bit his lip. 'Who are you from – AGLA?'

The man looked surprised and there was more than a little

admiration on his face. 'You've worked out something about AGLA? That is *good!* That priest at Rennes-le-Château was trying to steer you away from himself because he belonged to the penitents. He is the one who desecrated that church with the ancient symbol.'

'I knew it!' Rahn said, and then a thought occurred to him, *'Belonged?'*

The man looked down a moment, as if trying to broach what must be delicate matters. 'Poor Abbé Lucien is at this moment hanging by one leg upside down from a tree near Couiza. His hands dangle downwards and he has one leg bent backwards and tied behind him. After all, he is a betrayer of secrets.'

'You killed him?' Rahn screeched.

The other raised his brows, and the look was of mild incredulity. 'Me . . . personally?' He shook his head. No.'

Rahn remembered how Abbé Gélis's carcass had also been left in the shape of the hanged man tarot card – along with a calling card from Association Angelica. 'Was it AA?'

The man nodded, expelling his breath in a whistle again and in a conspiratorial tone whispered, 'But they are the least of your problems. You should be worried about AGLA. They are not far behind you.'

'How do you know?'

'Because we are watching them, watching you. It is only a matter of time before they catch you and then . . . well . . .' He smiled, as if this itself said all there was to say.

Rahn could hear the sound of a bird cawing, otherwise all was still. The fog was moving over the ground with stealth. He wondered if he was about to die here in this godforsaken place.

'Now . . . all you need do to rid yourself of this problem is to hand me the parchment.'

'What parchment?'

'The one in your shoe, the one Madame Dénarnaud gave you.'

La Dame said, 'Why should he trust you?'

The man's face was full of surprise, as if he had forgotten La Dame and would now put this terrible rudeness to rights. 'Professor! I'm so glad you have brought up the matter of trust because I—'

A shot rang out. It sounded more like a cannon in the stillness. Dragomir fell and began to cough, gasping to find any small puff of air as if he were choking. Blood was oozing from his mouth and from a hole in his neck. The sympathetic man with the gun had turned around and was crouching, looking in the direction from which the shot had been fired. Meanwhile Rahn took hold of a sizeable rock and was about to hit him over the head when another shot rang out, hitting the crouching Serbian in the belly. The man fell and pointed to La Dame but could say nothing. Rahn had no idea who had shot them and he didn't care.

There was a mad scramble to get into the Peugeot.

Rahn took the wheel and such was his agitation that he put his foot down on the accelerator with a force that sent the car skidding over the road.

Eva said calmly, 'I hear a siren!'

Rahn didn't know what to do, so he just kept driving. 'Does anyone know how to get to Saint-Just-et-le-Bézu?' he cried, at the end of his tether.

'Just continue on this road north and turn right at the turn-off to Granes!' Eva pointed.

He looked in the rear-view mirror: La Dame was touching at his lip to see if it was still bleeding. He was paler than his beard – not even while potholing had he looked more worse-for-wear.

'What happened back there, Rahn?' La Dame said, with a touch of melodrama.

'I don't know! Someone was either helping us or trying to kill us, take your pick.'

'Do you think the Serbian was right about Deodat?' Eva said.

'I can't think about that right now. We have the clue, let's use it and see where it leads us.'

'Didn't you hear what that man said?' La Dame pointed out, testily. 'They're probably watching us right now!'

'So what do you want to do, La Dame, sit here and wait till they kill us? So far no one else has any idea about what's on the parchment. That's our only insurance.'

'I don't agree,' La Dame protested. 'Once we find what we're, or rather, *they're* after, what's to stop them from killing us anyway?'

'Nothing,' Rahn said laconically.

'My God, I need a brandy!' La Dame mourned, and all conversation ended for a time.

They arrived at the dismal little village of Saint-Just-etle-Bézu in the dark. It was deathly cold and the medieval township at the foot of the mountain was turning in on itself. The fog obscured the way to the cheerless church; its entrance was in the street. A painted cross over the arched doorway told them they were in the right place. Luckily, they found the oak door ajar and stepped inside, where it was no warmer. Rahn felt the old familiar panic rise to his throat. His mouth was a dry, barren wasteland, his knees were broken hinges and his breathing was an engine running out of steam. He sneezed then, occasioning a cry from the sacristan who was sweeping the church. The old man's emaciated form, standing beneath the blue-vaulted ceiling, was lit by the dancing luminance of the altar candles.

'Who are you?' he cried. 'The church is closed!'

'We're terribly sorry, old friend,' La Dame stepped forward with a casual manner. 'We didn't mean to frighten you. We were just passing and stopped for a moment to take a look in your beautiful church. We're looking for . . . a veil – the veil of a goddess to be exact. Do you happen to know where we might find it? There was something about it in a magazine and we just had to see it.'

'A veil? A goddess, you say?' The squinting man considered this and said, with a modicum of suspicion in his voice, 'At this ungodly hour? City people! Why not come back tomorrow? It will be *All Soul's Day*, and the priest is coming again.' He made a sweep of the hand. 'I'm busy getting the church ready, as you can see.'

'Please, just a few moments. What harm can it do?' Eva cajoled, smiling.

The man sighed. 'Very well, the only veil we have is over there, behind glass. But it's only a copy.' He went to the altar, took a candle and gave it to Eva. 'I must see to some preparations in the sacristy, so you may look until I'm done.'

La Dame and Eva soon found the framed veil and Rahn, following behind, put a hand to his brow where a cold sweat had gathered and was snaking its way over his face.

'Come see this!' La Dame called out to him.

When Rahn joined them he gave another sneeze and it was a moment before he realised they were looking at an engraving hung precariously from a long nail protruding from the stonework. It was too dark in this corner to see it clearly.

'Take it down, La Dame, so we can have a closer look,' Rahn asked.

It was an image of a bearded face drawn over a stretched cloth. Below it was written:

VERA EFFIGIES SACRI VULTUS DOMINI
NOSTRI JESU CHRISTI QUAE ROMAE
IN SACROSANCTA BASILICA S.PETRI IN
VATICANO RELIGIOSISSIME ASSERVATUR
ET COLITUR

'*Veronica's print of the face of our Lord Jesus Christ, guarded in the Basilica of Saint Peter in the Vatican*,' Rahn translated it under his breath.

'That's it!' Eva said. 'On the way to the crucifixion a woman called Veronica took an impression of the face of Christ on her veil – Veronica's veil!'

'Veronica must be the goddess the clue is referring to.' Rahn turned the print around and looked at the back of it. He lifted the backing up a little and gave another sneeze, which bounced off the walls at them. 'There's nothing behind it.' He gave it back to La Dame, who replaced it on its hook.

'Wait!' Eva said. 'Beneath is not behind. Maybe it means underneath the print. Maybe on the floor . . . A print can be moved but a mark on the stone is there to stay and can go unnoticed.'

Rahn took the candle and squatted to look at the flagstone at his feet. He put his hand to it to see if he could feel any marks that may have been covered up by grime or wear. Nothing. But as he was rising something caught his eye on the wall directly below the painting. He found what looked like a plugged-up hole the size of a small walnut in the wall. He gave the candle to La Dame, took out his penknife and carefully inserted the end of it into the hole. It took a moment but he soon teased out the plug and what lay behind it: a narrow glass vial.

There was the noise of a latch as the sacristy door opened.

'All right! I have to close the church now!'

Rahn hid the vial in his coat pocket. 'A wonderful specimen!' he said to him.

'The veil?' The thin man came over to them. 'No, it isn't so rare. Other churches around these parts have them: Bugarach, Saint-Paul-de-Fenouillet . . . Brenac.'

'Saint-Paul-de-Fenouillet, that's Abbé Grassaud's church?' Rahn said, surprised.

'Yes.' The man's face opened into a toothless grin. 'Do you know him? He grew up in this town. He went to seminary school and was accepted into Saint Sulpice in Paris. He is a doctor of theology now. We are very proud of him!'

Rahn tried to take this in and wondered if it was coincidence or design. *Saint Sulpice! Could Grassaud be a member of Association Angelica?*

They thanked the sacristan and left. Once outside, Rahn felt both relieved to be out of the church and encouraged that they were one step closer in their search. 'We've got it!' he said.

'We've got *what*, dear Rahn?' La Dame said, whining. 'We don't know what it is yet.'

'Well, I aim to find out. We need light to have a look at this, and besides I think we deserve something to eat and a glass of brandy. What do you say?'

All were in agreement. They took the road out of the dismal little town and headed back to Granes. But they had only been driving a short time when they came up behind a hearse travelling at a snail's pace over the mist-laden road.

'What's a hearse doing about at this hour?' Rahn said.

'It is rather odd!' La Dame agreed. 'Perhaps it's like the curious incident of the dog in the night time, Rahn!'

'What?' Eva asked.

'From a Sherlock Holmes story – "Silver Blaze"' Rahn informed her.

'What did the dog do?' Eva said.

'The dog did nothing,' Rahn replied. 'Actually, it didn't bark when it should have and that was the curious incident.'

'In other words,' La Dame added, 'if something is odd or curious, there may be a good reason for it.'

Rahn nodded. La Dame was right. The forest of partially denuded trees stood sombre on either side of the narrow country road and there was no way to pass the hearse safely – if someone came from behind them, they would be trapped. Every now and again they would lose the hearse around a corner, but they could still see the fog glowing from its headlamps. The road narrowed even further and at this point headlights appeared in the opposite direction. The hearse stopped and began to reverse, forcing Rahn to follow until they had reached a point where the oncoming car could squeeze past them.

'I like this less and less,' La Dame said.

'Look, there's a car behind us!' Eva put in.

Rahn glanced in the rear-view mirror and realised she was right. His heart did a double somersault. Once again that potholer's sense of foreboding had been on the mark. *Could it be the black Citroën?*

'What are you going to do?' Eva said.

'I don't know!' he answered tersely. But now he realised that due to a peculiarity in the road he had lost sight of both cars. He saw a turn-off on the right and knew this might be their only opportunity, so he switched off his headlights and took the turn sharply.

This occasioned a cry from La Dame: 'What are you doing!'

'Shut up, will you?' Rahn said, concentrating, his heart in his throat.

He drove the Peugeot only a little way by the faint light of an unseen moon and switched off the engine. 'We'll wait here,' he told them, 'and for crying out loud, La Dame, don't light up your cigar. This could be nothing, or it could be something. The car behind us won't know he's not following us for a while.'

'What now then? You do realise that you must be a suspect in five murders and one kidnapping? Not to mention the man at the university!' La Dame said.

Rahn *hadn't* thought about it like that. It was true! There was Abbé Cros, that man in the barn at Arques, Abbé Lucien, and now those two Serbians lying dead in some desolate spot near Campagne-sur-Aude, and if all this weren't enough there was Deodat's fate to take into account, whatever that might be! He felt dismal, but there was nothing to be done about it now. He had to concentrate. When he felt it was safe, he turned the key and the lights came on again, illuminating the fog that, like a living thing, had grown to like their company. He reversed the Peugeot back to the juncture with the road to Granes and took to the road again, continuing until he found a shoulder on the left with enough cover to hide behind. He stopped the car and turned the engine off.

'What now?' La Dame cried.

'Look, it's like this, if that car *was* following us, whoever is in it will soon figure out we've given them the slip and they'll come back looking for us.'

Sure enough, within moments of Rahn having said this, the car drove past – it was the black Citroën. As soon as he saw those tail-lights disappear, Rahn pulled out again and set off for Granes at full speed, hoping the hearse was long gone.

At Granes they came to a little pension on the Grand Rue that was still open. They parked the car around the back of the building and met the owner of the establishment sitting at the front, smoking a pipe. He was a portly man, with a long moustache and a short disposition. He told them that there were two rooms available and that the kitchen was closed but that his wife could warm up some leftover rabbit stew if this sounded to their liking.

In the poorly lit kitchen, having consumed what was left of a delicious stew, La Dame sipped at his brandy and puffed on a Cuban, looking almost like his old self, except for the split lip. Eva sipped at her tea and Rahn unrolled the little yellowed parchment he had taken out of the vial. It was another encrypted message and it looked similarly constructed to the last:

VITA
XWNSOILSV
YIGSGIVRJQQDZLBEP

'So, what's the master word?' La Dame asked, sitting forward to see.

Rahn took out his Vigenère Square and looked at it.

'Vita. It's the only intelligible word and besides, it fits: life and death, vita and mors.'

Rahn wrote 'vita' underneath the cipher and used the Vigenère Square again to decipher each letter.

Master word	V	I	T	A	V	I	T	A	V
Plain text	C	o	u	s	t	a	s	s	a
Cipher text	X	W	N	S	O	I	L	S	V

'Coustassa!' Rahn said. The church of Abbé Gélis! Yes, of course it's on the list!'

He deciphered the second line:

Master word	V	I	T	A	V	I	T	A	V	I	T	A	V	I	T	A	V
Plain text	D	a	n	s	l	a	c	r	o	i	x	d	e	d	i	E	u
Cipher text	Y	I	G	S	G	I	V	R	J	Q	Q	D	Z	L	B	E	P

'*Inside the cross of God* . . . You know what this means? We have to go to Coustassa and we'll have to go there now. You heard what that Serbian said 0about tonight – think of Deodat!'

Despite protestations from La Dame, they left Granes discreetly, and headed north to Coustassa via Campagne-les-Bains, where the Serbians had accosted them. Rahn kept to the back roads, his eye on the rear-view mirror looking out for the Citroën.

He was glad to reach the town of Coustassa without incident.

The village appeared to be worn out and in decline and, like its church, looked for the most part to be sleeping except for a house here and there showing a light at its window. A fine rain fell and all three were wet and trembling by the time they got to the church. Their mood did not improve when they found it locked. Rahn took out his knife, and selected from its assortment of gadgets a suitable device and put it into the lock, moving it around this way and that. It didn't work. He heard Eva sigh beside him.

'Here, let me,' she said and took the penknife from his hand with an air of authority that was infuriating. 'A lawyer's secretary has to learn one or two unconventional skills.'

She moved the knife deftly until there was an audible click.

'Bravo!' La Dame whispered.

Rahn grunted. 'What kind of lawyers did you work for?'

'The ordinary kind – the kind that don't always obey the law.'

Inside, the only light came from the votive candles and the perpetual flame at the altar. Rahn reconciled himself to entering another church even though the thought of it made his every muscle and sinew scream for him to stop. He told himself that Deodat was still alive and that each step closer to the treasure was a step closer to Deodat. Keeping this firmly in his mind, he walked down the short nave, opened the little gate and took the three steps to the sacred space before the altar. Here the rabbit stew came to life, thumping its feet in his stomach as he took himself to the cross. His anxiety made his chest feel like a squeezed lemon.

Inside the cross of God . . . The cross on the altar looked to be solid and fixed. There was no way of removing it without making noise. Behind the altar there hung a large picture of Christ on his cross, a terrible rendition of His death that had been darkened by centuries of candle smoke. Rahn went to it now and inspected it. As he did so he thought it through:

Vita was the master word in the second parchment – the word for life in Latin.

The next clue was, *inside the cross of God.*

Could it mean that the clue was hidden inside that painting depicting death? If so, then someone had a sense of humour! He inspected the painting and noted that part of the canvas had been pulled away from the frame at the bottom left-hand corner. His heart sank. It looked like someone had beaten them to it. If there had been a clue here – it was gone.

'I think we're too late,' he said.

'Too late for what?' La Dame asked.

'The clue is missing.'

'But that doesn't make sense,' Eva said. 'Saint-Just-et-le-Bézu was intact and that was the second clue, the second parchment. To find this parchment they would have needed to have found the first and second parchments,' Eva said.

'I don't know, maybe it was Gélis?' Rahn said. 'Maybe he started tearing apart his own church, like Saunière did. It certainly looks renovated.'

'Then this may not be the original painting,' Eva pointed out.

Rahn told La Dame to bring him a candle and in the meantime pulled the painting away from the wall a little. 'Look at this. The original wall surface is still behind the painting. It must have always been here and they renovated around it. Now, if Gélis did find something hidden in it, he could have sold it to Cros. That would explain the money they found in his presbytery. It would also explain why Saint-Just-et-le-Bézu is intact. Cros could have used the clue in this church to find the clues in the other four churches and it may have been enough to point him in the direction of the treasure.'

'So it's gone and he has been buried with it,' Eva said. 'In that case I was right, Cros had been so secretive about his funeral arrangements because he wanted to hide the treasure in his coffin.'

Rahn felt the blood drain from his head. 'This has been for nothing and now Deodat will be killed – or worse!'

'Listen, Rahn,' La Dame said, 'something doesn't add up. If I'd found the treasure I wouldn't bother to hide the list and guard it so keenly. I'd be sunning myself on the Côte d'Azur, with a bottle of Luis Felipe and affectionate friends to keep me company.'

Rahn grabbed La Dame by the shoulders then and shook him with delight.

'Steady on, Rahn! Have you lost your senses?'

'No! The very opposite! I think you're right, La Dame! Why not just destroy the list? Why was Grassaud after it, if it had no value? And why would Madame Dénarnaud say that the moment Abbé Lucien looked at it he would know what to do?'

'There has to be something that we've missed!' Eva said.

'No, he always wanted someone to find the list, for a reason.' Rahn took the list from his pocket. 'After all, he gave us the clue to the tabernacle where it was kept.' He moved closer to the candles to study it.

> Jean-Louis Verger – Paris 1857 – *Penitents*
> Antoine Bigou – Rennes-le-Château – 1781 *AA*
>
> ~
>
> A J Grassaud – Saint-Paul-de-Fenouillet 1886
> A C Saunière – Rennes-le-Château 1885
> A K Boudet – Rennes-les-Bains 1885 – *AA*
> A A Gélis – Coustaussa *murdered* 1897
> A L Rivière – Espéraza *refused last sacrament* 1915

'The two names at the top of the list differ from the rest,' Eva pointed out.

'Yes, they're separated, as we said before, because those priests weren't contemporaries of Saunière,' Rahn reminded her.

'No, there's something else,' she said.

'What?'

'She's right!' La Dame erupted. 'Look, Rahn, Verger and Bigou both have their first names. The others on the list below only have initials.' He gave Eva a conspiratorial smile that annoyed Rahn so much that he was hard pressed not to kick him. Even so, he had to admit it was true.

'The A must stand for Abbé because it occurs before every name,' Eva said, 'so we'll ignore that. Now, logic would say that the other initials point to first names. But they don't, do they?

'Saunière's first name was Bérenger,' Rahn said. 'And that doesn't match.'

'And what about Abbé Grassaud?' La Dame said. 'What was his name?'

Eva gave Rahn and La Dame a significant look. 'His name was Eugene.'

'Another mismatch,' Rahn announced.

'I'll wager that all the initials are wrong,' Eva said, finally.

'Yes, it might be another cipher,' Rahn agreed. 'Let's see, if you put all the initials together it makes . . . JCKAL.'

Eva looked at it. 'What if it is meant to be jackal, but Cros had to conform to the number of priests on the list and so he had to leave one letter out. Is there a connection?'

'Anubis!' Rahn said, looking at the two of them. 'Anubis is the jackal-headed Egyptian god . . . the god of the Underworld!'

'That took you long enough to figure!' said a voice that made them all jump nearly out of their skins. Rahn saw a shape in the darkness. When it came into the light he wanted to faint.

42

WHAT DID KING DAGOBERT SAY TO HIS HOUNDS?

'The surprise was not all on one side I assure you!'
Sir Arthur Conan Doyle, The Hound of the Baskervilles

The man stepped out from the shadows. 'The mademoiselle is right. There is a church missing on that list . . . that is why the word JCKAL is not complete.' Rahn couldn't believe his eyes. 'Deodat! We thought—'

'Yes, I know.' Deodat looked perfectly calm and not at all tortured, harangued or abused. In fact he looked better than Rahn felt. Rahn had to sit down, and found a pew. He was breathless and feeling faint. The crushing weight of responsibility that he had felt until now lifted from him, leaving him completely unable to speak for a moment. He was thoroughly numbed.

'Come, come, dear Rahn, are you alright? I owe you a thousand apologies!' Deodat said, making his way to him.

Rahn stood a moment, looking at his friend's concerned face. 'Good gracious! I can hardly believe my eyes. I – I'm in shock!' Then, 'I've never been more glad to see anyone in all my life!' He was choked up, and took Deodat's hand and shook it vigorously, but his joy soon gave way to a sudden vexation. 'How dare you upset me like that!' he said, letting go the hand. 'For Heaven's sake, Deodat! Where have you been? What have you been doing? We found a note, the house was ransacked, you were gone . . . They nearly killed me!'

'Hold on, Rahn,' Deodat said, lifting up a hand to stay him. 'For things to make sense you have to tell me everything from the beginning.'

Rahn held in his annoyance and curiosity until he had told Deodat of his misadventures: his being locked in the boot of the Tourster; the man with his throat cut; the conversation with Grassaud at the hermitage; the Sator Square and what led them to Rennes-le-Château. He told him about the underground crypt; the desecration of the church; Madame Dénarnaud; the circle of abbés; the parchment; Saunière's dealings with Association Angelica, the penitents and the Freemasons. He told him about Abbé Lucien, the anchor and the snake, and about the Serbians who accosted them and were killed for their efforts. He told him how they had managed to decode the parchment using the Vigenère Square and how the solution had led them to Saint-Just-et-le-Bézu, where they had found the second clue, which had brought them here to Coustassa. He also told him about the hearse and the black Citroën that had been following them.

Deodat listened without interruption, nodding now and again as was his custom. When Rahn finished, Deodat was thoughtful for a long time before speaking. 'Well, Rahn, you've exceeded my expectations. Well done! Capital job. Things are falling into place, everything you've told me coincides quite beautifully with what I have discovered.'

'What are you talking about?' Rahn said. His vexation was not mollified. 'Are you telling me you weren't kidnapped – that this has been an elaborate hoax?'

'Let me start at the beginning. Yesterday morning, when we

decided to rest before seeing Abbé Grassaud, there was a knock at the door. It was Inspecteur Beliere. He told me he had gone to Bugarach to see Mademoiselle Cros to ask her some questions about the abbé's death. When he got there, he said the house was open and the maid was missing, as was the mademoiselle. Every room had been ransacked. It was obvious that whoever had done it was looking for something or someone, and the inspector said that he was very concerned for her safety, not to mention ours. He asked me what I knew about the mademoiselle. I told him we'd only just met on the day the abbé died. He then told me he was investigating La Cagoule because the police had been informed of a plot to assassinate the president and that there were various secret societies in the south involved. In light of this, I could no longer refrain from telling him about the list, and what we had discovered concerning *Le Serpent Rouge* and the key to completing it.' Deodat's eyes shone and his cheeks were flushed with exhilaration in recounting it. 'And so I gave him the list, knowing full well that we had made another one. He wanted me to come with him and asked where you might be; I told him you had gone to Espéraza with the housekeeper and that I would leave you a note where to find me.'

'That was the note?'

'Yes.'

'But you made it sound like you were kidnapped!'

'And I was.'

'I don't understand.'

'You see, at this point I already knew that the inspector was suspect.'

'What?'

'Yes, he was an imposter!'

'How did you know that?'

'After you went to bed I couldn't rest. I had suspicions about Beliere, so I called the Paris judiciaire and they told me that a certain Beliere had been sent to Carcassonne. When I asked them to describe the man they said he was tall, rather thin and balding. As you know, this description does not fit with our short, squat, Inspecteur Beliere.'

'But then, what made you think he wasn't the real thing in first place?'

'In all my years as a magistrate I have seen many inspectors, but I have never seen one who wears a suit that looks like it has been slept in—'

'Is that all?'

'But you haven't let me finish, dear Rahn! A crumpled suit and the most brilliantly polished shoes. Such polarities and enigmas do draw my attention. I then remembered something, which you will recall I mentioned to you. He was in possession of a military . . .'

'A what?'

'Le Francais Model 28. A revolver specifically designed for the French army.'

'I still don't see!'

'Of course you wouldn't. Only those who have some knowledge of guns, the army and the police would know. You see, the army and the police had both decided to pass on the design of that gun and none of those revolvers were ever taken into service. You will only find them in the hands of civilians nowadays.'

'Remarkable!' Rahn said.

'Observation is paramount, Rahn, as Sherlock Holmes often tells Watson. Seeing is one thing, observing another! Now, once I knew he was not the same man who was sent here, I realised that he must have done away with the real Inspecteur Beliere and taken his place. So, I called the Carcassonne gendarmerie, as I wanted to know if the man had ever arrived at all, because this would tell me one of two things: if he never arrived then he must have been killed en route, and the police should be looking for him if they are not also in on it; if he had arrived and he was the real Inspecteur Beliere, he might be completely unware that another man was impersonating him. So I called and asked to know the whereabouts of our Inspecteur Beliere and they said he was not in . . . that he was on the way to an address – my address! When they gave me his description I knew.'

'Oh!' Rahn said. 'Did you tell the police to come as soon as possible?'

'No. Are you mad?'

'Why not?'

'Because I didn't know if I could trust them. At this stage I thought the gendarmes might be in on it too. So I went upstairs to wake you and to take you to the Tourster. But that blow to your head must have done more damage than we had estimated because you got up like a sleepwalker, and it took me quite a time to get you to the barn. By then I could hear the sound of cars coming. I told you to get into the trunk and, because you were in some ways like a person who is hypnotised, you did so without complaint and I closed the lid, but only slightly, just enough to make it seem closed. I thought when you woke up you could just push the trunk lid open to get out. I had no time to escape with you, you see, so I did what was necessary. You must play your cards as best you can when the stakes are high. I went round the back of the house then, and entered it by the back door, and in a moment our fake inspector was knocking at the front door. Well, I knew that in the trunk you were safe for the time being and, if it came to the worst – if they did away with me – you would find the key before they did!'

'This is just like Sherlock Holmes in *The Hound of the Baskervilles!*' La Dame said, looking on with admiration.

Deodat sighed. 'As Dagobert said to his hounds: "Sometimes even the best of friends must part if there is to be a hunt . . ." I knew that if you could just keep out of Beliere's clutches, you would be safe.'

'Why did you think that?'

'Because your name was in Monti's diary, that's why! Monti

being the man he was, he no doubt told others that you were the one who could find the key. You were *tenet*, as I said to you that night in my study: the lowest common denominator, the only one capable of finding what had been lost for hundreds of years. That's why the groups looking for the *treasure* were not going to get in your way. In fact, it seems some groups were even willing to give up whatever clues they had to help you along, hoping that they would be the first to seize the treasure from your hands once you had found it for them.'

'But what about you – what happened to you?' Rahn asked.

'That's a long story too. To cut it short, they took me to Maison de Cros where I was detained in the wine cellar and that is where I finally met the real Inspecteur Beliere.

'So what did he say to you?' Rahn asked.

'Not much actually, it's difficult putting words together when you're hanging by your neck from the rafters! At any rate I wasn't there long. Last night I heard a commotion, some muffled sounds and this morning, the man who had been guarding my door seemed awfully quiet, so I ventured out carefully to take a look and found him sitting in the kitchen with his face in his dinner and his throat cut from ear to ear. That's when I took the Citroën—'

'The black Citroën!' Rahn said, suddenly illuminated. 'The one that had been parked outside the Maison de Cros!'

'Exactly so.'

'Then *you're* the one who's been following us?'

'Yes – you see, last night the fake Beliere told me he knew you were at Rennes-le-Château, and he was going to fetch you so that he could take turns at torturing us into telling him what we knew. This morning when I escaped I went straight to Rennes-le-Château to find you but the police were already there. The problem was, I couldn't tell if it was the fake Beliere, men working for him, or the actual police, so I waited outside the town. That's how I saw you leaving with La Dame and the mademoiselle, headed for

Couiza and the boulangerie. I sent the boy with the note but you didn't get my clue, did you? The rebus.'

'That was you? I thought your kidnappers made you write it. I feared they were becoming impatient and quite possibly about to cut off your nose or something equally as precious. Why didn't you just come into the boulangerie, or write something simple, for instance: "I'm outside in the Citroën"?'

'Because, dear Rahn, firstly, I knew you were being watched by those Serbians, so I wasn't about to just walk in and announce myself; and secondly, I thought you'd be smart enough to instantly recognise the note as a warning from me about the mademoiselle. I had to make it enigmatic in case the note was intercepted or the girl got a hold of it. I thought you would have put two and two together to make four, but instead, once again, you've come up with twenty-two!'

'Well, whatever the case, we gave you the slip!'

'Yes you did, and a good chase it was, until I finally found you lying on the ground with a gun to your head. So I did the only thing I could do. I shot those men.'

'That was you? You're a crack shot, Deodat!' La Dame effused.

Deodat gave him a sideways glance. 'Luckily, that Citroën came fully equipped with a virtually brand new Mosin-Nagant carbine rifle, with a scope mount, no less – any sniper would have been proud. A marvellous weapon for a hunt. It's the latest technology and deadly accurate, as those men found out.'

'I didn't know you could shoot like that!' Rahn said.

'Why not? Have you forgotten how we ate when we were potholing? Those rabbits don't grow on trees, you know. At any rate, after that I lost you for a small time and caught up with you again on the road back from Saint-Just-et-le-Bézu when you were behind that hearse! That was a clever manoeuvre, Rahn, quite ingenious. After that I drove around Granes looking for you and found your car in a side street. I waited and followed you here to Coustassa and now I have something to tell you . . . but first, where is she?'

'Who?'

'Mademoiselle Cros, or should I say – Mademoiselle Fleury!'

'What?' Rahn said. This hunt had more twists and turns than the Gorges of Galamus! 'Fleury?' He looked about him in the darkness and at that moment he heard the sound of the door to the church closing. Rahn took himself down the nave but by the time he was at the door he could hear the Peugeot starting and before he could reach her, she had taken off.

'Don't tell me you left the keys in the car, Rahn!' It was Deodat beside him.

'Why would she do that?' Rahn stood in the deathly cold feeling perplexed, watching as the tail-lights of the auto disappeared into the rain and fog.

'I'm not surprised,' Deodat said.

'What did you mean by "Fleury"?' Rahn looked at him, feeling a wave of vertigo and a sudden reviving of that bee in his ear.

'I found out from Beliere – or whatever his name is – that she is a direct relative of Gabriele Fleury, daughter of Marie de Nègre Hautpoul-Blanchefort! Marie Blanchefort had three daughters: Elisabeth, Gabriele and Mary. From what you say, she chose to leave her inheritance in the hands of Abbé Bigou instead. The mademoiselle is after what she feels is rightfully hers – the treasure of the Cathars.' He paused. 'Now I think she's realised that she is in way over her head and, if she's smart, she'll keep driving all the way to Italy.'

'And we were almost close,' La Dame said, wistfully.

'Oh that's right, *you're* here,' Deodat bemoaned, turning to him.

'It's a pleasure to see you too, Deodat,' La Dame said. 'So, what now?'

'Well,' Rahn said, 'the parchment clue in this church is missing, so, unless we can figure out what JCKAL means, we have nothing to go on. Besides, you're alive, Deodat, and now the imperative to find the treasure is no longer there.'

'What nonsense!' Deodat retorted.

'But we've hit a dead end!' Rahn countered.

'Have we? I don't believe so . . .' Deodat said, happily, looking like the cat that swallowed the goldfish. 'I think you were right about the list, ingeniously right. Think for a moment. There are five churches on the list; why is that, when there should be six?'

Rahn looked at Deodat's darkly lit face. 'Because Cros hadn't found the parchment at Saint-Just-et-le-Bézu!'

'Exactly so! Let's go over it: Cros knew of the parchment at Rennes-le-Château and I think this Abbé Gélis you mentioned must have found the parchment hidden in this church and he either sold it or gave it to Cros. And I don't think Cros gave it to the Bishop of Carcassonne; I feel certain of that. He kept it and made it his life's task to find the rest of the parchments. That would explain his obsession with puzzles. Now, the original parchment, he knew, was at Rennes-le-Château, that's one church; there was the parchment he didn't find at Saint-Justet-le-Bézu, that's the second church; this was the third church, Coustassa; so that leaves three more. Each parchment led to another. But here's the interesting part – years ago, Cros and I had a discussion on the tarot; remember I mentioned that to you before, Rahn? He was looking for information regarding the pope card. I remember it because it was so unusual. I gave him Éliphas Levi's book and he kept it for months. This is connected to it – I'm certain of it.'

'How?'

'Well, in my estimation, the family Perillos chose a circle of churches that were close enough for the priests to know one another, then they created an elaborate cipher and the master word to solving it was hidden in a painting by Poussin. The first church, Saunière's church, contained the original parchment given to Bigou by Marie de Hautpoul-Blanchefort on her deathbed. This parchment revealed the second church in which a second parchment revealed the third church and so on. Ingenious really! And if the chain was broken, it could be picked up at another point along the line, simply by understanding the rule.'

'What rule?'

'In every case the parchment was hidden in a church in which there could be found some connection, even if slight, to the tarot. Rennes-le-Château has its devil, the fifteenth card; Saint-Just-et-le-Bézu its goddess, the twenty-first card; and this church, Coustassa, has two pillars on either side of the altar, which to me signifies Joachim and Boaz, the second card. And I realise only now why Cros wanted Éliphas Levi's book. I believe that something in the parchment in this church must have led to the church at Rennes-les-Bains.'

'Why Rennes-les-Bains?' La Dame asked.

'Rennes-les-Bains has a painting depicting a pope straight out of the tarot, which signifies the fifth card.'

'Madame Dénarnaud also mentioned the tarot!' Rahn said. A thought occurred to him. 'What about Saint-Paul-de-Fenouillet?'

'The hermitage, Rahn; it signifies the ninth card – the hermit.'

'So, all the churches are on the list except for Saint-Just-et-le-Bézu, because Cros had never had the first parchment that led to it?' La Dame said.

'Yes, even you, La Dame, could figure that out!'

'But you've said nothing about that other church – Espéraza,' La Dame pointed out.

'I don't think that was one of the churches,' Deodat said to him.

'What do you mean?' Rahn said.

'I believe Cros may have thought it was one of them, but in the end, he realised it wasn't.'

Rahn shook his head. 'How on Earth do you know that?'

'I'll have to tell you how I came to my conclusion on our way.'

'On our way to where?' La Dame lamented.

'Get in the Citroën, it's over there – tempus fugit, tempus fugit!'

43

AND THE FIRST
SHALL BE THE LAST

'There is nothing more deceptive than an obvious fact.'
Sir Arthur Conan Doyle, 'The Boscombe Valley Mystery'

Enroute, Deodat told Rahn and La Dame of his discovery. Rahn drove the Citroën through the falling sleet, listening to Deodat. The night was dark and the road ahead was wet and barely lit by the headlamps.

'I have to start at the beginning. Yesterday morning, before Beliere came calling, and even before I had called the Paris judiciaire, I kept thinking there was something we had missed on the list . . . something obvious and yet elusive. I kept looking at it and eventually I figured out the same thing you did, Rahn: the initials were incorrect. When I put them together, I came to the same word . . . JCKAL. Now I can tell you what JCKAL has to do with it, but before I do so, I'll begin by explaining how I came to my conclusion. It's quite complicated and I can't prove it, not until we get to the church at Bugarach.'

Rahn could hear La Dame sighing in the back and striking a match to light his Cuban. 'My mind boggles,' he said.

'Well, La Dame, this should be right up your street, considering it's all about numbers. In fact it has to do with gematria.'

'Gematria! I know it: the study of numbers in connection with letters? Hebrew, isn't it?'

'That's right, you *are* good for something besides womanising and chalking in cave markings.'

'Are you never going to let me forget that?' La Dame said, sounding dejected.

'Never. Now, as I was saying, in the Hebrew mystical tradition, gematria is the secret of numbers. A text can be discovered through its connection to numbers because each letter has a numerical value, and the combination of letters has an esoteric significance. Now, in the wine cellar I had time to think about the word that Cros gave us – sator. In Hebrew, sator is made up of these letters: samech, which is sixty; vau, which is six; resh, which is two hundred; and tau, which is four hundred.'

Deodat looked at Rahn. 'Now, my point is, it doesn't really matter how it's spelt, whether sator or sorat, or taros or rotas, or any combination of those letters – they will always add up to six-six-six.'

'Burn my beard!' La Dame said, sitting forward and thrusting his head between them.

'The number of the *Beast of the Apocalypse of Saint John?*' Rahn said, incredulous.

'The number is all that is given in the Apocalypse,' Deodat said, 'and in a veiled way it indicates the name, Sorat.'

'Sorat?' Rahn said.

'Six-six-six is both the name and the seal of the sun demon Sorat, but *not* the sign – this is important. Grimoires are all about using spirits, demons and the like, to do the bidding of the living, but to control these beings one needs three things: a name, a seal and a sign – all three. If one of these three components is missing, the magician doesn't have full command over a demon or entity. Now, in the same way there is a Holy Trinity, there is also a Satanic one, a trinity of imperfect beings that is represented by six plus six plus six. It's not six hundred and sixty-six as many believe. The Antichrist is not just one being – that is a misconception – it is a collective of beings that work under the demon of the sun, Sorat. I think *Le Serpent Rouge* is able to summon this trinity of evil but not the demon Sorat. Monti quite rightly guessed that all grimoires are missing the most powerful key – the sign that summons Sorat. From the moment I saw that Monti had connected *Le Serpent Rouge* to the treasure of the Cathars, I had a sense that the missing key he was talking about was given in the original *Apocalypse of Saint John*. We had always said that the Apocalypse was part of that treasure, and now I feel sure of it. Imagine what this sign of Sorat could do in the hands of certain men? Do you see now why Cros had inscribed the sign of the Lamb of Christ into his tabernacle? He put it there to protect the sacrament from unholy forces, because the sign of the lamb repels the sign of Sorat – the demon of the black sun.'

'The black sun?' Rahn was in shock, remembering Wewelsburg. He was thinking the connections through out loud: 'The swastika is the symbol of the black sun – that's common knowledge among the SS. You know, I myself heard Hitler say to a group of the most senior SS dignitaries, his inner circle, something to the effect, that "all Germans must sacrifice their goodness, even their connection to Christ". I had a sense that there was something evil about Himmler and Hitler, but I mostly thought they were just madmen – I couldn't have been more wrong! This whole Nazi business is clearly part of an intelligent design to bring the German people under the worship of the black sun, under the worship of Sorat.'

'Sorat will bring about Apocalypse, Rahn, the end of the world, Armageddon! Yes,' Deodat confirmed. 'Hitler knew enough to reverse the swastika, transforming the ancient sun symbol into a symbol of evil. That is why you were sent here, Rahn – not to find *Le Serpent Rouge*, Hitler no doubt already has that; you were sent here to fetch the key. They need that key if Hitler is to invoke Sorat. Now you see the gravity of this entire affair? And soon we will know what JCKAL has to do with it . . . at Bugarach.

'Bugarach? Is that the sixth church?' Rahn said.

'Time will tell.'

When they arrived back at Bugarach church, Rahn parked the car behind some trees, feeling forlorn. He chose the same spot he had used two nights before and turned off the engine. The town lay dormant under a sky scattered with fast-moving clouds revealing behind them a tangle of stars. A thought occurred to Rahn and he turned to look at Deodat. 'What did you call that creature on the Countess P's clock?'

'A Leoncetophaline,' Deodat said.

'You said it was Hermetic, or Mithraic, right?'

'Yes, and it also represents the rogue sign, the thirteenth sign of the zodiac. The sign by which—' He looked at Rahn in the darkness and Rahn could just see the outline of his face. 'Ophiucus . . . it has two snakes winding around its body and in one hand it holds – a key! A key to the Underworld! A key to the forces of a living death . . . and a dead life . . . to Saturn forces – forces of the bottomless pit!' he said.

'Will someone let me in on what in God's name you're talking about?' La Dame said, from the back seat. His voice sounded anxious. He kept looking from this side to that.

'Are you expecting someone, La Dame?' Rahn said.

La Dame answered, 'I reserve the right to be moderately concerned for our safety. Have you still got that hunting gun, Deodat?'

'Actually I dropped it in the forest after I shot those men.'

But Rahn wasn't listening, his mind turned to a question that was bothering him. 'Deodat, what was that engraving on the clock, do you remember it? You know, I think the countess was leaving me a clue! Don't forget, she also died of a stroke on the same day as Saunière and Marie Blanchefort. Three people dying of strokes and all of them on the seventeenth of January, the date that Verger was sentenced; and it's also the same date in Monti's notebook. Don't forget that date marks the feast day of Saint Sulpice, and Saint Sulpice in Paris is the headquarters of AA, Association Angelica. I'm beginning to think, Deodat, that the Countess P was somehow mixed up in all this.'

Deodat was silent in the darkness. When he spoke his voice was grave. 'Rahn, I think you're right, and I can make sense of that riddle now. *This is a tomb that has no body in it . . . this is a body that has no tomb around it . . . but body and tomb are the same.*

This is a tomb that has no body in it – means the tomb is the corpse; after death the corpse has no spirit body in it. It is therefore a tomb without a spirit body. Now, *a body that has no tomb around it* – means the spirit body is free of the corpse and therefore has no tomb around it. But in certain cases the corpse and the spirit body remain united, even beyond the grave. In this case body and tomb, spirit and corpse, are one, do you see?'

'You mean, like a living death?' Rahn said.

'Yes, Rahn! In fact I'll wager that what we are dealing with here is a kind of suicide circle, wherein those who choose to die give over their spirits to the members of these groups as a form of immortality, but they may not know that this immortality is a sentence to Hell because those who run these groups are seeking to use them for the benefit of Sorat – the sun demon. That is the point! That would explain Saunière's sudden obsession with death and the penitents, and their cult of the dead, in which the sacrament that is administered to the dying is desecrated, mixed with excrement, to create a species of control after death.'

'I had a feeling that Cros had scratched the sign of the lamb in the tabernacle to protect his own sacrament!' Rahn said. 'Perhaps that's why he didn't want anyone knowing where he was going to be buried, because he was concerned they would somehow snatch his immortal soul.'

'Perhaps, but in order to invoke Sorat these groups need the sign, which they don't have – the key missing from *Le Serpent*

Rouge. So now we know what Hitler wants with the key and what the penitents want with the key, and perhaps also what this AA, and anyone else who is after it, are seeking – they are seeking to invoke Sorat, to bring about the end of the world so that they can install a New Jerusalem – a new world order that is to their liking. And we, my dear friends, are about to stop them, because the crucial ingredient, I believe, is in that church.'

'What makes you think Cros would hide it there? Wouldn't that be too obvious?' La Dame said, in the back.

'That's exactly why it's suspect!' Deodat said, with an emotion close to glee. 'And we are going to find it by using your Vigenère Square, Rahn. You are going to decipher JCKAL using Sorat as the master word.'

'So you think Cros wasn't intending to be buried with the treasure at all, and that the clues to the treasure's whereabouts are on the list – as I surmised?'

'Exactly so. Let's go, what are we waiting for?'

Inside the church, Rahn followed Deodat and La Dame to the altar like a lamb going to the slaughter. Once more, he wondered why in God's name he had answered that telegram in Berlin. Deodat was excited at the prospect of discovering the key, that much he could see, but for his part he wasn't relishing it, nor was he relishing the potential consequences of having it. Then again, perhaps it had always been his destiny to find it? If it was his destiny, he wondered how he would ever atone for it if his actions should lead somehow to an Armageddon of biblical proportions? But as Deodat had already pointed out, he was chin deep in responsibility. Feeling grim, he looked about with a creeping sense that he was being watched. Perhaps it was the Devil himself around the corner waiting to snatch away his soul?

At the altar his hands were shaking so much he could hardly hold the pencil, and his eyes were finding it difficult to focus. He gave them a rub and wrote down the cipher and the master word and deciphered each letter using the square. He came to his solution while La Dame held a candle close:

Master word	S	O	R	A	T
Plain text	r	o	t	a	s
Cipher text	J	C	K	A	L

'My God!' Rahn said, looking at his own handiwork. 'Rotas is the encrypted word! We seem to be going round in circles. Literally.'

'Rotas!' Deodat said, ecstatically. 'Yes, you are right! We have been going around in circles, like a wheel! Running around looking for something we could have known at the beginning. Rotas, arepo, tenet, opera, sorat! When Cros gave us sator, he must have intended to give us rotas.'

'Why do you say that?' La Dame said.

'Because rotas is the wheel in the tarot, the wheel of fortune – the tenth card. Now we see it: six parchments, six priests and six churches. Six plus six plus six. Cros was the sixth priest, and this was the sixth church. Let's see if I'm right.' Deodat went to the stained-glass window in the side chapel.

Rahn followed Deodat, taking a candle from the altar with him.

'Don't look at the window, Rahn, look instead at the altar beneath it. What do you see?'

Rahn noticed something very obvious and yes, the obvious was the most deceptive! Here, beneath the rotas window, there sat, innocently, a book bound in blue leather.

44

UNBROTHERLY QUARRELS

'How now, traitor!' exclaimed Don Quixote.
Miguel de Cervantes, Don Quixote

Perhaps Rahn had never expected to see the Cathar treasure in his lifetime, and this is what made him hesitate. After all, one could argue that to have one's dream come true might be a curse in itself. However, his hesitation was more to do with that part of him, a significant part, that didn't want to know the key – the part that wanted to leave the Devil in his place.

Deodat must have guessed his thoughts because he took the book in his hands and looked at Rahn gravely. 'To know the secret or the formula of God is to be God, and to know the secret or the formula of the Devil is to be the Devil. But to wish to be at the same time God and Devil is to absorb into one's self the two most strained contrary forces. I believe that in this book we shall find the sign of Sorat, which can make one both a god *and* a devil.'

Deodat had just begun to open the book when La Dame called out.

'Rahn!'

'Not now, La Dame!' he said, annoyed.

'Rahn, turn around!'

'What in the devil's the matter, La Dame?' Deodat said, and then: 'Put that down!'

When Rahn turned he saw his friend standing in the near darkness pointing a gun at them. The hangdog grin on his face made him look rather ridiculous but he held the gun as if he knew how to use it. This was a side of La Dame that Rahn had never seen before.

La Dame shrugged. 'Sorry, old boy, but you're going to have to hand it over to me.'

'What are you doing? Have you lost your mind?' Rahn said, pushing his fedora up over his forehead a little so he could see better in the dim light. He was still holding the candle in his hand and the wax was dripping onto the stone floor at his feet.

La Dame nodded as if to confirm the incredulous thought that was passing through Rahn's mind.

Rahn said, 'Don't tell me you're involved in all this?'

A frown crossed the landscape of his bearded face. 'I'm sorry, Rahn, really, I am.'

'But why?' Rahn moved forward. 'Who are you working for?'

'Don't try anything funny or I'll shoot you, and Deodat, too, for that matter,' he said, not sounding very convincing. 'Pass it over.'

Rahn couldn't believe it. 'What are you doing with that gun? You couldn't use it if your life depended on it!'

'Give me that book, Deodat. I'm warning you!'

With La Dame's attention turned to Deodat, Rahn realised he was in striking distance. He had to do something, but what? All he had was the candle in his hand. He needed to make La Dame drop his gun, so he did the most unexpected thing he could think of – he thrust the candle he was holding straight into La Dame's face.

La Dame flailed, trying to deflect it, but the flame caught on his beard and there was the smell of burning hair. The diversion created, Rahn went in for the kill. He struck a punch that grazed La Dame's left eye and hit the bridge of his nose.

'Oh!' His friend staggered back, one hand holding his nose, the other still holding the gun. Shock gave way to anger and he lunged at Rahn.

There was a struggle. Rahn left behind him any memory of their friendship, their hours of drinking, laughing, commiserating, Don Quixote and Sancho Panza, their potholing days and many adventures. He made himself blind to everything except the other man's struggle to point the gun closer and closer to his brow.

'Stop it, La Dame, for God's sake!' Rahn yelled at him.

'No! You burnt my beard!'

La Dame's cut eye was red and in it Rahn saw frenzy. His swollen nose was growing black, there was blood on his scorched beard and on his suit and he was breathing hard, gritting his teeth. Rahn managed to push the hand holding the gun away and caught a glimpse of Deodat coming from behind. He manoeuvred La Dame into position and then pulled at what was left of his beard with such fierceness that La Dame cried out in pain and turned his head slightly, enough for him not to notice Deodat approaching with a crucifix that he had taken from the altar and which he now brought down squarely over the hand holding the gun.

The gun fell to the floor with a clatter and Rahn took it up and gave it to Deodat. It was over. La Dame was now sitting on the floor panting and assessing his various injuries. Rahn's knees gave way then and he found himself sitting opposite La Dame.

'You've burnt my beard! You don't understand!'

'It serves you right for saying "burn my beard" all the time — it's what gave me the idea!'

'And I think I've lost a tooth,' he said, horrified, spitting out more blood.

'You were always a stupid bastard,' Rahn said, his anger waning. 'I should have listened to Deodat.'

'And I think you've broken my nose too! You didn't have to hit me so hard! There is an explanation!'

'I should have hit you *harder!* I don't want your explanations!'

'Oh God, it hurts!'

'You're not cut out for this, La Dame,' Deodat said, with no pity in his voice. 'You didn't even load the gun.'

'I know,' La Dame said miserably. He looked like he was about to weep but instead he found a handkerchief in one of his pockets and proceeded to wipe the blood away.

'What in the devil?' Deodat cried.

'I'll be taking that book now, if you don't mind.'

All three men looked into the darkness from which emerged the shape of someone else holding a gun! Rahn recognised him – it was that *ordinary-looking* man: ordinary height, ordinary weight and ordinary face. It was the man he thought was following him in Paris; the man in the café and the man who had been standing outside his hotel. Behind him now, unfortunately, there also stood two men who looked like prize-fighters.

'I promise you, my gun is loaded, and I am a very good shot, unlike our brother,' he said, indicating La Dame.

'Brother?' Rahn said to him.

'No time for pleasant chatter. I want you to stand up slowly and throw the gun over there.'

Rahn did as he was told.

'What are you going to do with us?' Deodat said.

'We're going somewhere a little warmer!'

'I demand to know where we're going!' Rahn said, knowing full well that he was in no position to demand anything.

'Why, Monsieur Rahn, you are going to Hell . . .'

45

In the Heat of the Moment

'Let me leap out of the frying-pan into the fire.'
Miguel de Cervantes, Don Quixote

Rahn and the others were bundled uncomfortably into the back seat of the black Citroën, a gun pointing in their faces. When they reached their destination, the Maison de Cros, the three of them were marched at gunpoint into the house. It was deserted, every room was littered from the ransacking two nights before and moreover, there was the all-pervading stench of death. The stench only grew in intensity the closer they came to the wine cellar where Deodat had been detained, and where the body of the real Inspecteur Beliere remained, hanging from the rafters.

'What are you doing?' La Dame said anxious, surprised. 'This isn't what we planned. I was supposed to bring it to you. You'd better speak to your superiors! Is this the way to treat a *brother?*'

The man looked on, impassively, aiming the gun at La Dame.

'You're more stupid than we anticipated. This was always going to be the end. Didn't you realise that, Professor La Dame? Besides, you were never really a *brother*. You were, let us say, nothing more than a provisional guest. And now you've worn out your welcome!'

Still incredulous, La Dame was tied with his hands behind him, back to back with Rahn and Deodat. They were made to sit down with their legs in front of them and then their feet were tied.

The man with the gun perused the leather-bound book in his hands. 'We are grateful to you for your wonderful work, Monsieur Rahn. We could not have done it better ourselves.'

'What are you going to do with that manuscript?' Deodat spat.

'It will be safe with us,' he said, his perfect, urbane English sounding strange in the present circumstances. He took a cigarette from his pocket and lit it, puffing on it until the end glowed.

'Who are you and what do you want with it, anyway?' Deodat said.

'I suppose it will not hurt to explain a few things, since you have been of great assistance. Consider it your last sacrament.' He exhaled a plume of smoke. 'I suppose you've already guessed that there *is* going to be a war, it is inevitable – even desirable.' He took a long drag on his cigarette, as if he could see the war in his mind's eye and it was a pleasant image. 'We English, I'm sure you know, Monsieur Roche, were always intended to be the leaders of this epoch. We have used the French before – your Masonic Lodge the Grand Orient, for instance, has always been in our pockets and we have used, and continue to use, the Germans. What was begun in the last war will continue with this new war, until we have achieved our aims. Try to view it, magistrate –' he ashed his cigarette, '– as the triumph of Sherlock Holmes over Monsieur Lecoq!' There was a curt smile. 'The superior English have outdone the arrogant French and the German peasants!'

'So,' Deodat said, 'the English Lodges were responsible for the last war?'

The British were known to have a particular fondness for talking about their conquests and Rahn guessed that Deodat was playing for time, but time for what?

He smiled. 'Plans for the Great War were made in London,' the man continued, 'and filtered into western Europe, where they were relayed to the Balkans and through them to Russia. Your history books won't tell you, magistrate, that Archduke Franz Ferdinand and his wife Sophia were assassinated by men paid by Russians, working for Englishmen.'

'The Serbians who shot Franz Ferdinand were working for you?' Deodat said.

'Yes, but they didn't know it, of course; the Black Hand always thought themselves quite independent – if only they knew who was behind them! Do you know that their catchcry is "Viva Angelina"? Angelina is, of course, a Serbian saint.' The man smiled, looking like a schoolteacher instructing his favourite students.

'Viva Angelina!' Rahn said. 'Gélis was killed by Serbians?'

The man shrugged. 'It was necessary. You see, Saunière was making friends with the Habsburgs . . . we couldn't allow that, it was a warning to him.'

'But I thought Viva Angelina was the call of AA?'

'Yes, but AA and the Black Hand are associated, as are other Serbian secretive organisations like Omladina and Narodna Odbrana. Many of their members are staunchly Catholic and happily belong to AA. Their common desire, in those days, was to rid themselves of the Austro-Hungarian Empire.'

'But the two Serbians who tried to kill us today acted as though they despised AA.'

'Of course! Those underlings know nothing of the intricate nature of these associations.'

'But I thought England was at odds with Russia?' Deodat kept him talking while Rahn tried to reach for his penknife but realised he didn't have it!

'Of course we are at odds with them, but if a British commercial empire is to be founded, there has to be an opposite pole of consumers – and the Russians do so hate commerce.

We leveraged off the animosity that has always existed between Austrians and Serbs and that's how the assassination came about – it had to look like a Serbian assault on the Austrian Empire. Austria then demanded that the assassins were handed over, Serbia refused and Austria-Hungary invaded Serbia. This now meant that Serbia had to ask Russia for help since they were allies, and in turn, France, having a treaty with Russia, was pulled in; on the other side of things Austria had to call on Germany, and Germany declared war on France and Russia and invaded Belgium, which brought us into the war, of course. We had a moral obligation to help Belgium, and also France. As Sherlock Holmes would say, elementary! You see, in the end, the fall of the Hapsburgs and Germany, as a central power, the curbing of Russia in her desire to expand towards India, and the reconfiguration of the Balkan states to give Russia her winter ports as consolation, was essential for the splitting up of Europe into two distinct regions – east and west. The commercial and industrial monarchy that we are wishing to establish meant we needed to get rid of the middle.

However, things did not go so smoothly, there were complications. Groups began sprouting up all over Europe: there was the revolution in Russia and the rise of the Bolsheviks; the Fascist movement in our own country; as well as an intrusion from the annoying American Freemasons who wanted to get what they could from the spoils. In the end the true aim was not reached, you see? Too many cooks stirring the pot! So a decision was made to make the best of a bad situation and that is how the Treaty of Versailles came into existence – as the seedbed of another war. The stab in the back was a good slogan, it stuck, and when it was combined with the Communist threat, inflation and unemployment . . . well, it was simple, really. The ordinary people are always led by the nose, all they need is a charismatic leader,' he said. 'The Germans, for instance, will follow Hitler into a bloodbath, while they sing a chorus of: "Deutschland erwache!"'

Rahn was fuming. 'You bastards!' he said.

'Your people, old chap, will welcome the destruction of their precious Germany rather than see it conquered. And when it is fully destroyed, we'll step in, of course, and with the help of the Americans, the Russians and the French, we'll change all the borders of Europe, once and for all!'

There was the strong smell of gasoline now, and Rahn assumed the men upstairs were preparing their cremation.

'So, you are saying Hitler is *your* man?' Deodat said, completely oblivious to everything around him.

'Hitler is an experiment, that's all.'

'And you think you can control him? He might turn on you, what then?' Deodat said.

'We have Himmler – and Hess – up our sleeves . . .'

'*What?*' Rahn exclaimed.

'Oh yes, Monsieur Rahn, the man you are working for wants the top job for himself, but of course we will doublecross him and Hess before the end.'

'But you haven't answered my question. How can you be certain you can control Hitler?' Deodat said.

'That is why we need the key found in this book, and why it is so important that it fall into *our* hands. We wouldn't want it to end up in the hands of the Nazis, or the different French Nationalist groups, or the Russians, or even the Jesuits! You see, Hitler and the Vatican are well connected. Why else do you think the present pope never speaks out against Hitler's crimes against the Jews and the disabled and mentally ill? They do not count in their mutual plans. Look at Goebbels – he was brought up in a Jesuit college, not to mention the fact that Himmler's father was a director of a Catholic school in Munich and his brother was a Benedictine monk!' he said, pleased with himself. 'All the popes since Honorius have known about *Le Serpent Rouge* and all of them have been after the key that completes it . . . And they still are, as you know. You see, when Pope Honorius made his pact with the Devil, he soiled the papal chair with excrement forever!' He laughed.

One of the burly men came down now and told the Englishman that 'it was ready' and to make sure that he extinguished his cigarette before he came upstairs. The Englishman paused. 'This, I'm afraid, is the end of our occult history lesson – something to take to Hell with you. You really should not have jumped out of the frying pan and into the fire!' He laughed, threw his cigarette on the floor and climbed the steps out of the wine cellar without looking back.

'What about my position at Oxford?' La Dame shouted after him.

'What job at Oxford?' Rahn said.

'Never mind, Rahn!' Deodat shouted. 'Use your penknife to cut the ropes!'

'Eva left with it,' Rahn answered.

'What?' La Dame said.

'Afraid so.'

'That beautiful Irene Adler will be the cause of our demise,' La Dame said.

'Well, perhaps if we bring our feet underneath us,' Deodat said to Rahn and La Dame, 'we can push on each other to get to our knees.'

They tried but this was impossible and they toppled, righting themselves again with great effort.

Rahn thought of something. 'Look, we can inch along on our backsides but we have to do it together, at the same time.'

Rahn pulled while Deodat and La Dame pushed. Rahn imagined they must look like a large octopus scurrying over dry land.

They could smell smoke.

'They're going to burn us!' La Dame cried. 'This is all your fault, Rahn – if you hadn't written that damned book we wouldn't be here!'

'What? *Me?* You're going to blame this on *me?*'

'You're at the centre of everything!'

'Don't you point the finger! We wouldn't be in this mess if it weren't for you, you traitor! How long have you been setting me up? Was it from before the manuscript of *Don Quixote?* Before the Pabst film set? Before our potholing . . . ?'

'Good heavens no, Rahn!' La Dame said, out of breath, behind him. They had almost reached the steps. 'It was while you were in Germany.'

'What was?'

'I was invited to a party put on by George Darmois, from the faculty of science.'

'Quite an honour,' Rahn said, sarcastically.

'Oh yes! Turns out he is a Freemason and he said he liked my paper on the demise of the Templars and the theory of probability,' La Dame said, coughing. 'One thing led to another and I was being made an offer I couldn't resist. And you know what that's like, Rahn.'

Rahn strained to breathe – the acrid smoke coming from the fire above them made his lungs shrink to half their size. 'What was that?'

'They told me if I helped them get whatever it was you found, they would give me a job at Oxford University.'

'Now I know why I never liked you, La Dame,' Deodat said, between gasps.

'Leave off, Deodat, it's not so simple as you think,' La Dame gave back. 'If I didn't agree to their conditions they were going to kill both of you as soon as you found what they wanted. And, as they had now exposed their plans to me, if I refused, they were going to kill me first – leaving no one to warn you! I was doomed no matter what, you see?'

A small part of Rahn had to admit he knew what it was like to be in such a position, but he was too angry to acknowledge it and, besides, there were other things to think about now because the fire had taken a hold of the house. They could hear it crackling and embers were floating down into the wine cellar. It was getting louder and hotter.

'The trouble is, you were always so damned interesting!' La Dame shouted. 'The adventurous Otto Rahn – the great Don Quixote!' He coughed. 'Author! Archaeologist! Historian!' He took in a strangled breath. 'I was boring old Sancho Panza, professor of Scientific Methodology, for God's sake! A man with only a little imagination and a small talent to match. And though I've always been dashingly good-looking, I'm also boringly dependable, and terribly uninteresting. Here I was finally given a chance to be a leading character and I took it.'

'And the picture's a flop – everybody dies!' Rahn said. 'You could have confided in me at least.'

'I was scared . . . I was confused. Think about it, Rahn, I could have just gone back to Geneva and let them kill you, but I didn't. Don't forget, they killed that man in my room to show me they meant business.'

'So it wasn't a case of mistaken identity?'

'No.'

'Liar!'

'For God's sake, don't be like that, Rahn!'

'Will the two of you shut up!' Deodat said, at the peak of irritation. 'Rahn, try to leverage off the step to stand up.'

Rahn tried to get onto his knees by bringing his tied feet under him and leaning his side on the step, but he was fettered by their collective weight working as an opposing force. It was no use. Rahn could hardly see now for the smoke and he was completely exhausted; the events of the last days had caught up with him.

He gave up, defeated. 'What about all that talk about liking your boring life?'

'It was all rubbish. I hate my life!' La Dame coughed. 'Dull routine. Endless days. But this . . . I could have done without this . . . Come on, Rahn, let's not die with this coming between us.'

Rahn's eyes were watering. 'You mean, like the gun you were

pointing at my head?'

'It wasn't even loaded! I didn't know they were waiting—'

'You didn't theorise that it might be in the realm of *probability?*'

The house upstairs erupted in a conflagration. They tried one last time to squirm out of the ropes but they were too tight and the knot would have made a sailor proud. There was nothing sharp they could try to cut the rope with. They were trapped.

'I don't want to die with this on my conscience, Rahn,' La Dame said, emphatic for a dying man. 'Say you forgive me!'

Rahn's lungs were burning from irritation, his lips were dry and he was sweating. 'For God's sake, La Dame!'

'Say it!'

'Alright! I forgive you!'

Deodat said, wheezing, 'It's over!'

Rahn knew it was true. He held his breath and closed his eyes. He saw himself in a cemetery, pointing to a gravestone on which stood the Leoncetophaline of the Countess P's pendulum clock. He sank then, for the third time in so many days, into a black mine, into a womb of darkness, into that tomb . . . He was going to die – perhaps he was already dead? But something made his eyes open briefly. There was a figure in the smoke and flames. It was coming towards him. He heard the sound of a bee . . . but it wasn't a bee at all. It was Esclarmonde de Foix! She had returned from the land of Prester John! Her hair flowed white about her face, she wore a crown of stars, and in her belly there was an effulgence like the sun. She stood on a crescent moon, whose body crushed a great red dragon with seven heads. She would take him out of this momentary terror and together . . .

'You certainly make it hard for me to keep you out of trouble, Otto Rahn!' she said.

ISLAND OF THE DEAD

46

AN END
WITHOUT END

'In the deepest slumber – no!
In delirium – no!
In a swoon – no!
In death – no!
Even in the grave, all is not lost.'
Edgar Allan Poe, 'The Pit and the Pendulum'

Venice, 2012

There was a knock on the door. I looked at my watch – twenty to midnight. A voice came from the other side. It was the Irish monk. I was to get dressed and to go to the library.

I found the Writer of Letters waiting for me with a coat and scarf in his hands.

'You'll need these; come, I have something to show you.'

He led me out into the fog-laden cemetery by the light of a lamp, without so much as an apology for the late hour. I asked him what we were doing and he was effusive in his reply.

'It's time to solve the puzzle,' he said. 'I hope you're up to it?'

I wasn't about to have him think otherwise. 'Of course.'

It was deathly cold. I blew into my hands to warm them. There were no sounds except for the hooting of an owl in a nearby tree and the gentle lapping of the lagoon. My drowsiness had by now completely deserted me and I kept a sharp eye out in case this man was planning to kill me – as a macabre solution to the puzzle of death that I had come here to solve. I didn't want to die but I knew that if I were to despoil the Writer of Letters of his dramatic end I would equally despoil myself of the final conclusion, the master work.

'This is all very dramatic,' I managed to say without sounding too nervous.

'Dramatic? Yes, metatheatre is dramatic,' was his cold reply. 'But you have always tried to keep reality at bay, isn't that so? Living your life as if it were a work of fiction. No, my desire is not to create drama but to unveil your life. Now, where did we leave Rahn last night?'

'He was dying in the fire and dreaming he was in a cemetery . . .' I looked at him, and it occurred to me – the Leoncetophaline! 'Surely you're not about to tell me he was dreaming of this cemetery, are you?' I asked him, unable to prevent a chuckle at this new absurdity.

'I don't know, was he? Why don't you tell me how the story ends?'

'Me?' I said, surprised.

'Yes; just write the end. If there is anyone capable of judging your abilities it's me. Perhaps this is the test you spoke of? Could you see yourself replacing me on this island, in this library of galleries?'

I looked at him. He wasn't joking. I realised I was being cheated of my ending. Perhaps that had been his intention all along, to drag me like a laboratory mouse, through his labyrinthine galleries, only to deny me my hard-earned cheese at the end.

'Think of it as an exercise in reasoning,' he said. 'What is the most likely thing to happen next?'

I was so annoyed I could say nothing in reply.

He paused and lifted the lamp to look at my face. I returned the look with a wild stare. I was angry, resentful.

'You're upset. You thought I was going to make it easy for you, didn't you? Every story gets the end it deserves, don't you agree? Now, what is the end this one deserves?'

'I have no idea!'

'Perhaps it would help you to see another gallery, then? I can tell it to you as we walk. It is the gallery called Penitence.'

47

PENITENCE, PENITENCE!

*'... and, as the saying goes, the dead to the grave
and the living to the loaf.'*
Miguel de Cervantes, Don Quixote

Rennes-le-Château, 18 January, 1915

The snow fell over the mountains in icy sheets, making the promenade dangerously glassy. Even so, Madame Dénarnaud insisted on wheeling the body of the Abbé Saunière to the greenhouse herself, so as to be alone with him one last time.

She was dressed in black silk. It had cost a fine fortune but it was the latest fashion in funerary wear from Paris. After all, people expected it. They would soon be arriving from every place to see the body and they would leave after taking a tassel from his gown, as was the custom – as if those old clothes had been impregnated with power. She smiled at the thought of it now – if only they knew.

She could hear the bell-ringer's son digging the grave in the cemetery, cursing the frozen ground. Yesterday, before the abbé had taken his last torturous breath, Abbé Rivière of Espéraza had come to hear Saunière's confession, but upon hearing it his face had paled and he had refused to give the abbé the prepared wafers and wine. It had delighted her to see the villagers' faces when they heard of it. They believed that Saunière had whispered something diabolical to the priest, but she knew Saunière had said nothing into that hairy ear – because he knew nothing. Yes, that greedy priest from Espéraza had been hoping to hear, in Saunière's confession, how he had come by his fortune. When the confession was not forthcoming he decided to take his revenge on Saunière by withholding the sacrament. In the end, Madame Dénarnaud had given it to him herself, in secret.

Well, she thought, let them all imagine that Saunière was the mastermind of everything: the refurbishment of the church; the building of the villa and the tower, the greenhouse and the gardens. As long as this was what they believed, she could continue with her work unnoticed.

In truth, her life had been filled with predestined events: at birth, she had been accepted into that section of the Grand Orient created especially for women; at the age of seven, her mother, also a member of the Lodge, had taken her to Toulouse to be initiated; and as a young woman, she was schooled to be the next Madame Blavatsky, the celebrated Russian theosophist. But she did not allow herself to become like that woman, who had been used by various groups for their own ends. She had decided long ago that she would do as she pleased; she would owe allegiance to no group!

In the beginning her powers had been crude and unsophisticated. Occasionally she would lapse into a trance in which disembodied spirits spoke through her; sometimes she saw visions of future events; and at other times she would write long sentences, pages and pages of them, automatically. But these childhood aptitudes had graduated, under expert instruction, into powers that were polished and chillingly exact. Moreover, she was a handsome woman, possessed of the dark good looks of her heretic ancestors, and intelligent enough to use them to enhance her talents. These, combined with her knowledge of the lesser magic of perfume-blending had taken her far.

Yes, she had been much admired by various suitors, and there had been many marriage proposals, but she had ignored them with a cold disdain. The ignorant, miscreant villagers of Rennes-le-Château had thought her a strange girl to pass up such advantages, choosing instead to remain a poor shepherdess, who wanted nothing more than to tend her family's little herd of goats or to work occasionally in the hat factory at Espéraza. They did not know that she was waiting for her time to come.

The day she and her mother had spied the disaffected Saunière toiling over the road to their village with his bags in his hands, dressed in his black cassock and hat, looking like a man who has been deprived of his birthright, they knew they had found their priest. Immediately Abbé Boudet, a member of their order, was informed and the entire affair was set into motion.

Saunière's arrogance had made him a willing servant, but they could not have known the extent of his incautious nature, or how obsessed he would become with finding the missing treasure for himself. His task had been merely to find the parchment and leave clues in his church for those who would follow, but his tongue was loose.

She bent down to look at the corpse's face. It still bore some resemblance to Saunière: the dimpled chin, the shock of dark hair, the brooding mouth. He never knew the true goal of the secret and yet he had been so full of his own importance! She wiped away some fluid from his shrivelled lips. And to think he had imagined himself an initiate! His journey to England had made him powerful, but it had been on her behalf and for another purpose entirely.

No, it had been a preparation for her task. For she had met the chosen initiate only two years before in Vienna, where at the time he had been undergoing instruction by members of the Thule Gesellschaft. They had seen in the young man called Adolf Hitler the perfect combination of stupidity and fervour, an empty vessel for the future impregnation of the seed of Sorat. Oh, it was exciting and difficult and frustrating to anticipate, to wait. But in the cards she had seen the one who would come to unlock the secret whereabouts of the key, the one destined to be tenet – and nothing could be accomplished without him. She would know him by his willingness to enter Hell. A question put to all true initiates.

She adjusted the gown on Saunière's shoulders, smoothing her hands over it and picking off some stray lint. She wondered what the villagers would say when they found out that their illustrious priest had died a pauper, his only income his priestly stipend. That the Villa Bethany, the Tour Magdala; everything had always belonged to her? Even now his spirit had joined the circle of those whose spirits would be used by the initiate – the circle of those who had willingly chosen to die and even those who were murdered to cleanse the world of riffraff. It had not taken much to convince Saunière to sell his soul and to join that circle in return for eternal life. They had enacted the ritual of excarnation, of suicide, in the crypt of the dames using the secret of sator, arepo, tenet, opera, rotas. It had been accomplished! The stroke had hit him in a matter of days. They always suffered strokes – so that way the spirit left the body gradually . . . excruciatingly. She didn't know how many had partaken of the bread and wine blessed by Satan to join the circle of the undead but she knew they were countless. Saunière was only one among many! How many masses for the dead had he conducted himself, using those wafers, trapping the unwary in that realm of midday, between life and death? She could feel his agonised presence nearby. Immortality has its price. Penitence!

People were arriving. She could see them in their finery, in their silks and furs and top hats, threading through the snow-covered garden. She looked down at her wrist, the snake entwining the anchor was showing slightly and she adjusted her lace-edged sleeve over it and donned the mask of the grieving housekeeper. With her heart full of an imminent thrill, she left the conservatory to greet them.

48

LADY IN WAITING

'What was the fair lady's game? What did she really want?'
Sir Arthur Conan Doyle, 'The Adventure of the Second Stain'

Maison de Cros, Bugarach, 1938

'You certainly make it hard for me to keep you out of trouble, Otto Rahn!'

It was Eva! She was busy cutting their bindings with his penknife. He coughed and his lungs burst into screams of pain. When they were loose she herded them without a word to an opening and they stooped to enter what seemed to be a low storeroom. After negotiating their way through boxes and barrels and bric-a-brac, she directed them on their knees through a small hatch into what became a low tunnel.

'Keep moving, don't stop, it leads outside!' she called out to them from behind.

They proceeded for a time, coughing and wheezing and stumbling in the darkness. Here the air was clear and earthy, and eventually Rahn came to some stone steps that led upwards to the garden. By instinct and without thought, he staggered as far as he could from the conflagration before throwing himself down. The others followed and the four of them sat, breathing fresh air into their tortured lungs, coughing and spitting. He could hear

Deodat vomiting and coughing. The sleet came down all around them and the ground was wet. Above, the clouded firmament was untouched by this human madness. There was lightning in the far reaches and he could tell the moon was rising behind it.

In the meantime the inferno had progressed. The roof caught alight and the thirteenth-century monastery that had survived revolutions and purges, ruin and desecration, now began its last song as the roof rafters caved in, one after the other, sending clouds of sparks into the cold air.

Eva was sitting beside him, wiping her face. She was a little breathless but otherwise unhurt, and even seemed exhilarated. 'I once saw a fire like this,' she said wistfully, sadly. 'It burnt the most beautiful building in the world, my building! The twisted metal of the musical instruments created the most wondrous colours and one could hear it like music whistling in the flames. Isn't it interesting?' She looked at him, coming out of her contemplation, her eyes still distant but only for a moment. 'Are you alright?'

'You mean, aside from my manly ego? Yes, I'll be fine, but you know, I was the one who was supposed to save the damsel from the fire of the dragon – not the other way around.'

'Don't worry, in saving you I am also saving myself – remember?' Rahn smiled a little.

'How did we get out?' Deodat said, panting.

'All medieval monasteries have at least one underground passage leading to the outside. Elementary!' she said to him.

'Now you're sounding like me!' Deodat smiled weakly.

'What are you doing here anyway?' Rahn asked. 'I thought you would be halfway to Italy by now.'

'Italy? Why would you think that? No, I was waiting for you to wake up.' But he didn't have time to ask her what she meant because she stood. 'Come on – we have to leave before the fire brigade arrives with the gendarmes . . .'

'Did you see anyone?' Rahn stood with his head light and his legs weak.

'Yes. Three men. I think they're going to the hermitage we went to that day.'

'The hermitage of Galamus?' Deodat said. 'How do you know that?'

'Just a hunch.'

Rahn frowned. 'You and your hunches.'

'We have to follow them,' Deodat made a grab for Rahn's arm and Rahn helped him up. Rahn was too exhausted to argue.

In a moment all four of them had left the Maison de Cros's sacrificial burning behind them and Eva was leading them to where she'd hidden the auto-car. Inside the Peugeot, Eva's single-minded profile was lit up by the reflection of the headlamps and this gave her, to Rahn's mind, an otherworldly look. Once again she exuded a detachment that seemed unnatural.

'How do you feel?' Rahn asked Deodat, who was coughing and wheezing in the back seat beside the traitor La Dame.

'My chest feels like I've been breathing in hot peppers but otherwise I'll be fine.'

Rahn passed a hand over his face full of cuts. He could smell smoke in his hair. 'You never mentioned what made you come back for us, Mademoiselle Fleury,' he said.

She looked at him a moment; her darkling eyes staring out from that pale face were as deep as the well of Democritus. She was remarkably beautiful, almost too beautiful to be real He fancied, in his exhausted state, that she was Joan of Arc: a mighty female warrior, her eyes replete with the visions of archangels and her heart full of strange tempers.

She shrugged.

She's an enigma!

'You followed us?' Rahn said.

'Yes . . .'

'Well . . . this entire hunt's been for nothing anyway. All we've managed to do is to lead them to it,' Rahn's words tasted sour.

'Do you mean the Cathar treasure – the key?' Eva asked, serenely, as if it didn't matter.

'Yes, it's a book. Cros had always kept it at Bugarach in plain sight. But the English Lodges have it now – it's all over!'

'No, they don't,' she said.

Rahn blinked. 'What?'

'When those men left the house there were others outside waiting for them.'

'Others?' It was the traitor, La Dame, speaking now, and it irritated Rahn.

'They looked like priests, but they were carrying guns. Two large men came out first and they were shot immediately, a third man exchanged shots with them but in the end he was wounded. They bundled him into the Citroën at gun point and took off,' Eva said, rounding a corner too fast for Rahn's liking.

'Where were you?'

'I was hiding in the bushes.'

Deodat grabbed the back of Rahn's seat and sat forward.

'We've got to get it from them, Rahn!' he said.

La Dame cleared his throat. 'I guess this is where my character exits then – stage left. I've been written out of the film, I'm afraid,' he announced. 'Look, this has always been your script, Rahn. You're the leading man and I'm just the greatest dolt in the world. I've always had the bit parts and I'm afraid I've come to realise that's all I'm cut out for. So, mademoiselle, if you would be so kind as to drop me off at the next town I'll catch a ride to back to Couiza and from there I'll find my way home. I'm going to lay low for a while . . . in the mountains. You know where I live, Rahn, if you should ever trust me again, I'd love you to come for a visit. I shall wish you a fair adventure, "O dear Rahn, perpetual discoverer of the antipodes, torch of the world, eye of Heaven, sweet stimulator of the water-coolers!"'

'Oh shut up, La Dame! Quoting Sancho won't get you out of this one. Trust you? *You?*' Rahn said, glowing with rage. 'You're nothing but a great scoundrel, dunderhead, and thief all in one! Why should I ever trust you again?'

La Dame frowned, obviously hurt. 'Now, Rahn, don't say things you'll regret. Remember, I saved your life!'

'You're a dirty, doublecrossing rat! You wanted the job at Oxford!' he spat, relishing his anger now.

'That's offensive! That was just an added bonus,' La Dame said, with indignation.

'Let me be precise. You're a cowardly, suppurating, dirty, doublecrossing rat – and a bastard!'

'Now you've gone too far, Rahn. You've wounded my pride.'

Rahn almost expected him to shout, 'Pistols at dawn!'

Instead, La Dame sighed, and his voice suddenly sounded full of remorse. 'You're just anxious – I understand.'

'Anxious? Why should I be anxious?' Rahn said, sarcastically. 'There are secret societies on our tail: some trying to burn us alive in car trunks; others trying burn us alive in cellars; some have a preference for shooting us to pieces; and others find it more amusing to drown us in crypts. I've been manipulated, lied to, messed about! I've got cuts and bruises everywhere. I haven't slept in days, there's a bee flying about in my head and the Eiffel Tower is snowed under! And what has all of it achieved? I've managed to lead evil-minded madmen to a secret that was elaborately safeguarded and hidden for centuries and now, to exonerate myself, I have to walk into the middle of a conventicle of black magicians to stop them from conjuring the evil spirit Sorat – who makes Satan look like a retarded demi-god – where I will most likely end up suffering moral and spiritual ruination. Or at best a grievous, agonising, living death for all eternity. Anxious? Yes, I'll admit I'm a little anxious. *But I'd say no more anxious than this insane story demands!*' Rahn finished, loudly.

'That's because, my dear Rahn,' La Dame countered, meekly, 'you're the hero of the script, I realise that now. The one prepared to march into Hell for Heaven's sake! And I'm, well, I told you, I'm a coward, I have no ribs to bear Hell and I freely admit it! Even when I'm holding a gun, the truth is, the gun is holding me. I couldn't even load the damned thing for fear it might go off and shoot something unintended. I'd be no good to you at all, you see? Better to be rid of me.' He sat forward. 'When all this is over we'll break open that numbered bottle I've kept hidden away for a special occasion and we'll have a jolly laugh.'

'You know where you can shove your numbered bottle and your jolly laugh, La Dame,' he said testily, 'where it's dark and the temperature's stable!'

'Rahn! There's a lady present!' La Dame cried, shocked.

Rahn gave him a sidewise glance. 'Shut up before I punch you again and break your nose twice.'

La Dame winced. Deflated and consumed by guilt, he said nothing more.

When they came to the little hamlet, Eva stopped in a small lay-by to let La Dame out.

As they sped off, Rahn caught sight of La Dame's pathetic form in the rear-view mirror. He stood by the side of the road like an abandoned dog looking for a good home. Rahn felt a sudden remorse. His temper had ebbed and he was already missing La Dame. He realised once again that he was no different to his friend and moreover he was at fault: La Dame was right, had he not mentioned the skeleton key in his book, had he not gone to that apartment in Berlin, none of this would have happened. He sighed, fighting a desire to tell Eva to turn back to get him. La Dame was better off staying away from all this. He had wounds to nurse and a life to live. He was right. Rahn was the one who had to walk into Hell.

'I don't know . . .' Deodat said, wrenching him from his painful thoughts.

'What is it?'

'At that moment in the church, when La Dame called out with the revolver in his hands, something occurred to me. Cros was a good chess player. He always found a way to create weaknesses in his opponent's position in two directions. He said it took at least two weaknesses to win a chess game, because an opponent couldn't be in two places at the same time.'

'I don't understand,' Rahn said.

'Two places, Rahn. The clever player creates a diversion to allow something else to go unnoticed. He even risks losing a valued piece to secure victory. Cros sent us in search of rotas but did we only find what he intended us to find?'

'You saw the manuscript, didn't you? It is the original *Apocalypse of Saint John*, isn't it?'

'I didn't have time to open it.'

'So what do we do now?' Rahn felt like throwing his hands up in the air.

'We have to assume, for the time being, that it is what we think it is.'

Rahn was so exhausted he didn't know when he fell asleep, or how long it took for them to reach the turn-off to the hermitage. He woke, perhaps sensing the sudden stillness, with his feet numb and his mouth tasting like charcoal. He sat up. Eva was staring straight ahead.

'Do you know what tonight is?' she said, buttoning up her coat, getting ready for a battle, looking practical and cool.

'Tonight?' Rahn said.

'Remember what Madame Corfu told us at Rennes-le-Château two nights ago, when she recounted Gélis's horrific murder over dinner? Remember what the Serbians said?'

He could hear the gorges below, water rumbling over the rocks. The moon was edging the clouds, filling the world with phantoms, spectres and demons disguised as rocks, trees and bushes.

'Today is *All Saints' Day* and tomorrow will be *The Day of the Dead*,' she said. 'Tonight is the cusp. This night, forty-one years ago, Gélis was murdered.'

'You mean, at midnight?' Rahn said.

She nodded.

Rahn allowed a smile to steal over his face. The creator of this script had thought of everything except for his choice of leading man! He took one look in the rear-view mirror and inspected his red eyes and his split lip. La Dame was wrong about him – he wasn't leading man material. He badly needed a brandy and his hands were shaking. Perhaps Pabst would one day make a film about such a man as he might have been, a wise-cracking, hairy-chested archaeologist – a larger-than-life Grail hunter who wore an ironic smile on his face, a tropical helmet on his head and a pistol on his belt. He sighed. It was a ludicrous thought. Now another thought occurred to him. Perhaps he had died at Wewelsburg; perhaps those shots had killed him and he was now in some hellish version of a story by Edgar Allan Poe? A story in which the hero is trapped in Purgatory and doesn't realise he's dead. Where he is made to live and relive Hell, over and over again, like the legend of Judas – stuck on that island where every day is Good Friday.

'The hour before midnight is used for good, the half-hour after is reserved for evil,' Eva said, cutting through his thoughts.

'How do you know these things?' Rahn asked her, amazed.

'I'm the personification of wisdom.' She smiled sadly. 'So few men are truly wise.'

'But the Cathars were perfect,' he gave back.

'Ah, but who in this world can truly say they are perfect?'

He sat stock-still. Where had he heard this before?

'When is midnight?' he asked.

'Soon,' she said. 'We have to go.'

'I won't go with you,' Deodat said, with disappointment in his voice. 'I'm not feeling myself. It's my heart, I think. Madame Sabine may have been right after all – I'm just an old fool trying to relive my youth.'

'You just need some rest, Deodat.' Rahn soothed.

'We won't be long. Lock the doors and stay out of sight,' Eva said, perfectly in control.

'Have you thought about what you're going to do, both of you?' He asked.

Rahn chewed on the inside of his mouth. He couldn't think. 'I don't know, we'll improvise.'

'Listen,' Deodat said. 'You're not on a movie set now. This is real. When evil wills are brought into communion in a circle, such a circle can be made stronger than the world. Don't let them use the key. Whatever you do, don't let them use it!'

'We have to hurry, it's nearly time!' Eva said.

Rahn had an idea; he reached into the back of the Peugeot looking for his bag. It was still there. He took out the Countess P's grotesque clock and put it under his arm.

'What are you going to do with that?' Deodat said.

'It's the only weapon we've got and it's heavy enough to hurt. After all, I don't have a candlestick,' he said, looking at Eva.

Her smile in return was wry.

They got out of the car and Rahn braced himself against the squall's cold teeth. 'So what do you propose, Dorothy? Should we trespass on the party, click our ruby shoes, demand the manuscript from the Wizard of Oz and then make our merry way back to Kansas before supper?'

'I don't know what you mean,' she said, flatly.

'Haven't you heard of the Wizard of Oz? Louise Brooks was from Kansas, you see . . .'

'Who is Louise Brooks?'

He sighed, feeling ridiculous. 'Never mind . . .'

'Shall we get started then?' she said, and with the philosophical mien of a captain about to enter the field of battle, added, 'Let's go!'

49

LE PAPESSE

'Then an unconquerable terror seized upon me
from which I could no longer get free.
I felt that a catastrophe was approaching before
which the boldest spirit must quail.'
Jules Verne, Journey to the Centre of the Earth

Rahn followed Eva feeling inept and clumsy, an emasculated hero. Trees hung across their path and their bare limbs stood out against the inky blackness, like bony fingers pointing to a half-worn moon obscured by drifting clouds. The wind carried the sound of an owl and a creature scurried in the undergrowth. That feeling came again, the feeling of peril ahead, and not just that: a pure form of terror began to seize him, not that same panic he felt going into churches but a calm terror that was visceral. No, there was no turning back.

Not far ahead he could see the outline of the hermitage set high over the gorge and the sound of water tumbling and foaming below was louder now. When they came upon firebrands lighting the way he knew they were expecting company. He had a sense for where they would be; Grassaud had mentioned an abbé who had entered the underground tunnels some years before and returned incoherent and lethargic. He had died soon afterwards, without elucidating what had happened.

Rahn's instincts were proved right when they reached the forbidden grotto of Mary Magdalene. Here a grilled door lay open with firebrands on either side, and beyond it there was a tunnel illuminated by torches. Rahn entered first with Eva following close behind. Soon there were stone steps and a steep descent; after that more steps, followed by more descending. It was cold and damp and easy to lose one's bearings. Strata and substrata passed by until they began to hear the low snarling and growling of dogs intermixed with chanting. They moved now with stealth until they reached the mouth of a great open gallery.

Eva signalled to a spot behind a high rock and he followed her to a position in the shadows from which they could see into the gallery below.

The gallery was wide and domed and lit by a large fire and black candles. Rahn saw the dogs now, three Dobermans tethered to a rock. A number of people were gathered in the cave, all of them dressed in black cloaks and facing a circle that had been drawn on the ground. Written around the circle at the four cardinal points Rahn could make out the letters ROTA. Inside this circle a pentagram had been drawn and in the middle of that, before an altar, stood a woman dressed in a black cloak, wearing a sword in a red girdle around her waist. When she turned around, Rahn gasped. It was Madame Dénarnaud!

The madame now addressed the group in a solemn voice: 'Aeons ago the great general council of all the masters was called. Fearing that the Church would destroy their work, the masters who came out of Naples, Athens and Toledo chose from one of them, a man whose name was Honorius, the son of Euclid, master of the Thebans. They gave the Theban Honorius the task of creating an illustrious compendium of magic, a work never seen before by human eyes. Upon its creation, copies were made for safekeeping, and these were given to men who swore an oath to pass them down only to those who had merit. One copy fell into the hands of a man destined to become a pope and so was born

Le Serpent Rouge, the *Grimoire of Pope Honorius III,* the finest distillation of our art – the most infernal grimoire ever written.

'But now, the time has come for priest to give way to priestess, pope to popess! You are all acquainted with the tarot card le papesse. That is how you must think of me. For I will take the title of Pontifex Maximus and I alone will hold the missing key that opens the way to Hell. This Night of the Dead, I will place that key into the sacred lock and call forth the master of all demons.' She looked around. 'Who brings me the blood of le sacrifice humain?'

A cowled man placed a large bowl on the altar.

'The blood of the English Freemason who used Gaston De Mengel as a puppet will serve us well this night!'

'Where are the cakes of light?'

Another man brought forth a bowl and Rahn knew this must be the desecrated sacrament.

She looked about again. 'Who brings the *Apocalypse of Saint John?'*

A tall, cowled figure came forth and offered her the blue manuscript from Bugarach. The madame took it and placed it on the altar.

'And finally, who is the guardian of *Le Serpent Rouge?'*

A rather portly figure shuffled forward, holding a red manuscript. When he removed his cowl a hush fell.

'I give you Aleister Crowley!' Madame Dénarnaud said with ebullience.

There was the tremulous sound of murmuring voices and muted applause.

Crowley had bushy eyebrows, a balding head and a bloated face. The geriatric Satanist looked happy with himself, as if he had just managed to escape from a hospital for the aged and mentally ill and was now going to have the time of his life. He placed the red book on the altar alongside the blue book and stood in the pentagram beside the madame – the witch and her warlock were perfectly matched.

He raised a hand and perused the crowd with a modicum of drama. A signal that he was about to speak. 'There is an inviolable occult law: just as Lucifer, the king of light, was incarnated six centuries before Christ in China, so shall Satanas the Prince of Darkness be given his chance to incarnate in a human vessel, Adolf Hitler.

The conventicle repeated, 'Adolf Hitler.'

'This glorious event has been in preparation for eons!' Crowley said. He took up the manuscript and began to read from it: 'In the beginning was the sign, and the sign was with Sorat and Sorat was the sign! And he was with the sign and nothing was made without the sign. And the sign is the sign of death, for he is the king of death and he is the darkness of all men – but men understood him not! A whore was set apart by Sorat to unite with him and give testament to the darkness so that all might become sons of Sorat.' He intoned: 'We believe in the mother, the womb, the prostitute, and her name is the Whore of Babylon.'

The congregation replied, 'The Whore is the wife, the sister and the mother.'

'We believe in the serpent, and his name is Sorat!'

'Sorat is the law, Sorat in our will!' the conventicle answered.

'Excitacio ventorum est principium operandi in illa hora diei operis sacri et debet fieri extra domum longe a circulo ad duo stadia vel tria . . .'

'Ad duo stadia vel tria.'

The tethered Dobermans were straining at their chains, snarling, barking and growling.

'The vessel of Satan,' Madame Dénarnaud took over, 'awaits his unification with a mighty spirit from the depths of dark space! The serpent that lives in the bowels of the earth runs from France to Germany over the spines of the mountains. Let it do so this night, from my soul's womb to his mind's genius! For I am the harlot that shaketh death and my whoredom is a sweet scent. I am like a seven-stringed instrument played by Satan, the invisible, the all-ruler. Let it begin!'

Aleister Crowley kissed *Le Serpent Rouge* and simultaneously the old woman kissed the *Apocalypse of Saint John*. Then she turned to a page in the manuscript and looked up, a maddened smile on her features.

She seemed puzzled, fascinated. 'Men have died and killed to know this key! It is a sign. And it could not be simpler. Like the philosopher stone, it is contained in nature. In every twig and tree does live the shape of the two-horned beast.'

'My God, we have to stop her!' Rahn whispered to Eva.

'I command you,' said Aleister Crowley, reading from *Le Serpent Rouge*, 'oh all ye demons dwelling in these parts, or in what part of the world soever ye may be, by whatsoever power may have been given you by God and our holy angels over this place, and by the powerful principality of the infernal abysses, as also by all your brethren, both general and special demons, whether dwelling in the east, west, south, or north, or in any side of the Earth, and, in like manner . . .'

The crowd swayed and buzzed, trance-like, mesmerised.

'Et debet prius,' said Madame Dénarnaud, 'esse bene pre-paratus de necessariis suis, de optimo vino de seven ensibus, de sibilo, de virgula coruli, de sigillis, de signo dei, de thure, de thuribulo, de candela virginea et sic de aliis ut prius patet . . .'

The conventicle intoned, 'Ut prius patet . . .'

Aleister Crowley read: 'I command all ye demons, by the power of the holy trinity of Hell, by the merits of the most holy and blessed Lilith and of all the dark saints! Sorat, Arepo, Tenet, Opera, Rotas! Rotas, Opera, Tenet, Arepo, Sorat!'

The madame took the bowl of congealed blood and drank from it. Aleister Crowley did the same and after that, the bowl was passed around the congregation.

'We offer you, Sorat,' Crowley said, 'this bloody sacrifice, and we ask, pray and entreat you, to send down your spirit into the whore here offered!"

'STOP! What are you doing?'

It was old Grassaud pushing through the crowd, gesticulating.

Aleister Crowley's face reddened with anger and he thrust out his hand to stop the abbé. 'Do not enter the circle!'

'I will do as I please. You do not frighten me, you old goat!' Grassaud wheezed. 'You are not authorised to conduct this ritual. The pope alone may do so!'

The old madame said coolly, 'Go back to Rome. Tell the pope and his mafia AGLA that they have been surpassed. Tell him the key to the gates of Hell has been snatched away from his gnarly grasp. Tell him that this night it has revealed the presence of the Prince of Evil, the origin of all darkness!'

Grassaud yelled at the top of his voice: 'Atah Gibbor Le'olam Adonnai!'

'Yes, yes, yes . . . thou art mighty forever, oh Lucifer! But you're forgetting that Sorat is more mighty than Lucifer and AGLA means nothing here,' she said, 'so shut up, old man, and go back to your bed. Leave me to my work.'

'Your ritual will not succeed, woman,' he said with authority. 'There is no priest to direct the power of the spirit into your soul. This man isn't a priest – he's a necromantic pretender, a pompous fool!'

The madame laughed. 'What do I need a priest for when I am a priestess?'

'When AA hears of this, you will have no tongue with which to swallow those words!' Grassaud cried.

'I have long since broken away with that association of fake angels. Their only desire is to lock *Le Serpent Rouge* away along with the key because they fear it. I do not fear it!'

The old man shouted, 'In that case, I will conjure Sorat myself, in the name of Jesus Christ to thwart you!'

She was aghast. 'What? No! You will not!'

'I will bind him to keep him from your clutches!'

'Get him out!'

But Grassaud had already begun. 'I conjure thee, Evil and Accursed Serpent, to appear at my will and pleasure, in this place, before this circle, without tarrying—'

'Stop him, you fool!' the madame shrieked at Aleister Crowley, who hesitated.

'Come without companions, without grievance, without noise, deformity, or murmuring. I exorcise thee by the ineffable names of God, which I am unworthy to pronounce: come hither, come hither, come hither! Accomplish my will and desire, without wiles or falsehood. Otherwise Saint Michael, the invisible Archangel shall presently blast thee to the utmost depths of Hell. Come then, do my will!'

'*Swine! Pig!*' Madame Dénarnaud flew into a rage, gesturing wildly. 'Remove him!'

But all were afraid and hung back.

'Why tarriest thou, and why delayest? What doest thou?' Grassaud continued to spit out with vehemence. 'Make ready, obey your master, in the name of the Lord, *Bathat, Rachat, Abracm, Ens, Alchor, Aberer!*'

There came now a scream from Madame Dénarnaud, loud enough to curdle the blood, and she put her hands over her ears. '*No! No! No!* I alone will now call forth the divine master of the Dark Sun, and to the Devil with you! I will call the demon of aeons past! Come to me!' She closed her eyes and swayed from side to side and moaned and groaned and turned her face to the vaulted rock ceiling. 'Come to me here – from the bowels of the Earth! I command thee, come to your saint, impregnate your prostitute! *Ecce formacionem seculi spiritus autem spiritum vocat!*'

'*Ecce formacionem seculi spiritus autem spiritum vocat!*' The crowd repeated.

'Behold the Pentacle of Solomon!' the old man countered, bringing forth a pentacle from around his neck, which he pointed at the madame. 'I have brought it into thy presence! Oh despicable spirit! I command thee by order of the great God, Adonay, Tetragrammaton, and Jesus!' he bellowed.

'The bowl!' she cried, signalling to Crowley. 'I will make the sign!'

Crowley hurriedly brought the bloody bowl to her and old Grassaud rushed forward, grasping for it, and in the struggle the altar toppled, the bowl was catapulted to the ground and the books fell at the edge of the great fire. A scuffle broke out between the two old men; Crowley took hold of the old man's ears while Grassaud scratched at his eyes.

'I conjure thee by the . . . ineffable . . . ah you devil – let go of me! By the name of God . . .' Grassaud said, between gasps, 'Alpha, Omega . . . AGLA . . . AGLA!'

The gallery erupted. Dogs snarled and people gestured and cried out. Some were objecting to the treatment meted out to old Grassaud while others were defending the old woman. These disagreements now escalated into pandemonium, replete with insults and blows. To Rahn it resembled a bar brawl. Crowley struggled to bring his face close to Grassaud's and then bit the old man on the nose, so that Grassaud yelled and dropped to the ground, moaning and whimpering and holding his nose with one hand while the other pointed at Crowley. 'You will pay for this!'

Crowley pointed at the old man and Grassaud began to choke, or so it seemed, from whatever power Crowley had called forth to assail him.

In the middle of the fracas, the madame cried out, 'Amor Satanas nos coniungat, sua potencia nos dirigat, sua misericordia nos coniunctos misericorditer nos custodiat!' She made a sign on her forehead with her bloodied finger and, ignoring the chaos around her, lifted her right hand and seemed about to trace the sign in the air when there was a sudden collective wheeze. All argument paused. The crowd drew back and Madame Dénarnaud was left with her arm in mid-air, breathless, dishevelled and once more deprived of her moment. *What now?* she said.

The agent of this second interruption walked into the circle surrounded by men at arms. The man was small. He wore a crumpled suit and an old Panama hat. Rahn couldn't see his face but he would have recognised that hat anywhere. It was Professor Moriarty, or rather, the fake Inspecteur Beliere! There was a murmuring of voices. Uncertainty reigned and people moved away.

The moment Crowley realised who it was, he picked up his skirts and melted into the receding crowd. Madame Dénarnaud was now alone, with only the whimpering Grassaud at her feet for company.

'Did you think you could get away with this?' came the man's unmistakeable voice.

Madame Dénarnaud was suddenly at a loss for words. She was an old woman again and not a priestess of Sorat.

'This is not authorised,' he said, as if he were chastising a foolish child. 'All of you!' He looked about. 'You should be ashamed! You are all here illegally!'

Taking a hold of herself and harnessing her melodramatic powers, Dénarnaud shouted, 'I do not need your authority and I care nothing for legalities!'

The man ignored her histrionics. He lit a cigarette, shook the match out and threw it into the pentagram. 'This place is surrounded and I demand that you give me the book!'

'No! You will never take it from me!' She snatched the blue book away from the fire then, and held it to her bosom.

'I won't ask again!' the fake Inspecteur Beliere warned.

'Why should I give it to you?'

'Because you are not authorised to have it.'

'Who says so?'

'I say so.'

'And who are you? I don't recognise you!'

He aimed the gun up at her head. 'Your recognition makes no difference to me.'

She smiled, and lifted the book imperiously over the fire.

'Perhaps this will make a difference to you!'

The fake Beliere stepped into the circle of protection and wiped the line that marked the pentagram with one shoe, rendering it powerless. 'You will die,' he said.

Her face was all rancour and her hand moved the book over the fire. 'I don't need this any more. I have the sign – it's in my head! The key to commanding Sorat, the greatest and most powerful demon the world has ever seen, is mine! If you kill me, I will die knowing it and you will have nothing!'

'You are being foolish – do you know who I am?'

'I don't care who you are!'

'Have you heard of the Black Lodge – the invisibles?'

There was a shiver of whispers.

She faltered, but only for a moment. 'This is an unpleasant fiction created by men to amuse themselves.'

'It is a reality,' he said flatly.

'Then if it does exist, I believe the Black Lodge will welcome this convocation.'

Rahn could see her hesitate. Despite her defiance she was erring on the side of caution.

The fake inspector casually smoked his cigarette, his gun pointing at her head. 'You are not only an impetuous woman, but also a misinformed one. Satan is not expected until seventy-four years from now.' His voice was conciliatory, paternal. 'The arrival of the vessel of Sorat will announce the dawn of a new age – a New Jerusalem. Time will begin again and it will be measured by His coming as a turning point. His time will be announced by cataclysms, earthquakes, hurricanes, volcanic eruptions and social unrest, because he will rise up from the centre of the Earth, on His own behalf, and *not* at the behest of an old woman!'

'No!' She held her chin up. 'Hitler is destined to be the embodiment of Sorat!'

'Hitler is not the Dark Messiah. He is only the tool of Lucifer. The full power of Sorat would kill him!'

She frowned, but her resolve had weakened. She looked to be standing on uneven ground.

'Only an incarnation of Satan could bear the full power of the dark sun's maleficence and he will not come until the year 2012! Now hand me the book, if you don't mind!'

'What will you do with it?'

'It is ours for safekeeping.'

'And I?'

'You will be bound to that little hovel at Rennes-le-Château,' he said. 'As punishment.'

Her hand moved, unbidden, away from the fire. She looked down at it in horror. She was being manipulated against her will. '*No!*' she cried.

Rahn could not let them have the book, but what could he do? At that moment fate decided that question because the Countess P's clock struck twelve. The noise of it broke into the silence like a horn blast. Its chime echoed from the stony walls and cowled heads turned this way and that to look for its source. Rahn did the only thing he could do then, being the inept hero that he was. He stood and threw the clock as hard as he could, aiming it at the madame. It hit her and the shock caused her to drop the book, and once again it landed close to the great fire.

The fake inspector leapt forward to grab it. At the same time the old woman let go an ungodly scream and lunged with an un-expected fierceness, colliding with him and causing him to lose his balance so that he fell backwards into the flames. He caught alight immediately. He dropped the book into the blaze as he tried to get up, yelling and screaming and flapping his flaming arms in a directionless, terrified panic of anguish and pain, be-fore falling again. His men at arms rushed to him, trying to pull him from the flames, but it was too late. There arose a cacophony of disapprobation and surprise and finally of terror and of dis-gust, and the gathering dissolved in all directions.

Rahn saw Eva get up but he hesitated, drawn by the horror of the spectacle. She nudged him with her shoe, breaking the spell, and in a moment he was following her through the passage, running, stumbling, falling, ascending, turning and ascending again. It seemed like an eternity before they reached the grilled door, out of breath and weary. Behind them, they heard the growls of the rabid dogs drawing nearer. There was no time to pause. Rahn followed Eva out of the grotto of Mary Magdalene and closed the gate. Eva stumbled and nearly fell but he caught her by the arm. There was a flash of lightning and the rumble of thunder as they clambered through the turmoil of leaves and dirt and branches that the wind had whipped up. He felt like a child again, running with lightning through the forests near his home. But once more, he didn't sense the sovereign protection of Michael the dragon slayer, the feeling that good always triumphs over evil, and he wondered, as he ran with his heart in his throat, how he had ever imagined that Hell could lead to Heaven.

'They're coming!' Eva said, beside him.

The dogs of the Underworld were not far behind; they would soon be at their heels.

'Don't look back!' Rahn shouted.

When they got to the Peugeot it was locked and it took a precious moment for Deodat to recognise their panic and to open the door. Rahn threw Eva in first, following her into the back seat and closing the door seconds before the hounds were at the car. Rahn climbed into the front seat and turned the ignition with a trembling hand. It wouldn't start. He tried again. Black figures were moving in the night towards them. The dogs threw themselves against the car with such fury that he heard the dinting of metal. He tried again and the car grumbled to life.

He backed out of the hiding spot and skidded off onto the narrow road, leaving behind the pursuing hounds and whatever else might be chasing them. Almost on cue, icy rain poured down in great sheets, lightning flashed again and thunder rumbled, as if Hell had broken loose.

50

TWO PLACES
AT ONCE?

'It is a secret about a secret that is based on a secret.'
Imam Ja'far Sadiq
Henri Corbin, Historia de la Filosofia Siglo

They arrived at the village of Rennes-les-Bains and, following Deodat's directions, they crossed the rain-slashed street and made their way over the footbridge that spanned the River Sals. Beneath them the river rushed, swollen and tortured. Deodat led them to a house near Place des Deux owned by an old and trusted friend.

Gaspar welcomed them without fanfare or question. He was a tall, thick-set man of about fifty, a veteran of the last war, and Rahn immediately felt safe in his company. Once inside, in the light, Gaspar took in their appearance but he didn't look particularly perturbed. He was obviously not the sort of man for effusive gestures. He said, 'I guess you'll be wanting a coffee?'

Rahn was shown to the bathroom and stood at the mirror staring at his unrecognisable reflection: his bloodshot eyes looked out from red-rimmed sockets; under the left one a gash had crusted over; above the right eye there was a sizeable bruise; he touched his swollen split lip and winced. He removed his fedora. Under it, his hair was filthy, in fact all his clothes were soiled beyond recognition. He filled the dirty sink with water and took the half-used cake of soap in his hands and began to wash.

He dressed in some spare clothes that Gaspar had given him and looked at himself in the mirror again. The shirt and jacket were too big and emphasised the lean, hungry look he'd developed these last days. But there was more to it. He felt like he had passed through some terrible illness that had left him inexorably changed, both physically and mentally. With those events at the hermitage locked behind his eyes, he went to the small room at the back of the house where Deodat lay. He tried to put on a brave face but Deodat looked terrible.

He found a seat near the bed. 'I'm sorry about all this, Deodat.'

'Don't speak nonsense! I've had the time of my life,' he said. A coughing fit took hold of him and it was a time before he could speak again. 'Tell me everything.'

'It was the fake Beliere!' Rahn said. 'As it turns out, he was Professor Moriarty, after a fashion – the organiser of half that is evil and nearly all that is undetected.'

'I see,' Deodat said, frowning.

Rahn recounted the events from the time he left the car to his return.

'So, Madame Dénarnaud was there, at the centre of it all, a popess, what nonsense! And Grassaud belongs to AGLA – the Catholic Mafia?' Deodat marvelled. 'And you say there was a battle of wills between them? My Lord, she drank blood!'

'I think it was the blood of that Englishman who tried to burn us at the Maison de Cros. But before she could make the sign of Sorat, Professor Moriarty came in and everyone scattered. He works for the Black Lodge – this sounds like the Cénacle you mentioned.'

Deodat sat up excitedly. 'The invisibles? Yes!'

'Oh! You were right, Deodat, it is a nest of vipers!'

'Fascinating!' he exclaimed. He was weak but it didn't prevent him from enjoying the moment. 'So, the madame took it upon herself to make Hitler the vessel for the demon of the sun! But you say the vessel is yet to come?'

'Yes, the year 2012 apparently, according to Professor Moriarty . . . He said it was going to be the turning point in time.'

'Diabolically ingenious!'

'But as we heard, before that they will need a reordered Europe, which they expect this coming war will create.'

'Yes. Don't let this buffoonery fool you, Rahn, there is real danger still looming ahead. The Countess P's clock may have saved the day, but Madame Dénarnaud still has the sign, even if it is only in her head. Did you see it, Rahn?'

'No, the old woman never made it. But there's something else bothering me now. Earlier when you said something about chess and being in two places at once, what did you mean?'

Deodat nodded, frowning. 'Yes, it is this: I think that perhaps old Cros has had the last laugh, after all. At least I'd like to think so.'

Rahn creased his brow. 'I don't understand.'

'Oh, it's just an old man's hope that—' But another bout of coughing prevented him from finishing. When he got his breath back he looked at Rahn with eyes that were losing their hold on consciousness. 'I'm afraid I'm going to need a few days in bed, then I will be as good as new.' He smiled weakly. 'Don't worry. I'll be safe with Gaspar. I'll lay low for a while. I am a magistrate, after all.' His words were slurring. 'There's not much they can do to me without raising a few eyebrows. At any rate, I didn't see anything and there is no longer any evidence, is there? Everything is burnt. It's all gone! All gone. The orders would have covered their tracks, you can be certain of it.' He faltered. 'I guess there is nothing left for the police. The old maison was empty – arson – who knows who did it? Listen, Rahn. Come close.'

Rahn leant in.

'Just remember what I said.' He closed his eyes. 'One can't be in two places at the same time . . . Two places, Rahn. Go to Eva . . .' And like that, mid-sentence, he fell asleep.

Rahn found Eva in the kitchen, sipping a coffee. She was the most beautiful woman he had ever known, or perhaps the most cunning at making herself seem so – he couldn't tell.

'So, how is he?' she said.

'He'll be alright, I think.' He sat down opposite.

'And you? Are you alright?'

'I don't know how I feel,' Rahn said truthfully. 'At least it wasn't all for nothing, I suppose. We did prevent the Lodges from getting the Apocalypse. My only regret is in losing the treasure of the Cathars. Perhaps I was never destined to see it. Madame Dénarnaud is now the only one who has seen the key, the sign of Sorat. She said it was in the shape of a two-horned beast.'

'Yes, it is, but not the way you think.' She set down her cup to look at him.

He blinked. 'How do you know?'

She smiled a little. 'Some years ago a scientist, a woman actually, discovered that men are born with something women don't have, they call it the Y chromosome. One day scientists will know how to distort this chromosome. They will add something to it, so that it resembles the sign of Sorat.'

'What? I don't understand.'

'This is how it will look.' She drew the sign on Gaston's dusty kitchen tabletop.

'The addition of the barb at the bottom of the Y will bring about a race of men who will be carriers of evil – vessels for the forces of six-six-six. You see, it isn't God who is found in the details, it is Satan.'

Rahn sat back a little numbly. He remembered Himmler's words in the crypt at Wewelsburg, about a program for children – Lebensborn, he had called it.

'In the future,' Eva continued, 'it will be a gift of grace to be born a woman, because a woman does not carry that chromosome and cannot be manipulated in this way to become a vessel of evil. These are the truths of the future that will begin with the year 2012. By then you will return again.'

'Return?'

Her deep eyes met his. At this point it may have been fatigue or that knock on the head, or those things she had said, but before his gaze her face seemed to change: one moment she was the evening star, the next she was Demeter, the mother of nature; she was the lady who stole into the heart of every troubadour; the ideal woman; the good, beautiful and true in the soul of every poet. She was Dante's Beatrice, Petrarch's Laura, Louise Brooks and Irene Adler. All women in one! When her face paused in its transformations, he realised with a sense of wonder and awe that he was gazing at a countenance he had seen only in his dreams. He may not be wise but something told him that he had been in the company of Wisdom all along.

Her gaze shifted to her coffee and the world returned to what it had been.

'Who are you?' he said to her.

Her eyes fell on his again, brown and liquid and tranquil. 'Who do you think I am?'

'Like everything else in this strange script, the writer has certainly created an enigma in your character, Mademoiselle Fleury.'

There was the slightest trace of a smile. 'You can call me the guardian of the Cathar treasure, if you like. I think Poussin managed a very good classical likeness of me.' She stood to go. 'One day, when you have time, you must go to Venice and when you get there, don't forget to look for the Leoncetophaline.'

'What do you mean?'

'You'll find it in the cemetery Island of the Dead, the island of San Michele. You see, Deodat was right – a man can't be in two places at once.' She walked to the door.

'Mademoiselle! Surely you're not going to leave without an explanation?'

She turned around. 'Since the beginning of time initiates have known about seven mysteries, seven keys.'

'*Seven keys?*'

'Yes, the key in the *Apocalypse of Saint John,* the sign of Sorat, was the Sixth Key. It was the key to the bottomless pit held in the hand of the angel in the Apocalypse.'

This struck Rahn. He recalled the poster of Dürer's woodcut in Pierre Plantard's apartment.

'The Seventh Key,' she continued, 'is, in fact, the most important of all, Otto. Cros knew he had to guard it with his life. To find it you will have to go to Venice. Don't worry, I will see you there.'

He had a last impression of that beautiful, haunted face, those fathomless eyes, and the calm mouth and then, she was gone.

ISLAND OF THE DEAD

51

WHO IS WHO?

'I fear there is some dark ending to our quest,' said he,
'it cannot be long before we know it!'
Sir Arthur Conan Doyle,
'The Adventure of the Missing Three-Quarter'

Venice, 2012

I realised that we had come to be standing before the grave with the Leoncetophaline, the figure of the lion-headed man holding a key and entwined with two snakes. This was the grave that the old monk had been cleaning . . . the grave without a name, the grave Eva had told Rahn to find. I looked at the Writer of Letters.

'So, Rahn did come here to Venice?'

'This is your story, what do you think?'

I considered it. 'I say he never had the chance . . .'

'Why not?'

'Because on the train back to Paris he sat next to a man.'

'Who?'

'A man he recognised from the Schloss on Lake Malchow, a Russian who belonged to the order of Black Swans . . .'

'Grigol Robakidze?'

'Yes, the one who handed him the card with a phone number

he was to ring if he was ever in need of a friend. Do you remember Rahn's old girlfriend Etienne? She was also a member of the Black Swans. It had been her job to assess Rahn's suitability for the order.'

'Oh, yes! The Russian cigarettes, the sudden departure.'

'At any rate, Robakidze told Rahn that within the Nazi organisation there was a kernel of men working against Hitler, the foremost of which was, ironically, the head of military intelligence, that man called Canaris. Robakidze also told Rahn that the only way forward now for Germany was to eliminate Hitler, and various groups were uniting around this cause. He then proposed to Rahn, that if he was inclined to join in this effort the Black Swans would allow him entry into their circle and provide him with protection. But before he could do so, he would have to prove himself by returning to Germany in order to carry out a mission for them. He warned Rahn that it would be risky, not only because he had failed in his mission to find the key, but also because some SS members had come forward to denounce him as a homosexual. If he agreed to return, the Russian advised him to immediately confess his crime to Himmler and to ask for his forgiveness before they seized him. Rahn laughed then, and told the Russian that he was mad; Himmler would send him to Buchenwald and that would be the end of him. What good would he be to the Black Swans then? The Russian reminded him of Canaris and his influence on Himmler.'

'And is that what happened?' the Writer of Letters asked. 'Did he go back to Germany?'

'Yes. In the end Rahn decided to take the risk but when he arrived in Berlin, he found that Weisthor had disappeared and he was now directly under the command of SS-Gruppenführer Wolff. After Rahn's confession, Wolff sent him directly to Buchenwald for reserve duty to wear away his homosexuality – in other words, to toughen him up. In the meantime, at Buchenwald he saw new heights of atrocities and this steeled his desire to work for the Black Swans in any capacity.'

'So what did he do?'

'When he was allowed to return to Berlin,' I said, 'Rahn continued his duties while managing to help fifteen young Jews escape
to Switzerland. He also gathered highly valuable information on
Himmler and others in his circle for Canaris. When things began to get too hot, however, with more accusations from diverse
quarters, this time about his genealogy and a possible Jewish heritage, he was advised to ask Himmler to approve his immediate
dismissal from the SS.'

'And?' the Writer of Letters asked.

'Himmler looked him in the eye and reminded him of Wewelsburg. He told him that a member of the Inner Circle could
never resign. He had only two choices – an enforced death in a
concentration camp, or suicide.'

'Which one did he choose?'

'He chose the latter . . .'

'He committed suicide?'

I nodded, having read it in a translator's note in that copy of
Rahn's book in the library. 'It was March 1939,' I continued. 'He
took a bus to Söll, a village in the Austrian Alps, and checked into
a small hotel. Here he wrote two letters, one to La Dame and
another to Deodat.'

'La Dame?' the Writer of Letters looked surprised.

'Yes, they had been corresponding for some time . . . The next
day he travelled deeper into the mountains by bus and alighted at
a stop known as Der Steinerne Steg, where he took a path that
led into the forest. After that, no one ever saw him alive again.'

'So, the official line was that he was caught in a snowstorm?'
the Writer of Letters asked.

'That's right.'

'But was he?'

The night hung heavy and it was cold; I could barely see the
Writer of Letters smiling at me, anxious to hear the rest. 'On the

twenty-fifth of May 1939, in an edition of the SS Newspaper *Das Schwarzes Korps,* there appeared a notice which read:

> During a blizzard in the mountains SS Obersturmführer Otto Rahn died tragically. We regret his death and we have lost a decent SS member and the creator of marvellous historic and scientific works.

'It was signed by the head of personnel, SS-Gruppenführer Wolff,' I said. 'In the inner circles his suicide was viewed as a declaration of his faithfulness, even in death, to the SS.' I felt like I needed a brandy.

'Do you mean that Rahn became a member of the undead?' the Writer of Letters asked.

'The body is, to this day, interred at Worgl Söll. It was badly decomposed when it was found on the eleventh of May 1939. Rahn was reported to have died on the anniversary of the fall of Montsegur – the thirteenth of March. However, his parents were never allowed to identify the body.'

'So what do *you* think . . . did he commit suicide or not?' the Writer of Letters asked.

'Personally, I don't know.'

He nodded his head, pensive. 'Do you know who this grave belongs to?'

I blinked. I wasn't sure I wanted to know. 'It can't be Rahn's.'

'I'm not asking you about Rahn.' He paused for a moment. 'Cros is the one who is buried in this cemetery. If you recall, he wanted to be buried in secret and no one was to know where his grave was; there was to be no name, no date,' the Writer of Letters said.

'Because he was afraid they would snatch away his soul?' I asked.

The Writer of Letters shook his head slowly. 'No.'

'Why the elaborate arrangements then, and all the secrecy?'

'Cros had very good reasons for his concern and I think it's time we take a closer look at him,' the Writer of Letters said.

To my great relief he now took up the reigns of the story and began to illuminate it for me. 'Cros was only a young man just out of the seminary when he was asked to investigate matters pertaining to the priest Saunière. The Bishop of Carcassonne had chosen him precisely because he was young and precisely because he belonged to no group and owed allegiance to no order. In the beginning, Cros had no idea about *Le Serpent Rouge* and had never heard of the Cathar treasure. He thought he was investigating corruption among a number of priests who were allegedly selling masses for the dead. He only realised what lay behind the investigation when Gélis approached him secretly, offering to sell him a parchment he had found in his church. Gélis told him he feared for his life and needed money to leave the country. At first Cros had refused but when Gélis told him the whole story, about what Saunière had found, he realised what the Bishop of Carcassonne was after, and that things were far more complicated than he realised. He bought the parchment from Gélis hoping to glean from it some information. But when Gélis was murdered soon after, Cros, now afraid, lay low, realising the danger he was in.

'Cros waited patiently as one by one, the priests involved in the matter died, leaving only Grassaud, who Cros knew was a member of AGLA. In the meantime Cros quietly set about solving the cipher in the parchment and eventually his pertinacity won out. He managed to find one parchment after another, in churches that were by now old and empty of priests. The last parchment pointed to the church at Bugarach, where the royal seal of AA was inscribed on its walls – the anchor and the snake. The treasure had been hidden right under their noses! With a word in the right ear he was made the priest of Bugarach, where he could look for the treasure unperturbed. Bugarach was the sixth church and he had now become the sixth priest, just as Deodat had figured out. When Cros finally found the treasure, he understood what they were all after – the key, the sign of Sorat. But he also discovered an unknown part to the treasure, a far more important part. He understood that he had to safeguard this part from the brotherhoods, even if it meant giving up the key.'

'What do you mean "another part to the treasure"?'

'There were three parts to the treasure of the Cathars: the first part was Isobel's child, the reincarnation of Saint John, the child that was whisked away to the Monastery of Saint Lazarus by Matteu; the second part of the treasure was the original *Apocalypse of Saint John* and its key; and the third part was what Bertrand Marty gave to Matteu, a roll of parchments, which he asked him to take away with him at the last minute – do you recall that?'

'Yes.'

'This roll of parchments that Bertrand Marty gave Matteu centuries ago was of utmost significance because, although the *Apocalypse of Saint John* and its "sign" was the Sixth Key, the third part of the Cathar treasure was the last key, the Seventh Key. And as Eva told Rahn, a clue to its whereabouts is secreted here on this island in Venice.'

'So is the clue inscribed on this headstone?'

'What do you think?'

'I think it is. I think that if the Sixth Key was found in the Apocalypse of John, the Seventh must have something to do with the Holy Grail, and this inscription points to it, am I right?'

He smiled. He wasn't going to give too much away. 'It was Rahn's task to come here to find it.'

'But Rahn never found it, did he? Because he committed suicide.' I thought that I had it all now . . . until the Writer of Letters shook his head again.

'Fortunately for Rahn, your account of his last moments was not completely correct. You're right in so far that he did travel

433

to Söll. It was late afternoon by the time he neared a farmstead on the outskirts of the town. He saw some children playing and he spoke to them a moment. It had been snowing earlier and he asked the children if they thought it would snow again. They said that it looked like it would, and then he continued walking.

You see, he wanted the children to be able to say, when questioned, that they had seen an SS officer. Now, the snow was a metre deep in places and it was cold but he kept up his walk. When he came to a large fir tree he took off his uniform, folded it neatly and placed it on a rock. From a bag he retrieved his pot-holing clothes and, after he had dressed again, he backtracked to a brook, covering his footsteps as he went. He walked part of the way through the water and then left again for Söll.'

'Just like Sherlock Holmes in "The Empty House!" He faked his own death, didn't he? But they found a body, so whose body was it?'

'Rahn had to tell Himmler exactly where he was going to commit suicide. You see, Himmler wasn't just going to let him walk away, he had him closely watched. But let us not forget that Rahn was a good potholer and he knew the area he chose very well. He was astute in ways of covering his tracks. When the search party looked for him and found only his clothes, neatly folded, Himmler was incensed. He realised that he'd been duped. Having to save face at all costs – Himmler had numerous enemies who would have made much of this blunder to Hitler – he organised two of his men to go to Dachau in search of a prisoner Rahn's age and size and colouring. It was then a simple matter to crush a cyanide capsule in the prisoner's mouth and to spirit him away. Stranger things happened all the time in the camps. Anyway, it was relatively easy then for Himmler's men to plant the body back in the forest along with the clothes and to place a bottle of pills beside it. By the time they found the body of the dead man that spring, it was so decomposed it had to be buried in haste before the parents could identify it. Those SS men who planted the body were later sent to the Russian front and were never heard from again.'

'So where did Rahn go?' I asked.

'He made his way to a predetermined location near Söll where he was met by his friend Dietmar Lauermann, who had arranged a Swiss passport for him. Lauermann drove Rahn over the border to Italy, to a place where La Dame was waiting for him. Rahn's death had been well publicised and so he was now free, not only of the Nazis, but of the brotherhoods as well.'

'He and La Dame did break open that numbered bottle that La Dame had offered as a peace offering in the car just before they parted ways. That is how their friendship was revived. In truth, Rahn had never meant to hold a grudge against him, and besides, La Dame had won his esteem by helping to smuggle those Jewish youths over the border to Switzerland. He had earned Rahn's respect again and La Dame, as a gesture of penitence, offered him something that touched his heart.'

'The Mexican edition of *Don Quixote?*'

'How did you guess? Yes, the one in that bookshop in Berlin, the very reason for their first meeting.'

'And?'

'We do know that Rahn went to France again to meet with Deodat. It was near a small village called Oradour-sur-Glane where he figured no one would recognise him. Incidentally, in 1944 a Nazi unit arrived at Oradour-sur-Glane supposedly looking for forbidden merchandise, or members of the resistance. The villagers were summarily rounded up and murdered, all in all, six hundred and forty-two men, women and children. These days the whole town is a memorial to those who died.'

'Were they looking for Rahn?'

'Who knows? The Nazis also sent a team to Montsegur and another, led by a man called Skorzeny, went to the Corbieres to search about in the mountains and caves. Perhaps they thought Rahn was hiding in them. In fact, legends told of him wandering about the mountains. But Rahn was long gone. He became an expert in disguise and he did live long enough to laugh out loud at all the conjectures about his death . . . Long enough to go to the cinema and to see himself portrayed as an American with a gun at his belt and a wry smile on his face. How he laughed! The scriptwriters even had their hero wearing a fedora and a leather jacket – just like that jacket Rahn had taken from the Pabst film set, but they didn't know that it was La Dame who was afraid of snakes, not Rahn.

'He also lived to learn from Deodat that Madame Dénarnaud had returned from her experience at the hermitage in a similar condition to that priest Albert Fonçay – the man who ventured into those tunnels under the hermitage years earlier. She had no recall of the events that had transpired that night in the gallery. Some say that the Cénacle placed her in an occult prison – as the American brotherhoods had done to Madame Blavatsky. Sometime later she willed the Villa Bethany and its grounds to a businessman from Paris, who agreed in return to look after her in her old age. Was he a member of one order or another, sent to keep an eye on her? Who knows? Whatever the case, she died at Rennes-les-Château after suffering a stroke. After that the businessman transformed the Villa Bethany into a hotel and the old cistern under the covered way of the Tour Magdala, into a restaurant, and began to attract tourists to the village.

'Do you remember that sour-faced youth, Pierre Plantard? Well, he became a grand master of his own order, an order he concocted from thin air, which he called the Priory of Sion. Together with a certain Monsieur De Cherissy, Plantard encrypted parchments carrying some aspects of the truth hidden behind an entire smoke screen of lies. He then placed these parchments strategically within genuine documents at the Bibliothèque National and waited to see who would take the bait. There were a few who did, and as a result, a number of books were written which called much attention to Rennes-le-Château.

'Monsieur Plantard now began calling himself a Saint Clair, and therefore from the lineage of Merovingians – the supposed true kings of France. These, he then postulated, were related to Jesus, making him a descendant of Jesus. What a load of nonsense!

'At about this time another parchment was found at the Bibliothèque National, called *Le Serpent Rouge*. Yes, don't look amazed. It is a poem containing thirteen stanzas, each devoted to one sign of the zodiac. If one reads it carefully one can discern Rahn's entire adventure in the South of France locked between its lines. Moreover it was officially published on the seventeenth of January. At any rate its discovery caused a great stir. Unfortunately for the three men who co-authored the parchment – Louis St Maxent, Gaston de Koker and Pierre Feugere – they all died within twenty-four hours of each other, in different locations; all three supposedly committing suicide by hanging. An associate of theirs, a certain Janjua Fakharul-Islam, a Pakistani, was found a month before, lying at the side of the railway line near Melun. Apparently, he had fallen from the train travelling between Paris and Geneva, though no luggage belonging to him was ever found. Unnoticed by the gendarmes was a strange tattoo on the man's right wrist, a serpent and an anchor – the sign of AA, as we know.'

I was shaking my head with amazement. 'Who killed them, the Cénacle?'

'It is obvious that there are *some* who will stop at nothing to keep Rahn's time in the South of France out of the limelight. In any event, the intoxication of the world with the enigma of that small circle of churches, remains even to this day. The brotherhoods will continue to proliferate and to squabble like children, to taunt one another, and to assassinate one another. These brotherhoods are completely oblivious to the fact that they are living in an endless performance of metatheatre where they, as both actors and audience, allude to a redundant secret, and in their collusion they perpetuate a reality that is really nothing more than an illusion.'

'But it's an illusion based on the truth,' I said.

'Most illusions are.'

'So, did Rahn eventually make it to Venice? Did he find this tomb?'

'He will.'

'What do you mean, he *will?*'

'First, he has to wake up.'

I must have looked at him blankly.

'Are you surprised?' he said.

'I don't understand.'

'Don't you know that you are in a dream?'

'What?'

'Yes.'

'You can't be serious?'

'The first time you dreamed this dream you were waiting for a vaporetto to bring you to the island. I have been asking you, over and over, why you are here, and this is because you have been here before, in those days . . . long ago. That is what I meant, when I said you invited yourself. You see, you wanted to remember Wewelsburg, and Rennes-le-Château, and the hunt for the Sixth Key.'

'Remember it? I still don't understand.'

'That was the promise Rahn made to the Countess P – that he would remember his destiny as the guardian of the treasure. You see, in a previous life, Rahn had been Nostradamus's secretary, Chavigny, and before that he was the troubadour Matteu.'

For some reason this made sense to me. 'What about Deodat – who had he been?' I asked.

'Do you not see Nostradamus in Deodat?'

'And La Dame?'

'He was the Templar knight who saved the young Matteu from Béziers. That is the bond between La Dame and Rahn – La

Dame had once saved Rahn's life.'

'And you? Who are you in all of this?'

'Don't you know yet?' He shot me a glance.

I was filled with a sudden realisation. 'You're Cros!'

'Matteu and I once sat together on the pog at Montsegur, aeons ago.'

'You were Cros and Cros was Bertrand Marty, the Cathar perfect!'

'Yes. You see, the Seventh Key is *my* bond with Rahn.'

I was numbed, shocked, amazed.

'Now, if you will permit me, I will tell you the rest.'

'Please.'

'Well, by the time I found the treasure in the church of Bugarach I was already ill. I felt I didn't have much time and I was unsure of what to do. I went to Paris to see my lawyers and while there I heard the fake rumour that Monti had circulated about *Le Serpent Rouge*. At first, I was surprised to hear about it after so many years, and then a plan began to formulate itself in my mind. I gave my lawyers those strict instructions regarding my funeral arrangements, which you know about. I then told them to expect something from me in the coming weeks and gave them instructions on what they should do with it.

'After that, I asked around about Monti. It wasn't difficult to contact him. In a note I informed him about a missing key to *Le Serpent Rouge*. A key to unlocking the powers of the grimoire. I told him that clues to this missing key's whereabouts could be found on a list somewhere in the south of France; clues that only one person could decipher – a German writer and Grail historian called Otto Rahn. I also included the name of Otto's book and the page number where the skeleton key was mentioned. I signed it, Eugene Grassaud.'

'So Monti went to Saint-Paul-de-Fenouillet to see Grassaud?'

'Yes, and that's how the rumour was spread about the list.'

'But how did you know about Rahn?'

'Deodat had often talked about him and had given me a copy of Rahn's book.'

'And after that you placed the *Apocalypse of Saint John* containing the key in plain view, under the ROTAS window – the wheel of fortune – in the church.'

'That is actually where it always was, I merely replaced it and planted clues to its whereabouts on the list of priests – JCKAL – and hid the list in the tabernacle.'

'And the sacrament?'

'I knew I was being watched by the Lodges and that it was only a matter of time before they used their Black Magic on me, so I gave my sacristan express instructions that I should have no other sacrament than the one I kept in the tabernacle, safeguarded by the Sign of the Lamb. But before I succumbed to the stroke I had a change of heart. You see, the arrival of Eva meant that the penitents couldn't get near me to give me their desecrated sacrament, so I removed the key to the tabernacle from the sacristan's ring of keys and hid it in the pond. Later, when AGLA tortured the poor man, knowing nothing on the list, he gave them the keys to the church, but the key to the tabernacle was long gone.

'The morning Rahn came to see me with Deodat, I had Eva wheel me as close as possible to the pond. You can't imagine my excitement when I saw Rahn. At this stage I didn't yet know of our past karma together, but I was happy that my plans had come to fruition and that I would soon be released. I gave Deodat the word sator, knowing the combination of Rahn's erudition and my dear friend's wisdom would literally lead them around in circles. When Rahn and Deodat left to go to the church with Eva, I saw my chance. I overbalanced my wheelchair – it was an old chair and only needed a little tilt of my weight on uneven ground – and fell into the pond.'

'So you committed suicide?'

'I was already dead, incapacitated, a vegetable, and I didn't want to end up like those others who had lost their souls.'

'I see.'

'Rahn and Deodat's hunt for the key diverted the attention of the Lodges away from my death and burial, as I had hoped it would.'

'You wanted to distract them from your burial because you had left instructions for the clue to the third part of the treasure's whereabouts to be inscribed on this headstone.'

'That's right.'

'Very clever. But if you are dead and this is your grave, how did you send me letters – how did you help me with my books?'

'I told you that when you fall asleep you also enter that same realm in which the dead live. Were they letters you received? Or were they messages, impulses, inspirations, intuitions?'

I had to pause to think this through. 'So then, what is *this* moment . . . past, present, or future?'

'It is the future, in Rahn's time, and the present in yours. It is the Day of the Dead in 2012 *and* the Day of the Dead in 1938. You should know by now that galleries stand side by side.'

'But who is the fearful monk who guards this grave? Is he just imaginary?'

'That monk tends this grave lovingly because it is his. He is me, as I was long ago when you first came here. He is a remnant, a memory of what I was.'

'And are you *undead*? Locked in limbo?'

He shook his head. 'No, I'm here of my own free will. I remained behind to guard the knowledge of the whereabouts of the third part of the treasure, the Seventh Key, until Rahn returned to solve the inscription. In those days I feared not only that the living would find a way to the grave, but also that the living dead would find it. You see, intrigues don't only occur in the world of the living, there are those who have crossed the threshold precisely in order to discover what I took to my grave.'

'So who was Eva?'

'On the physical level, she was the reincarnation of Isobel, the mother of the young boy who was taken to Montsegur, and Isobel, in turn, was the reincarnation of Mary Magdalene. On a spiritual level, she was the embodiment of wisdom.'

'I see . . . and the woman who reads to the dead?'

'You will meet her when we return to 1940.'

'She said she had given me the solution to the inscription. She said *they* knew, and that *they* were after me. Who are *they?*'

'Himmler, of course, and others . . .'

'Himmler?'

'Yes, don't forget Himmler knew Rahn wasn't dead and sent his men to hunt him down.'

'So you said we will return to 1940 – another gallery?'

'Aptly named "The First Return". It begins when Rahn takes up the hunt for the rest of the treasure. He will shortly wake up on a bench, waiting for the vaporetto that will bring him to this island. Rahn has to find this gravestone and to solve the cipher. At that time he had the freedom to turn around and take a different path – the same freedom you will have when you wake up. In fact, he nearly did take another path, as you will see, because he felt he was about to walk into Hell. The trouble with inspirations and intuitions is that we soon forget them when we wake up.'

'Will I forget all that you've told me?'

'It is likely that only a vague feeling will remain in your heart. If you choose to follow it, you will find the right course. If you forget everything else, remember this . . .' He paused to look at me and said, 'The way to Heaven is always through Hell . . .'

52

THE FIRST RETURN

'Holmes!' I cried. 'Is it really you?
Can it indeed be that you are alive?'
Sir Arthur Conan Doyle,
'The Adventure of the Empty House'

Venice, November 1940

Otto Rahn had fallen asleep on the bench waiting for the vaporetto. He woke with a dry mouth and a crick in his neck that he was still massaging when the boat pulled up at the Fondamente Nuove. He remembered dreaming about a conversation with a man; something about being in a garden with many paths that lead here and there, something related to a promise he'd made. As he climbed aboard the vaporetto he wondered if the dream had anything to do with his promise to the Countess P.

As the boat chugged lazily over the lagoon, he leant in to ask the boatman about their destination, 'Is that San Michele?'

'Yes, that is the cemetery island of Venice,' the man said, in a wonderful Italian voice.

The sun was rising, casting its golden hues over the old lagoon and the island, bringing to his mind the Egyptian river of souls and the boat of Isis in which one travelled to the realm of the dead. Well, he thought to himself, why not place a clue in a cemetery island in the middle of a lagoon? It all made a crazy sort of sense. It was something a man like Cros would do!

The vaporetto now arrived at the landing stage on the northwest corner of the island and Rahn climbed out, paid the boatman and watched the vessel pull away. He had an unnerving sense that he was about to walk into Hell again. After all, there was a monastery on the island, and a church. His mouth was dry again, his hands were shaking and he could feel his stomach churning. He seemed destined to find himself always at the gates of Hell, but it had never prevented him from continuing, even into the flames. Like his heroes Parzifal and Don Quixote, Jason, Hercules and Alexander, he would have to take the Thief's Path through Hell to reach Heaven.

'Well then . . .' he affirmed to himself, as he climbed those steps. 'I dare!'

AUTHOR'S NOTE

For some years now the south of France, its churches, its priests and its secrets, have captured the minds of writers and readers alike. Hundreds of books and a very substantial number of websites and blogs are dedicated to exploring and understanding every detail of the multilayered, deeply veiled, enigmatic mystery behind the churches surrounding Rennes-le-Château and its priest, Bérenger Saunière.

Likewise, Otto Rahn has been the subject of a number of books and some believe he was even the inspiration for Steven Spielberg's Indiana Jones. The true Otto Rahn was indeed a philologist, historian, explorer and amateur archaeologist, who found himself at the wrong place at the wrong time, becoming an unwitting member of the SS.

In 2004 I visited Rennes-le-Château as part of research for *The Seal.* I sensed something very sinister working there, in its peculiarly renovated church, in its Villa Bethany, Tour Magdala, restless cemetery and strange conservatory. The town filled me with a feeling of dread and I had an urge to leave as soon as possible. This intrigued me, and when many years later I began exploring the mystery of the churches in the area, I discovered a story that was quite bizarre and more complicated than I had ever imagined, a story that was tantalisingly stranger than fiction! I decided to explore the connection between Otto Rahn and these mysteries. *The Sixth Key* is a result of that exploration. The story is my own, but it is written around historical facts.

In *The Sixth Key* I have remained faithful to what is known about Rahn's life during this period, taking only some liberties with dates and leaving out events of lesser interest in order to focus on what was integral. Rahn did work in the south of France; he did write two books, *Crusade Against the Grail* and *Lucifer's Court;* he was indeed searching for the treasure of the Cathars; he did work for Himmler; and there is conjecture about him being sent on a secret mission to the south of France. To this day there is a question hanging over his official 'suicide' and as no efforts have been made to exhume his body for DNA testing, the entire affair remains a mystery – at least for those who haven't met Rahn, that is!

As mentioned previously, all secret societies and groups discussed in *The Sixth Key* are real. All rites that I have mentioned – white, grey or black magic – have been drawn from real and credible sources. All church artwork, including the magic squares, paintings, etc., given as clues, can be found by anyone. All grimoires and books quoted do exist, including the *Grimoire of Pope Honorius III*, which was indeed purportedly written by a pope.

As far as the supporting characters go, Pierre Plantard, as many may already know through books such as *Holy Blood and Holy Grail,* did have much to do with the mystery of this area and has been the focus of quite a lot of media attention over the years through his Priori de Sion hoax. Bérenger Saunière, the curé of Rennes-le-Château, is almost a figure of legend and myth but he is a true character and did renovate the church at Rennes-le-Château, building the Villa Bethany, the Tour Magdala and the conservatory, drawing from sources of wealth that were never explained. Madame Dénarnaud, Bérenger Saunière's housekeeper, is a true personality who survived Saunière to inherit everything. Like him, she died incapacitated, never divulging her secrets. The Abbé Gélis was actually murdered in the gruesome way described in this novel and his murder has never been solved. He and Abbé Boudet and Abbé Cros did all meet according to the diary kept by Saunière. Similarly, Abbé Bigou, Jean-Louis Verger, Abbé Rivière and Abbé Grassaud are all historical personalities, as were Paul Alexis Ladame, Rahn's best friend, the Countess Murat Pujol who was a member of the Polaires, and Deodat Roche, who had close links with Anthroposophy. Interestingly, Sir Arthur Conan Doyle, the creator of Sherlock Holmes whom I quote a lot throughout *The Sixth Key,* was involved in spiritualism and was known to have moved in the esoteric circles of Antonin Gadal, one of Otto Rahn's mentors.

The Book of the Seven Seals, the original *Apocalypse of Saint John,* is believed to have formed a part of the treasure of the Cathars. The sign of Sorat is real, as is the sign of the Lamb of Christ.

And the Seventh Key? To know more you will need to follow me into the galleries and Rahn's next adventure!

Acknowledgements

Some time ago my mother Rita introduced me to Otto Rahn after watching a documentary about him. Without this introduction, *The Sixth Key* would not be what it is and I thank her so much for that. I would also like to thank my husband, James, for his patience and diligence in reading and editing the manuscript in all its stages and for making many useful and practical suggestions.

I would also like to thank Sylvia Francke and Thomas Hawthorne for drawing my attention to Ophiucus in their book *The Tree of Life and the Holy Grail.*

Finally, thanks must go to Otto Rahn himself, whose enigmatic life was an endless source of inspiration and whose two books were more of an insight into his soul and personality than any biography of his life could have been.

See you in the galleries, Otto!

Printed in Great Britain
by Amazon